TYRANT
OF ROME

By Simon Scarrow

The *Eagles of the Empire* Series

The Britannia Campaign
Under the Eagle (AD 42–43, Britannia)
The Eagle's Conquest (AD 43, Britannia)
When the Eagle Hunts (AD 44, Britannia)
The Eagle and the Wolves (AD 44, Britannia)
The Eagle's Prey (AD 44, Britannia)

Rome and the Eastern Provinces
The Eagle's Prophecy (AD 45, Rome)
The Eagle in the Sand (AD 46, Judaea)
Centurion (AD 46, Syria)

The Mediterranean
The Gladiator (AD 48–49, Crete)
The Legion (AD 49, Egypt)
Praetorian (AD 51, Rome)

The Return to Britannia
The Blood Crows (AD 51, Britannia)
Brothers in Blood (AD 51, Britannia)
Britannia (AD 52, Britannia)

Hispania
Invictus (AD 54, Hispania)

The Return to Rome
Day of the Caesars (AD 54, Rome)

The Eastern Campaign
The Blood of Rome (AD 55, Armenia)
Traitors of Rome (AD 56, Syria)
The Emperor's Exile (AD 57, Sardinia)

Britannia: Troubled Province
The Honour of Rome (AD 59, Britannia)
Death to the Emperor (AD 60, Britannia)
Rebellion (AD 60, Britannia)
Revenge of Rome (AD 61, Britannia)

Nero's Rome
Tyrant of Rome (AD 62, Rome)

The *Berlin Wartime* Thrillers
Blackout
Dead of Night
A Death in Berlin

The *Wellington and Napoleon* Quartet
Young Bloods
The Generals
Fire and Sword
The Fields of Death

Sword and Scimitar (Great Siege of Malta)

Hearts of Stone (Second World War)

Writing with T. J. Andrews
Arena (AD 41, Rome)
Invader (AD 44, Britannia)
Pirata (AD 25, Rome)
Warrior (AD 18, Britannia)

Writing with Lee Francis
Playing with Death

The *Gladiator* Series
Gladiator: Fight for Freedom
Gladiator: Street Fighter
Gladiator: Son of Spartacus
Gladiator: Vengeance

SIMON SCARROW

EAGLES · OF · THE · EMPIRE

TYRANT OF ROME

HEADLINE

First published in 2025 by
Headline Publishing Group Limited

3

Cataloguing in Publication Data is available from the British Library

Hardback ISBN 978 1 4722 8724 3
Waterstones exclusive ISBN 978 1 0354 3987 4
Trade Paperback ISBN 978 1 4722 8723 6

Map and artwork by Tim Peters

Typeset in Bembo by CC Book Production

Printed and bound in Great Britain by Clays Ltd, Elcograf S.p.A.

MIX
Paper | Supporting
responsible forestry
FSC
www.fsc.org
FSC® C104740

Headline's policy is to use papers that are natural, renewable and recyclable products
and made from wood grown in well-managed forests and other controlled sources.
The logging and manufacturing processes are expected to conform to
the environmental regulations of the country of origin.

Headline Publishing Group Limited
An Hachette UK Company
Carmelite House
50 Victoria Embankment
London EC4Y 0DZ

The authorized representative in the EEA is Hachette Ireland,
8 Castlecourt Centre, Dublin 15, D15 XTP3, Ireland
(email: info@hbgi.ie)

www.headline.co.uk
www.hachette.co.uk

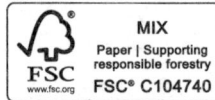

For the Parsatam family, with thanks for your kindness
and friendship – Rajesh, Nivedita, Fina, Yohan and Davish

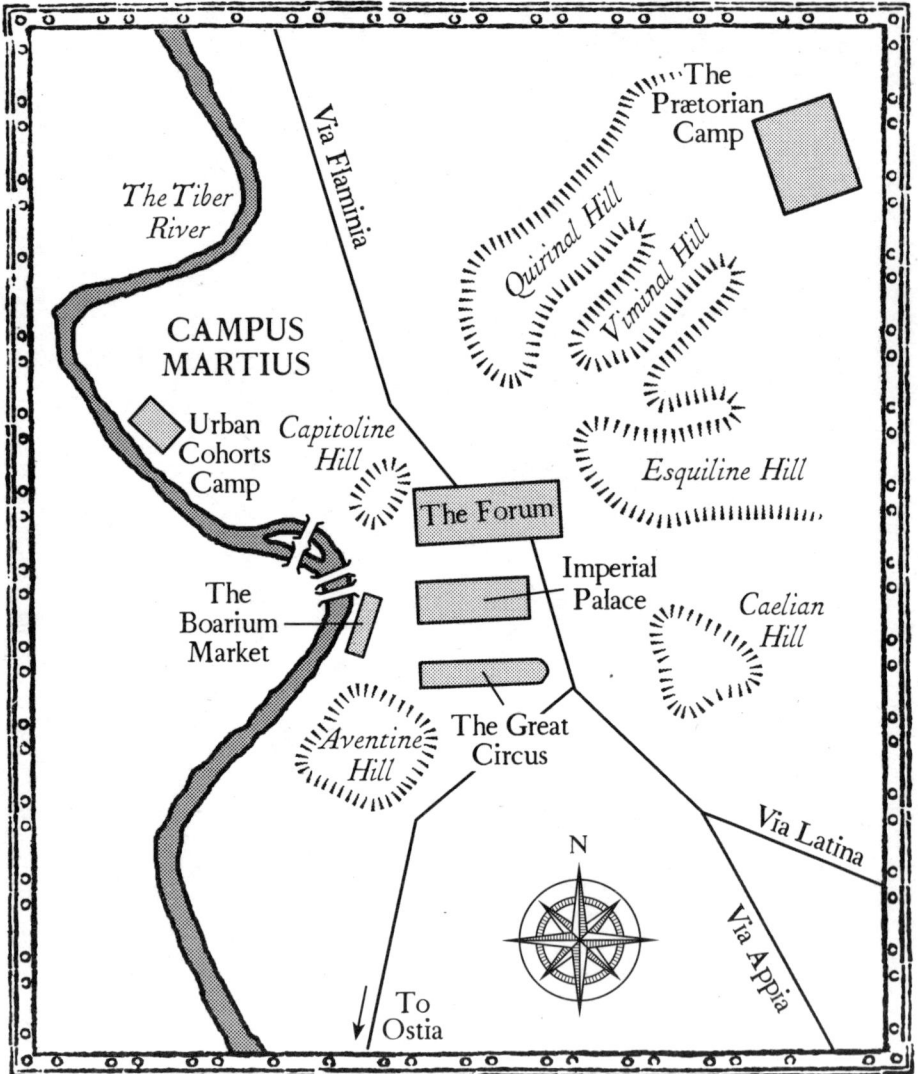

ROME AD 62

The Prætorian Camp

The Tiber River

Quirinal Hill

Viminal Hill

CAMPUS MARTIUS

Urban Cohorts Camp

Capitoline Hill

Esquiline Hill

The Forum

Imperial Palace

The Boarium Market

Caelian Hill

Aventine Hill

The Great Circus

Via Flaminia

Via Latina

Via Appia

N

To Ostia

ITALIA AD 62

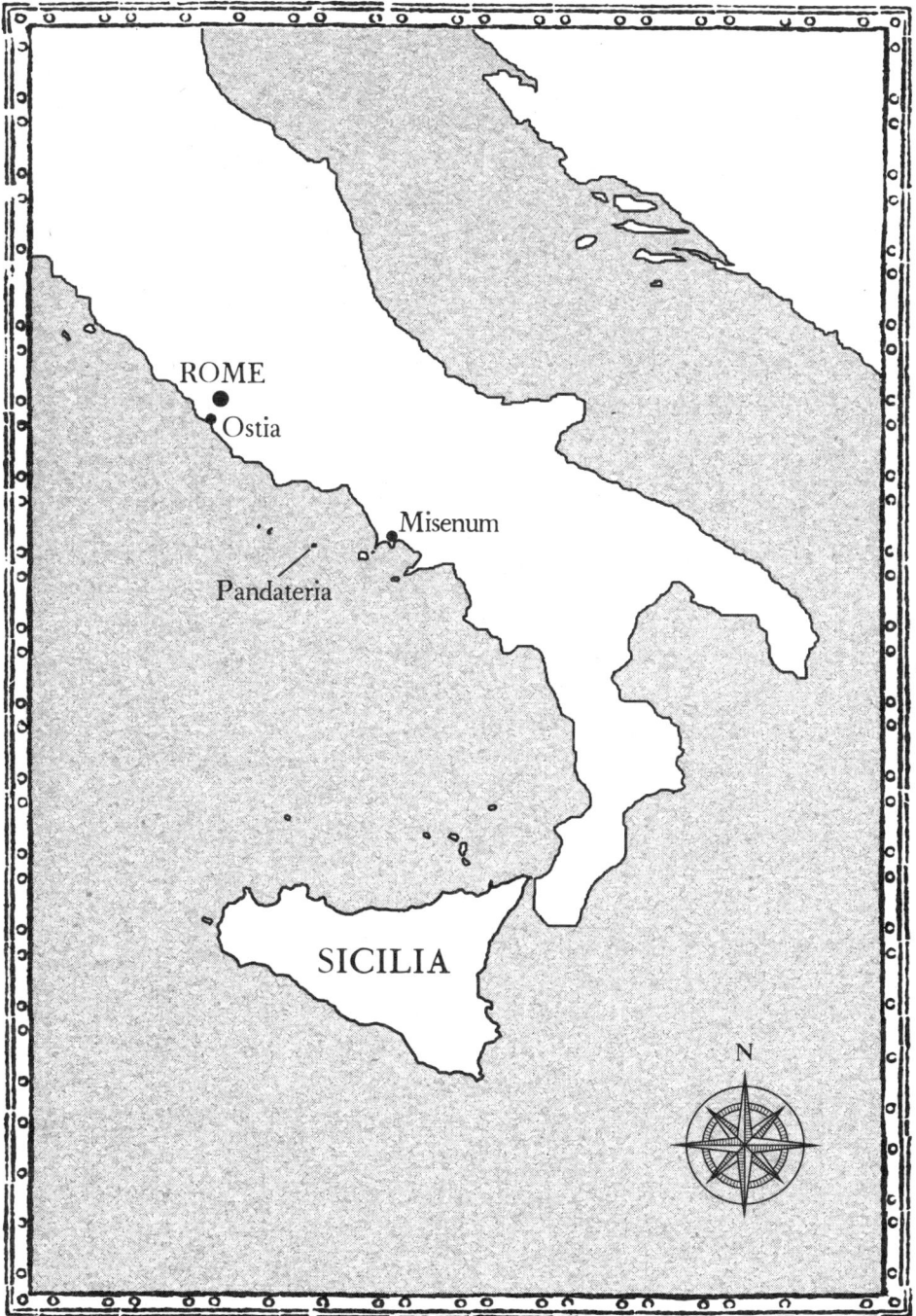

ROME

Ostia

Misenum

Pandateria

SICILIA

N

Emperor Nero

Prefect Burrus

Praetorian Guard

12 cohorts of
1,000 men based
in the Praetorian
Camp just outside
the walls of Rome.
Tasked with
protecting the
emperor and the
imperial palace.

**Acting Prefect
Cato and
Centurion Macro**

Urban Cohorts

3 cohorts based
within the walls of
Rome. Tasked with
providing public
order and supporting
the Praetorian Guard.

The Vigiles

Small units based
within the walls of
Rome. Operating
from neighbourhood
watch-houses, they
tackle low level
crime and serve
a police function.
They are not heavily
armed soldiers like
the men of the
Praetorian Guard
and the Urban
Cohorts.

CHAPTER ONE

Rome, AD *62*

Macro knew there was trouble before they reached the Forum. It had already started by the time he and Petronella left the house on the Viminal Hill. The cobbled street sloping down to the market in the centre of the capital was emptier than usual. On a normal day there would be the bustle of shoppers, street hawkers, men sitting on benches outside the small canteens, the odd pickpocket furtively fixing on his mark. Litters carrying the wealthiest of Rome's inhabitants, off-duty Praetorians in their white tunics, and bedraggled men laden with charms offering to tell the fortunes of passers-by or place a curse on thieves, frauds and love rivals. Today, most shops and canteens were hurriedly closing up in anticipation of trouble. A handful of men and women scurried past Macro and his wife as they made their way down the hill.

Even though it was early summer, the city was basking in an unseasonal heatwave. As they drew closer to the Forum, Macro could hear the clamour of a huge angry crowd. He could make out a peculiar shift in tone that seemed to alternate between rage and grief.

'What's happening?' Petronella asked, clutching his arm.

He shook his head. 'Don't know. There's nothing on at the racetrack and no games for at least a month, as far as I know.

Whatever it is, sounds like trouble.' He paused and turned to her. 'Do you want to return to the house?'

She thought for a moment. 'Do you?'

Macro chuckled. 'You know me. Always keen to know what's what.' His expression became serious. 'You can go back if you like. I'll see what's going on and report back.'

'More likely you'll get caught up in some trouble.' She clicked her tongue. 'You need to start acting your age. You owe it to me and Bardea.'

He gave a reluctant nod. Although he had been married to Petronella for some years, he had not yet grown accustomed to being a father. Bardea was the result of a brief relationship with an Iceni woman shortly after the legions had invaded Britannia. That the woman had gone on to be queen of her tribe and led the recent rebellion against Rome rather complicated matters. Bardea still suffered nightmares in which she relived her abuse by Roman soldiers. Macro had tried his best to make up for what she had endured, but he was not used to the role of parent and he did not feel himself suited for it.

At first he had not believed Boudica when she had revealed that he was the girl's father, but Bardea's short, solid build, dark hair and broad face were unmistakably inherited from Macro. The timing of her birth also matched up with Boudica's explanation. So he had accepted his responsibility for his daughter and taken charge of Bardea after the rebellion was over, bringing her to Rome to raise her. Not that the arrangement was without friction, over and above that to be expected from any child on the cusp of adulthood. Bardea mourned the loss of her family and those she knew who had died at the hands of the Romans. It took all Macro's limited sensitivity to manage her frequent dark moods.

'You're not a squaddie on a night out any more,' Petronella continued. 'Haven't been for a long time.'

Macro affected a hurt expression. 'I can still cut it with the rest of them.'

She smiled sympathetically. 'I know you can. Look, I'm coming with you. No arguments. There'll be less chance of trouble if I do.'

Macro arched an eyebrow. 'You think?' His wife was a solidly built woman, capable of flooring almost any man with her right hook.

They were interrupted by a wiry, bald man in a grubby tunic. One eye was milky, and a mere handful of stray strands of hair rose from his freckled scalp. His right leg was spindly and twisted inwards, almost useless and forcing him to depend upon a stout walking stick. He was looking behind him as he blundered into Macro.

'Oi! Careful,' Macro growled, pushing him away and steadying him at the same time. At once Petronella leaned in and grasped the man's free hand as it darted towards the folds of his tunic. Macro's purse, heavy with coin, was clutched in his claw-like grip. His eyes widened with fear, instantly replaced by a crafty expression as he took in Macro's red army cloak.

'Sorry, Centurion.' He hazarded a guess at Macro's rank. 'Must have grabbed at that when I thought I was going to fall.'

Macro retrieved the purse and thrust it to the bottom of his sidebag, covering it with his cloak. Then he raised a finger and prodded the man in the chest.

'Ever try that on me again and I'll make sure you need another crutch, just so you don't have a hand spare to rob with. Clear?'

The old man nodded vigorously.

Macro gestured in the direction of the Forum. 'What's going on down there?'

The man opened his mouth, revealing a handful of crooked teeth. 'The emperor's just turned down the appeal for clemency for Paetius Secundus's lot. There's some in the Senate not happy about it and they've been whipping up the mob. It's looking ugly down there, Centurion. The urban cohorts have been sent in. They're trying to clear a path from the Tullianum cells to the execution site, but the people aren't having it. Going to be trouble, you can count on it. Me? I'm getting clear while I can.' His eyes narrowed and his tone shifted to faintly whining self-pity. 'An old veteran such as me, who's given the best years of his life in the service of Rome and paid for it with the wound to this leg, ain't got much of a chance when things turn violent. And I'll not be able to beg for a few coins to feed myself today . . .'

Macro looked him up and down. 'Veteran, eh? Which legion?'

The old man hesitated. 'Fourteenth, Centurion. Fine bunch of lads. I was with them until five years ago. When I got this.' He tapped his wizened thigh.

'You must have been sorry to leave them behind, and that posting in Syria.'

'Indeed I was.'

'Bollocks. The Fourteenth has been in Britannia for the last twenty years.' Macro frowned. 'Now piss off before I drag you down to the nearest watchhouse.'

The man flinched at the prospect of being handed over to the law enforcers of the vigiles, who had a reputation for rough-handling street criminals. He hobbled to one side, giving Macro and Petronella a wide berth, before continuing up the street. Macro spared him a last glance and spat into the gutter. 'Bloody chancer.'

'Who is Paetius Secundus?' asked Petronella as they continued towards the Forum.

'It's old news. He was a senator, murdered last year by one of his slaves. Or so the story goes. From what I heard at the Gladiator's Rest, it took a few months of torture before one of the poor sods cracked and claimed to be the guilty party.'

'I'm not sure I'd believe every bit of gossip I heard at the Gladiator's Rest . . .'

Macro's brow creased in mild irritation. His wife did not approve of him patronising the inn strategically placed outside the bathhouse he frequented. But since many of the clientele were former soldiers like Macro, it was something she had to tolerate, even if she disapproved.

'Anyway,' he continued, quick to move off the subject of his favourite drinking hole, 'the way the law goes, if a slave murders their master, then all the slaves of the victim's household are put to death.'

'Surely not?'

He shrugged. 'Why do you think such murders happen so rarely? The onus is on the slaves to police each other so that one of their own doesn't turn on their master.'

'But how can the innocent be held responsible alongside the murderer? That's wrong.'

'Maybe, but it's the law. Come on.' Macro took her hand and drew her on. 'The reason it's causing a fuss this time is due to the number involved. Four hundred slaves are having to pay the price for the crime of an individual. If it had been a smaller household, like ours, for example, it would barely merit a mention in the gazetteer. It's because so many have been condemned that things have dragged on for months and roused the passions of the mob. The common people are little more than one step up from slaves, so they tend to feel sympathy for them from time to time. More than a few senators also raised objections to executing the lot when the matter was raised in the Senate. But in the end they voted against showing mercy and the matter was bumped up to the imperial palace. Nero's been sitting on it for a while before making his decision. Seems he has now.'

'Why the delay?'

'Who can say? He's young, and from what I understand he wants to be loved by the mob. Needing to feel popular tends to get in the way of being decisive. It's not a good trait in a leader.'

Petronella gestured towards the Forum as a fresh roar of protest carried across the capital. 'He doesn't sound too popular to me at the moment.'

'No . . . Let's hope it's all bark and no bite down there.'

They continued without speaking as the din rose in successive waves of anger and pity. As they reached the junction at the bottom of the hill and turned towards the Forum, they caught sight of the crowd pressed into the space between the ramshackle apartment blocks on either side. Across their heads, Macro could see protesters clinging to statues and standing on pedestals as they gestured in the direction of the imperial palace compound. He stopped.

'We ain't going to get through that lot. There's a terrace a few streets down. We should be able to get a view from there and see if there's any way we can get to the market.'

Petronella nodded, and they threaded through the dingy alleys until they came to the top of a narrow ramped street that overlooked the end of the Forum, where the rostrum, constructed to look like the bows of a warship, stood above the crowd. There was a waist-high wall running along the slope of the ramp, and from there they were afforded a view of the unfolding drama. The centre of Rome was packed with thousands upon thousands of the city's inhabitants, bellowing their anger towards the Palatine Hill as they brandished their fists and stabbed their fingers. Thousands more were besieging the Curia, where most of the senators sheltered from the mob, protected for the moment by a screen of lictors and bodyguards brandishing cudgels and shields. They formed a two-deep cordon at the top of the steps in front of the doors of the Curia. One of the doors was open and a handful of senators in their white togas with a red stripe peered out from the gloom within. Below them men and women in the crowd shouted and screamed abuse and hurled clods of filth and other missiles at the men protecting the aristocrats. As Macro and

Petronella watched, one of the senators was struck on the chest. Macro could not help grinning with pleasure at seeing the minor misfortune of one of the city's high and mighty.

On the other side of the Forum, a similar confrontation was taking place at the gates of the outer courtyard of the imperial palace. A hundred or so soldiers from the urban cohorts, fully armed and armoured, javelins at the ready, held off the crowd while suffering their own barrage of insults and unsavoury missiles.

'Looks ugly indeed,' Petronella commented.

'What's that?' Macro had to cup a hand to his ear and lean in to be heard over the cacophony.

'I said it's turning ugly,' she said more loudly. 'Maybe we should go back. Besides, we've no chance of getting through that lot to reach the market.'

'We're safe enough here,' Macro responded. He was loath to leave the scene without seeing how it turned out. 'We'll stay. For a while at least.'

Petronella knew her man well enough to know that when he made a decision he would not back down. She shook her head in frustration.

For the best part of an hour, they looked on as the crowd's mood gradually moderated, as was often the case when an impasse was reached. Those closest to the palace gates and the Curia drew back and hurled the odd insult, while the bulk of the mob milled around, their cries of anger giving way to a droning hubbub that reminded Macro of the atmosphere at the Great Circus once the last race of the day had been run. He took his wife's hand and started down the ramp.

'Come on, we can get to the market now.'

They made their way across the Forum towards the Boarium market. Macro put his arm around Petronella's shoulders and drew her close, while keeping an eye open for any more pickpockets.

They'd reached the rostrum when there was a fresh disturbance from the far end of the Forum. Shouting built up across the crowd like a great ocean wave breaking across a reef, and there was a surge that carried Macro and Petronella a short distance before he managed to brace himself and shelter her. He made free with his spare hand, thrusting people aside.

'They're bringing the prisoners!' a voice cried out, and Macro looked up to the rostrum to see a man clinging to the modelled ram of a warship that made up the front of the public-speaking edifice. His cry was taken up by others, and again the crowd flowed. This time Macro could not resist the pressure, and he and Petronella were swept along with the others towards the heart of the Forum. The man on the rostrum turned to stab his finger towards the Curia and cried out, 'Murderers! Them and the emperor! Murderers!'

Several men suddenly pushed against Petronella, and she let out a cry. Recovering quickly, she gritted her teeth and punched the nearest of them in the side. He turned to her with a furious expression and raised a fist.

'Oh no you don't!' Macro snarled as he threw a punch at the man's face, causing blood to spurt from his nostrils. As the man gasped in surprise and pain, Macro dragged Petronella away, making for the steps at the side of the rostrum. There was already a press of bodies, but he forced his way through, glaring at anyone who stood in his way. It was an expression that was more instinctual than cultivated, and it worked as well on Roman civilians as it did on parade-ground recruits or the shaken barbarians who had confronted him on battlefields across the Empire.

Holding on tightly to Petronella, Macro forced his way up the stairs and towards a corner of the balustrade, positioning himself across the angle to protect his wife.

'I told you we should have gone home,' she said as she recovered her nerve.

'Too late for that now. We'll just have to hold on here until it's over.'

From his raised position, Macro could look down the length of the Forum, and he could now see the commotion as the column of condemned slaves and their escort began to force their way towards the gentle ramp leading up to the outer courtyard of the palace to his right. The crowd closed in around the soldiers of the urban cohorts, bellowing their rage. Between their ranks, Macro could make out the pitiful line of slaves, men, women and children manacled and linked by lengths of rope fastened around their necks. As they drew closer, he could see their expressions. Some looked on blankly, unable to believe that they were moments from death. Others cried and raised their chained hands to beg for mercy. One woman who had been clutching an infant to her chest thrust the child towards the crowd so that it might be saved, but she was headed off by an officer and forced back into line.

The blast of a horn echoed across the Forum, and Macro looked to the left and saw the head of a column of Praetorians forcing their way into the crowd from the street leading to the military camp outside the city walls. Someone in the palace had called in reinforcements, and the sight of the elite soldiers only added to the rising fury of the crowd. They responded with a barrage of rubbish, loose cobbles ripped from the street and any other missile that came to hand. The Praetorians raised their shields and drew their swords, the points held high to threaten the faces of those in the mob. Those closest to the soldiers tried to fall back, but the press of bodies behind them held them in place and some could not escape the blades.

Macro felt his blood run cold, and for the first time realised the mortal danger that he and his wife might now be exposed to as the situation began to slip out of control. The column escorting the condemned slaves had forced its way through to the courtyard gates, and the Praetorians there drew aside to let them through. The long line of doomed slaves took a while to enter the open area bounded on three sides by a colonnade, with a further ramp on the far side that zigzagged up the Palatine Hill to the palace complex on the crest. There, a distant figure emerged on a balcony overlooking the Forum. He was wearing a purple tunic, glinting with gold trimming.

At the sight of the emperor, many in the crowd raised their arms and implored him to call off the executions. The deafening roar of tens of thousands of voices reached a new intensity, filling Macro's ears and seeming to press into his skull as if his head was caught in a vice. He could not hear Petronella as she tried to make herself understood inches from his face. She grasped him by the collar and drew his ear close to her lips.

'He can't let it happen. Surely?' She pointed. 'Nero.'

Macro had no firm idea what the young emperor might choose to do. Despite his whimsical nature since becoming Caesar, Nero had stuck by his promise to put an end to the secretive treason trials that had plagued the last years of Claudius's reign. He had also said he would not interfere with the responsibilities of the Senate. Fine words and intentions, Macro mused. In reality, the senators had grown so used to looking to the emperors and their highest officials for a steer on how they should vote that they were almost incapable of taking the initiative for themselves. It was the Senate that had condemned the slaves. Only Nero could intervene to save them now.

Macro had observed the emperor up close some years earlier, and it had been clear back then that Nero revelled in the affection of his people. Now the mob was making its change of sentiment abundantly clear with respect to the fate of the slaves. In his gut, Macro felt confident that the emperor would milk their grief for all it was worth before granting clemency and then basking in the relief, gratitude and love of the people. He was

10

struck by a further possibility. Maybe Nero had let the Senate think he wanted them to condemn the slaves so that he could overrule their decision, thereby pleasing the mob and delivering a reminder to the senators where the real power lay in Rome. Smiling ruefully, Macro wondered if he had spent too much time in the company of his friend Cato, who was perpetually inclined to look for hidden motivations and machinations.

The slaves had been led to the rear of the courtyard, where the ground was slightly elevated, so that they would be easily seen by those outside the gate and the cordon of Praetorians. They were ordered to kneel, facing the Forum. The cries from the crowd died away, and by the time the last of the slaves was forced to the ground, a hush had fallen across the heart of Rome. A curt order from a Praetorian centurion followed, and the men of the urban cohorts stood by as ten of the Praetorians downed their shields and took up their places behind the first of the slaves waiting to be executed.

Macro looked up at the emperor on the balcony. 'If Nero's going to put an end to this bloody drama, he's cutting it fine,' he muttered. 'Come on, man. Give the order.'

He found himself willing the emperor to call out. But Nero did not stir, did not appear to say anything as he stared down into the courtyard. The Praetorian centurion glanced up, as if waiting for a signal, then hesitated briefly before he barked the order in a clear voice that carried across the Forum. 'Carry out the sentence!'

The ten Praetorians leaned forward and placed the tips of their swords into the notch of the collarbones above the hearts of the waiting slaves. One of them began to struggle, then threw himself down and curled up, howling in terror. Before any of the others could react, the Praetorians plunged their swords down, twisted them from side to side and then wrenched the gory blades free as bright red blood spurted from the mortal wounds. The bodies jerked and were thrust away from their executioners so that they fell face-first on the flagstones.

A great keening cry of despair rose in the throats of those in the Forum as the Praetorians moved on to the next batch of slaves. Among them was the woman who had tried to save her child. The infant was ripped from her hands and hurled head-first at the base of the nearest column, where it lay still. The mother had time for one last cry of grief before she was silenced, joining her child and the others in death.

'I feel sick,' said Petronella. 'I want to go. Now.'

Macro nodded, and they began to work their way to the far side of the rostrum as the crowd roared with anger and began to seethe towards the gates. The Praetorian reinforcements had managed to cut across the Forum, and they now halted and faced out in both directions. Once the bucina sounded, they advanced slowly, pushing the crowd back on either side. The soldiers guarding the courtyard gates were outnumbered and were being forced back by a renewed barrage of missiles. One of the Praetorians punched his shield forward; it was instantly seized, and the soldier stumbled forward and was set upon by the mob. The officer in charge of the men shouted an order, and the other Praetorians advanced, flailing with their swords as they hacked at the crowd, driving it back. The rage of a moment before turned to terror.

Macro and Petronella tried to make for the ramp at the bottom of the Viminal Hill. Buffeted by the crowd, Macro held on to his wife as he fought to stay on his feet. Suddenly there was open ground in front of him, and he saw several Praetorians charging by as they chased a group of men. One of the soldiers spotted him and changed direction. From the gleam in his eyes, Macro could tell that the man was caught up in the bloodlust unfolding across the Forum. As the Praetorian raised his sword, Macro braced himself and stood erect.

'Lower your fucking weapon! You threaten a centurion and you see what happens to you!'

For a heartbeat the man hesitated, then his eyes narrowed and he came on again.

A lifetime in the army and on the streets of Rome as a child had sharpened Macro's reactions to a razor-sharp degree. He thrust Petronella behind him, then went into a crouch, hands raised. At the last moment, he ducked to the side of the Praetorian's oval shield, grabbed the edge and threw his weight forward, thrusting his opponent off balance so that he fell to the ground, with his shield and Macro crashing down on top of him, the breath bursting from his lungs with a groan. Instantly Macro was on his feet and grinding the nailed soles of his boot on the soldier's sword wrist until he released the weapon. Snatching it up, he smashed the pommel into the Praetorian's face until the man lay still.

'Let's go!'

Keeping the sword low and unobtrusive, he grasped Petronella's hand and hurried through the rush of fleeing civilians desperate to evade the soldiers. There were bodies scattered across the Forum, some writhing, some crawling to the nearest cover and some lying still. Cries of terror echoed from the walls of the temples and public buildings. Macro moved as fast as he could while keeping watch for any further encounters with the Praetorians running amok amid the protesters. He and Petronella hurried for the shelter of whatever corners, alcoves and pediments presented themselves until they reached the foot of the ramp and joined those escaping to the comparative safety of the warren of narrow streets and alleys on the hill.

He paused at the top of the ramp, heart pounding and breathing heavily, and drew Petronella close.

'Are you all right? Any injuries?'

She shook her head.

Macro looked back down into the Forum and saw that the Praetorians had cleared the ground in front of the imperial palace and were pursuing the last of those still lingering on the fringes of the Forum. A group of men armed with staves were staging a last show of defiance as they fought an unequal struggle with a party of heavily armed Praetorians near the Curia. In the courtyard, the executions continued, with over a hundred bodies lying in rough lines across the flagstones now running with blood. A similar number of dead and dying littered the Forum. Macro shifted his appalled gaze up to the palace balcony, where he could make out Nero leaning forward, hands resting on the balustrade as he surveyed the scene. He seemed to give a nod of satisfaction before he turned away and led his small retinue back inside and out of sight.

Macro paused a moment longer, scanning the ground below him until he caught sight of the Praetorian he had been forced to deal with. He felt a stab of anxiety as he saw the man sprawled on his back, unmoving. Two of his comrades were kneeling beside him while a third beckoned to an officer. Macro still had the sword in his hand. There was blood on the pommel and on the fist curled around the handle. He looked round before he let the weapon drop, then led his wife up the street towards Cato's house. She started at the sight of the blood on his hand.

'You're hurt!'

'It's not my blood. We'd better get out of here. Quickly.'

They left the slaughter behind them and hurried after the other people flowing past the crumbling apartment blocks on the lower slopes of the Aventine. Macro wiped off as much of the blood as possible using the bottom of his tunic. He tried to recall the confrontation with the soldier in as much detail as he could, and felt reassured that it had not been witnessed by any other Praetorians, or at least not by any close enough to be able to identify him. All the same, it would be wise to stay out of sight for a few days.

His thoughts turned to the execution of the slaves. Given Nero's previous demonstrations of sensitivity and his aspirations to deliver a golden age for Rome, it was hard to believe that he had failed to show them mercy. Something had changed. Macro felt that there had been a shift in the emperor's values. A colder, more ruthless streak in his nature had been laid bare, and the callous disregard for the fate of so many innocents indicated a gathering darkness of the soul.

For Macro, it seemed that the dangers and violence he had faced for so many decades on the frontiers of the Roman Empire had pursued him to the capital. He would have to be on his guard about what he said and who he was seen with in future. The dark days of the Claudian era might be returning to Rome, and with them the vermin who sought to profit from informing on or framing their fellow citizens. Macro, who had lost almost everything during the recent revolt in Britannia, was not worried for himself. His concern was for Cato, who had risen to equestrian rank and had come into a fortune through his first marriage, to the daughter of a senator. Along with his wealth, Cato was burdened with a measure of fame due to his military exploits. The kind of fame that many were envious of and resented given his humble origins.

Both Cato and Macro might have hoped to retreat into a more peaceful existence, far from the dangers of fighting on the Empire's frontier, but it was clear that there were perils of an equally deadly kind even here in the heart of Rome.

CHAPTER TWO

The road to Obriventum, fifteen miles outside Rome

The sun was glaring down from a clear blue sky and the shepherd was about to take a nap when he saw the rider approaching along the road a short distance from the slope where his sheep were grazing. The route to Obriventum was little more than a rutted narrow track, and the village itself consisted of a clutch of single-storey homes, stables and sheds. It boasted a single inn where the local men drank in the evenings after toiling in the surrounding fields and orchards.

The shepherd focused on the rider, picking out the quality of his cape, the red leather calf boots and the fine lines of his mount. A man of some status. In which case it was likely that he had taken the wrong road, since there was no obvious reason for him to visit a tiny backwater like Obriventum. With a tug on the reins, the rider slowed his horse to a walk and drew up a short distance from the shepherd, addressing him in the tone of a man accustomed to giving orders.

'You there. Where does this road lead?'

The shepherd pointed in the direction of the vale where the village was situated to take advantage of the small stream that ran down from the distant hills beyond. 'It goes to Obriventum, sir. Two miles or so that way. That's where it ends. If it's the village you're after, that is.'

The man regarding him from the saddle looked to be in his fifties, with a broad, lined face topped with thinning hair plastered down with perspiration. He was stocky and sat erect as he glanced in the direction of the village with a doubtful expression.

'I'm looking for the villa of Sempronius. I was told it was on the road to Obriventum.'

'You've already passed the turning to the villa, sir.'

'I have?' The rider glanced back down the road with a surprised expression.

'It's easy enough to miss, sir. If you ride back a half-mile, just over that rise there, you'll find it on your left.'

The rider swatted a fly from his neck as he mentally retraced his route and recalled the crumbling gateposts either side of an overgrown track that disappeared into some olive groves. Surely that could not be the entrance to the estate of the man he had come to visit.

'Are you certain about that? The place looked abandoned to me.'

'The villa's there all right. Been a bit neglected since old man Sempronius died, but his son-in-law, Master Cato, is living there now right enough. I can show you the way if you'd like, sir.'

The rider considered the offer briefly, then shook his head. 'You tend to your flock and I'll find my own way. A good day to you.' He wheeled his horse around and urged it into a canter.

The rider reined in as he reached the turning and examined the gateway and the overgrown track leading into the small estate surrounding the villa. Its appearance did not square with the wealth of the man he sought. Quintus Licinius Cato was an army officer with a well-earned reputation for courage and getting results. He had recently returned from Britannia, where he had won the final victory over Boudica and her followers that had ended their rebellion. Before that, he had served on most frontiers of the Empire with distinction as he had risen through the ranks.

17

The rider smiled as he recalled his first encounter with Cato, who had arrived as a raw recruit of the Second Legion Augusta in its fortress guarding the Rhine frontier. He had been appointed an optio on the orders of Emperor Claudius to honour the service of Cato's father, an imperial freedman. Since then, he had been promoted to the centurionate, followed by various independent commands as a prefect commanding a cohort, and had even been entrusted with the temporary command of a legion. His military success was matched by his climbing of the social ladder. He had married the daughter of a senator, an only child, and inherited Sempronius's estate after the latter had joined an ill-fated conspiracy that resulted in his death. Cato's wife had died around the same time, leaving him a son, Lucius. It seemed that Cato had decided to take a leave of absence from the army and retreat into the privacy and obscurity of his farming estate.

The rider steered his horse through the gateposts. The track went through a large plantation of olive trees, curving as it traced its way around the small hillocks on either side. After a mile or so, he emerged from the trees and saw the villa a short distance ahead, built atop a rise to take advantage of the views over the estate and any welcome breeze that would make the height of summer more bearable. It stood above and slightly apart from the stables, storerooms and slave quarters, and was surrounded by a wall with a gate opposite the façade of the main building. There was a short avenue lined with poplars leading up to the gate. The slopes below were planted with vines and cereal crops, and several figures could be seen tending them.

It was a bucolic scene, very different to the bustle, noise and stench of Rome, and for a moment the rider paused to enjoy the view. He had recently acquired his own villa in the seaside resort of Baiae, a fashionable location among the senatorial class with a taste for hedonism. There were frequent parties on the beach and competition to provide the most sophisticated banquets and entertainment. He felt envious of the quiet solitude that Cato had chosen for himself since his return to Italia. Solitude that was about to come to an end, the rider reflected with a trace of guilt. That was too bad. Rome could not afford to leave an officer of Cato's quality whiling away his life in such a backwater. His talents were required, one way or another . . . Besides, he had broken protocol in not reporting his return to the imperial palace, and the longer he left it, the more trouble he was storing up for himself.

'Are you certain that's the move you want to make?' Cato regarded his young son, sitting on a stool on the far side of the table. Lucius withdrew his piece and pulled at his dark forelock as he examined the painted board thoughtfully.

They were in the library, surrounded by the scrolls and books that Sempronius had amassed during his lifetime. Over by the window, Cato's second wife, Claudia, reclined on a couch reading a collection of poetry. Between Cato and his son rested the wooden board and playing pieces of the 'Game of Brigands' set that Macro had gifted them on his last visit from Rome. The small playing pieces were carved from ivory, with one set being stained a weathered brown. Despite their value, and his father's admonition not to treat them as toys, Lucius often used them for small battles he staged in the garden at the rear of the house.

Cato's eye caught the broken tip of the spear on one of the figurines. He was tempted to remark on it, but that would break the spell of concentration and the moment of bonding that he was enjoying with his son. Even though Lucius was ten years old, Cato had spent only a fraction of that lifetime in his son's company and was resolved to make up for it as best he could. If life in the army had taught him anything, it was to grasp whatever pleasures each day brought, since there was no guarantee that one would survive the morrow.

Lucius reached for a different piece and moved it to trap one of Cato's figurines, glancing up at his father warily before he committed to removing his hand. Cato did his best to keep his expression neutral as he saw that the decision would leave his son open to losing the game in no more than three moves. Which prompted the question faced by all parents trying to encourage their offspring to improve their skills. Should he let Lucius win to build his confidence, or should he deliver a hard lesson in defeat and trust that his son was mature enough to embrace the need to practise rather than give up? Experience had taught Cato that instilling competence and discipline was a matter of judicious use of the carrot and the stick. Too much of the former led to overconfidence and even arrogance, while too much of the latter led to resentment and incapacity.

He leaned back and stroked his chin as he cleared his throat. 'Hah–hmm . . .'

'Why don't you just tell him it's a bad move?' Claudia called out from her couch. She chuckled and rolled her eyes. 'Honestly, you think he can't see through your hah-hmming? You know what your father is thinking, don't you, Lucius? And if you know that, then you know enough to beat him at this game. Go on. Show him.'

Cato shifted to face her, ready to express his disapproval of her interruption. But the twinkle in her eye disarmed him at once and he could not stop smiling at her.

'You're right, my dear. I must let the boy make his own mistakes.'

'What mistakes?' Lucius demanded, his eyes flashing anger before he fixed his gaze on the board. 'Tell me.'

Claudia raised her head to scan the pieces, then nodded. 'Ah, I see what you mean, Cato. Now then, Lucius, think it through.'

Keeping his hand on the piece he had chosen a moment earlier, the boy examined the board. Cato saw the fingers of his other

20

hand twitch as he went through the permutations of the moves available to him, and his father's counter-movements. Then his eyes widened with realisation and he shifted the piece to a free space on the corner of the board, where he would be able to command two lines of attack. He sat back with a smile and folded his arms as he waited for his father's response.

Cato affected a disapproving tone. 'Thank you, Claudia. Just when I thought I had him on the ropes. Now he's got me . . .'

They exchanged a wink, and she returned to her book while Cato regarded her briefly. They had finally married shortly after taking up residence in the villa. It had been an intimate affair, with only Macro and Petronella as guests and witnesses. It could be no other way given Claudia Acte's past. She had been a mistress of Nero until his mother had forced him to discard her. Sent into exile on the island of Sardinia, she had formed a relationship with Cato, the officer in charge of her escort. A plague had been sweeping the island, and they had pretended that she had died from the disease in the hope that she could escape from exile and live with him. Since then, she had contrived to change her appearance by dyeing her fine blonde hair, and had kept away from anyone who might recognise her. Which was why they had come to live in the villa, letting Macro and Petronella take on Cato's house in the capital. In time, they hoped, Nero would either forget about her or perhaps die or be deposed, and they could live in the open without fear of the consequences arising from her past.

Cato heard footsteps and looked up to see his steward approaching. Trebonius had served as his servant during the campaigns in Britannia and had chosen to accept Cato's offer to take him on as a retainer. They had come to know each other's ways and preferred to stick with the familiar arrangement. Trebonius was some ten years older than Cato, with a spare physique and a weary and at times critical manner about him that expressed itself through subtle sighs, raised eyebrows and muttered comments. But he was reliable, trustworthy and loyal. Qualities to be prized in any man, let alone a servant.

'Pardon me, master, but it seems you have a visitor. The house boy says there is a rider approaching the villa.'

'Macro?' Cato wondered.

'No, sir. The boy says it is someone else. A stranger. Wealthy by the look of him.'

He exchanged a glance with Claudia. Apart from Macro and Petronella, there had only been one visitor to the villa in the two months since they had moved in – a servant sent by the owner of a neighbouring villa to invite them to dinner. An invitation Cato had been obliged to accept on his own while Claudia remained at home and out of sight.

'Stay here with Lucius. I'll deal with it.' He rose from the table and made to leave the room.

'Can I come?' asked Lucius.

'No. You need to think about your next move, lad.'

Cato followed Trebonius out of the library and through the decorated corridors of the villa to the atrium, where a handful of fish swam languidly in a small pond. The doors of the main entrance opened onto a courtyard in front of the villa. Beyond the portico Cato saw a broad-shouldered man handing over the reins of his horse to a servant. He was dusty from his ride, and as he turned to face Cato, his craggy face broke into a warm smile.

'Good to see you again, Prefect Cato.'

Cato grinned as he descended the steps and clasped the other man's arm. 'Senator Vespasian. By the gods, it's good to see you again, sir.'

'It's been a while.' Vespasian's eyes glanced over Cato. 'A couple of scars, a few more lines around the eyes and some grey hairs since we last met, but I dare say you could say the same about me.'

'And more,' Cato responded, still smiling. 'What brings you here, sir?'

'Besides a desire to look up an old comrade after a long, hot ride in the blazing sun?'

'Forgive me, sir. You honour me with your visit. Please enter and we can take some refreshments in the garden.' He nodded to Trebonius to make the arrangements before he bowed his head and beckoned his visitor towards the entrance.

The walled garden at the rear of the villa, a safe distance away from the library, had been created as a peaceful sanctuary by Sempronius. It was laid out in four lawned areas, surrounded by a trellised walkway where climbing plants provided shade. An open-sided pavilion with three dining couches faced a modest water feature fed from a stream that ran down from the hills. The soft splashing of water seemed to add to the coolness of the shade as the two men sat on the couches.

Vespasian made a face as he removed his cloak and rubbed the small of his back. 'I'm getting soft. It's been too long since I've been on campaign. Too long in the company of the gossiping aristocrats at the imperial court. Too many dinners and too little exercise.'

'You say that now, but I dare say you'd change your tune if you were still serving in Britannia over winter.'

Vespasian recalled the bitter cold and damp of the northern province and nodded. 'Yes, I try to forget that . . .' He turned to face Cato. 'You're a hard man to track down. I only discovered you had returned from Britannia after bumping into that rogue Macro at the theatre a few days ago.'

Cato could not hide his surprise. 'Macro went to the theatre?'

'Oh, it was just some knockabout comedy by Terentius, but he seemed to be having a good time. I think most of the audience heard his laughter. I caught up with him as the audience was leaving. Him and his plump wife. Quite a character, that lady. Anyway, I asked after you and he was reluctant to say much at first, but we traded a few old war stories over a jug of wine in a nearby inn and he let slip that you were back. Sounds like you both had a hard time of it.' The senator's expression hardened. 'The rebellion was a bloody business and nearly cost us the province. That can never be allowed to happen again.'

· 'No, sir. It can't. We lost a lot of good men, as well as many civilians. It makes me wonder if the whole thing was worthwhile.'

'Invading Britannia?' Vespasian shrugged. 'Maybe not. It was a bad decision and most reasonable people understand that. But it's too late to do anything about it now. For better or worse we're committed to the province. If we abandon it, the loudmouths in Rome and their followers will never forgive us. And with an emperor who is desperate to be the darling of the mob, I cannot see anyone admitting the mistake. That's politics, I suppose.'

Cato nodded. 'That's why I do my best to keep out of such matters. I'm happy enough living here, away from Rome.'

'So I see. But you can't do that indefinitely. From what Macro said, you haven't yet notified the imperial palace of your return. If I were you, I'd do that as soon as you can, before Nero's people start asking questions. They tend to see threats to the emperor everywhere and they'll wonder why you are hiding out here.'

'I'm not hiding, sir.'

'Really?' Vespasian raised an eyebrow. 'If that's the case, then their thoughts might run to asking if you are hiding something or someone else.'

Cato felt a chill ripple down the back of his neck, and it took all his willpower not to look past the senator to the house. He swallowed to calm himself before he responded. 'I can't imagine why anyone would consider my living arrangements a cause for such suspicion. I've served Rome loyally for the best part of two decades and I've earned the right to live in peace in a place and manner of my choosing.'

'If anyone can claim that right, it's you, Prefect. I have every sympathy for your point of view. But others won't, and you will need to allay their concerns if you are to be left alone. You and your family. How is your boy, Lucius?' Vespasian glanced round the garden and towards the house. 'Is he here?'

'Resting.'

'Resting? What would a spirited young lad of his age be doing resting on a fine afternoon like this?'

'He had a tiring morning,' Cato responded lamely. 'Helping me oversee the crops.'

Vespasian chuckled. 'I don't see you settling down to be a farmer. I really don't.'

Trebonius appeared from the house, followed by a slave carrying a tray with a wine jug, cups and some pastries, which he set down on the small serving plinth between the couches. The steward turned to Cato. 'Do you require anything else, master?'

Cato dismissed him with a shake of his head, his thoughts turning to the true purpose of Vespasian's visit.

'Forgive me, sir, but you seem to have gone to considerable trouble to pay me this visit. I take it that you didn't just want to remind me to report my return to the imperial palace.'

'Oh dear, am I so transparent? Ah, well. I might make a decent commander of a legion, but it seems I am doomed to be much less successful as a scheming politician.'

They shared a smile before the older man continued in a more serious tone. 'I take it you heard about the trouble over the execution of the slaves the other day.'

Cato nodded. Trebonius had been sent into Rome that day to buy some farming tools, and had been shaken as he described what he had seen.

'A bad business,' Vespasian continued. The only reason the Senate voted in favour of execution is because we were given the nod by Tigellinus that Nero would show mercy. Seems we were misled. And there was a riot as a result.'

'Tigellinus?' Cato prompted. 'I'm not familiar with the name.'

'You have no reason to be, given your absence from the capital for some years. He's the emperor's new blue-eyed boy, lined up to replace Burrus as the prefect of the Praetorian Guard.'

'Is Burrus retiring?'

'Burrus is dying. Poor sod is being eaten away by some disease or other. Hollowed out and thin as a rake. I doubt he'll last more than a few more months. At present Tigellinus is serving as the commander of the urban cohorts, but he's already spending a great deal of time at the Praetorian camp, buttering up the officers. When he's not there, he's at the palace, buttering up the emperor. It's been quite a swift rise to prominence for our friend since Nero visited his stud to buy some horses a few years back. From horse-breeder to the side of the emperor in a single bound. You'll see why when you get to meet him. The smooth bastard has fine looks and is as silver-tongued as any flatterer. Frankly, I'm astonished that Nero buys his praise at face value. A more sickening display of obsequiousness is impossible to imagine. Anyway, Tigellinus is the coming man and we had better get used to it.'

'Sounds like one to avoid. I'll be sure not to invite him to dinner.'

Vespasian gave a light laugh, then reached for his silver goblet and sipped the watered wine that had been poured for him. His gaze fixed on some point in the mid-distance for a beat before he turned his attention back to his host.

'Tigellinus is only part of the problem, I fear. You've returned to Rome at a difficult time, Cato. We're fast approaching something of a crisis, thanks to Nero. I dare say you're aware of that even if you have squirrelled yourself away in the depths of the countryside.'

'I know almost nothing about what goes on at the imperial court, sir, and I'd prefer to keep it that way.'

'Prefer what you like, but don't put too much faith in the old adage that what you don't know can't hurt you. You may not be interested in politics, Cato, but believe me, politics has a way of being interested in you, whether you like it or not.'

Cato frowned. 'Then I must do my best to keep politics at bay.'

'Good luck with that.' Vespasian took another sip as he collected his thoughts. 'The emperor does not have an heir. He's been married to Octavia for a number of years without issue. It's likely that she is barren. If she had given him a child, ideally a son, then he might be tempted to stick by her even if they despise each other. Word is that he intends to divorce her and marry his mistress, Poppaea Sabina. You know her?'

'The name is familiar, though I can't quite place it.'

'She is the wife of Otho, one of the emperor's circle of friends. Quite the looker. She caught Nero's eye a few years back and he found a neat solution to the problem by sending Otho off to Lusitania to serve as governor. Saved having to serve him a dish of mushrooms to get him off the scene.'

Cato recalled the unfortunate husband now. He had encountered him many years ago while serving in Britannia. A likeable enough junior officer, but he had made no secret of his yearning to return to Rome as soon as he had served out his time as a tribune.

'Anyway, the rumour is that Nero's little poppet is with child. The emperor needs an heir to cement his position, ergo Octavia needs to be pushed out and Poppaea needs to have her divorce from Otho and marriage to Nero rushed through. That's going to cause a few headaches for the happy couple, given Octavia's popularity. There will almost certainly be trouble once Nero makes his move.'

Vespasian paused, and Cato felt a growing uneasiness.

'What kind of trouble do you mean, sir?'

'Nero's legitimacy as Caesar is based on his adoption by

27

Claudius, and Claudius's legitimacy rested on the successful invasion of Britannia. A rather shaky foundation given the men and treasure Rome has committed to pacifying the tribes only for things to go to pieces when Boudica's rebellion threatened to torch the whole province and to annihilate every Roman on the island. Thank the gods she was defeated. I shudder to think about the consequences if she had not been. So Nero's authority has been called into question. Not that he has helped matters. All his poncing around playing the poet, actor and singer and neglecting his duties has unnerved and angered the Senate. Particularly given the power wielded by his freedmen and advisers, who seem to rule in his place.' Vespasian paused briefly. 'I like to think of the power of Rome as being founded on three pillars: the emperor, the Senate and the mob. At the best of times they work together. But now it's as if they are pulling in different directions, and the whole edifice may come crashing down. If that happens . . . who knows? Civil war, perhaps.' Vespasian gave Cato a sharp look. 'I can see you think I am overreacting.'

'No, sir. I'm just surprised at how far things seem to have gone.'

'Nero is becoming increasingly hostile to the Senate, and we may see the return of the political prosecutions of the last years of Claudius's reign. If that happens, none of us are safe. Not the senators, nor you equestrians on the next rung down. The question is, what can be done about it?'

Cato cleared his throat. 'What do you suggest, sir?'

'There are some in the Senate who are discussing the matter and considering a . . . solution, if that is what is required. Of course, they hope it won't come to that, and that Nero will be content to let the Senate carry out its duties without the interference of his cronies, or indeed the emperor himself. It's a question of balancing power really. I'm sure an intelligent man like yourself can see that.'

'I wouldn't know about that. I'm a soldier, not a politician.'

28

'If only it was that simple. The further you rise in the military, the more exposed to politics you become. You're no exception, Cato. But I can see that this is all very troubling for you. Forgive me. I did not come here to cause you concern. Just to set out the lie of the land, as it were. And to catch up with a former comrade-in-arms, of course.'

Vespasian drained his goblet and stood up stiffly, grimacing as he rubbed the small of his back. 'I'm getting to that age when too much rest is as uncomfortable as too much exercise. Now, I have to go. I thank you for your hospitality and look forward to having more time to talk on another occasion. Perhaps you might dine with me at my house in Rome.'

Cato nodded. 'I would be honoured to.'

'That's settled then.' Vespasian beamed. 'It's damned good to see you again . . .'

Cato escorted his visitor back through the house, and stood in the portico with a hand raised in farewell as Vespasian rode out of the gate and along the tree-lined avenue.

'What did he want?' asked Claudia as she emerged from the shade of the atrium. 'What did he say to you?'

Cato hesitated briefly. 'Unless I miss my guess, he was sounding me out to see if I would join a conspiracy against the emperor . . .'

CHAPTER THREE

The outer courtyard of the imperial palace was filled with aristocrats, provincials and petitioners hoping to be allowed to present their greetings to the emperor. Along with them were the usual crowd of philosophers, actors, historians and preening young blades trying to impress their peers while hoping to attract the attention of a moneyed patron. There were plenty of Praetorians, mingling with the crowd and guarding the outer gate as well as the inner gate that led to the anteroom to the emperor's audience chamber. They had put aside their usual white togas and this morning wore armour and carried spears in addition to their swords. The violence of a few days before was still fresh in the memory of their commander, Burrus. The show of force was intended to dissuade anyone from considering the emperor a viable target for assassination.

Cato had spent the night at his house on the Viminal and had dinner with Macro and Petronella. They had related the events of the day of the mass execution of slaves, and it was clear that Petronella had been badly shaken by the experience. Even Macro, battle-hardened as he was, expressed shock at the spectacle.

'Killing your enemy in combat is one thing, lad. Executing criminals and captives is unsettling enough. But massacring hundreds of innocent and harmless slaves? That's bad.'

'It's worse than bad,' Cato had replied. 'It's a mistake. Nero, or whoever is pulling his strings, is driving a wedge between the emperor and the mob. Rome is ripe for unrest at the best of times. How else could it be with so many people crowded into the slums and shanty towns outside the walls? This hot weather doesn't help matters. The city's a tinderbox, and it makes no sense to provide the spark that sets the lot ablaze.'

'Then you'd better be careful what you say about the situation back in Britannia. Someone is bound to ask, and you don't want them spreading the word about how close we came to defeat during the rebellion, or how loose our grip is on the tribes. That's the kind of information that goes round quickly, and if Nero and his advisers decide to make an example of defeatist rumour-mongers, you don't want them pointing the finger at you. You know what that would mean.' Macro had drawn his thumb across his throat.

Cato looked round the outer courtyard until he spotted a clerk making a list of those hoping to be permitted entry to the audience chamber and a chance to petition the emperor in person. As he approached, the clerk was being addressed in urgent tones by a corpulent man in a blue tunic with a small, active mouth set amid heavy jowls. His thin white hair was combed over his crown and held in place with some kind of sour-scented oil. He held his thumb and forefinger together in an oval as he gestured to emphasise his point.

'I own some of the finest tenement blocks in Rome. Everyone tells me they are the best. Some nasty people have been telling lies about my buildings being unsafe. I want the emperor to deal with them. You tell him that Titus Horangenus will be forever in his debt if Nero gives him justice.'

The clerk made a brief note and looked up. 'Horangenus?'

'That's right.'

'Very well. I'll pass your details to the director of petitions. If he thinks there is sufficient merit, then your name will be called out.'

Horangenus glanced around furtively, then stepped in front of Cato as he passed something to the clerk. 'Here's a little something to help you decide on the merit of my request,' he muttered. 'And tell the director there's more where that came from.'

He turned, glared briefly at Cato with a pair of watery eyes, then pushed his way over to the shade of the nearest colonnade.

The clerk quickly pocketed the coins and addressed Cato. 'Yes, sir? You have a request to make?'

Cato shook his head. 'I've recently returned from Britannia. I was commander of the Eighth Auxiliary Cohort there. I am reporting my return to the imperial palace, as required.'

'I see. Your name, sir?'

'Quintus Licinius Cato.' He held up his equestrian ring as proof of his status.

'If you'd follow me, sir.' The clerk led Cato the way towards the squad of Praetorians guarding the entrance to the hall and gestured for him to wait before disappearing within.

The civilians nearby regarded Cato with curious glances as they wondered who he was to be treated so preferentially. Certainly there was nothing in his appearance that set him apart from the others in the courtyard. He wore a plain red toga over a linen tunic and was shod in the army boots he had long since grown accustomed to. The faint scars on his face confirmed his military background but provided no clue as to his rank. The more observant would have spotted the equestrian ring that meant he was sure to be a centurion or above.

There was a brief delay before the clerk reappeared and beckoned to him. 'Sir, Prefect Burrus will see you now. Please be quick, he is a busy man.'

The Praetorians parted to let Cato through, and he followed the clerk at a swift pace through the large open doors into the inner courtyard beyond – a high-ceilinged chamber that was at least a hundred feet square. The air was filled with the cloying smell of incense rising from small burners in the corner tended by palace slaves. There were fewer people here than in the outer court, and from the quality of their attire it was clear that social class and wealth improved the chances of being permitted closer proximity to the emperor. Despite his bribe, Horangenus was unlikely to gain admission, Cato reflected with a degree of satisfaction. He knew the type well. Builders of shoddy accommodation that often proved a hazard to those unfortunate enough to become his tenants. His kind also fleeced suppliers and defaulted on loans from investors.

The clerk led Cato up a flight of steps into the palace complex and down a broad corridor to the anteroom outside the emperor's audience chamber which was guarded by a squad of praetorians. The clerk spoke in an undertone to a Praetorian optio. The doors were opened to admit Cato and immediately closed behind him.

Cato recalled the audience chamber from his childhood, but the staid paintings that had adorned the walls then had been replaced with fresh images of athletes, singers, musicians and what looked to be actors or poets proclaiming in theatres. It was a much smaller space than the anteroom. On the far side, Nero sat on a cushioned chair, listening intently to a group of plaintiffs.

Cato was ushered towards Burrus, the commander of the Praetorians. He had met him on a number of occasions, but was shocked at the change in his appearance. Burrus's features had shrunk so that his face now seemed to barely cover the skull beneath. The eyes seemed larger as a consequence and had a watery gleam. The once muscular torso had gone, and his limbs were withered and almost stick-like. It surprised Cato that a man who looked so ill could remain on his feet.

Burrus nodded a greeting as Cato approached. 'Prefect Cato.' He spoke in a hushed tone so as not to distract the emperor. 'I understand that you have returned from Britannia.'

'Yes,' Cato replied equally quietly.

'When?'

'Some two months ago.'

Burrus fixed him with a disapproving look. 'Two months . . . Why the delay in reporting your presence to the palace?'

Cato made to explain, but Burrus raised a finger to his lips and steered him towards an open side door that led out into a plain service corridor. Here they could speak without risking drawing Nero's attention, and possibly his ire.

'Explain yourself, Prefect,' Burrus demanded.

Cato had considered his answer the night before. 'I would have reported sooner, but I developed a fever on my return and only recovered a few days ago. I did not wish to report in person out of concern that the illness might spread to others.'

'Nevertheless, you could have sent a message. You know the regulation; all army officers and those of equestrian or senatorial rank have a duty to inform the imperial palace of their return from the provinces.'

'I know, but I was not in a fit enough condition to even write a message.'

Burrus regarded him for a moment. 'You don't have the look of a man who has endured such a serious illness that you were incapable of writing a note. Some of us manage to continue doing our duty despite illness.'

It was a pointed enough remark, and Cato felt a stab of guilt over the lame excuse he had provided.

Burrus sighed before he continued in a reedy voice. 'Be that as it may, I will have your presence recorded on the active officers list.'

'I had hoped to request a place on the reserve list. I've earned it,' Cato added with emphasis. 'Besides, there are certain to be more officers waiting for fresh commands than there are vacancies. I am surplus to requirements.'

'That is for Nero to decide. While there may be more officers waiting for a command, they are not necessarily of equal quality. You serve at the pleasure of the emperor. You do not get to choose whether you retire from active service. If Rome needs you, you will serve her. If you refuse . . . let's just say the consequences would be unfortunate.'

Cato felt a leaden sensation pull down on his heart as he heard the threat. After all the years of service he had given, he deserved a rest from war and the strains of campaigning. He deserved the chance to spend time with his son and his new wife. He craved peace. Now it seemed that he might not have the opportunity.

Some flicker of empathy seemed to spark in Burrus as he beheld Cato's world-weary expression. 'Listen, it's possible that you will be left alone. There are many officers chasing commands and most of them have powerful connections willing to further their cause. It would be easy enough for you to remain in the background and be overlooked. Even though I am not long for this world, I will do my best to let you rest a while.' He paused and glanced round, but there were only a handful of slaves in the corridor, and they were hurrying about their duties. 'I cannot speak for what happens after I am gone. Nero has said that he will revert to the old arrangement of having two prefects of the Praetorian Guard. One of whom is sure to be Tigellinus. You know him?'

'I have heard of him,' Cato said cautiously.

'And heard nothing much good, I'll be bound. He's of a kind with the emperor. One of his circle of dissolute friends from the early days. As Nero's favourite, he is sure to exercise more influence than whoever is appointed prefect alongside him. So a word of advice, Cato. While I may grant you a little licence in being tardy in reporting your return, Tigellinus might choose to use that as something he can hold against you, or to compel you to do his bidding. Tread carefully around that man.'

Cato nodded. 'Thanks for the warning.'

'I know your worth. It would be a considerable loss to Rome if you were to be exiled, or worse, due to some irregularity that Tigellinus might choose to exploit. My advice to you is to play by the rules and keep your head down.'

'Just like being a recruit all over again.'

'Yes.' Burrus smiled. 'The perennial burden of every good soldier, eh? Now let's get back in there. I'll present you to Nero once he's ruled on the case at hand. For all his faults, he has a good memory for faces and names and will readily recall your loyalty when Britannicus and his fellow plotters conspired to bring him down. It will be good for you to be seen to have the emperor's favour. At least it will make Tigellinus think twice in case he decides to target you. Come.'

He led the way into the audience chamber, and they stood to one side as Nero was delivering his verdict. The emperor eased himself back in his chair and took a deep breath as he reached his conclusions. His voice, slightly husky, nevertheless filled the chamber as he addressed the plaintiffs.

'I appreciate your commitment to your cause in travelling to Rome to make your case before your emperor. I have heard your grievances against those Roman officials whom you claim have imposed a considerable burden on the townsfolk of Metapolus, and I have a great deal of sympathy for the hardships you have endured. There is no doubt that egregious abuses have been carried out, and this causes us great concern and sympathy . . .'

The men who had come so far to see justice done could not help exchanging relieved and delighted looks as they listened to Nero. The emperor took a steady breath before he continued. 'However, the warrants issued by governors of the provinces that make up the Empire serve an important purpose. The smooth running of the administration of the Empire is in the interests of provincials as much as it is in the interests of Rome. If there is abuse of the system, that must be looked into on a case-by-case basis by the officials of the governor's office in each province. Moreover, the province in question is administered by the Senate, and when I became Caesar I gave an undertaking that I would not interfere in the running of such provinces. Therefore, I will not rule in your favour and the matter is referred to the governor of the province you come from. Caesar has spoken. Case dismissed.'

The plaintiffs looked aghast at the outcome. But Cato knew from experience that an emperor in Rome was unlikely to side with provincials against governors and their staff assigned to rule over them. The men from Metapolus would have to return home and try their luck with their local officials. Good luck with that, he thought.

The man who appeared to be their leader anxiously took a half-step towards Nero. 'Caesar, we beg you to reconsider . . . in the name of justice.'

A grey-haired man in a senator's toga, who had been standing to one side of the throne, stabbed his finger at him. 'How dare you challenge the decision of the emperor of Rome! You dog! Take your petition, and the rest of the curs who follow you, and scurry back to your hole in Asia Minor!'

The petitioner trembled as he bowed deeply, and he and his fellows backed away towards the entrance of the audience chamber, where the doors were opened by the Praetorians. As they disappeared, Nero let out a peal of laughter and slapped his thigh as he addressed the senator.

'By the gods, Seneca, you would make a fine actor. You delivered your lines like a veteran of the stage.'

Seneca smiled obsequiously and gave a slight bow of his head. 'I thank you, Caesar, but my outrage was quite genuine. These provincials must never be permitted to forget their place. When a decision is handed down by Caesar, no man is free to challenge it in the smallest degree. If your judgement is called into question, all that comprises the divine project of Rome is called into question.'

Nero considered this and nodded. 'How right you are, my friend. I am indeed fortunate to have such a wise head among my closest associates. You are as shrewd an expert on political matters as you are a most excellent arbiter of refined taste. Especially with regard to the sublime arts of poetry and music. My humble efforts in particular.'

'You are too kind, Caesar. I merely speak the truth. I am truly blessed to have been born in an age that has given rise to such divine talent, exercised with such unrivalled modesty.'

Nero smiled happily, and Cato did his best to keep his expression neutral. How on earth was it possible for the emperor to be oblivious to such absurd flattery? Yet glancing around the audience chamber, he saw that no one else seemed to be uncomfortable with Seneca's performance. Or at least they affected not to be. Even no-nonsense, plain-speaking Burrus kept a deadpan expression as he nodded approval at the senator's words. That was how things were arranged in the imperial palace, he realised. He wondered what it must be like to be the only man in the room who would never be told the full truth by those around him. Who would dare to?

Nero looked over the faces of his entourage with a dreamy gaze, then his eyes alighted on Cato and fixed there. He frowned momentarily, then rose from his chair, his smile broadening. The effect was unnerving, and Cato felt his pulse quicken with anxiety. There was nothing as worrying as being drawn to the attention of the most powerful man in the known world and dreading the slightest misstep that might draw his disapproval or anger.

'Why, it's that fellow Cato! Friend Cato, approach us.'

Burrus gave him a nudge, and Cato paced over to the edge of the dais and bowed. 'Caesar.'

Nero jumped down lightly and clasped his shoulders. 'My

saviour! I shall never forget the debt that I, and therefore Rome, owe you.'

'I did no more than my duty, Caesar.'

'You were motivated by more than just duty. I know genuine loyalty when I see it. And loyalty is a quality to be respected, and rewarded.' He looked Cato up and down. 'You appear somewhat older and more careworn since I last saw you.'

A similar line of thought was going through Cato's mind. Nero's fine youthful features had coarsened. His jowls were fleshy and his stomach betrayed his appetite for fine food. But the deep-set eyes still had the same lively glint as before. His hair, thinning noticeably, was fringed with carefully oiled curls that lined his brow, and was worn down his neck in what Cato assumed was some kind of thespian affectation.

'When was that?' Nero paused. 'Some five years or so ago. Yes, you were charged with escorting my dear Claudia Acte into exile in Sardinia not long after the demise of my rival to the throne. I was greatly saddened to hear that she had died of the plague,' he added. 'A sad loss.'

Cato swallowed and nodded. 'It could not be helped. She was one of many who died, Caesar.'

'Indeed. But none so beautiful as my Claudia . . .' Nero gave a guilty start. 'None save my darling Poppaea, I meant to say.'

Clearly anxious to change the subject, he released Cato's shoulders and turned to Burrus. 'Where has this fellow been these last years?'

'Prefect Cato has been campaigning in Britannia, Caesar. He only returned to Rome recently.'

'Britannia?' Nero mused, and his lips twitched with irritation. 'That island of barbarians is the cause of more trouble than any other province in the Empire. Except Judaea perhaps. I put it down to the insular and intolerant religious cults they subscribe to. What do you say, Cato?'

Cato swiftly gathered his thoughts. Having served in both places, he was aware of how stubbornly the Britons and Judaeans clung to their traditions and their faiths. 'You are right, Caesar. It is a pity they are so pig-headed. Why cling to their gods alone when they can share them with all of ours?'

'Quite so. And as for the notion of having only one god?' Nero shook his head. 'That is palpable nonsense. To make matters worse, there is even a sect among the Jews that believes their one god is composed of three gods who are one and the same. As if that makes sense. I am even told that they think one of the three divinities they worship is some criminal, Yeshua. Crucified thirty years ago.'

'I am familiar with the cult, Caesar. I came across some of Yeshua's followers when I was serving in Judaea. They seemed harmless enough.'

'Maybe so. But I can't say I care for the arrogance of those who insist their god is the only god. Still, as long as they keep to themselves and don't try to impose their convictions on other people . . . Anyway. I should like to hear all about your experiences in Britannia. Especially the rebellion. I've heard that their leader, Boudica, had hair of fire.'

'Fire?' Cato smiled. 'Not fire, Caesar. It was merely red.'

'You saw her yourself?'

'On many occasions.'

'Then—'

They were interrupted by Seneca clearing his throat. Nero turned to him. 'What is it?'

'There are five more cases awaiting your judgement this morning, Caesar. Perhaps the prefect could regale you with his adventures in Britannia another time.'

'Yes, yes.' Nero turned back to Cato. 'You see how it is. An emperor is a slave to his duties. Perhaps it would be best to hear you over dinner at the palace.'

'It would be an honour, Caesar.'

'Good. I look forward to it.' Nero patted Cato's cheek, then vaulted back onto the dais to resume his seat. As Seneca began to read the details of the next case from a waxed tablet, Burrus ushered Cato out of the audience chamber.

Outside in the hall, Cato breathed a sigh of relief. 'I take it the dinner invitation was just for the sake of politeness.'

Burrus shrugged. 'I couldn't say. Nero is like a butterfly, picking his way through life without ever settling on a firm direction. He might order an arrangement to be made, he might not. Who can tell? But I wouldn't make any other plans for the next few days if I were you, just in case. Oh, and never make the mistake of regarding such an eventuality as an invitation. It's more of an on-pain-of-death instruction.'

'Ah . . . I see. In that case, I'll await word, or not, at my house.'

'Yes. That would be wise.' Burrus nodded. 'Just watch your step, Cato. Rome is a more dangerous place than it has been for a long time . . .'

CHAPTER FOUR

A slave from the palace delivered a scroll after Cato had returned to his house on the Viminal Hill. He was relaxing with Macro and Petronella in the small courtyard garden, while Bardea was sitting in the corner reading some poetry to improve her Latin.

'How's it going?' Cato nodded towards the girl.

'You know how it is with kids and learning.' Macro shook his head. 'They spend twice as much effort avoiding their studies as it would take to do them.'

'Perhaps, but it can't be easy for her shifting from one culture to another. You might want to cut her some slack, brother.'

'What kind of advice is that?' Macro snorted. 'I've trained more men than Arpokras has eaten hot meals. If you want results, you have to push for them. If I go easy on Bardea, she'll never fit in.'

Petronella leaned forward and patted his thigh. 'Cato is right. She's a young girl, dear, not a recruit from one of your legions.'

'That's true enough,' said Macro. 'No recruit was ever trained in barracks as luxurious as this. She might want to count her blessings from time to time.' He gestured down the length of the garden.

Cato's house was situated on the crest of the hill to take advantage of any breeze and at the same time to avoid being overlooked by the tenement blocks that crowded the lower slopes.

To be sure, it was modest compared to the grand properties owned by the richest men in Rome. Particularly the small palaces of the imperial freedmen who had used their positions to acquire vast fortunes built on bribes and other forms of corruption. That in turn caused considerable resentment among the ranks of the Roman aristocracy, who did not hide their glee every time a freedman fell out of favour and was prosecuted, stripped of his wealth and sentenced to death.

The house was in a quiet area where other properties owned by modestly wealthy senators and equestrians nestled among shops above which Rome's poorer inhabitants lived in crowded apartments. The street-facing parts of the building were rented to a baker on one side and a potter on the other. A short corridor behind the sturdy iron-studded front door led to the atrium, with a small square pond fed by rainwater running off the roof tiles. The excess was directed along a pipe to feed further ponds in the garden and to water the plants. There were several rooms around the atrium and another corridor that led to the kitchen and the slaves' quarters at the rear, hidden behind the trellis that ran around the edge of the garden.

The palace slave was escorted by the steward of the house, Taurus, a muscular former gladiator with a pronounced limp, a legacy of the fight in the arena that had ended his career. The slave, in his white tunic with a broad purple stripe running down the middle, bowed from the waist as he handed over the small hinged tablet with the imperial seal fixed to the edge.

'From Pallodorus, director of the palace banqueting division, master.'

Cato took the waxed tablet as Macro raised an eyebrow and muttered wryly, 'Palace banqueting division, eh?'

Cato did not respond. He had been born and raised in the palace during the reign of Tiberius, and was familiar with the plethora of bodies and their hierarchies that surrounded the imperial family. He broke the seal, opened the waxed tablet and glanced at the message neatly inscribed within.

'*Your presence is requested at the imperial palace to attend a dinner at the first hour of the night,*' he read aloud. '*A toga is not required. Please confirm your attendance to the bearer of this message. Pallodorus, on the command of Caesar.*' He tapped his finger on the impression of the imperial seal at the bottom of the message. 'I have my marching orders.'

'Ah well,' said Macro with a gleam in his eye. 'A banquet at any rate. See if you can bring some dainties back for us, eh?'

'On past experience, you would be in for a disappointment. The only people who get decent food hot from the kitchens are the emperor and his circle. What is served to the rest is not so palatable, and lukewarm at best.'

'Better than army rations, at any rate.'

'When did you last eat army rations?' Petronella reached over to pat Macro's belly. 'You've been eating well ever since we got back from Britannia. I've made sure of it. More than a few pounds have been added to your middle.'

Macro frowned. 'Thank you for that, wife. Much appreciated.'

Cato turned to the slave. 'Tell me, have you ever delivered an invitation to dine with Caesar that was declined?'

The slave could not help looking surprised at the question. 'No, master. Never.'

'I see. Then perhaps it would be wise for me to accept, eh?'

'I would think so, master.' The slave gave an emphatic nod.

Cato sighed. The subjects of the emperor were obliged to bow to the will of Nero regardless of whether they were slaves or aristocrats. There was a hierarchy of subservience, but it was still subservience in the end.

'Very well. Please tell Pallodorus that I am honoured to attend and will for ever cherish the memory of being permitted to share the emperor's hospitality. Does that about cover it?'

'Admirably, master.'

'Very well. You may go.'

As the slave and the steward retreated down the garden path, Macro puffed his cheeks. 'Laying it on a bit thick there, weren't you, lad?'

'That's how it works at the palace, brother. Our emperor lives on a diet of unrelieved flattery. I may need some practice before this evening.'

'Then please don't try it on me. I may not survive the hilarity.' Macro scratched his jaw. 'There's always Petronella. She often says it would be nice to be paid a compliment from time to time. I try my best, but no man has yet managed to master the art of second-guessing what his wife really wants to hear.'

Petronella regarded her husband coolly. 'Being told I have a nice arse or great tits tends to wear thin after a while. You might learn a thing or two from Cato while he practises.'

'What? Something like "My most beloved princess, whose beauty shames Venus herself, whose eyes glitter and shimmer like the reflections of moonlight on the midnight sea. Whose voice is as sweet as a thousand songbirds greeting the morning sun . . ." That sort of thing?'

Cato and Petronella looked at him in astonishment before the latter nodded her appreciation. 'Something very much like that will do. Impressive.'

'Forget it. You know how I feel about you. I don't need to play the lovesick poet. You're the only woman for me. For ever. That's all you need to know.'

'A pity,' Petronella sighed. 'For a moment there . . .'

Cato smiled. 'I'm starting to wonder if it would be better if I sent you in my place, brother. What a great poet was lost when you chose to become a soldier. With a silver tongue like yours, you'd go a long way at the court of Nero.'

Macro rounded on him and raised a finger in earnest warning.

'Call me a poet again and I'll knock your head into the middle of next month. I ain't going anywhere near Nero. Had enough of his nonsense the last time we had dealings with him. Fuck dinner at the imperial palace. You go. I'd rather face Boudica's lot than suffer an evening among stuck-up senators, slippery freedmen and poncey poets, with a pudgy playboy prince lording it over them all.'

'My sentiments almost precisely,' Cato responded. 'However, you heard his slave. One does not turn down an invitation from the emperor.'

'Then one had better get his shit together and prepare a tactical advance to dinner.'

Pallodorus turned out to be an anxious man with cropped white hair and a short-sighted squint. He was waiting for the guests at the top of a flight of steps that led down into a sunken dining chamber open to the sky. The sun had already set and the stars gleamed in tiny pinpoints. A half-moon hung above the Temple of Jupiter, and its glow gave a ghostly luminescence to a band of thin clouds slowly drifting across the city. He made a mark by Cato's name on the guest list before one of the Praetorians guarding the entrance stepped forward.

'Raise your arms out to the side, please, sir.'

Cato did as requested, and the man expertly patted the folds of his tunic before stepping back and nodding to Pallodorus.

'You may enter, sir. Most of the other guests have already arrived. Caesar will join you in due course. Refreshments will be provided before the feasting begins.'

'How many other guests are there?'

'It's a low-key event, master. No more than twenty in all. You are the only one who isn't from the emperor's inner circle of friends.' Pallodorus regarded Cato curiously by the glow of the oil lamps suspended above the top of the stairs. 'It is an honour to be singled out in this manner. You must have achieved considerable fame in your field. A poet, perhaps? Or actor? Gladiator, maybe? Given your scars and build.'

'A soldier.'

'Ah . . .' The freedman's tone was vaguely disapproving. He dipped his head. 'You may proceed, master.'

More oil lamps burned in brackets fitted to the wall beside the stairs. At the bottom was a small stage, on the far side of which another flight of stairs led upwards. In front of the stage was a narrow pond that overflowed to create a miniature waterfall into another pond, with channels that ran around the dining chamber giving a pleasing sound of running water. The area in front of the stage had been prepared with the usual three-sided arrangement of couches. They were covered with purple cushions, with tasselled bolsters for the guests to prop themselves up on as they reclined. To either side were two further dining chambers, with a small water feature at the far end. Cato estimated that up to a hundred people could be entertained in the sunken chamber.

The other guests were clustered in small groups. Some were moving around and admiring the delicately painted rural scenes on the walls. In the arched ceilings of the alcoves polished stones dimly reflected the flickering light of the oil lamps and the small braziers that provided illumination. Despite its modest size, it was as opulent a setting as any Cato had seen. More so than any arrangement in the palace complex that he recalled from his childhood years. It seemed that Nero had a taste for fine surroundings with scant regard for cost. Cato mentally attempted to calculate the amount that would be needed to cover the complex water features, the fine frescoes and the expensive pigments that had been used by the painter, as well as the fees of the architects and engineers needed for the job. More than a king's ransom, he concluded.

A slave approached with a silver goblet and a platter of pastries, and Cato helped himself to a small pie. It turned out to be overly salty, and he was grateful for the sweetened wine to clear his palate.

Standing beside the small fountain and waterfall in one of the side rooms, he looked round, seeing how many faces he recognised. Most of the other guests were younger men, with carefully styled hair, showy tunics and the soft red leather knee-boots that were in fashion. There were a handful of older faces – a small group clustered about a slender man of middle height who had his back to Cato. When he turned, Cato saw that it was Seneca. As their eyes met, the senator muttered something to his companions before leaving the group and approaching Cato.

'Prefect, it is a pleasure to see you at such a select gathering. Nero must hold you in high regard. After all, it is not often that the same man gets to save your life, your throne and more recently your reputation.'

'I am not sure that I understand you, Senator.'

'I'm talking about you crushing the last of the rebels in Britannia and putting an end to that witch Boudica.'

'You flatter me. I merely served as one of Governor Suetonius's cohort commanders. The victory is his.'

Seneca's lips lifted in a brief, cynical smile. 'The victory, the triumph is Caesar's, like all victories since the days of Augustus.'

'Of course,' Cato conceded.

'Naturally, the corollary is that all defeats are seen as being the responsibility of the emperor as well, however much he might try to pass that on to his subordinates. Which is why the defeat of Boudica has been vital in restoring the reputation of Rome and the emperor. I am well informed enough to know that you played a significant part in the outcome. Therefore, Rome and Nero are in your debt. But don't let it go to your head. Nero's favourites come and go.'

'I have no intention of playing any such role at the imperial court,' Cato responded. 'I am here tonight because the consequences of not being here would be dangerous to me and my family.'

'That is so. And since you *are* here, I wish to give you some advice. You would be wise to accept it.'

'What advice?'

'Nero will want to hear your account of the rebellion. He has read the official reports and he has spoken to some of those who have returned to Rome since the rebellion broke out. But his grasp of the full details is fragmentary. You were at the heart of events. Not only that, but you have considerable experience of our campaigns in Britannia. I understand that you were an optio of the Second Legion when the invasion began nineteen years ago.'

Cato was unnerved by the depth of Seneca's research into his background. What else might he know? A sudden dread that the faking of Claudia's death had been uncovered caused him to flinch slightly. The reaction was noticed by the senator, who placed a hand on his shoulder.

'Rest easy, Prefect. Any misdemeanour you may have committed over the years is not my concern.'

'I am not aware of any aspect of my record that would give rise to concern, Senator.'

'Not yet, perhaps. But you know the old saying. "No good deed goes unpunished." There have been many men across the years who have served Rome loyally and in the end fallen victim to the whims of jealous rivals and anxious rulers. Nero is not so different to those who ruled before him. He has certain unfortunate character traits that I have done my best to teach him to control ever since I was appointed as his tutor. However, lately I sense that he is gradually turning away from those who have been able to influence his behaviour for the better.'

'Namely you and Burrus.'

Seneca nodded. 'He respects my intellect and my cultural accomplishments, and he respects Burrus's moral directness and soldierly authority. Between the two of us we have managed to keep him to his pledge to rule Rome with a light hand. But you have seen Burrus. The man is dying. Soon he will be gone, and Tigellinus is not inclined to maintain the same approach. Therefore Nero will inevitably listen more to the darker spirits of his soul. I doubt I will be able to prevent that, and I'm considering retiring from public life to spare myself the prospect of falling out with him.'

'All very interesting. But why are you telling me this? I have no interest in who is in and who is out at Caesar's court.'

'You may reconsider that remark sooner rather than later, if I am any judge of Nero.'

'What do you mean?'

'I may be wrong. We'll see. But listen to me, Prefect. Nero is like the wind. It can change direction in a heartbeat, and so can he. At the moment he is relieved that the rebellion in Britannia is over. He has been led to believe that the province is now at peace and will remain that way. It was quite different when the first news of the rising reached Rome. He was appalled to hear about the fate of Camulodunum, Londinium and Verulamium, along with the massacre of the Ninth Legion and the cowardice of the Second Legion's commander.'

Seneca raised his hand and almost, but not quite, pinched his thumb and forefinger together. 'Nero was this close to giving the order to recall the garrison and abandon the province. Can you imagine how that would have appeared to our enemies, outside the Empire and within? How many other provinces might have been tempted to throw off the Roman yoke? It's a gold coin to a brass one that Judaea would have been the first to rise up. Others would have followed, and Rome would have been facing war on more fronts than we could manage. We could have been looking at the collapse of our authority across the Empire and beyond.

'Frankly, the invasion of Britannia was a mistake. It served only to give Claudius a degree of credibility when he became emperor. It has been a thorn in the side of Rome ever since. Most of us who invested in the new province have already lost a small fortune. But we are where we are, as the saying goes. Now we have no choice but to make what success we can of that dismal island.'

He paused to let the weight of his words sink in, then tapped Cato on the chest and continued with icy intensity. 'The emperor will ask you about Britannia. He will ask you about the rebellion. You will tell him what you know. But you will weigh your words with utmost care to ensure that you give him no excuse to think there is any prospect of the rebellion being repeated. You will say nothing that might sway the young fool into deciding to admit defeat and withdraw from the province. And nothing that might cause him to think there is a way of presenting withdrawal as a prudent policy. Do you understand?'

Cato was shocked to hear the senator describe the emperor in such frank terms. But the shock passed as he realised the delicacy of the instructions Seneca had given him. The slightest slip of the tongue might have dreadful long-term consequences for Rome. Then again, even if he did inadvertently say something this night that might cause Nero's thoughts to turn to abandoning Britannia, it was equally possible that Seneca and Burrus might be able to persuade the emperor to change his mind the following day. All the same, he did not want to put himself in a position where he provoked hostility from the emperor or his two closest advisers.

A muffled shout for the Praetorians at the top of the stairs to come to attention caused all conversation to die away. Cato and the others turned towards the steps as four of Nero's German bodyguards came down the stairs and took their places around the imperial dining couch. They were followed by two officers, one of whom was Burrus. The other was tall and well proportioned, with handsome features and naturally curly hair of a fair shade. Next came Pallodorus, who made for the middle of the stage and clapped his hands together.

'My lords! Silence for his imperial majesty, Nero Claudius Augustus Germanicus, Caesar, and his consort, Poppaea Sabina.'

The other guests lowered their heads respectfully, and Cato followed suit as he heard the patter of footsteps descending the stairs. Tilting his head up slightly, he saw Nero hand his mistress down from the last step and then guide her to their dining couch. The emperor was wearing a pleated purple tunic fringed with silver lace. His hair was styled as formally as it had been earlier in the day. But it was the woman on his arm who drew the gaze of all the guests.

Even by the light of the oil lamps it was clear that she was a rare beauty. Her hair gleamed a tawny gold and was arranged in precise tresses that cascaded down her long neck. Her eyes, nose, lips and cheekbones were perfectly proportioned, so that her features seemed to have been sculpted by a master of the craft. Cato's attention was drawn to her eyes particularly, darkly lined so that they seemed to gleam and hint at a vivacity at odds with the demure and deferential glances and faint smiles she shared with Nero as they approached the couch and took their places.

'You may be seated!' Pallodorus called out.

The guests fell into place according to the rigid social hierarchy of Rome. Seneca and the other senators took the couches either side of the emperor; then came Burrus and the others of equestrian rank. Despite Nero's reliance on and friendship with the most senior of his freedmen, there were none of these among the guests. That would have been a social transgression that even he could not readily permit.

Cato hesitated before he made for one of the couches furthest from Nero. He had not gone more than a few paces before the emperor called out. 'Prefect Cato! Where are you going?'

He turned at once, saw the slight frown on Nero's face and responded warily. 'Caesar?'

'This dinner was arranged for your benefit, my dear fellow. You are my guest of honour. My friends and I are keen to hear of your exploits among the barbarians of Britannia. Come, sit at my side.'

Nero indicated the couch to his left, and the corpulent senator who had just settled down hurriedly shuffled along to make space. Cato swallowed and did as he was directed, propping himself up on his bolster so that he could face Nero directly. Behind them, slaves emerged from curtained service doors carrying the trays of delicacies that served as the first course of the night. Others carried silver decanters of wine, which were set down on the tables in front of the couches.

The guests began to sip and nibble, and conversation slowly built up. Poppaea whispered something in Nero's ear, and the emperor glanced at Cato and chuckled before he gestured towards him.

'My darling Poppaea thinks that scar on your face looks like a bolt of lightning.'

Instinct almost caused Cato to raise a hand to the slightly puckered scar tissue that ran diagonally from his brow to the bottom of his cheek. A memory of the Druid's face behind the blade that had torn across his face flashed into his mind's eye.

'She would like to know how you got it.'

'A battle wound, Caesar.'

'Yes, and . . .?'

'A Druid came at me before I could ready my shield. I was fortunate to have sufficient warning so that I could move back, and only suffered a flesh wound.'

Poppaea whispered again, eyes sparkling as she looked at Cato.

'She wants to know what happened to the Druid.'

'I struck him down.'

She let out a little gasp and clutched the emperor's upper arm. This time she addressed Cato directly in an unexpectedly husky and sensual voice. 'You are a great warrior, Nero tells me.'

Cato was aware that the exchange had caused conversations around them to die down, and the other guests were looking in his direction. Poppaea's comment made him acutely uncomfortable. The soldiers he had spent his life among were mostly hard, professional men who were inclined to underplay their own prowess and courage. They despised braggarts and those officers who devoted their time to promoting themselves to advance their military and political careers. 'Thrusters', they were called. They were reviled not just for their lack of humility, but because they often put those around them in danger.

Cato prided himself on not being such a man. It would be an easy thing to play the hero now and impress the young emperor and his mistress. That would surely gain him some advantage. Nero's generosity was well known. But it would also mark him out and incur the envy of those who saw themselves as rivals vying for the emperor's attention. The last thing Cato wanted at the moment was any kind of acclaim that would get him noticed and put not just himself at risk, but Claudia and perhaps Lucius as well. At the same time, he could not afford to come across in a manner that might displease Nero.

He felt like he was caught in a trap, as deadly as any ambush set by the enemies he had fought for the last twenty years of his life.

'Well?' Nero arched an eyebrow. 'Are you going to respond to my beloved . . . or not?'

CHAPTER FIVE

Cato swallowed hard as his mind raced to order his thoughts. Then he fixed Nero's gaze with his own, unwavering as he responded.

'I am a soldier of Rome. I have been since the first year of Claudius's reign. I joined the legions as an optio and was promoted to the rank of centurion during the first campaigns in Britannia. After that I was transferred to the army on the eastern frontier and fought Judaean rebels, Parthians, Nubians and Armenians. I put down a slave uprising in Hispania and have served in Britannia three times in all. I have fought many skirmishes and battles and been wounded and bear the scars to prove it. I have served alongside fine comrades who became closer to me than family, most of whom died from battle wounds, injuries and disease and who I have mourned as if they were brothers. We fought for the glory of Rome, yes, but more important to us was that we fought for each other.

'I have seen the snow-capped mountains and frozen forests of the north and have known the pitiless heat of the deserts of Aegyptus. I have fought on land and on sea. I have stood upon the walls of fallen cities and seen them burn to ash. I have woken on the previous day's battlefield and seen bodies garlanded with frost as crows feasted on their cold flesh. I have held a dying comrade in my arms as he breathed his last breath. I have known the joy of a great victory and the bitter taste of defeat.'

He paused. 'Am I a great warrior? That is not for me to say. Let others be the judge of that. Am I a hero? No. There were many times when my guts twisted with terror and I feared that I would be exposed as a coward. Times when it took the very last ounce of determination to make myself move forward and fight on, whatever the odds. I am alive today not because I am a great warrior, or the bravest soldier, but merely because fortune has favoured me across the years. At any time an unseen arrow, blow or spear thrust could have sent me into the shades. Is a warrior great because he is lucky?' He shook his head. 'I cannot say. I do not know the will of the Fates, nor the gods. All I can say is that I am a soldier of Rome and that I have survived.'

He drew a deep breath before raising his goblet. 'To absent comrades.'

Nero was regarding him with an astonished expression. Then Poppaea nudged him, and the emperor reached for his goblet and raised it, instantly followed by the other guests. 'To absent comrades.'

When everyone had drunk some wine, Nero shook his head and addressed Cato. 'By the gods, a soldier you may be, but you have the heart of a poet. It is as if your words were crafted by some Homeric hero, war-weary and longing for home. Prefect Cato, you are a man after my own heart. I salute you.' He inclined his head. 'Rome needs men like you. We need men familiar with steel and blood, just as we need those who are familiar with music, literature and art. It is rare to find a combination of such sensibilities as I believe you embody, despite your admirable modesty.'

'I thank you, Caesar.'

The emperor regarded him closely. 'You are an interesting man, Cato. I would like to get to know you better. But first I want to hear about your experiences in Britannia. My late adopted father never tired of going on about how the island was covered with mist and filled with barbarians who worshipped demons, and how it took huge courage for him to give the order to invade the place. He often boasted about the sixteen days he was in Britannia, masterminding the final defeat of Caratacus and his army. I can imagine how you and your fellows regarded such a Junius-come-lately. The old fool made Rome into a laughing stock. That's no longer the case since I became Caesar. I have made Rome great again. Now our enemies fear and respect us as never before.' He smiled. 'Tell us how the conquest of Britannia was experienced through the eyes of a common soldier.'

It was a poorly kept secret within the ranks of Rome's higher orders that Nero had little but contempt for his adopted father. Yet even while Nero mocked his predecessor, he was obliged to honour him before the general public in order to legitimise his inheritance. And part of that inheritance was the invasion of Britannia. To undermine that was to undermine Claudius and by extension his heir.

Cato was not going to fall into the trap of saying anything overtly critical about Claudius. An emperor was licensed to say what he liked about his predecessors in front of his inner circle. Someone of Cato's status was not. Moreover, he was irked by the implicit put-down of being called a common soldier. He must not let his irritation betray him.

'I only caught rare glimpses of Emperor Claudius from the distance,' he began. 'So I can't comment on what we felt about him. All I know is that we were greatly relieved by the reinforcements he brought with him when we faced the enemy at Camulodunum. Although we had won a great victory outside Caratacus's capital, we soon discovered that the conquest of the island was far from over. The hardest fighting was yet to come. The enemy avoided facing us in pitched battles and turned instead to harassing our supply lines and ambushing our patrols. It seemed that there was a barbarian hiding behind every rock and tree, ever watchful for the instant we dropped our guard.

'Worse still, the enemy was urged on by their Druid cults. Priests in dark robes, bearing mysterious tattoos on their faces and arms. They were fanatics, driving their followers on with shrill promises that their gods were protecting them, and using spells and curses against us. Some of the cults worshipped the very darkest of their gods and made human sacrifices of those Romans they took prisoner. They cut their hearts out on stone altars or burned them alive in wicker cages fashioned to look like giant men.'

Poppaea's eyes gleamed as she listened, and now she interrupted Cato's account. 'I should like to see one of these Druids. Perhaps have him displayed in the arena, forced to use his magic on the beasts sent to tear him apart. Nero, my love, can you find me a Druid?'

'Begging your pardon, my lady,' Cato said. 'It's too late for that. Governor Paulinus destroyed their last stronghold on the island of Mona last year. The Druids and their followers fought to the last. Not one of them was taken prisoner.'

She frowned and pouted. 'What a pity. It would have delighted the mob to see one of these wild men from the furthest-flung province of the Empire.'

'It can't be helped, my love.' Nero stroked the back of her neck soothingly. 'The Druids had to be annihilated if we were to break the will of the Britons.' He looked across at Cato and added in a hopeful tone, 'Are you sure none of the scoundrels escaped? Is there a chance that one or two may have survived?'

'Maybe, Caesar. They are a resilient cult. A number of them found their way to Boudica and helped stir her people up into revolt. Most of them died when her army was defeated. Only a handful escaped and followed her into the marshes that sprawl across the lands of the Iceni. When my men finally hunted her down, those Druids died with her. There may still be a few out there, hidden by the tribespeople and forever on the run from our soldiers. But too few to cause us any more problems.'

'That is for the best,' Nero reflected. 'Much as I'd like one to present to Poppaea and the people of Rome for their entertainment. Perhaps we shall find some undiscovered wild beasts in the hinterlands of the new province that will provide some sport in the arena.'

Cato nodded indulgently. 'Perhaps.'

Nero picked up his goblet and held it out. Immediately a slave, his chief taster, scurried from the shadows at the side of the room and gently took the goblet from his grasp, sipping the wine before passing it back to him. Cato noticed that the emperor had barely spared a glance for the man who stood between him and any attempt to poison him. Nero set the goblet down on the table, no doubt waiting to see if his taster was affected, and turned back to Cato.

'You have spent a good number of years in Britannia, so you must know the place and its peoples reasonably well. Would you say that we can make loyal subjects out of such barbarians?'

'Caesar is already aware that a number of their tribal kings have sworn loyalty to Rome and have adapted to our ways. The same goes for many of their aristocrats. There are others who are determined to continue resisting our rule, but they are weak and are too used to being at each other's throats to organise a coordinated campaign. In time, the remaining pockets of resistance will be mopped up. Then the only threat will be the wild tribes to the far north of the island. They live amid mountains and forests and scratch a living from what poor farmland is to be had in the region. It may not be worth extending our control into their lands. A frontier could be established to keep them out of the province. A barrier or wall, perhaps. As for the rest of the island, most of the people are farmers. They grow their crops and it makes little difference to them whether they pay taxes to their former rulers or to Rome. In time it is likely that they would be as content to be part of the Empire as they ever were to be ruled by their local kings.'

'That gives me some hope,' said Nero. 'I have heard much conflicting advice from those who say we must retain Britannia and those who say it is a worthless place that would cost more to maintain than it would ever generate in revenue. What is your opinion, Prefect?'

Cato tried to recall as much as he could about what the island had to offer its Roman masters. 'There's iron and silver to be mined, and rumours of gold to be found in the mountains to the west of the province. There's plenty of rich farmland that could be made more productive under Roman control. The tribes are partial to wine, cloth, pottery and other products imported from the rest of the Empire. Provided we establish a lasting peace, I see no reason why Britannia can't pay its way like any other province.'

'Provided there is peace.' It was the officer who had followed Burrus into the chamber who spoke. Nero glanced towards him.

'My friend Tigellinus is one of those who questions the wisdom of remaining in Britannia.'

Cato locked eyes with the younger Praetorian officer. He sensed at once the arrogance of the man in the way he tilted his head slightly back as he returned the scrutiny before turning to Nero.

'Caesar, we have four legions stationed in that part of the island that we presently hold. Of those, the Ninth Legion was almost annihilated during the rebellion and has been reinforced by drawing men from the legions spread along the Rhenus frontier. We are weakening the defences of Gaul in order to prop up Britannia. We only have one legion garrisoning our lands along the entire coast of Africa and we derive far more taxes and grain from there than Britannia will ever provide. Is it really worth deploying so much military power to derive so little in return? I think not.'

The man made a good argument, thought Cato. But as was

so often the case, prestige and the projection of power counted more than material cost in determining the policies pursued by those who ruled.

Tigellinus gestured towards Seneca. 'The good senator was one of those who was keen to recover the loans he had made to our allied kings in Britannia a year or so ago. He recognises a bad investment when he sees one. I recall him doubting the wisdom of keeping the province on more than one occasion in the past. What say you, Seneca? Do you still subscribe to that view? Or have you changed your mind yet again?'

Cato saw the veteran politician shift uncomfortably before he made to respond. 'That was my former belief, it's true. But the rebellion has changed that. If we withdraw now, it would be taken as a sign of weakness. For better or worse, Boudica and her followers have forced our hand. We are committed to maintaining the province for the foreseeable future. Much as I appreciate the military expertise offered by our friend Tigellinus . . .'

Burrus gave a soft snort of derision as Tigellinus made no attempt to hide his anger at the senator's sarcasm.

Seneca paused to let the other guests enjoy his goading of Tigellinus. 'This is not a matter for our military experts to decide. This is a matter of statecraft. There are more sophisticated forces in play. It only seems like a simple issue to the simple-minded.' He paused and smiled casually across the tables that separated him from Tigellinus. 'Not that I am suggesting that applies to you in the slightest, my friend. You have already demonstrated your appetite and aptitude for politics in a most spectacular manner. No one doubts your ambition to climb your way to the very pinnacle of power, albeit in loyal service to our beloved Caesar, of course.'

Tigellinus's face was rigid, his jaw muscles clenched tightly. He risked a quick glance at Nero to see what impact Seneca's words might have had. The emperor was only half listening as he nuzzled Poppaea's neck while she picked at a sprig of grapes and gazed speculatively at Cato over Nero's shoulder.

Cato looked away and reached for his goblet, relieved that attention had shifted away from him. The atmosphere on the couches either side of Nero was thick with tension and hostility, and the other guests were taking part in a strained discussion about a recent performance at one of the theatres in the capital to avoid being part of the confrontation between Seneca and Burrus on the one hand and Tigellinus, whose rising star the two men were desperate to dampen, if not extinguish. It would have made a good drama for the stage in itself, Cato mused, if only the enmity was merely theatrical and the potential for bloodletting not quite so real. He had no wish to play any part in it and forced himself to concentrate on getting through the dinner without making enemies or, for that matter, alliances, with those involved. Any hunger he might have had earlier had turned to gnawing anxiety, and he barely touched the savoury pie he had picked up to make it look as if he was too busy eating to take part in the discussions.

'Prefect Cato . . .'

He looked over to see that Poppaea had abandoned her grapes and was wiping some juice from the front of her stola. She tilted her head. 'This woman who led the rebellion. Boudica. What manner of person was she? Did you ever meet her?'

Cato swallowed and lowered the pie. 'I knew her as well as any Roman over the years, my lady. I had the honour of fighting alongside her when we faced mutual enemies among the Druid cults, and more recently when she came to our aid in putting an end to the criminal gangs terrorising Londinium. She was fearless in battle, loved by her people, admired by everyone else and loyal to her friends.'

'I see. It sounds as if you once counted her as a friend.'

62

He saw no point in denying it now that Boudica was dead and the rebellion over. 'I did consider her a personal friend, yes. And a worthy ally of Rome, for a long time.'

'A worthy ally of Rome?' Tigellinus intervened, his voice laden with irony. 'How can you speak so of that barbarian bitch? Have you already forgotten our fellow Roman citizens who were slaughtered by her followers?'

'By no means,' Cato protested firmly. 'I bore witness to the bloodshed she visited on our province. I have never seen the equal of the brutality and cruelty she unleashed. Pray that you never have to witness its like, Prefect Tigellinus, and be grateful that the Praetorians, urban cohorts and vigiles here in Rome will never be called upon to face such horrors.'

Burrus nodded. 'There's more to soldiering than spit and polish and parading around in your finery, my lad. You'd do well to listen to Cato.'

'Listen to him?' Tigellinus sneered. 'Why? He speaks openly of his friendship with this butchering woman. I almost wonder whose side he thinks he is on.'

'I know which side I am on.' Cato spoke clearly as he glared at the younger man. 'You all know of my military service. I dare any man to question my loyalty to Rome. It has been proven. If you wish to insult me, perhaps we might make an arrangement to continue this discussion on another day, face to face.'

Nero cleared his throat. 'My friends! There is no need for harsh words. Particularly over dinner, as my guests. Tigellinus, you overstep the mark. Our fine soldier has no need to defend himself against accusations of disloyalty. Now be a good fellow and tell him that no offence was intended.'

Tigellinus clenched his jaw and breathed in deeply through his flared nostrils. 'Pardon, Prefect Cato. I did not mean to question your integrity.'

Nero turned to Cato. 'There. He has apologised. The matter

is resolved. I do not wish to be informed that the two of you pursued any grudge after tonight. Do I make myself clear?'

Tigellinus nodded reluctantly.

'As Caesar commands,' Cato conceded. 'I am prepared to overlook his comments about matters he is not familiar with, nor qualified to speak on.'

Nero laughed nervously. 'Now, now! That's quite enough. This unseemly confrontation ends here, Prefect Cato.'

'Yes, Caesar.'

'That said, I get the impression that you entertain a degree of sympathy for Boudica. Am I wrong?'

It would be folly of the highest order to agree that the emperor was wrong about anything, and Cato weighed the words of his response carefully. 'It is my view that Boudica was a valuable ally of Rome, and would have remained so had she and her people received better treatment at the hands of the procurator of the province, Catus Decianus.'

Nero frowned. 'I don't recall the name.'

'He was a provincial, Caesar,' Seneca cut in. 'From Baetica. He was serving in a minor administrative capacity in Rome for a short time before he was appointed. It is unlikely that you would have met him.'

'I see.' Nero turned back to Cato. 'You disapprove of the man?'

'Yes, Caesar. If any person was responsible for causing the rebellion, it was him. He pressed Boudica's tribe for taxes they could not pay, then imposed penalties that only increased their sense of grievance. And when Boudica's husband died, it was Decianus and his hired thugs who stripped the kingdom of what little wealth that remained. He also gave the order for Boudica to be scourged and her daughters raped. Later, when the Icenians and the Trinovantians rose against us, his only thought was to save his own skin. He died while attempting to flee Londinium, or so I have been told.'

'That is a shame. If what you say is true, it would have been useful to have him prosecuted in order to encourage other procurators to carefully consider how they go about their duties. Anyway, the man is dead, the rebellion is over and, as Seneca says, we must ensure that there is peace in Britannia. One more such rebellion could ruin us.'

He regarded Cato closely for a moment before nodding as he came to a decision. 'You have impressed us, Prefect Cato. Rome has need of men like you. Burrus tells me that you have applied to have your name placed on the list of reserves and that you are living at a villa outside Rome.'

'Yes, Caesar.'

'It's no good having a man of action like you kicking his heels in the countryside when you could be doing something useful. I have an idea. Tigellinus is about to relinquish his command of the urban cohorts to take up the position of prefect of the Praetorian Guard alongside Burrus. In consequence of which a vacancy has arisen.' Nero cleared his throat and addressed his guests solemnly. 'I hereby announce that Cato be appointed prefect of the urban cohorts. There. A position he richly deserves.'

Cato felt his spirits sink at the prospect. Of the three bodies of armed men tasked with keeping order in Rome, the urban cohorts were the most despised by the city's inhabitants. They lacked the ceremonial glamour and pay afforded to the Praetorian Guard and were the first to be called out to control the streets if there was unrest that the watch patrols of the vigiles could not handle. As such they were looked down on by the Praetorians, resented by the vigiles and hated by the mob thanks to their heavy-handedness.

Tigellinus coughed. 'Caesar, the position was promised to my second in command, Gaius Albanius Ferox. He has a fine record and would be the best man for the job, in my opinion.'

'The decision has been made,' Nero said firmly, with a frown. 'Do you question my judgement?'

'No, Caesar.'

'Good. If Albanius is as competent as you say, I am sure we can find another post for him.'

Cato had been listening to the exchange with a growing sense of desperation. The last thing he wanted at the moment was a fresh command, let alone one in the heart of Rome, under the eye of Nero and his advisers. He would also be forced to leave the villa and Claudia to serve in the post Nero had conferred on him, all the while being undermined by Tigellinus and the crony he had earmarked to succeed him. He decided to take the risk of speaking up.

'Caesar, I think that Tigellinus's advice is sound. I am not familiar with the urban cohorts, so perhaps it would be better if the post was taken by a man with the requisite experience.'

Nero raised a hand to silence him. 'The decision is made. Do not presume to question me.'

Cato opened his mouth to protest, but saw the dangerous gleam in the emperor's eyes and nodded instead. 'As you wish, Caesar. You honour me and I am grateful.'

'Quite so.' Nero turned to Poppaea, and a look passed between them before he spoke again. 'There is another cause for celebration tonight, my friends. You all know that I have wanted an heir to secure my succession, and that my wife, Octavia, has proved to be barren. Therefore, it delights me to inform you that Poppaea Sabina is with child.'

He beamed at her, then dipped his head quickly to kiss her on the mouth. She clasped her hands around his shoulders and drew him in, and they kissed passionately without interruption while the guests looked on with increasing discomfort at the overt display of affection. Cato saw Burrus turn to Seneca with an arched eyebrow, and the latter gave a slight shake of his head, his shoulders slumping in resignation at what was sure to follow from the announcement.

When Nero finally drew away from his mistress, his expression became serious. 'This welcome development means that certain actions must now be put into effect. My marriage to Octavia is over. Arrangements will be made for the divorce as swiftly as possible in order that I can make Poppaea my wife and empress. Then no man will have cause to question the legitimacy of my child. Or dare to . . .'

CHAPTER SIX

'Prefect of the urban cohorts?' Macro could not help displaying his disdain. 'By the gods, why on earth did you accept?'

'I didn't have any choice in the matter. Nero made that quite clear. It was a case of accept or face the consequences.'

'Which would have been what?'

'I have no desire to find out, brother. The last thing I need is to get in the emperor's bad books and have his spies start looking into my domestic arrangements. If they find out about Claudia, she and I are as good as dead. Maybe Lucius as well. And all my property will be split between the informers and Nero. You know how it goes. That includes this place.' Cato gestured around the courtyard garden.

The dark mass of the house that he had come to know as home several years earlier suddenly felt vulnerable. It was past midnight, and the house was in darkness, save for the four oil lamps hanging from a frame beside the couches where he and Macro were sitting. From beyond the walls came the muffled sounds of the great city – the rumbling of carts using the night hours to avoid the densely packed streets of daylight, the raucous laughter and angry shouts of drunks staggering home, the cries of restless infants, and the occasional screech or scream as trouble kicked off in one of the crowded tenement blocks. The incessant noise that accompanied the lives of the million or so inhabitants of Rome. Along with the noise came the pervasive stench of sewage, woodsmoke, rotting refuse and sweat. All of which made Cato long for the quiet and fresh scents of the countryside about his villa.

'Do you really think he'd make so much trouble over a dinner guest who turned down a post he could readily fill with any of his cronies hanging about the imperial palace?' asked Macro. 'He'll probably have forgotten about it tomorrow in any case. The post goes to someone else and you're off the hook.'

'I don't think so. I got the sense that Burrus and Seneca will make sure he doesn't forget. They're happy to see me take up the command instead of Tigellinus's lackey. And then there's Tigellinus himself. He's lined up to be the new prefect of the Praetorian Guard. I'd say Burrus hasn't got long left. Soon the real power will be wielded by Tigellinus. It's safe to say that we didn't see eye to eye over a few issues, and I fear he considers me an enemy now. He's one of Nero's inner circle of friends and not the kind of man you want to hold a grudge against you . . .' Cato gave a deep sigh. 'This is not the kind of life I had planned for when we returned from Britannia. Why the fuck can't the Fates find someone else to play their games with? Just let a man live in peace rather than drag him into the bear pit of palace politics?'

'I hate to say it, lad, but a lot of that goes with the rank. You've carved out a reputation for yourself in the army and been rewarded with elevation to the equestrian class. You're running with the big boys now, whether you like it or not.'

Cato regarded his best friend bitterly. 'Thanks for the words of encouragement.'

Macro was silent for a moment before he cracked his knuckles. 'What are you going to do about it? Do you have any plans to find a way out of this fix?'

'Not at the moment. I'll keep my head down and wait on events. You might be right about this being a passing fancy; maybe Nero will go with Tigellinus's man, whatever Burrus and

Seneca have to say. Failing that, I might be inclined to make such a poor job of it that he has me replaced.'

'I wouldn't get your hopes up on that score. Incompetence seems to be a prerequisite for most of the appointments Nero makes. It's clear that he rewards craven loyalty over talent. Not that I'm suggesting that's why he chose you,' Macro added hurriedly. 'Frankly, you'd probably be one of the best men for the job under any circumstances. From what I've seen of Rome since Petronella and I moved in here, the city could do with a decent commander of the urban cohorts. The streets aren't safe, even in daylight. Pickpockets, footpads and bands of youngsters lording it over their patches. That's without even considering the crime gangs. It all needs a firm hand. Not only that, but the urban cohorts themselves are in pretty poor shape. Never there when they're needed and happy to take coin to look the other way when some gangster asks them to. Or accept a bribe to enforce a complaint against a neighbour. You'd be a good man to kick them into shape. It's a pity it's bad timing for you. On another day—'

'There's no other day I would consider taking it up.' Cato cut into his friend's line of thought. 'I'm a soldier. I have no grasp of the ins and outs of policing Rome. Tigellinus's man knows the ropes. He might be a crony, but at least he has the necessary experience.'

'What experience do you need? It's just a question of sorting out the rowdies and knocking a few heads together, surely?'

'You'd like that, wouldn't you?' Cato smiled. 'Are you already getting bored of retirement, Macro?'

His friend glanced towards the house before he responded in a softer voice. 'Let's just say Petronella is adapting to it better than I am. She's been good about me meeting up with the other old soldiers living in Rome, but the truth of it is, the more time I spend sitting in taverns talking about the good old days, the more I miss them. It's true that you can take the man out of the army but not the army out of the man.'

'Maybe I should suggest they give the command to you then.'
Cato was only half joking, and for a moment he imagined himself
making the case to Nero. Then he shook his head. 'I wish.'

'So like I said, what's the plan?'

Cato thought. 'I'll stay here for the next few days and see
what turns up. If I'm not summoned to the palace in that time,
I'll take my leave and go back to the villa, and hope that I'll
be forgotten or overlooked. In the meantime, I'll send word to
Claudia to let her know what's happened and to tell her to stay
there and keep out of sight as best she can. With luck, Nero will
change his mind, be grateful that I don't protest, and the matter
will be forgotten.'

'And if his nibs doesn't forget?'

'Then I'll have to go through with it. I'll have to take command
of the urban cohorts and bide my time until I can find a way
to be replaced. That means staying in Rome. I won't like being
separated from Claudia and Lucius, but I can't risk bringing them
here, where there's a danger of her being recognised. It's simply
too dangerous, with all the informers scenting change in the
wind and hoping to get richly rewarded for any dirt they can
find on Nero's enemies, real or imagined. And when Burrus goes,
Seneca will have to deal with Nero alone. If he runs up against
Tigellinus, he'll be sure to come off second best. I think he's
already aware of that and will be looking for his own way out.'

'Way out?' Macro drew his thumb across his neck.

'Not suicide. Some form of disengagement from Nero and
then retire to his estates. That will leave the field clear for
Tigellinus and Poppaea Sabina. From what I saw at the dinner,
she has her hooks into the emperor and he's lapping it up. Now
that she looks likely to give Nero an heir, her hold over him is
going to be unassailable. If Poppaea and Tigellinus form some
kind of alliance, they'll be playing Nero like a cheap cithara.
That's when the real danger will come if Tigellinus has decided

to make an enemy of me. With both of them influencing Nero, I won't stand a chance.'

The following morning, after breakfast, Cato sat down to write a letter to Claudia, explaining what had happened and the restrictions it would place on them until he could find some way to resolve the situation. He was deliberately vague about that, as he had no idea how he might be released from his new position. He concluded by trying to comfort her with the hope that there was a chance Nero would change his mind. In the meantime, she had to remain in hiding and look after Lucius. He sipped from a cup of heated wine as he read over the message and felt the inadequacy of his words. He had become used to making decisions and acting independently while in the army, and the powerlessness of his present situation frustrated and shamed him.

Not just him, he reflected. There was a wider shame that embraced all Romans. How had it come to pass that the fate of the Empire had been gifted to a feckless dilettante like Nero via a simple accident of birth? How was it that such a third-rate individual should be pandered to by a coterie of those wise enough to know better than to permit a fool to rule the most powerful state in the known world? It was not the first time Cato had found himself longing for the Republican era, when those who rose to the top were men of genuine ability, if not always genuine integrity. It seemed an offence against nature to live under a system of rule that threw up the likes of Caligula, Claudius and Nero.

He felt the stirrings of an ambition to prove himself better than their kind. Why should the imperial throne be the preserve of a dynasty? For that matter, why should the Senate be the preserve of those fortunate enough to be born into the aristocracy, with all the arrogance and self-entitlement that entailed? Cato himself had risen from a lowly background into the ranks of the equestrian class, earning his place through his years of service to Rome and his proven ability. And yet any further progress would be blocked because Roman society baulked at the notion of anyone moving up more than one social class in a lifetime. He would never be permitted to become a senator, and suddenly the thought filled him with bitterness.

He indulged the sentiment for a moment before he forced himself to reflect how pointless such anger was when it served no purpose other than to pander to his sense of injustice. He turned his thoughts to speculating on how it might be possible to change Rome for the better. If he could not rise to a position as potentially powerful as senator, then he needed to find, support and influence a man of ability who did have such authority. Such a man might one day, with the right encouragement, put an end to the role of emperor and restore power to the Senate and to the tribunes who had once represented the wider interests of ordinary Romans.

It was a sad fact of history that people did not cherish the institutions that made their nation great. Instead they listened to the siren voices of rich and powerful politicians, who persuaded them to surrender power. Once that was done, these unscrupulous leaders had no intention of renouncing the authority granted to them by the gullible. And so the lineage of increasingly inbred imbeciles led to the point Rome had reached today. As long as the mob was fed and distracted with spectacular entertainments to remind them of the greatness of Rome, they would come to forget the craven manner in which they had succumbed to those who now ruled them, and slip into the false belief that their interests and reputation were aligned with those of the emperors.

Change must come, Cato resolved. When the opportunity arose, he needed to be ready to find and serve the right man. He already had one in mind. Vespasian might not yet harbour ambitions to take power, let alone appreciate that he had the potential to be the one to put an end to the corrupt imperial dynasty that had originated with Augustus. It was early days, and he might yet fall victim to the poisonous schemers surrounding Nero. He might also fail to live up to the moral standards Cato thought he detected in the man. Time would tell.

Meanwhile, Cato had to focus on simply surviving the present regime and protecting his family and those who depended on him. If that meant serving as prefect of the urban cohorts, then so be it. He hoped he would not have to go down that path for long, beset as it was by the dangers faced by every high-ranking official negotiating the complicated politics and patterns of patronage in the capital.

Three days passed, and Cato began to hope that Nero's whimsy had caused him to reverse his decision. Cato's appointment would be sure to anger Tigellinus. Even now he could imagine the man fomenting a plan to have him framed for treason and arrested, to clear the path for his own crony to take command of the urban cohorts. In such circumstances, no news was definitely good news, and getting better with each day that passed. He even allowed himself to look forward to escaping Rome and returning to Claudia and Lucius.

Then, at dawn on the fourth day, the household was awoken by a loud pounding on the front door. By the time Cato pulled on his tunic and made his way to the atrium, Macro was already there with the steward.

'Open up! In the name of the emperor!' a harsh voice shouted from outside.

Although Cato and Macro had served far from Rome over the years, they had heard of the Praetorian death squads that had been a feature of the reigns of Caligula and Claudius. They came at first light and either bundled their victims away to the cells beneath the palace or executed them on the threshold of their own home. Macro pointed to Cato and raised a finger to his lips before he went to the door and responded.

'Who is it? What is your business here?'

'Praetorian Guard! We've come for Quintus Licinius Cato. Open up!'

'A moment!' Macro called out, and turned to Cato. 'There's time to make yourself scarce, lad. I'll delay them as long as I can.'

Cato quickly considered the option, but if the Praetorians failed to find him here, they would be sure to send riders to the villa to search for him there, and that would put Claudia and Lucius at risk. Whatever the purpose of their presence at his house, it would be best to face them here and now. He shook his head. 'Let them in.'

Macro raised an eyebrow as if offering his friend a last chance to change his mind. Then he slid the bolts back before easing open the heavy studded door. Outside in the dim light of dawn stood a squad of six men in white tunics and cloaks with swords at their sides. Their leader, an optio, eyed Macro. 'You took your time. Where's your master?'

'You took your time, *sir*!' Macro snapped back at him in his parade-ground voice. 'I am a centurion of the reserves. You will treat me with respect, or by the gods I will have you on an insubordination charge and broken back to the ranks as sure as day follows night! Stand to attention, damn you!'

The optio stamped his boot down and stiffened his spine, and his men did likewise. Macro glared over them for a moment before his gaze returned to the optio. 'Better. Now, what's the reason for making this gods-awful row first thing in the morning?'

The optio reached a hand to his sidebag and fished out a sealed roll of papyrus. 'I bear a message for Prefect Cato, sir. I was told I would find him at this house. Is he here?'

Macro moved aside and indicated Cato standing on the threshold of the atrium. The optio stepped up from the street and paused before glancing back at his men.

75

'No,' said Macro. 'Just you. My wife is particular, and she won't have a bunch of squaddies treading muck into the house.'

'Yes, sir.' The optio gestured to his men to hold their position, then approached Cato to hand over the scroll. 'From the director of the imperial secretariat, sir.'

'What am I charged with?' asked Cato, certain that his fears about Tigellinus had been realised.

'Sir?'

'Never mind.' Cato took the scroll, his heartbeat quickening as he anticipated dealing with whatever fate had been decided for him. Taking a calming breath, he broke the seal and unrolled the papyrus, glancing down at the lines written in neat cursive by a palace scribe.

From Polydorus, freedman, on the instructions of Caesar, to his good servant Prefect Quintus Licinius Cato, greetings. You are hereby requested and required to take up command of the urban cohorts of Rome with immediate effect. You will report to the cohorts' lines forthwith to be sworn in and take up your duties.

Cato repeated the message aloud for Macro before he rolled the papyrus up. 'Seems like the matter is decided.'

'Indeed. Better make the most of it.'

He turned to the optio. 'The message has been delivered. You and your men are dismissed.'

The optio shot an anxious look at Macro before he responded. 'Begging your pardon, Prefect, but my orders were to deliver the message and then escort you to the headquarters of the urban cohorts.'

'As your prisoner?' Cato said, only half joking.

'I think the idea was more along the lines of an honour guard, sir. So that you make an impression when you arrive.'

'I see. Wait outside. I'll need a moment to dress for the occasion.'

'Yes, sir.'

Once the door was closed, Cato spoke urgently. 'Get word to the villa to let Claudia know what's happened. Tell her I'll do my best to stay out of trouble. She's to stay put for now. If any strangers arrive there, Trebonius is to tell them that the master and his family have gone away.'

'I'll see to it.'

'And tell her . . .' Cato paused, a pained expression on his face.

'No need for more words, lad. I'll make sure she understands what you mean to say.'

Cato forced a smile. 'Thank you.'

He hurried to his sleeping chamber and crossed to the large chest where his military kit was stored. He took out his red tunic and army cloak, boots, sword and belt, scale cuirass and helmet. The crest had seen better days, and he ruffled the stiff dyed horsehair to get it into shape. He dressed steadily, not rushing, as he took in the change of circumstances and where it might lead him. Finally he fastened the buckles at the side of his cuirass and adjusted the position of his sword belt and cloak. Satisfied with his appearance, he picked up his helmet and returned to the front door.

Macro smiled at him. 'You look the part. In fact, it's been odd seeing you out of uniform since we returned from Britannia.'

It was true, Cato thought. Long years in the army had habituated him to his present appearance, and it felt natural somehow, despite his intention to enjoy his time as a civilian before returning to active service – if ever he chose to.

The friends exchanged a glance, then Macro opened the door and Cato stepped down into the street as the optio called his men to form up on either side. Settling the padded skullcap into place, Cato put on his helmet and tied the straps beneath his chin.

'All right,' he said steadily. 'I'm ready. Let's go!'

CHAPTER SEVEN

The camp of the three urban cohorts was located in the loop of the Tiber close to the old Fields of Mars. The large plain that had once been used for drilling troops, and where the people of Rome had exercised, had long since given way to temples, Rome's first arena made of stone, theatres, baths and a market complex. During the reign of Augustus, the cohorts had been assigned temporary accommodation in a set of dilapidated barracks arranged around a parade ground. They were still waiting for new lodgings over half a century later. Despite the sprawl of grand prestigious building projects across the Fields of Mars, the district surrounding the camp was one of the most impoverished in the capital.

The grimy, cracked walls of tenement blocks crowded along the bank of the fast-flowing river. When heavy rain came, the narrow alleys flooded. Sometimes the currents were strong enough to cause the weaker buildings to collapse, burying their inhabitants in the ruins, where they were crushed or drowned. And when there were fires, many people were unable to escape and were either burned alive or choked by the smoke. The buildings were bitterly cold in winter and sweltering in summer, and the air was thick with the odours of humanity and the sour stench of the local tannery that flushed its residue into the streets.

It was mid morning by the time Cato and his escort had worked their way across the city and approached the main gatehouse of the camp. On either side a two-storey wall stretched out, the rear of the barrack blocks that encompassed the parade ground. There were no openings on the ground level and only small shuttered windows on the upper level. Rubbish was piled at the foot of the wall, which was adorned with graffiti featuring the usual mix of insults, curses, boasts and advertising for local shops. The gates were propped open on ancient iron hinges and the two men on duty sat on small benches on either side, leaning back against the wall, thumbs inserted in the wide military belts worn around their brown tunics. The man on the left stirred at the sound of the tramping boots of Cato and the Praetorians. He rose unsteadily, knocking over a jug at his feet. A thick trickle of red liquid swirled across the cobbles. His companion did not stir, but snored loudly, his jaw slack.

Signalling the optio to halt his squad in front of the gatehouse, Cato approached the standing man, who was trying not to sway as he looked straight ahead.

'What the fuck are you supposed to be?' he demanded.

The man frowned. 'Sir?'

'Are you on duty?' Cato took a step towards him so that their faces were less than a foot apart. The man's breath stank, sour with wine.

'Y-yes, sir.'

'Then why haven't you made any challenge?'

'Challenge?' The man's eyes flicked towards Cato.

'Don't bloody look at me. Look ahead. Answer my question.'

'We haven't been issued any passwords, sir. We're just supposed to keep the civvies out. That's all. Until we get relieved.'

'Then I'll relieve you in just a moment. Stand still, damn you.'

Cato strode over to the other man, raised his foot and gave him a savage kick that knocked him off his bench and sent him sprawling on the ground. The man let out a howl of surprise and anger and scrambled to his feet, fists clenched, eyes blinking as he swung a lazy blow at Cato's head. Cato warded it away with his left hand and delivered a jab to the man's nose so that he staggered back, blood coursing from his nostrils. Then he turned back to the first man.

'You are both relieved and under arrest. Take this drunken piece of shit with you and report to the guardhouse. Tell the duty officer to put you in a cell.'

The man hesitated, and Cato stabbed a finger at him. 'Do it now or it'll be the worse for you both.'

'Yes, sir.' The man scurried over to grab hold of his friend.

Cato turned to the Praetorians and indicated the two nearest men. 'You and you. Stay here until further orders. The rest, follow me.'

They marched between the gates into the large open drill ground, a hundred or so paces square, Cato estimated. There was only marginally more order here. Although the walls were free of graffiti, they were in poor shape, and the original whitewash had faded to a dull grey, streaked with grime and patches of damp. On the far side a centurion was inspecting his men as they stood with their shields and spears grounded. Around the rest of the open space other men were sitting in groups outside their barrack blocks, hanging clothing out to dry, or hunched over as they cleaned or repaired items of their kit.

Cato stopped one of the soldiers and exchanged a salute. 'Where's the headquarters?'

'Over there, sir.' The soldier pointed to the corner nearest the river, where a squat tower rose one level higher than the rest of the grubby complex. There was a small porticoed entrance, and Cato led the Praetorians towards it. He was aware of the attention they were attracting as men turned and stared curiously. There were no sentries on duty at the portico, and he entered the small vestibule, dimly lit by narrow windows. There was a long counter on the far wall with shelves beyond, stacked with waxed slates, scrolls, writing implements and other stores. Three men were sitting on stools, dealing with administration tasks. One by one they stood up as Cato and the Praetorians entered the building.

'Who is in charge here?' Cato demanded. 'Where is the duty officer?'

One of the clerks answered. 'Centurion Brocchus is in his quarters, sir.'

'He should be here. Go and fetch him . . . Wait! Where is Tribune Albanius?'

'The tribune is not here, sir.'

'Then where is he?'

'I don't know, sir. He might be at his house on the Quirinal Hill. He's something of a late riser.'

Cato regarded the man more closely. There had been a distinctly disapproving tone in his voice. Either he had the guts to speak up about Albanius, or he was a troublemaker. Cato could not determine which. The man was in his mid thirties, thickset, with cropped hair and a prominent scar on his cheek.

'How long have you been in the urban cohorts, soldier?'

'Four years, sir.'

'And before that?'

'Tenth Legion. Optio. Or was, until I had a disagreement with a green tribune who wanted to lead my men into a trap.'

'I see.' Cato nodded. 'Name?

'Vibius Fulvius, sir.'

He resolved to take a look at the man's military record when he had the time. At the moment, there were more pressing matters.

'Tribune Albanius is the ranking officer at the moment, right?'

'Yes, sir.'

'Then he should be here too. Send for him. I also want the three cohort commanders and their centurions to report here at midday.'

Fulvius looked at him warily. 'Yes, sir. May I ask on whose authority?'

Cato took out the scroll and held it up. 'I am the new prefect in command of the urban cohorts. This confirms my appointment, on the authority of Caesar. Now get the word out to my officers. If they want to avoid having my boot up their backsides, they'll be here double quick when the third hour of the day is sounded.'

With the summons issued, Cato dismissed his Praetorian escort and made a preliminary inspection of his new command. The tower had been adapted to serve the usual functions of a headquarters. The pay chest, records and unit standards were secured in a basement shrine, under guard. The ground floor comprised offices for the clerks, their stores, and a stock of spare kit – a limited amount, as the urban cohorts were not intended for the wear and tear of campaign service. The only times they had to don armour and weapons was when they were on parade, or when they were needed to deal with unruly crowds or confrontations between the capital's criminal gangs.

The second floor was taken up with more offices, mostly empty, while the top floor was reserved for the accommodation of the commanding officer. There were some sleeping cubicles, a latrine, an office and a dining room, and stairs that led up to a roof terrace with views over the river, the square, the barracks and surrounding neighbourhood. Although the rooms had been neatly kept, there was little sign that anyone lived there. There were no scrolls on the shelves in the office, no personal items of clothing in the sleeping cubicles, no sign that Tigellinus or Albanius had ever made use of the space.

That would change now that Cato was in command. Not just because he believed that a commander should live alongside his men. He was also concerned to keep his distance from his house and his villa to protect his friends and family. If ever he fell from grace, it would be better if he was not taken in front of them. Macro, for one, would be sure to resist, and that would only get him into deep trouble. Besides, the prefect's quarters were perfectly comfortable, and the view from the roof terrace was one of the better prospects on offer in Rome.

He left the tower and extended his inspection to the other buildings. Most of the barrack blocks on the side that faced the Tiber were stained with damp inside and smelled musty. The men were slow to react to his presence, and their apathy and resentment at his intrusion were apparent. There was little evidence that their quarters were cleaned regularly, and their kit was left wherever convenient rather than stored in the places set aside for the purpose.

The neglect and lack of pride in their appearance and that of their quarters rankled with Cato's professionalism. It angered him that these men were taking the same pay as the soldiers of the legions, in addition to the emperor's frequent handouts, and offering such slovenly standards in return. He would never have tolerated this in the army, and he resolved not to tolerate it now, even if he did not want the command and was keen to ensure that he did not hold it for too long. The fault lay with their former commander and his officers for allowing the cohorts to get into such a poor condition. If Tigellinus was about to be promoted to command the Praetorian Guard, then the gods only knew what would happen to that prestigious body of soldiers. Cato hoped they were constituted of better material than the men he saw around him.

The granary was on the opposite side of the square, and was an old Tiber warehouse that had been incorporated into the camp when the barracks were constructed. Fortunately, its original builders had installed a raised floor supported by brick pillars to help preserve the contents from damp and rats, as well as occasional flooding. A small colony of cats thrived on the rich pickings of any rodents that attempted to invade it. The stocks of grain and jars of oil and wine took up only a small proportion of the building, which felt cavernous as a consequence. Cato made a mental note to discuss the matter with Fulvius. To have run the stores down to this degree was not acceptable. He suspected that someone was selling them off on the side. If so, he would put a stop to that and punish those responsible as severely as regulations permitted. It was one of many object lessons the men and officers of the cohorts desperately needed, from what he had seen so far.

There was a quartermaster's store with similarly empty shelves, and a stable block that had not seen any horses or tack for a long time and had been converted into a soldiers' mess, filled with tables, benches and dicing pits. A bar stretched across one end, with wine jars and clay cups stacked on the shelves behind, and a large bald man with a paunch was languidly wiping down the counter. As Cato entered, the handful of men at one of the tables rose to salute him.

He had not drunk anything since first light and had built up a thirst. Ordering a cup of watered wine, he sipped at it as he looked over the establishment.

'Are you in charge here?' he asked the man behind the bar. The latter swung the cloth across his shoulder as he shuffled opposite Cato.

'I just manage it. Tribune Albanius owns the concession. Sir,' he added as he took in Cato's armour and obvious senior rank.

'Concession? Then you're a civilian?'

'Yes, sir. Retired from the Third Cohort a few years back. Seemed like a good way to stay in touch with old comrades.' He nodded to the men at the table. 'Half of that lot are former muckers.'

'Are they indeed?' Cato noted. He drained the cup, set it down with a nod of thanks and left the stable.

Outside the next block, he encountered the men he had seen

being inspected by the centurion earlier. They had just been dismissed and were filing back to their quarters, sweating and tired. There was a different air about them compared to the other soldiers he had seen since entering the camp. They stiffened and stood to attention the moment he approached them, and their kit seemed to be in better shape, with neatly polished belts, helmets and shield bosses. He ordered one man to present his sword, and held it up to the sunlight to examine it closely. The blade gleamed and the edge was sharp. There was no trace of rust, and even a glimmer of oil to ease the drawing of the weapon. As he handed it back, the centurion came over and saluted.

'Sir, can I help you?'

He was a tall man, perhaps a few years older than Cato. Mid forties at most. He had a spare build, with dark features and almost black eyes under a deep brow that gave him a hawklike appearance, further exaggerated by his thin curved nose and high cheekbones. He stood straight with shoulders held back, and obviously took considerable care to ensure his kit was maintained to the highest standard. Cato assumed he was another of the regulars, like Fulvius, who had transferred to the urban cohorts from one of the army units.

He cleared his throat. 'I am the new prefect of the cohorts, as of today. Quintus Licinius Cato.'

'The new prefect?' The centurion arched an eyebrow. 'We were given to understand that Tribune Albanius would be taking over from Tigellinus . . . sir.'

'That arrangement was superseded a few days ago.'

'I see.' He nodded with the fatalism of a professional officer of long-standing service, then patted his chest. 'Centurion Aulus Lemulus, First Century, First Urban Cohort, sir.'

'You'll be another one who joined the cohorts after an army career, I'll be bound.'

'Yes, sir. Served in the Ninth Legion until five years ago.

85

Was tired of chasing hairy-arsed barbarians around the bogs of Britannia and fancied continuing my soldiering closer to home.'

'The Ninth?' Cato mused. 'Then you were lucky to get out before they had that run-in with Boudica's rebels.'

'I heard about that. Bloody criminal incompetence by the legate. Cost us a lot of good men.'

Cato nodded. 'And they were only the first of many we lost.'

Lemulus tilted his head slightly. 'You were in Britannia?'

'I was with the Second Legion during the invasion. Commanded an auxiliary cohort later on and was there during the rebellion.'

'So you know the province well.' Lemulus held out his hand and they clasped forearms. 'Be good to have a real soldier in charge here, sir. It's long overdue.' He turned and gestured towards the rest of the camp. 'It's a poor show. Things were not in great shape when I arrived. Got steadily worse under . . . under the previous management, sir.'

His reluctance to name Tigellinus spoke of caution with respect to his former commander, and Cato approved of his professional loyalty.

'Then it's time things began to improve. You're the senior centurion here. You'll be the man to lead the way as far as training and discipline go. I'll be counting on you to bring the men of your cohort up to the standard of your own century.'

'Yes, sir . . .'

Cato picked up on the hesitation at once. 'You have a problem with that?'

'Well, sir. It won't be the first time I've tried to improve standards. Some of the other centurions, men who owe their appointments to Tigellinus, protested to the prefect that I was pushing the men too hard and undermining their spirit.'

'Since when did training and good discipline ever undermine a soldier's spirit?'

'Quite so, sir. Frankly, there are a number of centurions here

86

who have never served in the legions or auxiliaries. They're more familiar with the inns and brothels around the Circus Maximus than they are with the requirements of soldiering, let alone being a serving officer of the urban cohorts. Bunch of fucking wasters and five-day warriors, sir. Pardon my Gallic.'

'Useful to know,' said Cato. 'I'll be addressing you and the other senior officers at headquarters at noon.'

They exchanged a salute, and Cato paced slowly across the square, hands clasped behind his back as he considered what he had heard and seen since entering the camp, all the while aware of the eyes of the men watching him. Wondering what kind of man their new commander would turn out to be.

'You'll find out soon enough . . .' he muttered to himself through gritted teeth.

'Attention!' Lemulus called out sharply. 'Commanding officer present!'

There was a scraping of benches and boots studs on the flagstones of the main hall of the headquarters tower. The hall was no more than twenty feet on each side, and the three tribunes and eighteen centurions of the urban cohorts filled the available space. They parted to allow Cato to pass through and take his place in front of the bust of Nero that looked down on the men from a niche on the far wall. The sculptor had obviously imitated an official portrait, and Nero's youthful features were uncorrupted by the fleshy jowls he had developed over recent years. The carefully trimmed facial hair was intended to honour the family nickname of 'red beard', though in reality Nero was clean-shaven, having given up on any attempt to grow a convincing beard of his own.

Cato turned to face his officers and slowly scanned their faces to try and determine which of them might be cronies of Tigellinus and which might be army veterans. In some cases it was clear enough, but there would be some army men who had been seduced by the soft living afforded by the urban cohorts and had gone to seed. Regardless of what had been permitted under Tigellinus, Cato was determined to set things right. By the time he handed the command to his replacement, these officers and their men were going to be a far more professional body of soldiers than those he had taken charge of.

He took a final glance round the room before he drew a deep breath and held up the scroll.

'By the authority of Caesar, I, Quintus Licinius Cato, assume command of the urban cohorts of Rome.' He turned to the clerk who was holding the standard bearing the likeness of the emperor and indicated to him to approach. Placing his left hand on the wooden staff, Cato raised his right and issued the oath. 'I swear, on my honour and on my life, that I will faithfully serve Caesar, the Senate and people of Rome. I will obey the orders of Caesar and any officer he should place over me. I swear to fight any and all enemies of Rome to my last breath, and may the gods punish me if I should fail in my duties. This I swear, before my officers and before the gods.'

He lowered his hand and turned to the officers as Lemulus led them in administering their oath of obedience to their new prefect. When they were done, he did not give them permission to resume their seats. He wanted them on their feet to hear what he had to say. He wanted them to know that things were not going to be as free and easy as before.

'Which one of you is Tribune Albanius?'

A short man in his late twenties stepped forward. His fleshy face was pockmarked and his dark hair glistened with the oil that held the tight curls of his fringe in place. Despite his stature, he managed to affect an aloof expression as he faced Cato.

'I am Tribune Gaius Albanius Ferox.'

Cato could see that the man's eyes were bleary. 'You will use the correct form when speaking to a superior, Tribune.'

It took Albanius a moment to grasp the point. 'Yes, sir.'

'That's better. Don't make the same mistake again. How long have you been the acting commander of the urban cohorts?'

Albanius lowered his eyes as he calculated, and Cato winced inwardly at the slowness of his thinking.

'Over two months, sir.'

'Over two months,' Cato mimicked. 'So that could be three, four or many more months, could it?'

'Two months and, er, five days, sir.'

Cato had no way of confirming this, but at least Albanius had managed to give a specific answer. That was a mark in his favour, albeit a small one. The army valued decisiveness above doubt and prevarication, even if that entailed a degree of deliberate inaccuracy or dishonesty.

'During those two months and five days, did you deliberately degrade the discipline and effectiveness of the men under your command?'

Albanius looked stunned. 'Sir? I . . . I don't understand.'

'What don't you understand? Was clear and concise Latin not good enough for you? Would you prefer that I point out your deficiencies in Greek, double Batavian or some other barbaric tongue if that makes it easier for you? No? Then I'll continue. I have served nearly twenty years in the army, and in all that time I have never seen a camp in such shit order. The barracks would shame a whorehouse in the backstreets of the most barbarian hellhole of the Empire's most backward province. The men are little better. Slovenly, slow to respond to orders, with one sentry too drunk to stand up on his own. Their kit is poorly maintained, and I dare say incomplete. The standard of many of the officers would appear to be no better. You, Albanius, don't even occupy your quarters, but prefer the comforts of your home and roll up here in such a drunk or hung-over state that you can barely think straight. From what I have seen in only a couple of hours, the urban cohorts are a den of cronyism, corruption and incompetence. That will end now.'

He glared at the officers, daring any to protest. Some returned his scrutiny with defiant expressions, some with contempt. Others looked fearful, and a few were too anxious to even meet his gaze. There were nods of approval as well as stern expressions that gave nothing away. There was material here he could work with, he decided. But there was also rot that he would need to cut away if the three cohorts under his command were to improve. An example was needed to show these men that he was serious. He turned to Albanius.

'You are a disgrace to your rank. Having seen the shitshow here in the camp it's clear that you fall so far short of the standards required as acting commander of the urban cohorts that you could slip into the Great Sewer without anyone noticing. I wouldn't trust you with the role of the most junior centurion in the unit. Fuck that, I wouldn't even give you an optio's rank. I want you out of the camp at once. You are suspended from all duties pending disciplinary procedures for a dishonourable discharge. You will not be permitted to enter the camp, nor speak to any of the officers or men. Any man who has dealings with you that come to my attention will be punished. Get out!'

Albanius had withered under the invective of his new commanding officer. His eyes were wide and his jaw trembled as he swallowed and replied, 'Just who in Hades do you think you are? I don't know you. Never heard of you. You wait until my friend Tigellinus hears about this. He'll destroy you, swat you aside like the whining insect you are.'

'Silence!' Cato took two steps towards the man and thrust his face within inches of Albanius's fleshy features. He was gratified to see the loudmouth recoil. 'You go running to your friend and see where it gets you. I was directly appointed by Caesar. You want to take it up with him, be my guest. You ask who I am?

I'm a real soldier, not some drunken oaf playing at being one. Now go, before I have to kick your fat arse all the way out of camp in front of the men.'

Albanius looked round for support from his cronies, but none dared draw Cato's wrath down on them.

'You cowards!' he spat. 'I'll be back. When the day comes, you'll regret this. I swear it.' He turned and pushed his way through to the door and left the room.

There was a tense silence as his footsteps faded, and Cato returned to his position under the bust of the emperor. He lowered his voice as he continued, but maintained a cold, uncompromising edge.

'I dare say Albanius won't be the last officer to lose his place here. I will give every one of you a fair chance to prove yourselves worthy of your rank. Those who fall short will be replaced. The same goes for the men. We are part of Rome's military. Our emperor and our people depend on us to keep order on the streets of the city and its environs. We will not let them down. When I am done with you, the urban cohorts will stand alongside the Praetorians as the showcase units of the Empire. I will tolerate nothing less.

'If any of you can't or won't measure up to the standards set, I suggest you submit your resignation before the day is out. For the rest, I promise you, the camp will be run with a firm hand from now on. There will be discipline. There will be order. There will be smartness and there will be hard training. I will make you sweat, ache in places you never knew you had, and curse me from dawn to dusk, day in, day out . . .'

He paused to make sure that every one of them understood what lay ahead.

'There will be a full inspection of all three cohorts and their barrack blocks an hour from now. Dismissed!'

CHAPTER EIGHT

'Hmm . . .' Trebonius mused as he looked over the prefect's quarters. 'Not too shabby. I think I can turn this into a comfortable place for you, sir. Not quite as bad as some accommodations we have shared in Britannia, but not as good as the set-up at the villa.'

There was a resentful edge to his last words that was not lost on Cato. In the letter he had written to Claudia, he had told her to send Trebonius to join him at the camp. He hoped that both of them would return to the villa as soon as he could persuade Nero to find a new commander of the urban cohorts. It would take some finesse to achieve that end; he must not make himself indispensable in his new role, but nor must he perform it so badly that he drew down the wrath of Nero, egged on by the fawning Tigellinus. In the meantime, there was plenty of work to be done to bring the men of his new command up to the standard required.

Trebonius emerged from the headquarters kitchen at the bottom of the tower. 'There's no stores there for the commanding officer.'

'I'm not surprised. Tigellinus and Albanius were hardly ever here. I'll draw some coin from my banker in the Forum for you to buy stock.' Cato paused. 'I want you to prepare all my meals. And I want anything you buy for the larder to be stored up here. For now.'

Trebonius raised an eyebrow. 'Are you expecting trouble, sir?'

Cato hesitated from sharing his thoughts with his steward. Poisoning was one of the favoured methods of the political toolbox in Rome. In a city where disease and agues were prevalent, poisons were easy to obtain and administer while passing off the consequences as the result of natural ailments. He felt a little ashamed at ordering Trebonius to take such precautions, but his appointment as commander of the urban cohorts was not approved of by some of the most powerful men in Rome. The kind of men who would not lose any sleep over having him murdered. Even though Albanius had been removed, there would be others among the officers and men who were hostile to him and loyal to their previous commander. He would have to be on his guard.

'Trouble? Maybe. This is a rather different situation to the one we faced in Britannia. At least we knew who our enemies were there, and that our backs were covered by loyal comrades. Here? I'm not so sure. Better to play it safe.'

Trebonius nodded. 'I'll see to it. You can rely on me, sir.'

'I know I can. Until I find my feet, it's going to be something of a challenge to work out who I can trust. Speaking of which, I need to speak to Lemulus. Find him and bring him to me.'

'Yes, sir.'

They exchanged a salute, and Trebonius left the tower and made for the barrack blocks occupied by Lemulus and his men. Cato climbed the steps to the roof and looked out over the camp. Two days had passed since he had arrived, and this morning, like the last, he'd had the men cleaning out their quarters, repairing any cracks to the walls and whitewashing the buildings. Already the camp was looking more like an army barracks: neat, clean and uniform in appearance. Precisely the qualities that professional soldiers with Cato's long experience cherished.

But appearances were not everything. In fact they counted

for little if not accompanied by discipline and training, instilling pride into each man and the section, century and cohort he belonged to. That would be the real challenge facing Cato, given how far Tigellinus had let standards decline under his command. The men would need a stern hand to get them back into shape and to give the urban cohorts the kind of corporate spirit they desperately needed if they were to become anything other than a band of armed louts occasionally deployed to beat up the mob while their officers slacked off and lived the high life on the emperor's coin.

Scrutinising the activity across the camp, Cato was encouraged by the thought that he had done this before. He had taken command of units in a similarly poor state and turned them round. But this was different, because the previous cases had involved men on the frontiers of the Empire, where their lives depended on being good soldiers. Here in the capital, there was no enemy to face in battle. Only a vast and occasionally unruly population, whose petty rivalries might spill over into street violence or whose hunger and simmering despair might cause them to rise up and demand action from those who ruled them. Which was why so much was invested in chariot races, gladiator spectacles and distribution of grain and other largesse. Distraction was everything. It was the secret whereby the rich and powerful maintained control over the masses, fleecing them while simultaneously posing as their benefactors.

All the same, the urban cohorts were a military unit, paid the same as the men of the legions, and Cato was determined to ensure that they performed their duty in line with the pay they received. Anything else would be an affront to all that he believed in.

He saw Trebonius and Lemulus striding across the parade ground and turned to descend to his quarters to receive the centurion.

Lemulus was wearing a neatly brushed tunic, a chain-mail vest and his medal harness, and he snapped to attention and saluted his commanding officer. As he returned the salute, Cato noticed the streak of whitewash on the man's forearm and stifled a smile. The centurion had obviously been working alongside his men when the summons came, but had quickly changed from his fatigues tunic to more formal attire. His stock rose further with Cato.

'At ease. Please be seated.'

Lemulus drew up one of the stools on the far side of the office and sat opposite Cato as he took his place behind his desk.

'The camp is already looking much improved,' Cato began. 'It's a good start.'

'Yes, sir. The place was becoming a slovenly pit. A disgrace.'

'Indeed. But the work is only beginning. The men will need training to get them back in shape and ready to carry out their duties effectively.'

'Duties?' The centurion raised a slight, mocking smile. 'Such as they are.'

'I can understand your scepticism, Lemulus. But they are a military unit, and even if the prospect of battle is remote, they are still required to be ready to meet any emergency effectively. Even if they spend the rest of their days keeping order in Rome, I want them to go about it with pride – and I want the people of Rome to have pride in them too.'

'Yes, sir.'

'Good soldiers need good leaders. Men like yourself, if I am any judge of character. To that end I am making you acting tribune of the First Cohort while Albanius is dealt with. It won't be a permanent promotion, you understand. Once Albanius is pushed aside, another will fill his place, inevitably some favourite of Nero or one of his close advisers. We can't do anything about the way patronage works in Rome. But I'll do what I can to delay it while you shake down the cohort and get them ready for their new commander. I'll see to it that you get the extra pay and privileges while you are in post.'

'Yes, sir. Thank you.'

'I expect the best from you in return, and I know I will not be disappointed.'

'You can count on me, sir.'

Cato nodded. 'Which brings me to the question of the other officers in the camp. I need to know what you can tell me about them.'

Lemulus shifted slightly. 'I don't think it's my place to comment, sir.'

'Of course it is. If we are to improve things, I must know about the quality, or otherwise, of the officers who lead my men. You know that's true. Whatever you say to me now is between us and will go no further than this room.'

Lemulus reflected before he nodded. 'Very well. Ask away.'

'Let's begin with the tribunes.' Cato considered the commanding officer of the Second Cohort. A young, sallow man, prematurely bald and thin. 'Marcellus to start with. His record looks clean enough. Did his military service as a junior tribune out east in the Tenth Legion. On his return to Rome, he served as quaestor in the corn supply department for another year before he was appointed to the urban cohorts, where he has been for the last year and a half. What's your opinion about him?'

Lemulus weighed his thoughts before responding. 'Even though his old man secured the appointment via a hefty bribe to one of the palace freedmen, Marcellus is a sound lad. Knows his stuff and would make a good cohort commander in one of the frontier units, given the opportunity. I imagine he thought this would be a stepping stone on the road to such a post and now he's starting to worry that he might be stuck here and be overlooked when new commands are allocated. There's no glory to be won in the urban cohorts. No battle honours. No way for him to stand out. Especially since he wasn't one of Tigellinus's blue-eyed boys.'

'I see. Do you think there's a chance he might respond well to the new regime I want to put in place?'

'I'm sure of it, sir.'

'Good. What about the other tribune, Pantella?'

Lemulus made a face. 'Not so impressive, sir. He's an officer in name only. Tends to leave everything to his senior centurion while he enjoys the high life of the capital. Just signs off on everything that Centurion Macrinus puts in front of him. When he's in the camp, that is. And that ain't so often. So Macrinus has a free hand in drawing up requisitions for kit and rations, which he sells on for a tidy sum. He also draws pay for men who were discharged from his century years ago. He has a nice sideline in taking bribes from men who want to avoid duties or take leave. Has thumbs in many pies, does our Macrinus.'

'Good gods, how on earth does he get away with all that?'

'Like I said, his commanding officer just signs off on it all. Besides, he was one of Tigellinus's appointments. Plucked out of the Praetorian Guard, where he was serving as an optio, and promoted to centurion. He was one of Tigellinus's favourites, so if any complaint was made against him . . .'

'It would go up the chain of command,' Cato continued, 'and stop dead the moment it landed in front of Tigellinus.'

'Exactly. Now that you're in command, I dare say he'll rein it in while he gauges how far he can push things. If you try to bring charges against him, he'll go straight to Tigellinus to complain about you. I'd be careful how you deal with him, sir.'

'As long as there's proof of his guilt, I should be on solid ground.'

'I'd suggest that you check the accounts of his cohort and you should find what you're looking for.'

'Noted. What about the other centurions in his cohort?'

'Three of them are his cronies, picked for promotion by him. The others were serving before he arrived. They're sound enough, but they wouldn't cut it in an auxiliary cohort, let alone one of the legions. Of course, that might change if they were forced to make some improvements.'

'And the other cohorts?'

'A mix of good and bad. Some have served most if not all of their time in the urban cohorts and have done little to prevent the slide in standards since Tigellinus took over. The rest are decent enough. A few transferred in from various legions and auxiliary cohorts. Veterans who know the ropes. They're as frustrated as I am about the way things are. They'll be glad to see a bit of discipline restored.'

'I'll need to rely on such men. The others will have to be licked into shape or removed. If anyone wants to play games and run crying to Tigellinus, then two can play at jumping the chain of command. I'll take it up with the emperor directly. He appointed me and he'll back me up.'

Cato saw that his words surprised the other man.

'Sir, I'll be straight with you, since you've said that whatever is discussed in here stays between us. From what I've seen of Nero, he's like a weathervane. He'll change his mind on a whim. More often than not he'll change it according to who has flattered him most recently. I wouldn't put too much store by the fact that he picked you for this command. He may show a little interest. He may approve of the changes you make. He may even set aside any complaints Tigellinus might make on behalf of his cronies. Equally, he might just have moved on to the next thing to take his interest. Give him a few months and he might even forget why he gave you the job and will appoint a new favourite to replace you.' Lemulus paused. 'I'm not saying I'm against the emperor, you understand. Just pointing out the facts. We have both sworn an oath of loyalty, but that doesn't change the truth.'

Cato nodded. He understood the man's caution. Even speaking sub rosa, the centurion was wary enough to qualify his remarks. He had placed his trust in his commanding officer as far as he could, and for that Cato was grateful. He needed men around him he could be honest with. This was not the imperial court, where the man at the top was relentlessly told only what he wanted to hear.

'I'll do my best to keep Nero onside for as long as I can. Meanwhile let's make a decent job of turning the urban cohorts into something worthwhile.'

'Yes, sir.'

'I'll have the confirmation of your temporary rank written up and entered into the records.' Cato stood and extended his hand. 'Congratulations, Tribune Lemulus. Do me proud.'

Lemulus rose and clasped Cato's forearm with a solemn expression. 'I swear by all the gods that I will, sir.'

After Lemulus had been dismissed, Cato sent for the accounting records of each cohort and studied them briefly. Then he summoned each senior officer in turn and set out his intention to improve the cohorts. He made it clear that it would entail hard work and discipline from all the men, regardless of rank, and any who were found wanting or who opposed him would be disciplined. Repeat offenders would be discharged and replaced by men who shared their commander's vision. Tribune Pantella and Centurion Macrinus were the last men to be summoned.

The interview with Pantella was brief. He was an overweight man in his early thirties, his age proof enough that he was content to remain at his present rank and draw his pay while indulging in the company of similarly dissolute aristocrats amid Rome's inns and fleshpots. Cato did not offer him a seat, but kept him standing at ease as he addressed him. The tribune had puffy cheeks and the spidery red blood vessels on his jowls and nose that showed he was a hardened drinker.

'Tribune Pantella,' Cato began, 'I understand that you exercise your rank and duties with what might be called a rather light touch. You delegate far too much to your senior centurion and make little effort to ensure that he is carrying out his duties diligently. That will cease. Until further notice, all my officers will be required to live in the camp and will require written permission to leave it when off duty. You will be drilled alongside the men until you are in a fit state to lead them. You will also be responsible for ensuring the integrity of your cohort's administration. I will be looking through the records of all three cohorts over the next few days. If I encounter any instances of corruption in your cohort, I will hold you responsible for making good any misuse of funds from your own resources. Failing that, I will have you prosecuted for corruption. Dismissed.'

Pantella opened his mouth to protest, but Cato shot his finger towards the door before the man could speak and snapped, 'I said dismissed! Get out!'

The tribune hesitated, the blood draining from his face. Then he turned about and marched out of the room, leaving the door open behind him.

Cato took a deep breath and braced himself for the most serious confrontation of the day. He had met men like Macrinus before. They abused their position to extract bribes and line their purses at every opportunity, with no regard for the effect this might have on the men under their command, who had no choice but to endure their vices or face punishment. Ever since he had been appointed to his first command, he had rooted out such individuals as soon as possible and replaced them with men of integrity.

He cleared his throat. 'Centurion Macrinus! Step inside!'

A huge man with brutal features came through the doorway. He was as broad as he was tall, and had the physique of a champion wrestler. Or boxer, Cato corrected himself as he saw the broad nose and deformed ears and the scars that marked his face. His hair was dark with streaks of grey, and two almost black eyes gleamed from deep sockets beneath a pronounced brow. He was wearing a tunic cut from expensive-looking cloth, trimmed with laced cuffs in a silvery oak-leaf pattern. He wore a gleaming leather harness over the tunic, and a sword hung at his side. In his left hand was a centurion's vine cane with an ivory carving of a wolf's head fixed to the top of it. Despite his size, he carried himself with a lightness of foot that confirmed Cato's impression of him as a trained fighter. His heavy lips parted in a casual grin.

'You wanted to see me, sir. How can I be of help?' He made to reach for one of the stools.

Cato was briefly taken aback by the confident forwardness of the man. He kept his own expression neutral as he shot back, 'Stand to attention when you are before your commanding officer!'

Macrinus arched a thick eyebrow and smiled insolently as he shifted into a passable approximation of coming to attention. He fixed his eyes on a point directly ahead of him.

Cato took some time to look him over, every detail seeming to confirm his initial unfavourable impression. There was an air of intelligence as well as imperturbable arrogance about the man that concerned him, and he knew he must handle him with caution.

'I understand that Tribune Pantella has abdicated the responsibilities of his position to you, and that you are the de facto commander of the Third Cohort.'

Macrinus affected a surprised expression. 'I don't think that is an accurate representation of the situation, sir. The tribune is a busy man. I merely carry out his orders and deal with day-to-day matters of administration, as is the duty of any conscientious subordinate.'

'Conscientious? That's a bit rich coming from you. I would

have thought a more accurate word would be corrupt. Do you deny that you are using your position to enrich yourself by fraudulent means?'

'Such as?'

'Claiming the pay of discharged soldiers. Selling the cohort's clothing, equipment and food to your black-market contacts. Taking bribes from the men you command to be excused duties and for the purposes of their privileges and preferment . . . Well? What do you say?'

Macrinus tilted his head before he responded. 'I say that someone has an overactive imagination, or perhaps malicious intent, to make such disreputable smears against me.'

'You deny them?'

'Of course.'

Cato narrowed his eyes. 'Sir.'

'I deny them, *sir*. Furthermore, I would ask you to provide proof to back up these allegations.'

'Proof, eh?' Cato reached over to the waxed tablet on which he had made some notes. He flipped it open. 'Let's see. To start with, there's the matter of the requisition of grain. According to the records, you have drawn enough from the imperial granaries to fill your cohort's stores twice over in the last year. And yet there's barely enough there to feed your men for more than a few days. How do you account for the discrepancy, Centurion.'

'There are a number of reasons, sir,' Macrinus said smoothly. 'Firstly, there are unfortunately a number of miscreants in the ranks who have been stealing from stores. You will find that the punishment logs of the cohort back that up. Secondly, we have had problems with occasional flooding from the Tiber, which has ruined a considerable amount of the grain. Again, this is documented in the cohort's records. Thirdly, we have serious rat infestations from time to time. They consume grain and spoil much of what they leave . . . If you like, sir, I can go to my quarters and return with the documents that will back up what I say.' He gestured towards the door as if asking for permission to leave.

Cato considered calling his bluff, but it was already apparent that Macrinus was wily enough to cover his tracks with a set of false records that would bear out his claims. It would be easy to exaggerate the quantity of grain ruined by floods or rats, if indeed there had been any significant loss at all. He decided that he would have to switch the direction of his attack.

'It will be a simple enough matter to check the disciplinary records by interviewing the men concerned. If, for example, it turned out that they had not been punished, or had been disciplined for other reasons, you would have a hard time explaining any discrepancies.'

'I imagine so, sir. If there are any discrepancies. Be my guest. Talk to the men who were charged and punished for theft. I dare say they will back me up. I should say, back up the official record. I am certain of it.'

Macrinus had assumed the weary expression of a teacher explaining something simple to one of his slower pupils, and Cato felt a surge of anger. No doubt the centurion had a hold over the men whose names appeared in the punishment log. Either they were afraid of him and would confirm what he had said to Cato, or they were his cronies and had been paid off to allow their names to be falsely entered in the log.

'Trust me, Macrinus. I will be speaking to them. I will also be going over the records in detail, and you will be required to answer for anything that does not add up.'

'I imagine there may be some gaps, sir. That is only to be expected. But whatever small discrepancies you may find will be no worse than any other unit in the army. To try to make an example of one of your officers over such matters would only reflect badly upon you. Some might say you were a petty jobsworth using one of your subordinates as a scapegoat for the incompetence of those who were in command at the time the alleged offences took place. *I'm* not saying that. But others might. In any case, I dare say that Tigellinus would not be particularly happy to have his reputation tarnished by such allegations. And since he has the ear of the emperor, I wonder who would come off worst if you pressed the matter?' The centurion cocked an eyebrow.

Cato strained to control his rising temper. Macrinus seemed to have covered his tracks well, and would doubtless be a dangerous adversary if Cato chose to go after him without hard and irrefutable evidence. Nonetheless, he *was* guilty, and he could not be permitted to continue getting away with it. There would be a way of dealing with him, but it would take some time and thought to lay the groundwork to put an end to his grift.

He cleared his throat. 'Make no mistake. I will be watching you closely from now on. One misstep and I'll be on to you faster than shit through a goose.'

Macrinus returned his glare impassively. 'Will there be anything else, sir?'

'There will be another full inspection of all three cohorts first thing tomorrow. You'd better make sure your men give me no cause for complaint. Dismissed.'

CHAPTER NINE

Trebonius rapped lightly on the door frame of Cato's office. 'Visitor for you, sir.'

Cato had been working through the cohorts' accounts since dawn. He looked up with a sigh, then lowered his stylus on the line of the inventory to mark the place. 'Visitor?'

Trebonius stepped aside with a slight grin and made way for Macro to enter the commanding officer's office.

'Hello, lad, thought I'd drop by on the way to the Forum and see how things are going with your new command.'

'On the way to the Forum?' Cato cocked an eyebrow. 'Lose our way, did we?'

Macro shrugged. 'I needed some exercise and took a diversion. Not intruding, am I?'

'I could use a break. Trebonius, bring us some refreshments. We'll be up on the terrace.'

'Terrace?' Macro made a face. 'Rank hath its privileges, eh?'

'One of the very few good points with respect to this command, brother.'

Cato rose from his chair and led the way up onto the top of the tower. Macro spent a moment taking in the view across the city before turning a professional eye on the interior of the camp. There were parties of men at work repairing the neglected walls before applying a fresh coat of whitewash. Other men were carrying out weapons drill, while a century marched in formation to and fro across the middle of the camp.

'Looks like you have things in hand here.'

Cato joined him at the wooden rail that ran around the terrace. 'I'm barely getting started. Tigellinus had let the cohorts run to rot. Poor discipline, corruption, idleness and insubordination of the worst kind. Frankly, I've never seen the like. There are some good men here, though.' He pointed out Lemulus, leading the century that was marching across the heart of the camp. 'There's one. Transferred from the legions. He's acting tribune. A good, reliable man, I think. However, there's a lot of dead wood. Take those two, for example. Over by the weapons training posts.'

Macro squinted towards the two officers.

'Tribune Pantella and his senior centurion, Macrinus,' Cato continued. 'The centurion is running just about every con you can imagine while his playboy superior looks the other way. While I have scoundrels like that in my command it's going to be hard to get the cohorts knocked into shape.'

'Why not just get rid of them?'

'Not so easy.' Cato jerked his thumb in the direction of his office. 'I've been looking for evidence to justify disciplinary action against Macrinus, but he's as smart as a whip and has covered his tracks. He's also got a tight grip over his men and none of them dare step out of line and speak against him.'

'Hmm,' Macro mused. 'You've certainly got your hands full.'

They were interrupted by Trebonius, who carried a tray across to a small table positioned in the shade of an awning that Cato had rigged up in the corner of the tower looking towards the heart of the capital. Once the wine jar, cups and a platter of snacks had been set out, the steward withdrew and the two men sat down. Cato poured them both a cup of watered-down wine. Macro took a sip and made a face. 'I take it they aren't paying you well enough to provide your guests with a decent drop.'

Cato knew that his friend preferred a more liberal proportion of wine to water and smiled. 'I need to keep a clear head these days. It's bad enough having to kick the cohorts into shape. Then there's the rather more difficult, not to say dangerous, business of negotiating the cross-currents of politics here in Rome. A man can be counted a favourite of Nero one day and be condemned the next, through no fault of his own. We live at the whim of a capricious and thin-skinned man who thinks he's a genius. The emperor is surrounded by a nest of backbiting vipers whose craven flattery he takes as the truth. I tell you, Macro, I'd rather face any of the enemies we have encountered on the battlefield than live with the worry of having a knife planted in my back.'

'And to think we were returning to Rome to enjoy a bit of peace and quiet . . .'

'Quite.'

They sipped their wine for a moment as they looked out over the city. The air was filled with a cacophony of noises. The sharp ringing of hammers from a small foundry in a nearby street. The cries of street hawkers, shouted greetings and arguments, and tens of thousands of other voices merging into a background thrum. Gulls and other birds circled lazily before swooping to snatch up some morsel of food they had spied from above. Others lined the ridges of roofs and perched atop temples and statues, depositing their droppings on the faded white streaks left by generations of their predecessors. A more fitting epitaph for those depicted by the statues than the vainglorious plaques commemorating their achievements, thought Cato. He glanced at his friend.

'How are things with you? Still enjoying your retirement with Petronella?'

Macro breathed in deeply before he replied. 'It's all right, I suppose. We live comfortably, thanks to you.'

'The least I could do,' Cato responded. 'I'm glad to make the house available to you.'

'It's kind of you, lad. After we lost everything in Britannia, I had no idea how my lady and I were going to get by. I'll make it up to you one day, I swear.'

'You owe me nothing. You've always covered my back, and you've saved my life more times than I care to recall.'

Macro shifted uncomfortably. 'All the same, I'll find a way to return the favour.'

They were on sensitive ground, Cato knew. His friend had lived his life standing on his own feet, beholden to no one for handouts, billets or favours. Thanks to Boudica and her rebels, he had lost his home, his lands, the business he had owned in Londinium and the savings he had lodged with a banker in the town. He was dependent on Cato, and that was an acutely uncomfortable condition for a man as proud as he.

'I heard that there's an opening for a trainer at the imperial gladiator school,' said Macro. 'The money's good, and if I got the post and stuck with it, I could move up to become a lanista. If I save enough, I might even set up on my own. Either way, I could pay our way and sort you out some rent.'

'I wouldn't take it,' Cato said firmly. 'Besides, can you really see yourself spending your life training good men to fight for the pleasure of pampered aristocrats and the mob?'

'I suppose not. But I have to find something to do. Some way of earning an income so I can pay you back. In any case, I'm starting to get bored. There's only so much a man can take of swapping tales with other veterans in the inns under the arches of the Great Circus. War stories and tall tales of army life tend to get repeated far sooner than you think. I need to do something else. Petronella's been nagging me about that. She can see that I'm slowly going to seed, and I ain't happy about it.' He patted his stomach. 'There's more padding there than I've ever had before. At this rate I won't be able to get into my armour.'

'You shouldn't have to. That's the point of retirement.'

Macro frowned. 'Dammit, lad! I ain't ready for that. I can still wield a sword as well as most men in the legions, and I ain't going to spend my days growing fat and lazy in the company of old soaks who live on the memories of when they were still real men. I deserve better than that. So does Petronella.'

Cato nodded sympathetically, weighing up the right moment to make his offer. 'Truth be told, I didn't think I would ever see the day when you finally accepted your military career was over. Many soldiers look forward to retirement. But not you. You were born to be a lifelong soldier. The kind of man who doesn't die in his bed. I always thought you'd go into the shades sword in hand and blood in your mouth, shouting your war cry to the last. Though I hoped that wouldn't happen for a long time yet, obviously.'

'Obviously. Petronella would throw a fit otherwise. And that's one woman you want to placate more than any of the Furies if you value your life.'

Cato laughed and refilled their cups before settling back on his chair and looking across the table at his friend. 'There is a way we can meet your needs and hers at the same time.'

Macro took a sip. 'You think?'

'I told you that I was short of good men here. There are some I can rely on, but I still don't know them well enough to trust them completely. Fortunately, I exercise control over most of the officers' appointments. I need someone at my side I can count on without reservation. Who better than you?'

Macro lowered his cup. 'You mean it?'

'I wouldn't say it if I didn't.'

'You're not just offering this out of pity?'

'That would be an unworthy sentiment for both of us. Truth is, I need you to help me get the cohorts back on their feet and root out those who have no right to serve alongside decent men. Will you do it?'

'Does the emperor shit on the Palatine?'

'Strictly between us, Nero shits on everything in Rome.'

They laughed, and Cato raised his cup. 'To comrades in arms. To the end.'

After the toast, he lowered his cup and adopted a more serious tone. 'Before you accept the post, you need to understand that this won't be like it was back in Britannia. It was us against a common enemy. Here it's different. The enemy is disloyalty, and it's already in our camp waiting for a chance to strike. I won't sell you any smoke about this – it'll be dangerous work. If I play it badly, I may be marked for death. And if they come for me, chances are they'll come for you too.' He paused to let his friend consider his warning. 'So, Macro, what do you say?'

'Since you've been honest with me, I'll return the favour and tell you that Petronella will never forgive you for making the offer. If you can live with that hanging over you, then I'm the man for the job.'

'Why not? I've faced mortal danger before.'

Macro rolled his eyes. 'You have no idea . . .'

'Will she really take it that badly?'

He shrugged. 'She knows who she married. She knows what comes with that. There may be a few tears, but she'll come round.'

'Fine. I'll have you entered on the strength as camp prefect. Your first duty is to take charge of the training and instil discipline. I'll have quarters prepared for you. For now, both of us are going to be living here, along with the rest of the officers and men. It's the best way to forge closer ties between the ranks and re-establish the spirit of the cohorts. Those are the terms. Are you quite sure you want to accept the job? I'll understand if you change your mind and go for the gladiator trainer position.'

'Fuck that,' Macro said emphatically. 'I'm in. For better or worse.'

'All right then.' Cato stood and held out his hand. They clasped forearms to seal the arrangement, then drained their cups.

'I'd better get back and tell her the news,' said Macro. 'Look for thunder and lightning over the Viminal Hill.'

Cato escorted him downstairs to the entrance of the tower, where they paused to say their farewell. 'How soon can you take up the position?'

'I'll be back before dark. Just need to break the news and collect my kit.'

Cato chuckled.

'What?' Macro fixed him with a look.

'If I didn't know better, I'd say this is precisely the outcome you'd hoped for when you decided to pay me a casual visit.'

'Then I'd say I'm almost as transparent in my motivations as you are, my lad. I'll see you later.'

Cato watched his friend striding across the camp, glancing from side to side, back straight, chest out – the model of a camp prefect already. The brief moment of pleasure faded, and he turned back towards his office. As he climbed the stairs, he considered the implications of Macro taking up his offer. There was no denying the risks he was exposing his best friend to. But the thought of Macro standing beside him to face the coming challenges was a great comfort for him personally, and a step towards remedying the lamentable state into which the urban cohorts had been allowed to fall.

He sat at his desk and resumed his scrutiny of the records. 'I'm on your trail, Macrinus,' he muttered. 'You'll slip up, and then I'll nail your arse to the cross as surely as I breathe.'

As the brassy notes of the bucina sounded midday across the camp, Cato eased back from the desk and sighed with weariness and frustration. He had found nothing that would justify bringing corruption charges against the centurion. There were some small discrepancies, but they could easily be explained away or owned up to by Macrinus without incriminating himself.

He stood up and rubbed the small of his back as he paced over to the window overlooking the interior of the camp. The men who had been conducting weapons drill were stacking their training swords and shields against the nearby wall before they headed for their barracks and the mess hall. Lemulus had called his century to attention and briefly scrutinised their ranks before dismissing them. Cato tried to gauge the mood across the camp, and was aware how quiet the men were as they made their way off the drill ground. Elsewhere, others who were tasked with repairs went about their work in sullen silence, without the speed or diligence he wished to see. Their officers made no effort to spur them on. In the far corner of the camp, a group of optios sat in the shade as they shared a jug of wine and played dice.

Cato was on the verge of leaving the tower to berate them when his gaze was drawn to two men approaching from the direction of the main gate. One was Macrinus. The other was a slender man in the blue livery of the imperial palace. As they drew closer, the centurion caught sight of Cato standing at the window, and his lips parted in a smile – or perhaps a sneer. He tapped his forehead in a mock salute, and then the two men disappeared below as they entered headquarters. A moment later, Cato heard footsteps on the stairs, and Macrinus appeared on the threshold of the office.

'What is it?' Cato demanded tersely.

'Begging your pardon, sir, but there's a lad from the palace with a message for you. Or rather, a summons.' Macrinus did not hide his pleasure as he added, 'I thought it urgent enough to escort him here directly, sir.'

'I bet you did. Send him in.'

Macrinus waved the other man through. The slave bowed low, then drew himself up and announced, 'Prefect Quintus Licinius Cato, you are ordered to attend the emperor at once.'

Cato felt an icy sensation ripple down his spine.

'Now I wonder what that could be in connection with,' said

Macrinus. 'What could be so pressing that the emperor would tear you away from your duties without warning? It could be some petty matter like asking you to pass judgement on his latest poetic endeavours . . . Or it might be something else. Something more serious concerning arrangements at the urban cohorts. What do you think, sir?'

'Shut your mouth,' Cato snapped. 'Before I have you on a charge of insolence and insubordination.'

'I wonder how that might turn out.'

'Get out!'

Macrinus saluted casually and turned away in the direction of the stairs. The palace slave stood still, his expression registering no reaction. Cato took his scale cuirass from the frame behind his desk and hurriedly put it on, fastening the straps before retrieving his helmet. He hesitated as he reached for his sword belt, then withdrew his hand. The blade would only have to be handed over before he was allowed into the emperor's presence.

'Well?' He turned to the slave. 'Where am I supposed to attend him?'

'The garden terrace of the palace, master. I am ordered to show you the way.'

'I know the way,' Cato replied. 'I was raised in the palace complex.'

The slave regarded him uncertainly for a moment. 'There have been significant changes there since Caesar inherited power, master. You may not be as familiar with the layout as you once were.'

'Very well. Let's get on with it.'

As he followed the slave out of the tower, Cato addressed him quietly. 'Are you aware of any reason for summoning me?'

'I am just the bearer of the message, master.'

They continued a short distance before he tried again. 'Am I in trouble?'

The slave slowed fractionally and looked over his shoulder as he replied. 'Define trouble . . .'

113

CHAPTER TEN

The emperor was attended by a small group as he surveyed the white-painted blocks laid out on a large diagram painstakingly detailed on a broad expanse of parchment that covered an even larger table. As Cato approached along the wide garden terrace that overlooked the Forum, he could see that the diagram depicted the layout of the city, and the blocks represented halls, colonnades and other structures that formed what appeared to be a modest city in its own right.

Nero's entourage stood a short distance away as their master conferred with two men in white togas. Cato scanned the faces of the others until he saw Tigellinus watching him with a cool smile of satisfaction. At once he guessed that it was Tigellinus who was behind the summons, and it was easy to piece together the purpose of it. Burrus intercepted him and steered him to the rear of the group as the slave who had escorted Cato bowed his head and backed off a few steps before turning to trot away.

'Well, you've made a fine start,' the Praetorian whispered harshly. 'What in Hades were you thinking when you dismissed Albanius? Not only that, but humiliating the other tribunes and spreading rumours about the integrity of one of the senior centurions?'

'Rumours? I've spread no rumours. The bloody man is corrupt. And I'll prove it soon enough. As for the tribunes—'

'Be quiet,' Burrus hissed. 'I don't give a shit about them or that bloody smarmy swine Macrinus. What matters is that they have all complained to Tigellinus, and he's been dripping his poison into Nero's ear. Now the emperor wants a word with you. When the time comes, you'd better be careful if you want to keep your head. Understand?' He glared at Cato. 'So much for your reputation as an intelligent officer with good prospects.'

Cato made to defend himself, but Burrus raised a warning finger. 'Don't.'

Cato waited as the others around him regarded the emperor in silence. Nero was examining the details of the plans, making observations and asking questions of the two men standing on the opposite side of the table. Cato looked round at his companions, some of whom he recognised. There was Seneca, standing slightly apart with a young man at his side, slender and delicately featured. The latter tilted his head and whispered something that made Seneca smile. There were a handful of other senators and a cluster of young men in brightly coloured chitons. Further along the terrace, he saw a group of women gathered around Poppaea, who was reclining languidly on a couch. Her golden tresses tossed as she chatted happily with her coterie.

'This isn't what I had in mind,' Nero announced loudly, folding his arms and moving slowly around the table until he stopped alongside the two men, who watched him anxiously. 'It won't do. Severus, I asked you for a palace fit for an emperor, not merely some squalid extension of the Palatine complex.' He unfolded his arms and pointed at a large block in the centre of the plan. 'What is that supposed to be?'

Severus, a short, portly man, flexed his fat fingers as he replied. 'That is the audience chamber, Caesar. If you recall, you asked for it to be the heart of the new palace.'

'I did not ask for it to be the size of a rabbit hutch.'

'It is twice the size of your existing audience chamber, Caesar. To make it any larger would mean a significant increase in cost,

115

and the rest of the complex will already exceed the budget you set me.'

'Damn the cost!' Nero threw his hands up. 'Such things do not concern me. I demand a palace that will be the envy of the world. A structure that will stand for all time as a reminder of the golden age I have conferred on Rome and its people. I want a palace to grace the greatest kings and princes, the finest poets, writers, musicians and actors. It is to be like nothing that has ever existed before. It will be the envy of the world and fit for the gods themselves. Do you truly think such an ambition should be concerned with anything as trivial as a budget? Well, man?'

Severus opened his mouth to reply, then thought better of it. He swallowed and bowed his head in apology. 'As Caesar wishes. I will redraft my plans to suit Caesar's intentions.'

'Not just you.' Nero rounded on the other man. 'I am equally displeased with the scale of the parkland that will extend around the palace. I want a landscape that would grace the Elysian Fields. Rich with game and with every variety of tree, fruit and flower. Not some miserable avenues of poplars arranged around a square pond.'

'It's hardly a pond, Caesar. There is nothing to compare it with in even the largest of Rome's bathhouses.'

'If I'd wanted a bath I'd have asked you for one, Celer. I want a lake. And I want the parkland to extend east as far as the city walls and stretch from the crest of the Caelian Hill to the south to the Viminal in the north, with the heights of the Esquiline in the middle.'

Celer's eyes widened. 'But Caesar, that would take up nearly half of the present city.'

Nero turned to him with an unconcerned expression. 'Yes. So?'

'It would mean countless tenement blocks, villas and businesses being demolished, Caesar.'

'As the saying goes, you can't make an omelette without breaking a few eggs.' Nero smiled emolliently. 'Come now, I am only asking for both of you to use a bit more imagination. Dare to imagine, my friends. Perhaps then your names will occasionally be mentioned along with mine in the ages to come, when people talk about the wonder we shall create together.'

Neither of the architects could find any response to Nero's exhortation, and he turned away from them with an exasperated expression to address his entourage. 'My friends, it seems that Severus and Celer need our assistance. This gathering represents the finest minds and tastes to be found in Rome. Let us see what we can come up with to inspire their imaginations.'

He beckoned, and his inner circle hurried forward and jostled for places close to the table. Cato found himself directly opposite the emperor, behind a short, swarthy youth in a chiton whose hair was shiny and slick with oil and who wore an overpowering sweet scent. Nero looked over his companions, eyes bright with excitement. 'I need suggestions, my friends. Who is to be first? How about you, Seneca?'

Cato saw the senator purse his lips as he looked over the diagram before responding. 'You are right, Caesar, naturally. There is a distinct lack of ambition as things stand. That said, Severus and Celer must be congratulated on providing an admirable initial sketch of the new palace. There is much that can be improved. Take the banqueting hall, for example. It's too small. It should be large enough to feast Caesar and his guests. It should be decorated in such a manner as to dazzle the eyes and beggar the imagination. I can barely conceive of the brilliance of the designs already fomenting in the mind of Caesar . . .'

As Seneca continued, Cato realised that he was doing his best to protect the two architects from further criticism. At the same time, his words fed Nero with the praise he obviously expected, and the young ruler nodded in satisfaction, seemingly unaware of the hyperbole washing over him. Cato wondered if Seneca might not go too far and sow the seeds of doubt about his sincerity.

Doubt might swiftly move on to a moment of self-awareness, and thence embarrassment and the most dangerous of imperial sentiments – shame. It seemed to Cato that Nero must surely see through it all at any moment.

Looking round the table, he searched the expressions of his companions for signs of the discomfort and disgust he felt stirring within himself. But all he saw were carefully contrived masks of bright-eyed adulation and nods of agreement as they listened to Seneca's oratory. Then a thought struck him. Suppose they were not masking their true thoughts? Suppose most of them were as blind to the truth as their emperor?

'Let a palace be built that is a monument to the golden age we are blessed to be living in,' Seneca continued. 'A palace made of gold . . .'

It was too much for Cato. 'A golden house,' he muttered. 'For fuck's sake. That's all Rome needs.'

Burrus shot him a furious look as Nero looked up from the table and raised a hand to silence Seneca. 'What's that? Someone spoke . . .'

Tigellinus cleared his throat. 'I believe it was Prefect Cato, Caesar. I am sure we are all fascinated to hear what suggestion he has to add to those of Seneca.'

Nero's eyes fixed on Cato. 'Well? Step forward and speak.'

Cato felt his stomach clench as he eased himself round the man in front of him and stood at the edge of the table. 'Caesar, I humbly suggest that the new palace be called the Golden House. "Palace" is too inadequate a description for any poet whose work touches the minds and hearts of all his people. This,' he indicated the design, 'will showcase your talents to the world. It will be the very home of the arts. So the Golden House is the most fitting name for it.'

Nero thought a moment. Cato saw the delighted sneer on Tigellinus's face as he anticipated his rejection of the name.

The emperor gave a light cough before he spoke. 'The Golden House . . .' He repeated it with a more resonant, stagey declaration. 'The. Golden. House!' Then he smiled with delight. 'By the gods, you have it, Cato! The Golden House it is. Bravo!'

Those around the table nodded effusively and clapped before Tigellinus spoke up again. 'Does our war hero have any other thoughts on the design he can share with us?'

Cato shot him a hostile glare. He had hoped he had said enough and was off the hook, but now the emperor was regarding him expectantly.

'Indeed. Yes . . . There is something missing at the heart of the design . . .' His mind desperately struggled to fabricate a fresh idea. Then the most apposite image struck him, and he continued confidently. 'Those who look on the Golden House will see buildings. Great buildings. Tremendous buildings, it's true. But what is the good of building such a palace if the people now and in the years to come cannot see the image of the man from whose imagination the concept sprang? I propose that a great statue be erected to depict Caesar. It should be the tallest statue ever built, and yes, it should be covered in gold.'

Nero's jaw sagged in awe, while at his side the two architects exchanged a look of horror.

'By the gods, Cato,' the emperor said in a hushed voice. 'You are truly inspired. A golden statue then. A colossus. For all my people to see. What could be more fitting?'

There was more nodding, murmurs of approval and muted applause before Nero silenced his entourage by raising his hand.

'One thing, though, Cato. The concept does not spring from the mind of a mere man. It is my divine inspiration that calls the Golden House into being.'

Cato bowed his head. 'Of course, Caesar. That is what I meant to say.'

'Good.' Nero smiled briefly, then frowned. 'Why are you

present?' He snapped his fingers. 'Ah yes, you are here because I summoned you.'

'Yes, Caesar.' The fear and tension surged back through Cato's veins.

'Then come and walk with me. The rest of you, wait here. Severus, Celer, pack that up and take it away, and draft me a better plan. I want to see it by the end of the month.'

The two architects bowed deeply and began to bundle up the parchment and the white models. Burrus tilted his head towards Cato and spoke quietly.

'That was quick thinking. Maybe I was wrong to rush to judgement. All the same, I'd choose your words even more carefully now. Good luck.' He patted him on the shoulder and moved aside to let him work his way around to the emperor.

Nero beamed at Cato and reached up to give his cheek a light pinch. 'You have a fine eye for detail and good taste. I like that in a man.'

'Caesar is too kind. I am merely a simple soldier at Caesar's command.'

'Nonsense. We both know you are far more than that, and you don't need to pretend otherwise. I am well aware of your military reputation and the great services you have rendered to Rome over the years, so let's not play games.'

There was a seriousness in his tone that put Cato on his guard. He nodded deferentially. 'As you wish, Caesar.'

'Good, then come with me.'

The emperor strolled a few paces in the direction of Poppaea until she noticed him. They exchanged a wave before Nero blew her a kiss and she gave a coquettish laugh in return. As he turned about and headed towards the opposite end of the terrace, his entourage broke up into small groups and chatted among themselves. Cato saw the calculating looks directed at him by Tigellinus, Seneca and Burrus as he followed Nero at a respectful distance of a pace behind and to one side of the emperor.

'I rarely get the chance to talk frankly with anyone from outside my coterie and those grovelling foreigners. Speaking of which, a delegation from Parthia has just arrived to discuss the situation in Armenia. I understand you served there some years ago.'

'Yes, Caesar. I commanded the column sent to put Rhadamistus on the throne.'

'That didn't go well, did it?'

The implied criticism stung Cato. The man chosen to rule Armenia had been an arrogant warmonger who had completely undermined the interests of Rome in that troubled region.

'No. It did not, Caesar.'

'And the situation hasn't been resolved since. Things go our way and then they go Parthia's way. Our replacement for Rhadamistus has been an equal disaster. After invading a neighbouring ally, he drew down the full wrath of Vologases and his army, and now our influence in that part of the world hangs in the balance. General Corbulo is in charge there. You know him?'

'Yes, Caesar. A fine commander and a man I respect.'

'You respect him?' Nero gave Cato a sidelong look. 'Interesting . . . He commands the largest field army in the Empire. Such power would be sorely tempting for an ambitious man.'

'I am sure Corbulo's ambition is to serve Caesar and Rome to the best of his ability.'

'For now, perhaps. In any case, I will see to it that he is kept too busy to entertain any personal ambitions. He has suggested that peace with Parthia might be achieved by both sides withdrawing from Armenia. Vologases is keen on the idea and has sent envoys to secure such a peace. They will return empty-handed, however.'

'Oh?'

'Indeed. I will not permit Rome to be seen as too weak to maintain its control over Armenia. We will make further demands of Parthia. Demands that Vologases will be sure to reject, and so the conflict will resume. If Corbulo is victorious, I will claim the credit. If he is defeated, the disgrace is his. Either way, he poses no threat to me. And if he does one day, I will offer him the free choice of death. The same goes for any senior army officer whose loyalty becomes questionable. Something to bear in mind, Prefect Cato. Not that I am questioning your loyalty, of course.'

Cato's mind was seething as he contemplated the emperor's blasé comments. He well recalled the difficulties faced by Corbulo and his army. Too few men to pin down and defeat the highly mobile Parthian forces. Too few men even to hold any ground that was gained. The political infighting between Corbulo and the other governors and army commanders of the eastern frontier. Most of all, the harshness of the terrain. Great expanses of desert to traverse, as well as towering mountain ranges that favoured the enemy. The region had already become the graveyard of Crassus and his ill-fated legions. There was every chance that Corbulo and his men would suffer a similar defeat if they carried the war too deep into the lands of Vologases.

Worst of all was Nero's casual admission that Corbulo and his men would be ordered to fight and die for no better reason than to satisfy the emperor's need for glory and allay any anxieties over the loyalty of his senior officers. Cato could not help wondering if all the perils he and Macro had faced over the years at the direction of rulers like Nero and the other Claudian emperors had been worth it.

For many years he had been at the sharp end of imperial might, facing death along with his comrades in the belief that on balance their cause was just. The light of Rome versus the rapacious barbarity of her enemies. He was certainly not blind to the injustices and incompetence perpetrated by those who decided on imperial policy, but he had seen enough of the world to come to the view that Rome was the least bad option for the peoples living under her control. They could have peace and prosperity in exchange for their taxes and submission to the laws and authority of the Empire. It was as good a bargain as any. And maybe a part of that was the recognition that such order depended on rule by one man. Or in the name of one man, at least. It was clear that Nero was largely a figurehead, whose authority was dispersed across tens of thousands of functionaries here in Rome and throughout the Empire. The most significant decisions he made were largely the result of the advice he was given by wiser men, who were motivated by what was good for Rome, and often themselves. For his part, Nero was more concerned by the quotidian pleasures of life, forever pursuing his artistic interests amid the surroundings of every possible luxury that the Empire could afford.

They had reached the far end of the terrace, and Nero rested his hand on the balustrade as he gazed down on the teeming masses in the Forum and streets below. He said nothing for a moment before he turned to Cato. 'No one knows what it is like to live with the burdens that fate has heaped upon my shoulders. The Empire and all who live in it look to me for decisions great and small. They look to me to ensure order. It is not helpful for dissent to be sown among those who serve me. That is the reason I have sent for you.'

Here it comes, thought Cato.

'When I appointed you to command the urban cohorts, I had not anticipated that you would cause me any difficulties.'

'Difficulties, Caesar?'

'My good friend Tigellinus tells me that you have upset a number of your officers, and have even removed some of them from their posts. Is this true?'

'Yes, Caesar.'

'Why have you done that? One of them at least is a man I personally appointed.'

'Albanius has served you poorly, Caesar. He has been neglecting his duties and has fallen short of the standard expected of a servant of Caesar. The same goes for the others. When you entrusted me with the command of the cohorts, you did so because of my reputation as a soldier. As such, it is my professional duty to ensure that the men of the cohorts are worthy of serving their emperor. You would expect no less of them, Caesar.'

'That's true . . .' Nero stroked the folds of flesh beneath his weak chin. 'All the same, could you not extend some leniency towards the friends of Tigellinus? He's been terribly upset on their behalf, and I hate to see how this has affected him. The poor man has been quite angry about it. He has called you all sorts of names. I really would rather the two of you were not at loggerheads over this and found it in yourselves to get on together. For the good of Rome and all that, I would be pleased if you resolved this matter amicably.'

Cato struggled to conceal his contempt for the emperor's words. Despite being the most powerful person in the Empire, Nero was someone who backed down almost the instant he was confronted. He took a calming breath before he replied in an even tone, 'Caesar, if it is a choice between making the urban cohorts a body of men you can be proud of and trust to be loyal, and appeasing the hurt feelings of the incompetent companions of one of your friends, then as one of your soldiers, I would choose the former every time. Tell me if I am wrong to do so.'

A pained look flitted across the emperor's face before he raised his hands in a helpless gesture. 'You make a good point. Soldiers must be soldiers. The fate of Rome depends upon those who take up arms in her cause. I suppose I will have to explain that to Tigellinus.'

'I am sure he already understands the situation, Caesar. May I take it that you are still confident in my ability to carry out my duty?'

'Yes . . . yes, of course. You have my backing. Do what you need to do, Prefect Cato. There, the matter is resolved. Now I can devote a few hours to the delightful company of my darling Poppaea. I have neglected her for too long today. Ah, but the work of a ruler is never done, and there are so few opportunities to indulge myself. Count yourself lucky you only have a few cohorts to run rather than an entire empire.'

Nero smiled and turned to walk off at a brisk pace. Cato watched him for a moment, glad that he had managed to defy Tigellinus. For now at least he had the emperor's backing to deal with Macrinus and the others. Part of him wished that Nero had taken the other man's side and given Cato the chance to request that he be dismissed from his post and allowed to return to his farm. He pushed the unworthy thought aside. The command was his for the time being, and he and Macro would make a good job of it. Nero might change his mind the next day, the next month or maybe even further into the future. Until then, the urban cohorts were Cato's to shape and lead.

He left the terrace, and after a wrong turn found a slave to direct him back to the courtyard at the main entrance of the palace. There were still plenty of petitioners waiting to register their requests with the imperial clerks sitting at a table outside the archway guarded by the Praetorians. There were also groups of senators and equestrians discussing business and making social arrangements. One of them raised a hand in greeting as Cato approached, and he saw that it was Vespasian.

'Prefect Cato! A pleasure to see you again so soon.'

'And you, sir.'

They clasped hands, and the older man held Cato's grip as he spoke. 'What brings you here?'

'A difference of opinion over how I lead my men.'

'The urban cohorts? I'd heard that you had been appointed their prefect.'

'Oh?'

'Word travels fast in Rome. Gossip even faster. I must admit that I was surprised to hear the news, given your reluctance to quit your farm when I saw you. I was under the impression that you had decided to hang up your sword for good.'

'That was my intention. The emperor decided otherwise.'

'That's too bad. For you, I mean. However, your loss is Rome's gain. I mean that sincerely. You're too good a soldier to be left rotting in some rural backwater.'

'It's kind of you to say so, sir.'

Cato shifted his hand slightly, and Vespasian released his grip.

'Listen, Cato. Now that you are back in Rome, I would appreciate seeing a bit more of you. As it happens, I am hosting a dinner tomorrow night. A gathering of friends and political acquaintances, some of whom you already know. It would be an opportunity to put your face about. Be good for your career. You never know when you might need the support of men of influence. What do you say?'

Cato would rather avoid the occasion, but it would be foolish to turn down his former commanding officer's invitation. He had made an enemy of Tigellinus and his cronies. It would be wise to curry favour with other men of influence. He forced a polite smile.

'I would be delighted to join the party, sir.'

'Good! You know where to find me. Be there before the second hour of the night. I shall look forward to seeing you. Now, if you will excuse me?'

Vespasian indicated the group of senators he had detached himself from. A couple of them had been watching discreetly and now exchanged nods with Cato before he turned away and headed back to the camp.

CHAPTER ELEVEN

'How does it feel to be back in the army?' asked Cato. The sun had barely risen above the city, and long shadows lay across the interior of the camp as the men of the urban cohorts formed up on three sides of the parade ground. Behind him, Macro was busy putting the final touches to his appearance.

'Like I never left it.' Macro smiled happily as he adjusted his harness so that it sat as neatly as possible over his mail vest. His medals had been given a fresh polish, and the leather straps had the dull gleam of the mixture of oil and fat that had been worked into them before being brushed ruthlessly. He put on his felt skullcap and lowered his helmet carefully before fastening the straps under his chin. Last of all he reached for the vine cane that marked him out as a centurion. Hefting the gnarled length of wood, he patted the end in the palm of his hand. 'I'm ready.'

Cato turned away from the window of his office. 'You look it. I dare say there were a few tears last night.'

'Petronella knows better than that. She helped prepare my kit and gave me a hug and a kiss to send me on my way. She knows what this means to me. Bardea, on the other hand . . . You know how she is at the sight of Roman soldiers. When I tried this lot on, she went to her room. Didn't see her after that. Anyway, let's get on with it.'

As Cato put on his own helmet, Trebonius came forward with

the red band that signified his rank and tied it about his waist, looping the ends evenly on either side. Then he helped Cato with his red cloak, arranging the folds so that they hung as elegantly as possible from his shoulders, before stepping back and casting a critical eye over his superior.

'Well?'

'You'll do, sir.'

'Thanks for the underwhelming compliment.'

'You're welcome, sir.'

Cato raised a finger in warning. 'One day you will go too far. Your familiarity borders on insubordination.'

'I should live to see that day, sir,' Trebonius replied with a straight face.

'Come on, Macro. Let's go where discipline still has some hold on this world.'

They emerged from headquarters just as the sun appeared above the roof tiles of the camp. The horsehair crests of their helmets were burnished a fiery red.

'Stand to!' Lemulus bellowed from his position in front of the First Cohort. 'Commanding officer present!'

The men stamped their feet together, gripping the trim of their grounded legionary shields, then snapped their arms to their sides, chins lifted and shoulders squared. It was by no means a smart display of soldiers responding in unison. Many moved too slowly and shuffled into position, leaving irregular gaps in their lines. Two men even managed to drop their shields, and were instantly pounced on by bawling optios.

'Dear fucking gods,' Macro muttered. 'Have you ever seen such a shambles?'

As the two officers made their way to the open side of the parade ground, quiet fell across the camp. Cato waited a moment to gain their attention, then drew a deep breath before he addressed the cohorts.

'You men are aware of how far standards have been allowed to fall. You know that it is my priority to put an end to that and turn you into proper soldiers. I will not accept excuses from any of your officers and I will not permit any man who does not meet my requirements to remain in uniform. To that end I have obtained the services of one of the finest drill instructors in the legions. He will make sure you become soldiers worthy of the name.'

Cato indicated Macro, who stood legs braced apart, hands clasped around the vine cane held behind his back.

'This is Centurion Macro, who has accepted the post of camp prefect. His authority is second only to mine. From now on, all disciplinary action, complaints and petitions from the ranks go through him. Any decision he makes with regard to such matters carries my support without reservation. If any man seeks to try and worm his way round this arrangement to take a grievance to officials outside the cohorts, he will be summarily punished with a dishonourable discharge and be denied his service bonus. You gentlemen should be clear that I was appointed by Caesar, and Caesar stands behind my determination to make you men earn your pay and do your duty.'

He took a long look around the faces of the soldiers before nodding to Macro. 'Over to you.'

Macro paced slowly forward until he stood in the centre of the parade ground. He wore a sour expression as he took in the demeanour of the ranks around him. Then he drew a breath and spoke in a voice well practised at carrying across such a wide space, so that all would clearly hear every word.

'You men, and I use the term lightly, are an utter shower of shite. I have seen the greenest of recruits to the shittiest of town watches in squalid settlements in the farthest-flung reaches of the Empire stand to attention with more competence than you arseholes just demonstrated. What the fuck was that supposed to be? You looked like a bunch of blind cripples fumbling around a geriatric orgy.'

There was some laughter from the ranks, and Macro immediately roared back at them, 'Shut your fucking mouths! You think I was joking? You are a disgrace to your uniform. You shame the standards at the head of your cohorts. When I tell a joke, you will know it, because I will give the order to laugh. Until then, you will keep your dirty traps wired shut and obey every order I give you like your life depends on it. Because if I have my way, it will. I hate slackers. I hate dirty uniform tunics. I hate grime. I hate rust on sword blades and armour. I hate boots with broken laces and without the regulation number of nails in their soles. I hate belts and straps that don't gleam with polish. I hate barrack-room floors that ain't clean enough to eat off. In short, I hate anything and anybody that comes between me and my mission to turn you worthless bastards into something vaguely resembling the warriors of my beloved legions. Right now, that means I hate every one of you with a passion that passeth all fucking understanding. Do I make myself quite clear?'

Cato was barely able to suppress a smile. His friend was on excellent form. Those men who had previously served in the legions or auxiliary cohorts would be lapping this up. Those who were either fresh recruits or who had experienced nothing like it before would be quivering in their boots at the prospect of incurring Macro's wrath. But none of them would be in any doubt that he would be merciless with those who failed to measure up to his high standards. That was the unwritten contract between soldiers and the men who trained them. Because that level of discipline, competence and effort was what stood between them and death at the hands of the enemy. In the case of the urban cohorts, of course, the enemy was likely to be the mob, but the formation was also supposed to serve as part of the final reserve of Roman power. Not that any such emergency had happened since the terrible days of the civil war that had brought down the Republic, Cato reflected. Still, the men had to be trained for such an eventuality, even if they were never called on to defend the last redoubt of their empire.

'I said, do I make myself clear!' Macro shouted, his voice echoing from the surrounding buildings.

There was a rumbling chorus of assent that he cut short with a howl of anger.

'What in Hades do you call that racket? That doesn't sound like the voices of men. You sound like a bunch of mewling eunuchs bitching over the scraps from the table. Try again. I want to hear you. I want to hear your lungs bursting with the bloody effort to be heard across the whole of the fucking city . . . I said, DO I MAKE MYSELF CLEAR?'

'Yes, sir!'

The interior of the camp resonated with the reply, but Macro was still not satisfied. He cupped a hand to his ear and frowned. 'Did someone squeak? Again!'

'YES, SIR!'

As the bellow died away, Cato noted that the sounds of street life beyond the camp were muted for a moment, and he could imagine the denizens of Rome pausing in their labours and journeys to stare in the direction of the din.

'Better!' Macro conceded. 'That's what I want to hear from now on when I ask you a bloody question. Make it so. Now then, having a good voice is only the start. Every man here is going to give me their best. If you don't, you can count on having my boot up your arse, or my vine cane across your back. And if you have any complaints about the treatment, you can fuck right off and find yourself a billet with those pansy wankers up at the Praetorian camp. They may get better pay than you, but they have smaller dicks and all the ladies of Rome know it.'

There was more laughter, which instantly died away as Macro

shot round towards those responsible. 'Did I say you could laugh? No. Then shut the fuck up. Centurions, optios! I want the names of any man who so much as titters from now on. There's always room for more when it comes to cleaning out the latrines . . .'

He leaned his cane against his shoulder as he proceeded along the front of the cohorts. 'Today you start as scum. If you obey orders and bust a gut to do everything I demand, you may improve enough to be considered human. If you work hard enough to eventually win my approval, you may one day become soldiers worthy of the name. But let's not get ahead of ourselves. Right now you are scum, and the first step to not being scum is to be clean and tidy. To that end, we'll start with your kit and your quarters. I want to see leather so polished I can see my handsome face reflected back at me. I want to see armour and weapons free of even a speck of dust. I want to see barrack rooms spick and span from the floor to the rafters. And I want to see it all before the inspection at the end of the day.

'Any man who persists in his scum habits will be signed up for latrine duties. And if I find anything that disagrees with me in more than half of the sections of each century, the centurion will be joining his men there. In this military formation, the shit flows up. No one is excused from duties, officers included. One thing is for sure – I fully expect us to have the most spotless latrines in the whole bloody army in the days to come, thanks to your efforts. Or lack of them.'

He turned about and strode towards Cato before standing to attention and saluting.

'Cohort is ready to commence training, sir.'

'Very good, Centurion Macro.'

'Permission to proceed, sir.'

Cato could not help being amused by the formalities they were playing out for the benefit of the assembled cohorts. He forced himself to adopt a stern expression as he looked past his friend and cleared his throat to ensure that he was heard across the parade ground. 'The men are in good hands, Centurion. Now make me a band of soldiers I can be proud of. Permission to proceed granted.'

They exchanged a nod before Macro turned on his heel.

'You have a few hours to make good, boys. Then I'm going to be all over you like shite on a shovel. Parade . . . dismissed!'

The formations broke up, and the officers shouted at their men to pick up the pace as they trotted back to their barracks to change into their fatigue tunics and set to work. Macro glared at them, extending his most withering look to any man bold enough to meet his gaze. As the last of them entered the surrounding buildings, Cato approached him and grinned. 'You haven't lost your touch.'

'I've just been taking a short break from the job.'

'I'll bet that's not how you explained it to Petronella.'

'She might just think I'm taking a short break from retirement,' Macro conceded.

'I wonder how long that little fiction will endure . . . Anyway, I'm delighted to serve with you again, brother.'

Macro gave a lopsided smile. 'You didn't really think you'd seen the last of me in our adventures, did you?'

'The thought never once occurred to me. Looks like we're both in it until the very end, come what may.'

'I suppose.' Macro tapped the vine cane against the side of his boot. 'I'd better get on. The men tend to keep their minds on their work when they know their officers are watching them like hawks.' He turned away and marched towards the entrance of the nearest barrack block.

Back at his desk, Cato ordered Trebonius to bring him some heated wine. While he waited, his thoughts turned to that evening's dinner engagement at the house of Vespasian. The more he considered it, the more misgivings he had over the wisdom of accepting the invitation.

Roman high society was where political connections were made, conspiracies hatched and treachery and betrayal thrived. The selection of Vespasian's guests would be a deliberate process driven by whatever imperatives the senator was serving. Cato, cautious by nature, had doubts about the seemingly casual manner in which the invitation had been extended. Of course, it was possible that his encounter with his erstwhile commander at the palace had been fortuitous, and that Vespasian was simply delighted to catch up with him and introduce Cato to his circle of friends. Possible but unlikely, given the effort the senator had made to track Cato down on his secluded farming estate. So what was his real purpose in inviting his former subordinate to his home? Cato would have to think carefully about every comment he made and consider the motives underlying everything that was said to him.

He paused in his thoughts and smiled at his suspicions. For all that, it might well be merely a light-hearted social gathering of friends out to enjoy each other's company.

Trebonius entered and set down a goblet and a small jar of wine from which faint wisps of steam curled. 'Will there be anything else, sir?'

Cato nodded. 'I need to look my best tonight.'

'Yes, sir.'

He raised the goblet and saw that Trebonius had not moved. 'Is there anything else?'

Trebonius shifted uneasily. 'Well, yes, sir . . . There's a girl at the villa, sir. Columnella.'

'The swineherd's daughter?' Cato recalled her features. Tall, fair-haired, with a broad face and an easy smile. More of a woman than a girl, he reflected.

'Yes, sir.'

'What about her?'

'She and I have got together, sir. Started shortly after we got back from Britannia, and . . . I think she's the one for me.'

'That's barely three months.'

'That's all it takes sometimes, sir.'

Cato recalled the circumstances in which he himself had met Claudia. 'True. So, do you intend to marry her?'

'Yes, sir. With your permission.'

'You'll need rather more than that. She's a slave. I'll need to arrange for her manumission first. And pay the tax on that.'

'Begging your pardon, sir. I have some savings, and there's silver due to me from my share of the booty proceeds from the campaigns in Britannia. Enough to offer you a fair price for her and cover the tax.'

'You seem to have thought this through.'

'Yes, sir.'

Cato regarded him for a moment as he considered the request. 'If I agree, what are your plans? Do you intend to leave my service and settle down with your woman? How would you support yourself and a family?'

It was a pertinent enough question. Cato was loath to lose a servant who knew his moods well and navigated around them. Moreover, Trebonius was intelligent, generally honest and, above all, loyal. The last was a decisive factor.

'If you'd be willing, sir, I'll continue as before. There are a few empty huts on the farm estate, close to the villa. If I could rent one of those, Columnella could live there and develop the surrounding plot of land. It would not interfere with me serving you.'

'I see . . .'

'She could continue to help her father manage the swine,' Trebonius hurried on, anxious to press his case.

Cato held up a hand to still his outpouring. 'I'll consider it and let you know my decision.'

Trebonius frowned. 'With respect, what is there to consider, sir? The arrangement will work, and you can trust me when I say I have no intention of leaving your service.'

Base flattery or true loyalty? Cato wondered. Either way, he needed men at his side he could trust. Men like Macro and Trebonius. Especially in a place as dangerous as Rome.

'Very well. You have my permission. I will have her manumission records drafted as soon as I have the time. As for my compensation and the tax, I'll make those my wedding gift to you and your lady.'

The look of relief and gratitude on the servant's face was a pleasure to behold, and both men laughed at the sudden release of tension. Then Cato recalled the matter that had begun the exchange.

'My best toga is at the villa. I need something for tonight. Something formal, befitting a man of equestrian rank who commands the urban cohorts. Some decent footwear too. Army boots won't do. Go to the Forum and see what you can find.'

'Yes, sir. How much do you wish me to spend?'

'Given the cost of what I have just agreed to, drive hard bargains and save what you can. Or else I might be tempted to think again.'

'I'll do my best, sir.'

'I'm sure you will. Dismissed.'

Trebonius hesitated, and Cato let out a weary sigh. 'There's something else?'

'Yes, sir. If I am to be married and supporting a family, I'll need a pay rise.'

Cato fixed him with a steely stare. 'I think it would be wise for this conversation to end and for you to go about your duties immediately . . . Get out.'

CHAPTER TWELVE

'And you are?' The steward of Vespasian's household looked Cato up and down as the latter took off his plain army cloak and handed it to a slave.

'Quintus Licinius Cato. Prefect of the urban cohorts.'

The man ran an expert eye over Cato's plain green toga and tunic. Although lacking in decorative trimming, the material was of sufficient quality to satisfy him that here was a man of status. A conclusion firmed up by his expensive red leather calf boots and the equestrian ring on his finger. When Trebonius had returned from the Forum markets with his purchases, Cato had thought the boots garish and delicate-looking.

'Why, man, these wouldn't last a month on campaign.'

'Then perhaps you shouldn't wear them on campaign, sir,' Trebonius had replied. 'I am told that this style is being worn by the most fashionable figures about Rome. Even the emperor has adopted the style. Or so the merchant said. Personally, I find the overall effect rather too sudden.'

Cato could believe it. The red dye was as bright as blood, and the fussy laces running down the front of the boots were impractical and time-consuming to do up. However, once Trebonius had helped him put them on and fasten the laces, and Cato had paced up and down the length of his office a few times, the comfort of the soft leather and the give in the soles were a revelation.

All the same, Vespasian's steward regarded them with unmistakable distaste. Cato was used to the peculiar double standard that existed in the ranks of Rome's aristocracy and those who served them. While a man would be judged a miser for any failure to display his wealth, overt displays were considered crass and without class. It was a challenge to tread the line between the two. Which was how the aristocrats who could trace their lineage back many generations liked it. No matter if they were rich or struggling financially, they could always use the double standard to belittle the arrivistes in the Senate.

A cough from the steward brought Cato's thoughts back to the present.

'The master mentioned that you had been added to the guest list. At least you are not the last to arrive. If you would follow me . . .'

He bowed his head before escorting Cato across the atrium, past the large shallow pool whose intricate mosaic depicting fish shimmered beneath the rippling water. Cato's glance took in the busts of patricians glowering from niches on the walls surrounding the pond. Rooms opened off the atrium, but the interiors were concealed by heavily embroidered curtains. On the far side a corridor led out into a large open space surrounded by a colonnade. Awnings covered all but the centre of the space, where there was a pool of murky water in which some teenage boys were splashing about. Three long dining couches had been arranged to one side, while musicians played on flutes and drums in the corner. Vespasian and his guests, some thirty or so, were standing in small groups to one side of the couches.

There were faces Cato recalled from those who had been with his host two days before. Amid the senators were a handful of younger men, including a tall, well-proportioned figure who was talking to a slender woman with her back to Cato. The steward coughed again gently as they approached Vespasian.

138

'Master?'

The senator turned and greeted Cato with a broad smile, clasping him by the shoulders. 'Ah! Here's my young protégé! I'm delighted you decided to join us.'

'I could hardly turn down the invitation of my old general.' Cato smiled back.

The other man's craggy features wrinkled into a frown. 'Old? Old, you say? Why, I could still give you younger officers a run for your money. In any case, you're not so young yourself these days, Cato. There's a few streaks of grey in those dark curls of yours.' He paused and thought a moment before his bushy eyebrows rose. 'By the gods, it's been nearly twenty years since you turned up at the Second Legion with the other recruits, thin, pale and drenched, as I recall. I wager neither of us would have guessed back then that you would rise so far through the ranks to become one of the most respected soldiers in the army.'

'You flatter me, sir.'

'Nonsense. Praise where praise is due. Now then, there's a couple of young men I want to introduce you to. Or reintroduce, I should say, as far as the older boy is concerned. Titus!'

The young man and woman Cato had noticed earlier turned towards Vespasian as he and Cato approached. She was almost as tall as her companion, with dark hair simply arranged. Her eyes were grey or pale blue, although it was difficult for Cato to determine which by the glow of the torches that illuminated the courtyard garden. Her nose was long and thin, and sensitive lips stretched into a warm smile above her small chin as she looked from Cato to his host.

'Is this the soldier you were telling us about? The new prefect of the urban cohorts?'

'It is indeed. Cato, this is Claudia Octavia, the wife of Caesar.'

Cato was momentarily startled by the introduction as he stood before the empress of Rome. He recovered his wits quickly,

139

bowing his head in respect and speaking as clearly as he could. 'It is an honour to meet you, uh . . .'

'Claudia Octavia will suffice.'

He looked up and saw her eyes twinkle with amusement as she continued. 'I suspect my days as the wife of Caesar are numbered, so please don't stand on ceremony, Prefect Cato.'

'As you wish.'

Vespasian indicated the young man who had been talking to her. 'So, Cato, do you recognise this strapping lad?'

Cato's discomfort went up another notch in front of the expectant expression of his host, but fortunately he deduced a likely answer from the younger man's broad face and cleared his throat as he replied. 'Unless I miss my guess, this is your son. Your older son, I should say.'

Vespasian grinned with delight. 'Exactly. The last time you two met, at the Second Legion's camp on the Rhine, he would have been little more than a toddler. And now? He's just returned from service in Germania with a commendation from his legate for his good service. He's done me proud, this one. He's going to be a fine soldier. I hope his little brother, Domitian, follows in his path. He would have been here to greet you had he not misbehaved and been sent to his room. Ah well, at least he has the shining example of his brother to look up to.'

Titus shook his head modestly before he clasped hands with Cato. 'A pleasure to meet you, sir.'

Cato noted the firmness of his grip as he responded. 'If you are as successful as your father, you will be a fine soldier indeed.'

'Pah!' Vespasian snorted. 'Enough of the flattery! Let's leave that sort of thing to the imperial household, eh? Here we can talk as former comrades and friends. We can speak freely, and have no need of buttering anyone up. By the way, I've heard that you were forthright in your views about Britannia when Caesar questioned you on the subject. Some might say that was foolhardy. Others might say it was brave of you.'

'It was simply the truth,' said Cato. 'When in doubt about how your words might be received, the truth tends to be the best way.'

Titus chuckled. 'It's as well you are a soldier and not a politician with views like that.'

'It's as well that there are still men in Rome who speak from their hearts,' said Octavia. 'I've found precious few of them in the palace. That place seems to be the realm of the obsequious and the incompetent. Those whose only qualification for the offices and rewards that Nero bestows on them is their unquestioning loyalty and private ambition and greed.' She turned to Cato. 'I do not include you in that. You are the exception that proves the rule. My . . . husband inadvertently chose the right man to appoint as prefect of the urban cohorts. I congratulate you on your appointment. Genuinely so.'

'Thank you.' Cato nodded. 'In truth, I did not wish it and I will serve only for as long as I enjoy Caesar's confidence. Then I will return to my farm and live in peace there.'

'You think so?' Octavia arched a finely plucked eyebrow. 'It is no secret that you have angered Tigellinus, and he is the kind of man who harbours a grudge. Should you fall from favour, he would find a way to get his revenge. He would arrange for your death with no more thought than swatting a fly. I find it strange that so many of you senators and men of equestrian rank assume that you are less vulnerable than the common people of Rome. If anything, you live in far greater danger than they do. Particularly if you come within the purview of Caesar and those close to him.'

'I had hoped to put politics aside tonight, my dear,' Vespasian intervened. 'Poor Cato has only just arrived. Let's enjoy ourselves while we can, eh? Titus, why don't you show Octavia those marvellous sculptures I bought the other day?'

'Sculptures? I hardly think—'

'Then perhaps it's time you started to.' Vespasian gestured to the far end of the courtyard, where Cato could make out a handful of statues mounted on podiums. 'There's a good boy.'

Taking Octavia by the elbow, Titus did as he was bid. His father waited until they were several paces away before he turned to address Cato in a low voice. 'You must pardon her directness. She's living from moment to moment these days. Her marriage to Nero is the stuff of nightmares. He hated her from the moment he was brought into the imperial fold when his mother married Claudius. The old boy was persuaded by Agrippina to give his daughter in marriage to Nero. The idea was that it would provide a line of succession. That's not how it worked out, sadly. Octavia turned out to be infertile. It was bad enough that she had to be subjected to being bedded by Nero, without him trying to strangle her on a number of occasions. Now that Poppaea is expecting his child, he has no further use for Octavia. If she's lucky, he will just end the marriage.'

'End the marriage,' Cato repeated with emphasis.

'Oh, I don't think he will do her any further harm. Octavia has too many supporters in the Senate, and the mob adores her. She carries herself like a queen and stands by all the old patrician values that command the respect of the people. As long as that's the case, it would be risky for Nero to make an attempt on her life.'

'He was willing to have his mother killed.'

'Fair point,' Vespasian conceded. 'But that didn't go down too well with many in Rome. Agrippina wasn't to everyone's taste, but she had plenty of supporters, and some of them are sure to be biding their time while they contemplate how to avenge her. Take Calpurnius Piso over there.' He pointed out a tall man with dark hair and a cheerful expression who was involved in an animated discussion with several other aristocrats next to a large tureen of heated wine, into which they were dipping their goblets.

All of this weighed heavily upon Cato, who had no desire to be drawn into political cross-currents that threatened to be as perilous as the enemies he had fought on the frontiers of the Empire. His host appeared to sense his mood and gestured towards the tureen.

'You could do with a drink, I'm sure. All this talk of the ins and outs of Nero's regime has left me with a dry throat. Come.'

They joined Piso and his companions, and fresh introductions were made before Piso patted his belly.

'Any chance that we might be fed before the night is over?'

'Patience, my friend,' said Vespasian. 'We're waiting on the last of my guests. It would be unseemly to start eating before they join us.'

'Bah, Seneca is always late, and you know it. Why not just invite him an hour earlier than the other guests? It's the only way to get him to arrive on time.'

'He is a busy man,' Vespasian countered.

'Busy worming his way ever further into Nero's affections, you mean. Why, the fellow is so far up Caesar's arse you can barely see the soles of his boots.'

Vespasian waited until Piso's cronies stopped laughing before he continued. 'I wonder if you would be so bold as to say that in front of the man who has the ear of Caesar. In any case, you should be grateful to him. We all should.'

'How so?' Piso challenged him.

'Because Seneca's influence is one of the few remaining constraints on Caesar's behaviour. Without him and Burrus to temper his decisions, who knows what Nero might do? We should worry about what happens when they're gone. Burrus is dying. And when he passes, there will be only Seneca to act as the voice of reason against the chorus of sycophants led by the likes of Tigellinus. How much worse do you think our lives will be then, Piso? So show a little respect to Seneca, eh? To his back as well as his face. Ah! Here he comes.' Vespasian turned as he caught sight of movement from the direction of the house.

Cato looked round and saw Seneca approaching, arm in arm with a young man in his early twenties. Their host crossed the courtyard to greet them, kissing each man on the cheek in the manner of aristocrats who were friends and equals. Cato saw Seneca stiffen, and could guess at the reason. Even though his family had settled in Hispania generations before, Seneca was descended from a long line of aristocrats. By contrast, Vespasian was the first of his family to be admitted to the senatorial order.

Now that the final guests had arrived, the steward indicated to the slaves to begin bringing out the food. Vespasian, Seneca and Octavia settled in the centre of the row of couches at the head table, and the others sat according to their social rank. Cato found himself towards the end of the left-hand row of diners, with only Titus and his younger brother, Domitian, positioned below him. Directly opposite reclined the young man who had arrived with Seneca.

The first course was served, fried sausage and onions in a rich garum sauce. The intense, salty flavour of the garum was almost overpowering, and Cato picked at the food before spreading it around the platter. His tactic was noticed by Titus, who leaned towards him and spoke in an undertone. 'The old man has always been rather taken by garum. He has it added to almost every dish he eats. Takes a bit of getting used to. Never been fond of it myself, to be honest.'

'It's fine in moderation,' Cato replied with a smile. 'And there was never much of it around on campaign.'

'That's one aspect of army life to be thankful for then.'

The two shared an amused chuckle before Cato continued. 'So you served in Germania?'

'That was my first posting as tribune. Not much to write home about. Gloomy forests, barbarians scraping a living in squalid little settlements and only a handful of roaming brigands to break up the boredom.'

'Not so different from when I was there twenty years ago.'

'And it'll be no different twenty years from now. Or two hundred, I imagine. I was lucky to get a temporary posting to the Second Legion in Britannia at the end of the rebellion. My father's old unit was in pretty poor shape at the time. Morale was low and discipline crumbling. Pitiful to see.'

'To be expected, given the way they disgraced themselves – deserting their comrades and turning tail when the rebels reached Londinium.'

It wounded Cato to think of the shame that shrouded the legion he had first served in. Back in the day, the Second had been at the forefront of the army sent to conquer Britannia and had earned an enviable reputation under the hard-driving command of Vespasian.

'At least the camp prefect did the decent thing,' said Titus.

Cato made a non-committal noise. The officer in question had failed his men and blackened the name of his legion. However, in the desperate days of the rebellion there had been much confusion, and it was possible that he had acted correctly in preserving his command rather than following the example of the column from the Ninth, which had advanced recklessly to its destruction. With the privileged perspective of hindsight, rational decisions were often seen as foolishness or, in this case, cowardice. Cato had some sympathy for the camp prefect's predicament, and his decision to try and salvage some of his honour by falling on his sword.

'Anyway, I wasn't in Britannia for long. Once the last of the rebels were defeated, I was sent back to Germania to serve out the rest of my tour. Glad that's over.'

'What's next for you? Will you stay in the army or pursue an administrative post in Rome?'

'I'd be better off in the army. I don't think I would be content to be a simpering political upstart using flattery and bribery to worm my way up.'

'Well put.'

'I'm hoping there'll be a tribune's post available when things kick off with the Scythians. That, or something in the army that's forming in Alexandria.'

'Oh?' Cato stopped shifting the scraps around his platter and looked up. This was the first he'd heard of any build-up of forces in Aegyptus. 'Trouble brewing there?'

Titus shook his head. 'Not yet. The word is that Caesar is looking for a military adventure to burnish his credentials. I'm told he has ambitions to turn the Euxine Sea into what he calls a "Roman lake". Of course the Scythians might have a thing or two to say about it. They've demanded that the city of Heraclea Cheronensis pays them tribute, and there's no question of Caesar permitting that. Unless the Scythians give way, there will be war. And if that's not bad enough, we've had reports that a powerful tribe of Sarmatians are pushing towards the Danube frontier. Then there's the prospect of Nero extending the frontier south from Aegyptus and taking Ethiopia. And if negotiations with Parthia fall through, there'll be another war over Armenia. Take your pick.'

'I am sure there will be a place for you,' Cato said. 'War has a way of creating vacancies for ambitious officers.'

'I'll raise a cup to that!' Titus grinned.

Cato felt an instant's sorrow for the younger man's blithe thirst for adventure. He himself had served long enough to experience most of the good and the bad of army life. To be sure, there was an intensity to it that made him feel more alive than in any other context. And there was the bond of comradeship, which was often deeper than that of family in civilian life. But there were also the moments of fear, of dread of being thought a coward or dangerously incompetent. There were the frequent and often shockingly abrupt and random deaths of friends. The despair of defeats and retreat and the raw, trembling awe of surviving a desperate battle. For young officers like Titus, death or a crippling injury was something that only happened to others, and war was seen as a fine adventure in a noble cause along the road to fame and reward. He would learn that the truth was a little more complicated, if he lived long enough.

Titus drained his cup and let out a soft burp before he spoke again. 'Can't help wondering why men are being sent to Alexandria if we're going to need them to fight Scythia or Parthia, though. They'd be more use if they were sent to Syria.'

'Easy enough to understand,' said Cato. 'Aegyptus is an imperial province under Caesar's direct control. If he was to send forces to the east and swell the number of legions under the control of one of the governors there, particularly Corbulo, they might be tempted to use them in pursuit of their personal ambitions. It's safer to send his soldiers where they won't provoke such unworthy sentiments in their commander.'

'You have a cynical frame of mind, Prefect Cato,' said the man sitting opposite him, the companion of Seneca.

Cato stared back, waiting for more, and the younger man sat up.

'I'm sorry, I have you at a disadvantage, Prefect. I am Lucanus, the nephew of Seneca.'

Cato regarded him for a moment, weighing up his response. He glanced briefly at Seneca, who was deep in conversation with Octavia, and thought he saw a family resemblance. 'I do not mean to be cynical. I merely meant to explain the practicalities Caesar needs to contend with.'

'I'm sure my friend Titus is well aware of such . . . practicalities.'

When Cato looked to his neighbour for a response, he realised that the younger man was in his cups, and barely aware of the conversation. He turned his attention back to Lucanus.

'Are you also a soldier?'

147

Lucanus laughed. 'Good gods, no! I am a poet.'

'A poet?'

He looked affronted. 'Surely you have read, or at least heard of, my epic the *Pharsalia*? I won a prize, from the hands of Caesar himself, at the Neronia festival two years ago.'

Cato shrugged. 'Sadly not. I was in Britannia at the time, campaigning against the mountain tribes. My hands were too full to spare any time for keeping up with progress in the realm of poetry.'

Lucanus smiled appreciatively. 'Well answered, Prefect Cato. At times I tend to forget that poetry is not the be all and end all for other men. Particularly soldiers who are obliged to deal with more practical matters.'

'I know many soldiers who are partial to poetry when their duties permit. Killing barbarians and making the Empire safe for poets is not the be all and end all for us either.'

'I see I have offended you. I apologise. I should not try to demean a man my uncle holds in high regard.'

Cato's gaze switched back to Seneca. If the senator respected him, as Lucanus claimed, he had shown little proof of it in their previous encounters.

All at once such thoughts were swept aside as Octavia sat up abruptly and let out a despairing cry before clasping her hands over her face and starting to sob. Seneca reached out a hand to her shoulder to comfort her, but she shook it off and scrambled off the couch, scurrying towards the darkness of the far corner of the courtyard. Seneca muttered something to Vespasian, and they hurriedly rose and went after her.

Titus lowered his goblet and unsteadily made to stand.

'I wouldn't do that,' said Lucanus. 'Leave it to my uncle. He knows what he is doing.'

'What *is* he doing?' asked Cato.

Lucanus regarded him closely before he replied. 'You'll find out soon enough, Prefect Cato . . .'

CHAPTER THIRTEEN

Vespasian, Seneca and Octavia did not reappear for the rest of the evening. In the absence of the host and his principal guests, the party continued in a subdued manner before people began to make their excuses and leave. Cato engaged in occasional exchanges with his neighbours, but the topics were trivial and conversation tailed off the moment it veered towards political matters. The wariness of his companions – even Titus, who had drunk enough to loosen the tongue of a mute – created an oppressive atmosphere and made Cato long to return to his farm to be with Claudia and Lucius.

An hour or so after Octavia's outburst, Cato calculated that over half the guests had left, and he would be able to depart without causing offence. Only a handful still occupied the dining couches. He picked up one of the scented cloths to wipe his lips and fingers and sat up.

'It's getting late. I have to return to the camp.'

Titus turned to him. 'So soon?'

'As a soldier yourself, you know the drill. A soldier rises early and his commanding officer rises even earlier.' Cato made to shuffle off the couch, but Titus took hold of his arm.

'Not yet.'

'I'd love to stay, but I really must go.'

'Not yet,' Titus repeated, but with quiet intensity this time.

Cato saw the abrupt change in his expression and realised that the young man was not nearly as drunk as he had seemed. He made to move, but the grip tightened, and Titus hissed, 'Stay.'

The first glimmer of fear stirred in Cato's guts as he nodded at Titus's hand. 'Let go of me. Now.'

Titus hesitated, then relaxed his grip and withdrew his hand, resuming his slurred demeanour. 'Apologies, Prefect. I've been enjoying your company and it would be a shame for you to leave so soon. The party's only just beginning.'

'Not for me it isn't, but you and your friends have fun. I need to go.'

'Please stay,' Lucanus interrupted from his couch. 'I can assure you the conversation will be stimulating and worth your time.'

The evening was taking an unexpected turn, even allowing for the earlier drama with Octavia. Cato sensed a trap was being laid for him by his host. It no longer felt like a coincidence that he had encountered Vespasian at the palace, and the social gathering was clearly a pretext to lure him to his former commander's house. The purpose was as yet uncertain, but Cato suspected that it related to the seething undercurrent of politics and conspiracy that flowed through Rome like blood through a man's veins. And he wanted none of it.

'I ask you to stay a while longer,' said Titus. 'Out of the respect you have for my father and out of the respect he has for you. Besides, you owe him for setting you on the path to your current position.'

'I am no patrician's client,' Cato replied coldly. 'I have more than repaid your father through my service under him, and the service I have rendered to Rome.'

'I understand that, and so does he. We ask that you stay as a personal favour. If you choose to leave now, I won't try to stop you and no one will think the worse of you for it. If you choose to stay, I am sure you will find what is said of interest to you.'

'What is going on here, Titus? Tell me.'

Titus glanced quickly at Lucanus, who gave a slight shake of his head.

'I can't say anything for now,' Titus continued in an undertone. 'Too many guests are still here. And walls have ears.' He nodded towards the slaves standing around the dining area, alert to the need to rush forward to clear away discarded platters or top up wine. 'I ask you to trust me. It's important that you hear what we have to say.'

'I do not wish to be a part of any plot,' said Cato. 'I am a soldier. That is all that matters to me.'

'But you are not just a soldier, Cato. Not by a long way. You are a man of action. A man of principle, like my father. Both of you have been placed by the Fates in positions of influence. So please, spare me the false modesty of the common-soldier rhetoric. It doesn't work on me.'

Cato hesitated a beat too long, and in that moment he saw Lucanus give a knowing smile before leaning closer. 'Admit it, Prefect Cato, you're too curious to want to leave. Like my friend says, just hear us out, and if you still have no desire to continue the conversation, we can all part as friends and say no more about it. Come, what is the harm in that?'

There was plenty of potential harm, thought Cato. He had learned enough about the aristocrats who jostled for power in Rome to know that most of them were not to be trusted. Nor were they particularly competent. Those who called themselves the Liberators had been plotting the downfall of emperors for generations, but had failed to achieve their aim and restore the Republic. Their botched conspiracies had only succeeded in decimating the ranks of the senators and their followers. Driven by a toxic mixture of high-minded integrity, naked personal ambition and dread, they lurked in the shadows and offered little but a life of constant anxiety and danger to those they drew into their net.

Even if the conversation Titus alluded to had nothing to do with the Liberators, Cato feared that it represented the tip of a similar type of conspiracy, every bit as inept . . . And yet if these people were to oust Nero and replace him with a republic, or more likely a fresh despot of their choice, then Claudia would no longer live in fear of her presence being discovered. If there was a chance of that, it might be worth hearing out Titus and his companions. If he concluded, as he anticipated, that they were just another band of misguided idealists, then he could walk away.

He eased himself back down onto the couch and Titus gave a small, relieved smile. 'Let me get you a fresh cup of wine.' He gestured to one of the slaves, who swept forward with a jug and topped up Cato's goblet.

Cato took a sip and cradled the vessel in his hands as he looked round the remaining guests, trying to assess who was in on the secret and who had simply been invited to make up the numbers and conceal the true purpose of the gathering. The conversation returned to safe topics and Titus did the rounds of the other guests, playing his part as the genial and slightly drunk host. One by one the others left, until there was only Lucanus, Cato, Titus and a handful of others. At once Titus dropped his act and indicated the bulk of the house looming over the garden.

'Come! It's time we joined the rest of them.'

They entered the house and proceeded through dimly lit corridors and up a flight of steps to one of the chambers overlooking the atrium, with its dark pond now reflecting the starlight and a sliver of moon. Cato detected a movement in the shadows, and a burly figure emerged from the gloom.

'It's all right, Gordio,' said Titus. 'It's me. Make sure no one comes into the room or eavesdrops. No one. Understand?'

There was a dull grunt of assent before the man moved back out of sight. Titus drew the door hanging aside and ushered the others through.

The room beyond was illuminated by two stands of oil lamps placed on a long table next to the windows. At one end sat Seneca, Vespasian and Octavia, along with a few others. She seemed to have recovered her composure, although her expression was weary and her hair disordered.

'Come in, gentlemen, and sit down.'

They did as they were bid, and Cato positioned himself at the far end in order to express a measure of detachment from proceedings. But Vespasian fixed his gaze on him at once. 'Welcome to our group, Prefect Cato.'

'I am not a member of any group,' Cato shot back firmly. 'I am here to listen. Nothing more than that.'

'Very well.' Vespasian nodded. 'You already know some of us. It's time for a few introductions. The man to your left is Senator Calpurnius Piso. Next to him is Rufrius Gallo, a tribune in the Praetorian Guard. To your right is Publius Nerva. Then there's Lucanus—'

'We're already acquainted,' the young man interrupted. 'And established a healthy disdain for each other.'

Seneca leaned forward. 'Hush, nephew. This is not the time to play clever. Just listen.'

Lucanus sat back and folded his arms as Vespasian continued.

'Thank you. Cato, I dare say you saw through my ruse a while ago and already know that the reason for your presence is something other than a social obligation.' He smiled faintly. 'I apologise for the deception, but I needed you to hear what we have to say. Perhaps Octavia most of all, given the news she received earlier today.' He gave her a gentle nod and she cleared her throat, collected her thoughts and spoke.

'Caesar has decided to divorce me. He was too cowardly or ashamed to tell me to my face. The message was delivered by that loathsome creature of his, Tigellinus. How he seemed to enjoy the task . . .' Her features twisted into a look of disgust before she continued. 'Now that Poppaea is expecting his child, Nero has decided to discard me to marry his mistress so that she can produce a legitimate heir to the throne. Assuming the child is a boy and survives infancy, of course. I am utterly redundant to Caesar now. Our marriage was only ever a sham in any case. A political union. That is all. He has hated me from the start. For my part, I was prepared to do my duty and I endured his hatred, suffered his violence and subjected myself to his degrading perversions. Twice now he has tried to murder me, and only been restrained by the intervention of others, Burrus being one of my saviours.

'Nero's abuse has only become worse since his mistress and Tigellinus came on the scene. They have steadily worked together to undermine me and cement their influence with Caesar. I have little doubt that they will encourage him to have me killed as soon as they can, once the divorce takes place and he marries Poppaea. She knows that the mob respects me and has affection for me in deference to my father, Claudius. She also knows how they ridicule her, despising her love of luxury and the power she holds over Nero. My life will be measured in months, perhaps days from the moment Poppaea becomes the new empress.' She paused and swallowed. 'That is why I reacted as I did at dinner. I apologise to you all for the unseemly display.'

Vespasian took her hand affectionately. 'There is no need for apologies, my dear. You have been cruelly used by Caesar and his helpmates. And it is not just the mob that holds you in high esteem. Most of the aristocracy sympathise.'

She smiled sadly. 'Sympathy is fine, but rarely extends to action these days.'

'That is unfortunately true,' said Seneca. 'Even among those who sympathise, few dare to come out in open support. The Senate was once filled with proud and principled men, but that has not been the case for over a hundred years now. Under the

Caesars, their integrity has withered away, and now the majority look to their own prosperity rather than the good of Rome and the prestige of their family name. Then there's the coterie of fawning second-raters who surround Caesar, flattering him whenever possible and treating his every utterance and change of policy as if his words carried the wisdom of the gods themselves.'

Cato was listening with growing contempt for Seneca's hypocrisy. He had seen for himself how Seneca played the very role he now criticised others for. The veteran senator seemed to sense Cato's mood as his gaze shifted to the end of the table.

'I know there are some who accuse me of being little better than the likes of Tigellinus in this regard. The truth is that I have long understood that Nero is a poisonous influence. Why, his own father said as much when he was born: that any child sired by him and birthed by Agrippina would have a black heart and be nothing but trouble for all who encountered him during his life. When Agrippina appointed me as his tutor, I saw the darkness in his heart and the hollow self-regard in his mind, and I knew that if I acted to manage and suppress his worst instincts I could limit the damage he did to the Senate and people of Rome.

'I was fortunate to have Burrus as a partner in this endeavour. Where I strove to divert Nero's attention towards his love of the arts, Burrus imposed his blunt and unshakeable moral standards on him. Between us we have done our best to hold his demons at bay for several years. But now our influence is on the wane. Burrus is dying, and when he is gone, I fear that what is left of Nero's self-control will wither, and he will abase himself, and Rome, in the years to come. His reign will become a stain upon the reputation of the Empire. And that won't be all. The emperor is running the imperial treasury dry. Every day he lavishes wealth on his cronies. Wealth that often comes from the victims of his persecutions. If all this continues, it can only offer hope and opportunity to our enemies. It has taken Rome hundreds of years to establish her primacy in the world. It takes only a few years under a ruler like Nero to destroy that inheritance.'

Seneca took a deep breath. 'I have reluctantly come to the conclusion that Nero is the enemy of Rome and the enemy of humanity.'

Piso spoke up. 'For a man who prides himself on his high-minded restraint of a dictator, you have grown rich as a result of the same largesse you claim to despise.'

Seneca pursed his lips. 'I don't deny I have done well out of the arrangement. Be that as it may, it does not undermine my pointing out the crisis we face if Nero is permitted to act without restraint. Octavia's murder will just be the start. Those who are identified as her supporters will be next. After that, it will be those who are suspected of being sympathisers and anyone Tigellinus accuses of failing to show unquestioning loyalty to Nero. Then those who have the temerity to be superior to Nero in any of the endeavours in which he claims to be best. Woe betide any poet, or actor, or musician, or charioteer who garners any popular acclaim that Nero takes as a slight on his own paltry achievements. Piso, you are a poet of some repute, like my nephew Lucanus. How long do you suppose you would survive Nero's piqued pride if an audience applauded your efforts more loudly than his? The man's vanity is without limit. As is his envy and cruelty.'

A silence fell across the room before Vespasian cleared his throat. 'My friends, Seneca speaks the truth. We all know it. We all know the danger posed to Rome, and to every one of us. If Octavia is murdered, each of us will fall in turn, as sure as the rising of the sun. The only hope of surviving is to utterly abase every value we have and surrender to Nero's will and his need for craven worship. That is the choice before us. The question is what we, and others, decide to do about it.'

He turned his attention to Cato. 'You have heard our words,

Prefect Cato. We have made our case. Now it's time for you to speak up. Where do you stand?'

Cato felt his scalp tingle with anxiety as he swiftly thought through what he had heard and composed a reply.

'Sir, I am not sure what case you think has been made. All I have heard is attacks against the character of the emperor. I'm not saying I disagree with what has been said, but only some of it coincides with my own personal observations of Caesar.'

'The man is a monster!' Titus said loudly. 'You heard what Octavia said about him!'

'Quiet!' Vespasian admonished him. 'Do you want the whole bloody city to hear us?'

'You said we could trust this fool.' Piso gestured towards Cato. 'You said he was a man of impeccable integrity and ability.'

'And so he is,' Vespasian said firmly. 'Now let the man speak without further interruption. Cato, continue.'

'Thank you . . . You have painted a picture of Caesar in the blackest of terms. Supposing it is wholly accurate, rather than the sour grapes of those who have not profited under his reign. Supposing what you say is true and Nero is a monster, what do you propose to do about it?'

Piso clenched his fist and thumped it down on the table, making the stands judder and the flames from the oil lamps waver. 'He has to go.'

'Go?' Cato tilted his head. 'You mean he has to be assassinated?'

'Let's not get ahead of ourselves here,' Vespasian responded quickly. 'There may be other outcomes.'

'Really? What would they be, sir?'

'It's possible that the Senate might be won over to censure Nero, and if the army and the Praetorian Guard fell in behind us, he might be persuaded to relinquish his powers and accept exile.'

Seneca gave a dry, dismissive laugh. 'Knowing him as I do, I doubt he would accept exile. As for the Praetorians, they used to be loyal to Burrus, but they must know he hasn't long to live and then there will be a new commander, Tigellinus. And he will be sure to advise Nero to hand over a lavish bonus to the men to buy their loyalty.'

'There's still the army,' said Vespasian.

'The nearest legions are hundreds of miles away,' Cato pointed out. 'It would take them months to reach Rome in the event of an attempt to depose Nero. By then the Praetorians would have hunted down and executed every one of the conspirators in the capital. Who would be left to lead a coup? Besides, how do you know the legions would support such a thing? Have you sounded out the army commanders?'

'Not yet,' Vespasian conceded. 'But I dare say most feel as we do about Nero.'

Cato shook his head. 'Gut instinct is not enough. How can you be certain? If I were Nero, I'd make damn sure the Praetorians weren't the only soldiers I bribed to stay onside. I'd bribe the most powerful of the generals and governors too. And let's not forget that they have family here in Rome. He could arrest them and hold them hostage.'

'The prefect is right,' said Seneca. 'We cannot depend on outside forces. We have to use the resources we have here in Rome. I know that the loyalty of some of the Praetorians is wavering. If their officers were promised promotions and other rewards after Nero is deposed, we might persuade them to side with us. As for the rank and file, if I am any judge of common soldiers, money talks louder than any oath sworn to obey and protect the emperor. They are little better than mercenaries.'

Cato felt a surge of anger at the senator's words. 'It's thanks to the sweat and sacrifice of common soldiers that we have the very empire you are talking about.'

Seneca eyed him coolly. 'My, the prickliness of you military men . . . Has Rome ever forgotten to thank you and reward you for your service? Now she is calling on her soldiers again. Yes, you swear an oath of loyalty. You swear to serve and protect Rome and you swear to obey the emperor. So tell me, what happens when the latter poses a threat to the former? Which side would you come down on, Prefect? Your loyalty to Rome or to Caesar? At some point you will be forced to choose. That day will come sooner than you think.'

'Maybe, but then the choice will be mine to make, not yours. Even supposing you succeed in forcing Nero out, who or what replaces him?'

'The Senate, of course,' said Piso. 'We restore supreme power to the Senate.'

'And how well did that work out for us in the past?' Cato demanded. 'The rival factions tore Rome apart in one civil war after another. Anything Nero does will pale in comparison to the blood that flowed on the streets back then. With regard to the senators, as has been said, there are too many cowards and venal men among them to have any hope of a restored Republic holding together.'

'Then we replace Nero with a man with the integrity and wisdom to restore sanity to Rome.'

'Which man would that be?' asked Cato. 'You? Seneca? Or Vespasian? I don't doubt you all have the quality and good intentions required for the task. But who is to say that once power is in your hands you won't turn out to be as bad as Nero, in some respects at least.'

'I think we are better men than that,' Seneca retorted irritably. 'Do you really think that any of us would turn out to be worse than what faces us now?'

'Who can say? Better men than those present have been corrupted by power. And you know it.'

'Perhaps,' he conceded. 'However, the best guarantee against that outcome is the quality of the men in charge, whoever is the figurehead of the group that takes power. That's why we need the best men in Rome to be part of this. Men like you, Prefect Cato.'

'High praise indeed, Senator. But I am not so easily swayed by flattery as Caesar.'

'It's not flattery,' said Vespasian. 'You are being approached because of your quality and incorruptibility. I vouched for you on my reputation.'

Cato was moved by his former commander's words, but he was still overwhelmed by doubt, and by the magnitude of what these men proposed.

'I thank you, sir. But I am not convinced that anyone in this room could resist the lure of power when it is laid before him. Besides, there are too few of you to carry this out.'

'We're not alone. There are others.'

'Then where are they?'

'Do you think we'd be foolish enough to reveal their identities before we could be certain of attaching you to our purpose? You'll have to trust me when I say there are many more who feel as we do.'

'Enough to make a difference?'

'I believe so. Many in the Senate. Others among the equestrian class, and officers like yourself and Titus.'

'What good can a handful of officers do against the Praetorians? You need Burrus, and time is running out in that regard. Will you be ready to strike before he dies and is replaced by Tigellinus? Well?'

Seneca gave a light cough. 'Perhaps we don't need to rely on Burrus. An officer with the urban cohorts at his back might be in a position to decide the outcome.'

Cato could not help a despairing laugh. 'The urban cohorts? You must be aware how poor their condition is. The people of Rome regard them as little more than a joke at the moment.'

'But that will change. I've heard that you have already made significant improvements to morale and discipline. You've been joined by your friend Centurion Macro. A fine soldier, but also a

160

fine trainer, if my friend Vespasian is any judge. How soon would you estimate before they are fighting fit?'

Cato shook his head in disbelief. 'Fighting fit? Right now they couldn't fight their way through a damp sheet of papyrus. That's not the only problem. There are many who are loyal to Tigellinus and would side with him in the event of any attempt to depose Nero.'

'Then get rid of them. Identify Tigellinus's cronies and make their lives so difficult they quit or give you grounds to discharge them.'

'Easier said than done,' Cato responded as he recalled how well Macrinus had covered his tracks. 'If I did as you say, it would only draw attention to my efforts to weed out Tigellinus's men, and questions would be asked at the palace. I'd be the one pushed out and then you can be sure that the urban cohorts will side with your opponents.'

'They're not just our opponents, Prefect. They are the enemies of Rome and all that she should stand for.'

'I don't disagree.'

'Then you support our aims?'

'I didn't say that.'

'No. But as has been pointed out, you will have to choose. You cannot remain neutral. You are either for or against us.'

'I thought I was free not to become involved if that's what I chose.' Cato pointedly turned towards Vespasian.

'You are free to do that. You can leave this house right now, and no harm will come to you from our side. You have my word on it.'

'Thank you, sir. I've heard enough for now.' Cato stood. 'I'll leave you to continue your plotting. You have my word that your secret is safe with me. But that is as far as I am prepared to go. My advice, for what it's worth, is to abandon this conspiracy. I see no evidence that you have the necessary support to carry it through. You'll get yourself executed, along with many others, and have Nero jumping at shadows and ready to condemn anyone he even thinks is an enemy.'

'Aren't we already heading in that direction?' asked Seneca. 'As Vespasian points out, we're not the danger. It's Nero and Tigellinus you have to protect yourself against. You've already made an enemy of Tigellinus. I wonder how long you will last.'

'Who can say how long any of us has got?' Cato replied. 'One thing being a soldier teaches you is that we live at the whim of fate. But I'll tell you this. I think you represent more of a danger to me than Tigellinus does. If one of you slips up and says something that is overheard by the wrong ears, you are dead. And the same goes for those Tigellinus accuses of being your friends and acquaintances. That includes me if he learns that I was here tonight.'

Lucanus leaned forward. 'Then what have you got to lose? Join us, Cato. Put an end to tyranny and save your life.'

'What have I got to lose? My life is not my prime concern. I used up my share of luck a long time ago on the battlefield, and I'm living on borrowed time. It's my wife and child I fear for.'

'Your wife . . .' Seneca said very deliberately. 'You mean Claudia Acte.'

Cato froze. How in Hades had Seneca come to know that? Suddenly he felt the same vulnerability and danger he had last experienced during the rebellion.

Seneca seemed to be enjoying his reaction. 'You are not nearly so accomplished at keeping a secret as you think, Prefect. One of my contacts in Britannia happened to visit Camulodunum in the days before Boudica's revolt began. He saw Claudia and recognised her, despite her attempts to hide her identity by dyeing her hair. She's living at your farm, I believe. Along with your son, Lucius.'

Cato did his best to appear calm. 'Are you blackmailing me to support your cause?'

'We don't have to. Now you understand that we know about

Claudia. If our conspiracy should be exposed, and we are tortured by Tigellinus's thugs and forced to name our contacts, who is to say that her name might not be prised out of one of us?'

'You bastard . . .' Cato took a pace towards the senator and Vespasian hurriedly rose to step between them.

'Let's have no talk of blackmail or any notion that we would betray Cato or his family. I won't stand for it. He's an honourable man and this is a dirty business we are engaged in. If he chooses not to be a part of it, I will honour his decision and so will all of you.' There was a silence as he looked round the table, daring any of the others to defy him.

Then Octavia spoke up. 'I understand your desire to protect your family, Prefect Cato. But yours is not the family at risk under the monster that sits on the throne. Is my life worth any less than that of your wife? Think on it. I won't judge you, but I suspect you will be judged by a more exacting person . . . Yourself.'

Cato felt a pang of guilt and shame at her words as Vespasian took his arm. 'Come, my friend, let me walk you to the door.' He held the heavy folds of the covering aside and ushered Cato out of the room. The slave standing guard moved aside to let them pass. They descended to the ground floor in silence and halted in the atrium as the doorkeeper hurried to unfasten the bolts.

'Don't worry about them,' said Vespasian. 'They will do as I say. You are safe.'

'I don't feel safe, sir.'

The older man sighed. 'Then you are no different to any other man of our rank in Rome. Death leers at us from over Nero's shoulder, and I fear that it is only a matter of time before he comes for us all.'

'Unless we strike first.'

Vespasian nodded. 'I bid you good night, my friend. May the gods protect you.'

CHAPTER FOURTEEN

'I don't like the look of the weather,' said Cato as he peered up at the heavy clouds rolling in from the west in the direction of Ostia. A cool breeze was blowing, and it had swept away most of the haze that had hung over the city for days. 'Looks like a storm is headed our way.'

'A little bit of rain never did anyone any harm,' said Macro.

They were standing on the parade ground, waiting for the First Cohort to assemble for the route march that Macro had in store for them that day. The men were in full armour and armed with spears in addition to their swords. Unlike the soldiers of the auxiliary and legionary units, they were not issued with marching yokes, as their duties generally confined them to Rome. Should they be ordered to march any distance from the capital, their camping kit and rations were carried by wagons.

'Are they ready for this?' asked Cato.

Macro had been drilling them hard ever since he had been appointed camp prefect. Mornings were taken up with exercises to increase their fitness, and weapons practice with wooden swords and wicker shields twice the weight of their real weapons. This built up their strength and fighting skills while Macro moved among them shouting reprimands at those who moved too slowly or failed to show the right spirit when attacking the training posts. By midday the men were exhausted and dripping with perspiration. But there was only a short respite to take water before they were back on the parade ground to practise formation marching for the next two hours, before being sent back to barracks to clean their kit and quarters ready for the evening inspection. Only when Macro and their centurions were satisfied by their turnout were they dismissed for the day and allowed to prepare their evening meals. As Macro had promised, they had grown to hate his guts and fear his ever-watchful gaze, sharp enough to pick out any failure to meet his exacting demands.

'Ready as they'll ever be,' he replied with a happy grin. He sniffed the early-morning air with relish. 'Be good to stretch our legs. Living the easy life the last two months hasn't done either of us any favours. The question is, do you think you're ready for it, lad?'

Cato snorted at the notion. 'I can hold my own.'

'I'm not so sure. You've been squirrelled away in headquarters for most of the time and traipsing around the palace whenever Nero has sent for you.'

'I'll be fine. I need the exercise.'

'Good, because you're going to get it. I'll be pushing the pace. I want to see how many of those bastards can keep up with me. I'm not so long in the tooth that I can't outmarch any man under my command. Whatever Petronella says.'

'She's still not best pleased about your returning to the ranks, I take it?'

'You've said it. Even though I go back to the house every few days, she complains that I'm too tired to be up to much. By the gods, Cato, you'd think she'd slow down after the number of years we've been married. But no. She's all over me, and no matter how tired I am, I have to perform. That night, and again first thing in the morning before I return to camp.'

'Some men might call you fortunate in that regard.'

'Ha-hmm! I'd like to see them try to keep up with her. If I

can't, I don't know who can. Such a man would need the staying power of a ram.'

They were interrupted by Lemulus coming forward to report that the First Cohort was formed up and ready to march. Macro made a quick inspection of the ranks to ensure that every man was carrying the required kit and that it was in good order before he announced his grudging satisfaction to Lemulus and turned to face Cato.

'First Cohort of the urban cohorts present and correct, sir. What are your orders?'

Cato returned the salute. 'We march towards Ostia! Centurion Lemulus, lead the men out of the camp!'

Lemulus bellowed the order and took his place at the head of the small colour party holding the standards of the cohort and the image of the emperor in gold surrounded by a silver back piece. Cato and Macro fell in at the head of the column as the cohort tramped out of the camp, century by century.

It was a rare sight for the people of Rome to see a column of soldiers marching by, and as the way cleared ahead of them, many stopped to stare. Children slotted themselves in the gaps between the centuries and marched with the soldiers for a short distance with an exaggerated swagger. Some young women cast longing looks at the taller and more handsome of Cato's men, and the prostitutes called out their blandishments from the doors and windows of brothels and inns. There was a cheery sense of a public holiday as the men stepped out and made their way through the capital.

To their left rose the mass of the Capitoline Hill with the Temple of Jupiter seeming to tower so far above them that the god himself could reach down from the heavens to touch the roof tiles. Cato directed them along a side street to avoid crossing the packed Boarium marketplace, and they continued along the bottom of the Palatine and Aventine hills before reaching the

Trigemina gate in the city wall. The archways echoed the crunch of their boots, and then they were outside the official boundary of the city, though they still had to negotiate the sprawl of shacks and crude shelters that stretched around the walls.

There were no cobbled streets here, just muddy alleyways winding between the crudely built structures. The poverty that characterised much of the capital was nothing compared to the living conditions of those in the shanty towns, which had accreted like barnacles on the hull of a ship. It was a lawless place, where people scratched a living however they could, and where the weak were forever victims of the strong. Most were not citizens but the flotsam of the Empire, washed up around its capital. Every hue of skin, every brand of religion and superstition gathered together in abject squalor amid a miasma of the foulest of stenches.

Cato unconsciously quickened the pace so that the cohort might reach open country as soon as possible. But first they had to negotiate the necropolis, less fashionable than that which had grown up either side of the Appian Way. The more recent of the tombs were still patrolled by watchmen hired by the rich to ensure they were not damaged or looted. The older tombs, long abandoned by succeeding generations, were now used by squatters, those too poor or too vulnerable to find their place in the shanty towns. Every so often the column passed an emaciated body, ravaged by hunger, sickness, age or all three, stripped of any clothing and mauled by feral dogs and cats before being picked at by carrion birds. The good humour of the first miles of the march quickly faded.

Two miles from the city wall, the Ostian Way at last emerged into open country, and Cato filled his lungs with air scented by the wild flowers and herbs that grew alongside the road. Even though the barges that plied the Tiber between Rome and Ostia carried most of the freight and passengers, there were still plenty of carts, wagons and people on foot passing along the road. Most were in a hurry as they noticed the dark clouds carried on a stiff breeze coming in from the coast. Cato sensed the drop in temperature.

'That storm is definitely on its way.'

'Storm? Pfft!' Macro glanced up at the sky. 'Mere drizzle. Nothing like it for brushing away the cobwebs.'

'A light brushing I can deal with. But those clouds look like we're in for a damn good soaking.'

'All the better for teaching this lot how to cope with a bit of discomfort. It'll go some way towards toughening them up a bit. They need it. Been living too long in the lap of luxury.'

'All the same, let's rest them at noon before we march them back to barracks. Should be more than halfway to Ostia by then.'

Macro did a quick mental calculation and glanced back down the column before he replied. 'We're making good time, and no stragglers so far. Not that there should be.'

Cato caught the meaning of his last sentence and nodded. There had been no trouble from Macrinus or the other malcontents. Either they were biding their time or they did not want to become the object of Macro's ire.

As they passed the next milestone, a light rain began, angled into their faces by the freshening breeze. Macro lifted his head and smiled. 'Ah, that'll help with the slight sweat we've worked up.'

They marched on as the rain became heavier and the breeze strengthened into a wind that tossed the boughs of the poplars on either side of the road, filling the air with a rustling roar that whipped the men's capes. Most of the travellers had moved off the road to seek shelter beneath the trees and the awnings and trellises of the inns scattered along the route. They watched in bemusement as the soldiers paced by, heads hunched down into the folds of their drenched cloaks.

Cato and Macro were familiar with the landmarks along the

road, and at length Cato saw the shrine that had been erected halfway between Rome and Ostia. Despite the enjoyment his friend took from the exercise and the chance to push the men, he was relieved that they would be turning back soon. He was looking forward to a session in the steam room of the small bathhouse just down the street from the camp gates. And after that a hot meal in the inn next door.

By the time they reached the shrine and Macro gave the order to halt, the rain was slashing down in steely streaks slanted by the wind, and the men were cold and shivering.

'Not sure it's wise to let 'em rest too long,' he said. 'Best we get back to camp quick as possible.'

Cato grinned. 'Not enjoying this so much now, eh?'

'Gets to my bones more than it used to,' Macro admitted, before adding in a defensive tone, 'Not that I'm complaining.'

'No, of course not.'

They were interrupted by the approach of a rider tearing down the road at full gallop. As he drew closer, Cato saw that he was wearing the livery of the imperial messenger service.

'What's his hurry?' asked Macro.

'Only one way to find out.'

Cato stepped into the middle of the road and raised his arm. The rider slowed and drew up a spear's length away, the horse's nostrils flaring as foam flecked its muzzle. Under normal circumstances the emperor's messengers rode at a steady canter between waystations. The speed of this rider indicated that he was carrying a dispatch of some importance. He was about to upbraid Cato for delaying him, then realised he was talking to a senior army officer and saluted instead.

'What's the rush? Is there trouble we should be aware of?' Cato called out above the din of the strengthening gale.

The rider steadied his mount before he spoke, breathlessly. 'There's a storm at sea. Came up with little warning and caught

169

the grain fleet as they were approaching harbour. They're being swept towards the shore.'

Cato and Macro exchanged a look. Every month a large convoy sailed to Ostia from one of the provinces that served as the breadbasket of Rome. They carried grain within their large holds, enough to keep the mob in Rome fed and largely content. Grain was the most vital food source for the inhabitants of Rome. There were times when the harvest failed or bad weather prevented the ships from sailing, and the poor went hungry. If nothing was done to fill the people's stomachs, a hungry mob quickly turned into a dangerous one.

'Please, sir,' the messenger said. 'Stand aside. I must deliver my report to the palace.'

'Go!' Cato waved him past, and the rider spurred his horse back into a gallop, pounding past the soldiers drawn up along the road.

'If we lose the grain convoy, the urban cohorts may be called on to keep order,' Cato reasoned. 'If it comes to that, we have to make sure they are ready for it.'

'Aye.' Macro glanced in the direction of the capital. 'If we pick up the pace, we can be back before nightfall. Shall I give the order?'

Cato was looking in the other direction, towards Ostia, thinking quickly.

'Sir?'

'Just a moment . . . No. We're not going back. We're marching on to Ostia. Our help may be needed to deal with the consequences of the storm. Send an optio back to the barracks to notify Tribune Marcellus and order him to take temporary command of the other cohorts until we return.'

While Macro strode off to carry out his instructions, Cato looked up at the dark rainclouds scudding overhead, blinking away the drops that spattered his face. It did not take much effort to imagine the conditions of the approaches to Ostia. The grain fleet rising and falling on the huge swells rolling in to break on the shore in thunderous bursts of spray. All the while the onshore wind would be bearing the ships towards the coast and the doom that awaited them there. The desperate crews would be doing all they could to claw their way out to sea. But their vessels were ponderous and stood little chance in a wind as strong as the one swirling around Cato and his men. A wind that would be even stronger out on the open sea. Only the gods themselves could prevent the disaster that Cato saw in his mind's eye.

As the optio of the rearmost century turned back towards Rome at a steady trot, Macro ordered the men to re-form the column and prepare to continue the march, his booming voice straining to carry above the sound of the storm.

'We need to quicken the pace,' Cato said as Macro rejoined him at the head of the cohort. 'We'll not stop until we reach Ostia.'

'This route march is going to be a little tougher than everyone bargained for. I'll see that the men are up for it.'

'What about you?' Cato asked with a wry smile.

'I'm doing fine.' Macro's reply was terse. 'I may be getting on in years, but I ain't some fucking lazy cunt. And I can still outmarch you any day.'

'We'll see about that, old man.'

They trudged on through the wind and rain, down the glistening length of the paved road. Cato smiled briefly. If nothing else, it was good to slip back into the lightly mocking banter that had been a feature of their army life for so many years. The thought provided some comfort as he lowered his head to shield his face from the driving rain. It was reassuring to have Macro at his side, come what may.

With every passing mile, he felt the cold seeping through his sodden clothes and into his bones. He could not prevent himself shivering, and clenched his jaw to stop his teeth chattering. Any hope that the storm might pass crumbled as the rain and wind continued to sweep across the landscape with increasing violence. On either side of the road people were fastening the shutters of farmhouses and wayside shops and inns. In the fields, cattle and sheep huddled together, lowered heads facing away from the driving rain.

Two miles from Ostia, the road passed over a rise. From its crest Cato could make out a few details of the town and the port beyond. Out to sea he could just about discern a handful of ships being tossed about by the waves as they surged towards the coast.

'Stand aside!' called a voice from some distance behind, and Cato stepped to one side of the road to look back as the head of the column continued by. The shout was repeated closer to, and he saw a party of riders approaching at a canter.

'Who do you suppose that is?' asked Macro as he joined Cato.

'Can't tell . . .'

As the riders drew closer, they could see that they were led by a troop of mounted Praetorians. Their officer could be heard shouting hoarsely as he gestured frantically with his hand. 'Clear the way! Clear the way for Caesar!'

Cato and Macro hurried to the verge a moment before the Praetorians thundered past. A short distance behind them rode the imperial party. Cato recognised Burrus, Nero, Tigellinus and a handful of others. Burrus slowed down and reined in.

'Prefect. What are your men doing here?'

'Training march, sir. We had word that the grain fleet was caught in the storm, and I decided to march on to Ostia in case we were needed.'

'I am sure you will be.'

Nero edged his mount alongside, and Cato and Macro saluted. The emperor was wearing a purple cloak, the saturated folds clinging to his form. The artfully curled hair that Cato had seen in the palace was now plastered to his scalp, and rain streaked his face and dripped from his brow and nose as he looked down at the two officers.

'Cato, it seems that when you are not fighting our enemies, you are fighting the elements.' Nero forced a smile before he gestured towards Ostia. 'Get your men down to the port as swiftly as you can and wait there for orders.'

'Yes, Caesar.'

Tigellinus edged his mount forward. 'Caesar, there's no time to waste. You are needed in Ostia.'

'Yes, quite.' Nero nodded to Cato, then tugged his reins and urged his horse into a canter as the imperial party hurried to catch up with the Praetorians.

As soon as they had gone, Cato ordered the cohort to continue its march at the quick step. Even though the distance from the camp in Rome to Ostia was no more than a standard day's march for the men of the legions and auxiliary units, the harsh conditions had taken their toll, and he could see the weary expressions on the faces of the men at the head of the column.

'Surprised that Nero is out in this weather,' Macro commented. 'Have to admit, he's the last man I would have expected to see on the road.'

Cato nodded. He was equally surprised. But then again, the fate of the grain fleet was of critical importance to the people of Rome, and perhaps to the survival of Nero if the mob began to starve and turned against him. The line between altruism and self-preservation was very thin as far as the lives of emperors were concerned.

When they reached the gates of Ostia, Cato could make out the roar of the surf and the thump of waves crashing against the mole that shielded the harbour from the open sea. Dusk had come early, and now bursts of lightning illuminated the clouds from within and added to the awesome spectacle of the violence of nature. There was more shelter in the streets of the town than out in the open country, and there were still people abroad, many making their way down to the harbour to witness the raging seas and the plight of the ships fighting to survive the wrath of the storm.

Cato and Macro led their men down the main thoroughfare, passing through the forum and on until they reached the warehouses that stretched back from the wharf. Above the roof tiles Cato could make out the tops of the masts of the moored ships weaving against the grey sky. As they emerged onto the open ground that stretched around the harbour, they could see groups of spectators staring out to sea with shocked expressions.

Macro drew up with a start and took in the scene, his jaw sagging with disbelief. 'Sweet Jupiter, Best and Greatest . . .'

CHAPTER FIFTEEN

The scene before Macro and Cato was like none they had witnessed before. The storms that they had seen off the coast of Britannia paled in comparison to the violence of the tempest striking Ostia.

Even within the harbour the ships and smaller vessels were being tossed about by the swell sweeping in through the gap between the mole and the headland. Some had poorly laid anchors, which were dragging and causing them to collide with other ships and the spars and rigging to become entangled. A handful were overladen, and their crews were desperately dumping cargo over the side to lighten them. Others were already awash and settling sluggishly amid the swell. Small craft from abandoned vessels were struggling to reach the wharf and steer clear of the jumbled rocks at the base of the mole. A few had already come to grief, and their shattered hulls littered the inside of the breakwater. Those crewmen who had survived the impact were clinging to the rocks and trying to climb to safety, timing their efforts between the waves breaking over them. They beckoned to those on the wharf to come to their aid, and Cato could hear their pitiful wails of despair between the thunderous roars of the crashing waves.

Beyond the mole the storm raged with unrestricted power. The ocean swell dwarfed the vessels caught on the open sea. They rose on the crest of each wave, bows and sterns canting at extreme angles before plunging down out of sight in the following trough. As Cato watched, a large cargo ship was caught on its beam and rolled over, the mast snapping like a twig and tearing down the sail and rigging as the hull disappeared momentarily and then rose like the curved, glistening back of some vast sea monster. As the waves smashed into and over the mole, they exploded in vast sprays of white, the last droplets hanging in the air for a moment before falling and fading. Each wave struck with a boom, and Cato and Macro could feel the impact through their feet as they watched. Above them the lightning burst, no longer content to be obscured by the clouds. Vivid bolts stabbed down towards the sea, stilling the scene for an instant in a vivid white marble frieze crafted by some insane sculptor.

There was a swirl of motion amid the crowd gathered along the wharf as Burrus drove his horse through the throng towards Cato.

'Thank the gods you are here,' he called out as his mount slewed to a halt. He pointed towards the end of the mole. 'Get your men over there on the double. We need to save those we can from the rocks.'

'Where is Caesar?'

'He's directing the rescue effort. Be quick, man.' Burrus wheeled his mount round and headed back the way he had come.

Cato gave the order for the cohort to follow him, and they forced their way through the crowd, shoving aside those too slow to move out of their path. Some protested angrily, until Macro raised his vine cane, and then they scurried aside. Most were numb and mute as they looked out to sea, and needed little prompting to clear the way for the soldiers.

Ahead, Cato could make out the group of Praetorians gathered about the base of the lighthouse at the start of the mole. Above them, lining the parapet of the viewing platform below the beacon, were Nero and some others. They were illuminated in the ruddy flickering glow of the lighthouse pyre, which was

176

tended day and night by those whose duty it was to keep it alight come what may. Intended to guide ships to safety, it served no purpose that evening other than to warn vessels at sea of their proximity to the storm-ravaged coastline. The more experienced and courageous of those ships' captains would do their best to stand out to sea and attempt to ride out the storm. Those whose good sense had abandoned them were still hoping to gain the entrance of the harbour and the comparative safety beyond.

Halting his weary men, Cato entered the lighthouse with Macro at his side. As they climbed the steps, the sudden respite from the wind and rain was stark, and their footsteps sounded abnormally loud in the still air of the confined space. A pair of Praetorians stood guard at the top of the staircase and crossed their spears to prevent the two officers gaining access to the viewing platform.

'Let them pass!' Burrus ordered, before turning to the handful of men on the parapet. Cato and Macro bowed their heads and Nero waved them forward.

'It's as if the gods, in all their fury, have declared war on man . . .'

Cato saw the wild gleam in the emperor's eyes as he gripped the stonework, staring into the rain and wind without flinching. His expression was one of stricken wonder for a few heartbeats before Burrus addressed him.

'Caesar . . .'

The spell was broken, and Nero turned to him, blinking. 'What? What is it?'

'You must give the orders.'

'Yes . . . of course.' Nero turned to Cato briefly and indicated the mole. 'Those people on the rocks must be saved. Send your men to do the job. At once.'

Cato regarded the wave-lashed breakwater. The walkway that ran along its length was shielded from the storm by a shoulder-high parapet, but there were already a number of gaps where the force of the storm had carried away sections of the stonework. Any attempt to reach those still clinging to the rocks would be fraught with peril. Nero's brow furrowed as he saw Cato's hesitation.

'Dammit, man! What are you waiting for?'

'Caesar, we risk losing more men than we save,' Cato responded.

'The emperor gave you an order, Prefect!' Tigellinus snapped. 'Carry it out.'

Cato breathed in deeply, ready to defend his view that it might be a pointless waste of lives, but Nero spoke first.

'There's no need for concern, Cato.' His voice was calm and reassuring. 'I will be there with you.'

Tigellinus's eyes widened in shock. 'But Caesar . . .'

Nero silenced him with a swiftly raised hand. 'I will be safe. Do you really think the gods wish me harm? Besides, the prefect and his men need to see that Caesar stands with them.'

Tigellinus shook his head, mouth gaping slightly, and struggled to form a response. Nero was already heading for the stairs, beckoning to Cato and Macro to follow him. Burrus paused and then made to join them.

As they descended the stairs a few paces behind Nero, Macro looked at Cato and arched an eyebrow, then nodded at the emperor and gave a thumbs-up of approval. Cato was not so convinced. He was as surprised by Nero's gesture as his friend was, but it would be interesting to see how far the emperor's resolve carried him once he was exposed to the violence of the waves breaking over the mole.

'We need rope,' said Cato as they emerged from the lighthouse. He sought out Lemulus. 'Take the first four sections and search the warehouses and the decks of the nearest ships. I want as much rope as you can find.'

'Yes, sir.'

As the centurion hurried away, Cato turned to see that the

emperor was already striding out along the walkway with Burrus at his shoulder. The first hundred paces of the mole were wider than the spine stretching out towards the harbour mouth, and the waves broke a safe distance from the two men and only served to drench them as they advanced.

'Have the first three centuries leave their spears and shields here,' Cato ordered. 'Helmets and armour too.' There was no sense in risking the men falling into the sea and being drowned under the weight of their kit.

Macro saluted and relayed the orders, bellowing above the howl of the wind, the hiss of the rain and the thunder of breaking waves. Cato started to unbuckle his own straps as he hurried after Nero, dropping the helmet and then shifting out of his scale vest before casting it aside. He was fascinated by the apparent coolness of the emperor as he continued unhesitatingly towards the point where the mole angled away from the open sea and became thinner and more exposed to the waves. The first gap in the parapet was no more than fifty paces further on and stretched for a similar distance before there was more shelter. Three men were clinging to the rocks just beyond.

Cato caught up with Nero and Burrus just as they reached the break in the parapet. He saw a big wave rolling in, bursting along the mole in a succession of enormous clouds of spray and gushes of seawater. Nero was several paces ahead, in the open, and he slowed as he became aware of the wave. Then he braced his shoulders defiantly and took another step along the glistening walkway, as if daring the sea to do its worst.

'Caesar!' Burrus called out. He lurched forward, but lost his balance on the slippery surface and fell onto his hands and knees.

Cato sprinted past him, scrambling for footing as he made for the emperor. He reached him just as the rolling wave thundered along the outside of the mole, grabbing him by the shoulders and pushing him down, trying to cover him with his body as an avalanche of seawater broke across the open walkway and swept both men towards the edge. At once the water was in Cato's eyes, mouth and ears, dragging at his body as he desperately held on to the emperor with one hand while the fingers of the other scrabbled for purchase. He felt the uneven edge of a paving slab and clamped his fingertips over it as the sea surged over the two men, the muscle along the length of his forearm burning with the effort before the water flowed away, leaving them both spluttering and gasping for breath.

Burrus came scurrying forward with Macro and several of his men. They snatched up the two prone figures and rushed them to the shelter of the next undamaged stretch of the parapet, ducking down just as another wave struck. Cato's heart was beating wildly as he slumped against the stonework.

'You all right, lad?' Macro asked, crouching over him.

'Fine . . . Just fine. Caesar?'

Macro nodded to one side and Cato saw Nero a few feet away, coughing hard as he cleared his lungs of seawater. Otherwise he looked unharmed. Burrus regarded the emperor with alarm.

'You must return to the lighthouse, Caesar. It's too dangerous for you here.'

Nero made to reply, but retched instead, shaking his head as he thrust Burrus away. When he had recovered, he managed to gasp his response. 'No . . . My men . . . need me.'

'Your people need you, Caesar. If anything was to happen to you, it would be a disaster for Rome.'

Macro caught Cato's gaze and gave a discreet roll of his eyes.

'I am not leaving while there are lives that can be saved,' Nero said firmly, and rose unsteadily into a crouch, grasping the edge of the parapet as more spray burst over them.

Burrus looked helplessly at Cato. 'For Jupiter's sake, help me persuade him to go back,' he whispered hoarsely.

Cato considered the notion for a beat and was tempted to

urge the emperor to follow Burrus's advice, but a feeling stirred in his heart and he realised that it was respect, for the first time in all the occasions he had been in Nero's company. The young man's casual arrogance and vanity had gone, and in its place was a determination to overcome his fear and do the right thing. It was a rare opportunity for him to test his mettle away from the comfort of his flatterers, and Cato decided he deserved the chance to prove himself. He ignored Burrus's plea and pushed past him to squat beside the emperor.

'Caesar, we must be careful not to be carried off by the waves. Stay close to me.'

Nero stiffened slightly and seemed about to say something, but paused and nodded instead. There was a glimmer of doubt in his eyes, and Cato gave him a reassuring grin as he leaned closer. 'Keep calm and follow my lead and you'll be fine.'

'Here's Lemulus,' said Macro, and Cato turned to see the centurion and a score of his men hurrying along in the shelter of the parapet, laden with coils of rope. Lemulus halted them as they reached the gap and let a wave surge across the mole before he led them in a dash to where Cato and the others were waiting. The centurion did a double-take as he recognised the emperor and gave a clumsy salute as he waved his men past.

'Keep your heads down, lads. Unless you fancy swimming back to camp.' He turned to Cato. 'What's the plan, sir?'

'Use the ring bolts to secure the ropes.' Cato indicated the heavy iron rings driven into the parapet at regular intervals, dating back to the safety lines used during the mole's construction. 'Then get them down to the men on the rocks as fast as you can, before their strength gives out. We'll deal with the nearest group. You move your men further up. And keep your eyes on the waves. Only move when it's safe. Understand?'

'Yes, sir.'

They exchanged a nod before Lemulus scrambled off, leaving

181

Cato with a coil of rope. He carried it to the nearest bolt and fastened the end securely, then moved to the edge of the walkway and looked down. The last of the dull light of day was fading fast and he could just make out the three men clinging to the rocks below him. As the nearest caught sight of him, he raised his hands and pleaded for help, though his cries were lost amid the din of a fresh cascade. Cato gathered up the line and cast it out so that the end fell as close to the man as possible. He stretched his hand out, but it was beyond his reach, so Cato hurriedly pulled it back and tried again. This time it fell close by, and the man snatched at it with both hands and held on tightly.

'He's got it!' Cato turned to Macro and Nero. 'Pull him up!'

Macro worked his way in between Cato and the emperor and turned to the latter. 'I'll give the count. On three, you pull for all you're worth.'

Nero gave a nod, grasping the coarse rope and bracing himself. 'One! Two! Three! Pull!'

They took the strain and heaved, slowly drawing the man up towards the walkway. A fresh wave crashed behind them and deluged them with seawater. Macro heard Nero give a surprised cry as the rope slipped from his fingers.

'Hold on, you daft bastard! It's just a piece of rope, not a fucking snake!' Macro shouted without thinking. 'Don't you bloody dare let go again!'

At once Nero grasped the line tightly again and they resumed their efforts until the first man reached the walkway, rolled over the edge and crawled towards the parapet. Cato took the rope from his trembling hands.

'Next one! Get ready!'

The rope reached the second man at the first attempt and he was quickly drawn up. Cato could see that the third man was in a more precarious position. Lower than the others and half immersed in the cold surge within the harbour. When the end of the rope landed close by, he stared at it helplessly, unable to make himself release his grip on the rock and grab the line.

'Take it!' Cato shouted down at him. 'For the gods' sake, take it!'

The man looked up in abject terror but didn't move, instead pressing himself into the rock as a wave swept over his body, leaving him spluttering as it passed on.

'Shit . . .' Cato muttered. He snatched the rope back and threaded the end through his belt twice, then tied it off and gave it a firm tug to ensure it was secure.

'What do you think you're doing?' Macro demanded.

'I'm going down there.'

'Like fuck you are. Let me do it.'

'No time for that.' Cato looked past his friend and fixed Nero with a firm stare. 'You make sure you don't let go of the rope. Whatever happens.'

'I will.'

Cato slid to the edge of the walkway and began to climb down the wet rocks towards the third man. He paused every time a fresh deluge swept over him and clutched the wet rock tightly until it was safe to resume his descent. The man was losing his grip and sliding lower, his limbs shaking with the effort to cling on. It took longer to reach him than Cato had anticipated, but at length he was able to grasp his hand and haul him up.

'Hold on while I untie the rope!' he shouted into his ear. 'I'll fasten it to both of us, then we climb up. Clear?'

The man nodded. Cato could see that he was no more than twenty, pale-skinned and probably from one of the northern provinces. The knot had pulled tight, and Cato had to work at it to loosen it, pausing as water swirled over him. At last it came free, and he reached towards the young man to secure the rope to him first. A hand shot out and snatched the rope from Cato's fingers and the man began to scramble up the rocks, making for the safety of the walkway.

'Stop, you fool!' Cato shouted.

The order was ignored. Cato felt a surge of panic and anger before he heard Macro's voice bellowing above the storm, 'Hold on, Cato! Big one coming!'

Flattening himself against a boulder, Cato clenched his fingers around the edge and held his breath. An instant later, there was a thunderous roar as the wave smashed into the far side of the mole and a huge cloud of spray exploded overhead. Water burst through the nearby gap and cascaded to both sides. He heard Macro shout at Nero to cling on, and then he was engulfed in the salty torrent. There was a muffled cry and something struck his shoulder as the sea rushed over him. Then it had passed, and he gasped for air. The rope lay over the rocks to his side. He glanced around, but there was no sign of the young man, neither near at hand, nor amid the wild waters below the rocks. The sea had claimed him and left no trace.

With a leaden heart, Cato steadied himself, then grasped the rope and climbed back up, assisted by Macro and Nero. They hauled him onto the walkway, and he flattened himself as another wave struck, then crawled to the parapet and sat with his back against it.

'I couldn't save him,' he said.

'I saw what happened,' Macro replied. 'It was on him. He lost his head. Lucky he didn't take you with him.'

Cato nodded. He was trembling from the terror of a moment before and wondered if he would have done the same as the young man if their positions had been reversed. There was no time for such thoughts now, he told himself firmly, and looked along the walkway to see how Lemulus and the others were coping. In the gloom he could just make them out as they did their best to save the stricken men, helped by the long stretch of parapet that held the tempest at bay. There were only a handful still awaiting rescue, and he realised there was nothing more for him to do on the mole.

Across the harbour he could see ships crushed together, rigging entangled, with some of the masts snapped. Loose sails billowed wildly and men frantically tried to save their vessels from further damage by lowering the spars and trying to fend off other ships bearing down on them. Many had foundered or capsized, and their hulls rose and fell leadenly across the breadth of the harbour. Cato wondered how many ships of the grain fleet had fallen victim to the storm and been wrecked along with their precious cargo. It seemed inevitable that Rome would go hungry.

'At least we saved these two,' said Nero.

Cato turned to the emperor and nodded. 'We did . . .' He swallowed and they shared a grim smile before the weight of the vast difference in their social rank reasserted itself in Cato's mind. 'I am grateful for your help, Caesar.'

The moment of peril had passed, and with it the brief moment of comradeship in adversity. Macro cleared his throat anxiously before he addressed the emperor. 'About the, uh, words I used earlier to address you, Caesar . . . My apologies. Heat of the moment and all that.'

Nero appeared to ignore him as he rose to his feet cautiously, rearranging the folds of his cloak before he grasped the top of the parapet and stared out to sea, heedless of the spray. Cato nudged Macro's shoulder and leaned closer to speak into his ear. 'Better get these two back to the wharf while he's preoccupied.'

'Right!' Macro nodded and gestured to the survivors to follow him. They stood in a crouch, waiting for the next wave to pass the gap, then scurried along the walkway to the relative safety of the next stretch of parapet. Cato watched them until they were safe, then moved to Nero's side.

'We should get away from here, Caesar,' he said gently.

The emperor did not seem to hear him, and Cato wondered if the experience had stupefied him. He cleared his throat and spoke more loudly. 'Caesar?'

Nero continued to stare, and Cato turned to see what had transfixed him. Less than a quarter of a mile away, a large vessel was being carried towards a cluster of rocks. Raising a hand to shield his eyes, Cato could make out that it was a bireme, perhaps one of the escorts of the grain fleet. The mast lay across the deck, festooned with cordage and wildly flapping shreds of sail. The crew, sailors and marines, were desperately using their swords and axes to cut the wreckage free. At the same time, the men at the banked oars on each side were struggling to claw the warship away from the rocks. It was a hopeless task, as the raging seas made it impossible to coordinate the strokes and the long oars flailed in confusion. It was clear that the vessel was doomed.

'Poor bastards . . .'

'What?' Nero glanced at him. 'What did you say?'

'There's nothing that can save them, Caesar.'

'Nothing? NO! I won't have it.' Nero raised his arms and took a deep breath before shouting out to sea. 'Nero, son of the divine Claudius and descendant of Augustus, commands you, O Neptune, to grant salvation to that ship and the men aboard her! I command it in the name of Caesar! Calm the seas and let them return to shore in safety! It is my will!'

Lightning burst overhead, the dazzling glare for an instant making a marble sculpture of the emperor, arms outstretched, shoulders back, with an imperious tilt to his chin. In the same instant the warship and the sea around it were frozen as if encased in glittering ice, before the dusk and rain blotted out the image. Cato saw a towering wave roll in from the open sea. It gathered height as it approached the shore and lifted the bireme, tilting the deck at a sharp angle and hurling several men into the water. Then the ship lurched forward onto the rocks with a tearing groan that could be clearly heard from the mole.

'No . . .' Nero shook his head. 'It cannot be! How dare you!' He clenched his fists and shook them as he raged at the waves.

'Neptune, I curse you! Do you hear me? May Jupiter tear out your eyes and tongue! May he scourge your flesh and rip it from your limbs!'

Cato recoiled a step, astonished at the insane wrath etched on the emperor's face. Then his gaze returned to the stricken vessel, pinned to the dark rocks as wave after wave crashed upon it, steadily battering it to pieces. The storm had worked the bireme round so that its stern was closest to the shore, and soon all that was recognisable of the once proud warship was a short length of the aft deck and the decorative fan tail that arched gracefully over the steering position. Perhaps a dozen survivors still clung to the ship's rail.

'Spare them!' Nero howled. 'For pity's sake, Jupiter, Best and Greatest, I command you . . .'

Another huge wave approached and exploded over the remnants of the hull, and when it passed on, there was nothing recognisable left. Just fragments of the ship swirling amid the foam. Cato caught a glimpse of one man, arms flailing as he tried to swim clear, before he was pulled under by the vicious currents and vanished from sight.

Nero slowly lowered his arms, and his head dipped in grief and despair. Cato hesitated before he reached out and grasped the emperor's shoulder.

'Caesar, come with me . . . There's nothing more to be done here. Please.'

Nero raised his head and nodded. Cato glanced over his shoulder and saw that Lemulus and his men, along with the handful of sailors they had managed to save, were working their way back along the walkway towards him.

'Let's go,' he said firmly, steering Nero ahead of him. They bolted past the gap in the parapet between waves, then hurried towards the safety of the shore, where Macro and the others were waiting for them.

CHAPTER SIXTEEN

The storm blew itself out in the early hours of the following morning, so that when dawn broke over Ostia, the sky was clear and only a light offshore breeze blew in across a gentle swell. The calm after the storm seemed to mock the scenes of devastation in the harbour and along the shore on either side of the port. Scores of ships had foundered, only their masts protruding from the still waters. Others had capsized, and their barnacle-encrusted hulls lolled gently like dead fish in a pond. Smaller craft – fishing boats, tenders and pleasure boats – had been pulverised by collisions with larger vessels or been crushed between them and the wharf, and all that remained were shattered timbers amid the flotsam and bodies spread across the surface of the harbour. Boats were making their way over the water to retrieve the dead, and the air was filled with the wailing of their relatives as the corpses were laid out in a long line along the wharf. It would be many days before the last of those lost at sea washed up on the shore and could be afforded a funeral, or, if unidentified, consigned to a mass grave.

The port itself had also suffered damage. Tiles had been torn from buildings, and the entire roof of one warehouse had collapsed, with the contents spoiled by the rain. The most concerning loss, however, was the vast quantity of grain that had gone down with the convoy that had been sailing up from Sicily when the storm struck. Only five of the grain ships had survived, and even then the violent motion of the storm had caused the cargoes to shift, amphorae to shatter and the contents to fall into the bilges, where the foul water rendered them unfit for consumption.

Cato's men had been kept busy most of the night helping with the rescue work and retrieving the cargoes that could be saved from the ships moored along the wharf. They also had to stand guard around the warehouses and patrol the dark streets to deter those who had taken advantage of the storm to rob and loot. Now that dawn had broken, the port seemed quiet, even allowing for the sounds of grieving, the excited cries of the gulls swooping on the spoils of the storm, and the orders being barked by the captains of the surviving vessels as they struggled to cut them free of each other and bail out the water that had been shipped. One of the centuries kept watch over the warehouses and harbourfront while their exhausted comrades slept wherever they could find shelter.

'What a fucking mess,' Macro said quietly as he looked out from the platform upon which the lighthouse stood. 'It's going to take a while to clear it up and get the harbour operational again.'

Cato was sitting nearby, his back to the base of the lighthouse. He nodded and yawned before rubbing his bleary eyes. His tongue felt thick in his mouth and he took a swig from his canteen before pouring the rest of the contents over his face to try and refresh himself.

'Several days at best before the harbour is cleared,' he decided. 'And longer maybe before the wrecks can be broken up and removed. If the emperor sends for more grain, it'll take at least a month for a fresh convoy to arrive.'

'That's going to cause a bit of a stir when the news reaches Rome.' Macro looked towards the harbourmaster's headquarters, where the emperor and his small retinue had sheltered for the night. A squad of Praetorians leaned on their grounded shields as they guarded the entrance to the building. He scratched the bristles on his chin. 'Nero's going to have his hands full. Which may be a bit of a blessing as far as I'm concerned. Do you think he'll overlook the, er, choice language I used last night? I don't expect he's used to being spoken to like a squaddie.'

'Probably not.' Cato forced a quick grin. 'That said, I'm sure he has rather more pressing matters on his mind. That'll be true for the next few days. I wouldn't worry too much about what you said. If anything, I'd be willing to bet he's secretly proud of himself for being treated like one of the men, albeit briefly.'

Macro took some small comfort from his friend's words before he continued. 'Have to admit, for all the bad opinions about the lad, he showed some guts last night.'

'Yes . . .' Weary as Cato's mind was, it had no difficulty in summoning up the terrifying images of the storm, and he recalled the dread he had felt when the rope had been snatched from his hands and he had clung to the rock, waiting for a chance to escape the waves breaking around him. There were many ways for a man to die, but the prospect of drowning was the one he feared most. He forced himself to put aside the memories and consider his friend's evaluation of Nero. He himself saw the emperor in a different light as a result of his courage the previous night. There were not many men who would have willingly shared the dangers faced by Cato and Macro, who were bound by their duty to act as they had. Certainly not among the ranks of the aristocrats and those at the court of the emperor.

He wondered if the plotters who surrounded Vespasian would have put themselves in the way of harm as willingly as Nero had.

'He surprised me,' Cato continued. 'I'll say that for him.'

Then he recalled the moment Nero had stood at the parapet and demanded that the gods hear and obey him. His wide eyes and shrieking voice had had a disturbingly fanatical edge. Worse, Nero's presumption that he was not only on speaking terms with the gods but also in a position to command them smacked of delusion at best and perhaps more than a little measure of insanity. The kind of madness that no ruler should possess, and no people he ruled should tolerate. An unfortunate consequence of being treated like a living deity was the temptation to behave like one. Such men were a danger to all others, in Cato's estimation.

But if not Nero on the throne, then who? Who else could command the loyalty of the legions and the mob and maintain the delicate balance of power that preserved Rome from the horrors of the civil wars that had plagued the dying decades of the Republic? Certainly not most of those who had gathered at Vespasian's house to discuss replacing the emperor. Of all of them, the only one who inspired any hope of becoming a decent ruler was Vespasian himself, and he had given little sign of putting himself forward for the role.

Cato paused his line of thought. Perhaps his former commander did harbour such ambitions. What if he was playing a long game? Building his support and paving the way to the purple one small step at a time? Was the blunt exterior of a seasoned soldier merely a façade behind which he was already scheming his way to the throne, using those around him, including Cato, to make it possible for him to take power one day? Cato hoped not. He hoped he knew the man well enough to know that Vespasian held himself to a higher moral standard than that. But then ambition was often a thing gradually uncovered rather than apparent from the outset. It might even become a matter of necessity in order to serve the common good . . . or self-preservation. The pursuit of power for virtue's sake was the aberration rather than the rule. Ambition should be made of much stronger stuff.

His speculations were abruptly halted by the sight of the emperor and his followers emerging from the harbourmaster's headquarters. While they waited for their horses to be brought from the stables, Tigellinus hurried over to address Cato.

'Get your men on their feet. Your cohort has been honoured with the duty of escorting Caesar back to Rome.'

Cato looked at him blankly as his exhausted mind processed the order.

'What are you waiting for, Prefect Cato?' Tigellinus cupped his hands and gestured. 'Up! Get moving.'

Cato rose stiffly, rubbing his back as he replied. 'We need to leave some men here to protect the warehouses. The town watch can't manage it by themselves.'

Tigellinus glanced along the wharf, where small groups of men had gathered, looking as though they might cause trouble. He turned to Cato. 'All right. Leave two centuries for now. They can be recalled or relieved depending on the circumstances. But I want the rest of your men formed up at once. Better not tarry, Prefect. Nero is impatient to return to Rome.'

'Then why not ride on without us?'

Tigellinus's nostrils flared slightly, and he had to control himself as he responded. 'Because Caesar wishes to honour you and your men for the lives you saved last night. Frankly, I see that as no more than your duty. But he regards it differently. All the same, I wouldn't push your luck by delaying him unnecessarily.'

Without any further word or pause for reply, Tigellinus strode back towards the emperor and his party.

Cato rolled his head to crack his neck. 'You heard the man. The Second Century can remain with Lemulus and his men. Send him to me.'

Macro stood with a grimace and cupped his hands to his mouth. 'First Cohort! Third, Fourth, Fifth and Sixth centuries fall in and prepare to march! Centurion Lemulus!'

The men stirred reluctantly, and Macro's eyes blazed as he strode over to the nearest group of soldiers and delivered a swift kick to a man who was still asleep. 'Are you bloody deaf? Or are you already dead? Because you're going to wish you were if you lie there sunning yourself like some leftover turd in the depths of the latrine! On your fucking feet, soldier!' He shrieked the last sentence to impart the requisite urgency to the hapless man, who cringed as he scrambled to retrieve his kit before scurrying away to join his comrades. Macro moved on, delivering equally savage treatment and invective to those who moved too slowly for his liking. The other centurions and optios followed suit, rousing their tired men and driving them into formation.

Lemulus came trotting over and saluted. 'You sent for me, sir?'

Cato was gratified to see that the veteran appeared tireless and alert, despite the previous day's march and the dangerous labours of the night.

'I'm taking most of the cohort back to Rome. We're to be Caesar's escort, it seems.'

Lemulus raised an eyebrow. 'That's quite the honour for our lot. Hasn't ever happened in my time, and certainly no chance of that while Tigellinus was in command.'

Cato ignored the comment. 'The Second Century will remain here with your lads, under your command. I want you to make sure there's no attempt to raid the warehouses and no trouble on the streets. Use whatever force it takes. You're to remain here until you receive further orders.'

'Yes, sir.'

Cato sensed the strain in the other man's voice and guessed that Lemulus was disappointed not to be included in Caesar's escort. 'Tell your men they did well last night. They can have a day's leave when they return to camp.'

Lemulus smiled. 'That'll please them.'

'One day, mind. Then it's back to training.'

'Can't wait.'

They exchanged a salute and Lemulus trotted back to his men, who were looking on with delight at the men getting ready to march. It never failed to amuse Cato how much soldiers enjoyed watching their comrades carry out duties more onerous than their own. For their part, the men of the other centuries called out insults and promises to look up the women of those remaining behind in Ostia.

As the last of the men moved into position, Macro called them to order. The soldiers formed their ranks and stood at ease.

'Cohort is ready to march, sir!'

'Very good, Centurion.'

Fastening the straps of his helmet, Cato took his place at the head of the century that would lead the column out of the port. The imperial party and the Praetorians had mounted up, and now Nero rode past, acknowledging the cheers of each century in turn. He reined in as he reached Cato and spoke loudly enough for his voice to carry to all the soldiers.

'It gives us great pleasure to see such a fine body of men, Prefect Cato. Be sure that Caesar will not forget the fine work they did last night. They can be proud of themselves.'

The praise was gilding the lily, thought Cato. His men had done no more than their duty, and most of that had consisted of keeping order. It was only Lemulus and his men who had faced danger. But he was content to take praise when it was offered. It would be good for the morale of the men.

'Caesar is too kind.'

'Not at all. Nor shall I forget the courage of their commander.'

Cato dipped his head in thanks, but not before he saw the bitter look Tigellinus shot him from a short distance behind the emperor.

'Let's be off!' Nero announced, and he led his small mounted contingent down the main thoroughfare in the direction of the town gate. Cato allowed a ten-pace interval before he led off the lead century, and the others followed, keen to return to the comforts of their barracks back in Rome.

★   ★   ★

The sky was still cloudy, but as the morning drew on, it was occasionally pierced by sunlight, which shone warmly across the landscape. Despite the discomfort of their still wet clothing and kit, the men's spirits were raised, and there was no trace of the disgruntled mood of the previous day's march. They had changed in that subtle way that a shared experience of hardship could bring. They were now more like the soldiers Cato wanted them to become.

Someone in the leading century began a marching song, and it was quickly taken up by the entire column. Ahead, Nero turned in his saddle and grinned as a commander with upbeat men at his back was wont to do.

'They're a happy lot today,' Macro commented to Cato.

'Long may it last.'

He regarded his friend closely, troubled by his tone. 'What's the problem, lad? We've got fair weather and good morale and we're the emperor's blue-eyed boys. Enjoy the moment.'

'I am.'

'If that's your happy face, then fuck knows what disgruntled looks like.'

Cato could not help a slight smile.

'That's better!' Macro clapped him on the shoulder. 'We'll make an optimist of you yet.'

'I'll settle for being a realist every time.'

'Oh yes? Then realistically speaking, what's not to enjoy right now?'

'Besides most of the grain convoy being at the bottom of the sea? There's going to be trouble in Rome.'

'Won't be the first time there's been a hold-up in the supply of grain. That's why there's always a healthy reserve kept in the Boarium warehouses. Sure, the price will go up in the short term, but if there's any grumbling, Nero can throw together a few days of gladiator games or chariot races to distract the mob. That's worked well enough in the past. So chin up and stop moping.'

Cato knew that his friend was speaking the truth, but a nagging sense of anxiety and anticipation of trouble continued to plague his mind. He was self-aware enough to know that this was a fault of his character, and neither reason nor Macro's cheery influence would make any difference to his mood. All the same, he decided that he would put on a smile for the benefit of the men.

'That's better!' Macro laughed and took a big breath before he began to sing along with the others, his deep voice booming out the more salacious lines of the marching song with gusto. After a moment, Cato joined in, and began to feel some release of the tension coiled inside him.

They had marched nearly halfway back to Rome when Nero steered his horse aside and waved his escort forward before dropping back to the head of the cohort. Macro and Cato stopped singing and bowed their heads in salute as the emperor turned his horse to ride alongside them. Despite a fresh change of clothes, Nero's hair was an unruly tangle, and instead of his usual pasty complexion there was colour in his cheeks and a more relaxed demeanour than Cato had seen before.

'Not far to go now, gentlemen,' he began a little awkwardly. He nodded back over his shoulder. 'Your soldiers are in good voice. I have half a mind to deploy them as a chorus for the next play I write. What do you say?'

Macro gave a little snort. 'I don't know about that, Caesar. The prefect and I have a full-time job just turning them into decent soldiers. I wouldn't know how to begin making actors of them. That's work for a politician, I'd say. They know far more about that than I ever will.'

Nero laughed heartily. 'You are right there, my friend! They are actors all right. Every last one of them. Fortunately, they are not very good at it. I know the craft well enough and can spot poor acting a mile off.'

Cato found that hard to believe, given the emperor's predilection for taking the most obvious flattery as sincerity.

Nero was warming to his theme. 'I need good men around me. Oh, I know I am fortunate to have the likes of Seneca and Burrus to offer me advice, and those like Tigellinus to serve as boon companions. But I also need men I can trust. Men who aren't afraid to call a spade a spade. Men who are prepared to speak out . . .' He paused a moment. 'Those honest enough to say . . . what was it again? Ah yes! "Hold on, you daft bastard! It's just a piece of rope, not a fucking snake!" – that sort of thing.'

Macro choked and missed a step before he continued, eyes lowered. Nero laughed heartily again. 'I might use that line in my writing one day. So inspiring. Fear not, Centurion Macro. I appreciate your candour and earthy language . . . Just don't make a habit of it, eh?' He leaned from his saddle and patted Macro's helmet. Then he urged his horse forward to rejoin his entourage.

Macro let out a long sigh. 'Fuck me . . .'

Cato shook his head. 'You lead a charmed life, brother.'

Macro looked round with a horrified expression. 'What was I bloody thinking when I said that?'

'Thinking?' Cato repeated wryly. 'What's the problem? You've just got away with speaking to Caesar in a manner that would have cost anyone else their head. Enjoy the moment!'

Macro glowered at him. 'Ha-fucking-ha.'

Ahead, Nero and his retinue had reined in and were in earnest conversation. Cato shouted the order for the column to halt, and the singing stopped abruptly.

'Wonder what's up now?' Macro craned his head to regard Nero and his companions.

Cato's gaze shifted beyond them in the direction of the distant capital. Being taller than Macro, he could see what had caused the sudden consternation. Even on a fine, clear morning like today, there was still a grimy haze hanging over Rome. Only this time a thick column of smoke was rising amid the haze. Large enough to betoken a huge blaze.

'There's a fire,' he said.

'Fire? Where?' Macro looked round.

Cato pointed. 'Rome.'

Macro rose on his toes and swore under his breath.

'First the storm and now this,' said Cato. 'I fear the worst is yet to come.'

Macro gave a start. 'Petronella . . . Bardea . . . Dear Jupiter, Best and Greatest, spare them. I beg you.'

CHAPTER SEVENTEEN

The emperor and his party rode away at speed and Cato gave the order for his column to resume their march, picking up the pace to reach the city as soon as possible. All trace of the earlier good mood faded as the men hastened along the road with grim expressions. Ahead of them the column of smoke steadily swelled in height and breadth, and soon towered over the haze. As they drew closer, Cato and Macro could see the billowing swirls of black smoke and then the glittery ripple of the flames against the backdrop of the temple complex on the Capitoline Hill. The fire was spreading in the direction of the Viminal, and Macro chewed his lip anxiously.

'Petronella will be fine,' said Cato. 'If there's any danger, she'll get away with Bardea.'

'I pray you're right . . . What if there's panic, though?'

It was a fair point, Cato knew. Most of the streets of the city were narrow and difficult to navigate on days when there were games or public festivals. If people were afraid and fleeing danger, the same streets could become congested and quickly turn into a death trap.

'Petronella will know what to do,' said Cato. 'If anyone can find a way out of trouble, it's her. You know that.'

Macro nodded. 'True.'

There was no question that the fire was growing in strength.

The heart of it seemed to be in the region of the Boarium market, next to the Tiber, rather than the residential neighbourhoods. That was some small comfort, Cato reflected. There would be time for most of those living in the path of the blaze to get clear before the flames consumed the tightly packed apartment blocks, shops and private houses that were ever vulnerable to the fires that broke out from time to time. Even so, many lived above their businesses in the Boarium and would lose their livelihoods.

Coming on top of the destruction wrought by the storm, the fire was ominous. It was as if the gods had turned against Rome and were heaping punishment upon punishment. For what reason? Cato wondered. Whatever the cause, it was certain that some would use these disasters to point the finger at those they had a vested interest in undermining or destroying. There would be those who blamed the fire on one of the smaller communities of the capital. Others would claim that the impiety of the times had provoked the wrath of the gods. Some would look to the man who ruled the Empire, and who, by virtue of his divine status, served as the conduit between the people and the gods. They would hold Nero accountable for the storm and the fire and question whether Rome might not be better off without him. The very people who had attempted to draw Cato into their conspiracy some days earlier. He felt a sudden surge of hostility towards the notion that they would exploit the suffering of the people in such a cynical manner. Besides, his view of Nero had shifted, and he was no longer sure if the emperor was the monster they claimed he was.

From the last rise before the city gates Cato and Macro could clearly see the scale of the fresh disaster faced by the people of Rome. Sure enough, the heart of the blaze was centred on the Boarium, particularly the sprawl of warehouses that lay back from the river. Great flames roared up from the buildings along the wharf and the densely packed barges that were moored alongside.

Even craft anchored further out were alight, and several burning hulks were carried off on the current and drifted past Cato and his men as they marched close to the river. People were flowing out of the gates, carrying their most valuable possessions or pushing small handcarts with as much loaded onto them as possible. Their flight was constricted by the shanty towns that surrounded the walls, and it was only when they reached open country that they stopped to turn and look back on the city with despair.

A Praetorian optio came running down the road and fell in alongside Cato. He saluted and struggled to catch his breath before he spoke.

'Prefect Cato . . . Burrus orders that you and your men . . . report to him at the near end of the Great Circus.'

'Tell him we'll be there as soon as we can, but we'll have to force our way through the people coming out. What about the rest of my command? The two cohorts that were in the camp?'

'They've already been deployed to fight the fire, sir. Same with most of the Praetorians. But it's a losing battle so far.'

Cato nodded. 'Report back to Burrus.'

The optio turned away and retraced his steps through the crowd streaming out of the city. In the light air the smoke was spreading out, creating a pall through which the sun was only dimly visible. Although it was only late afternoon, it already felt like dusk. Cato turned to Macro.

'We're going to have to force our way through the gate and the streets to get to Burrus. Pass the word down the column. I want the men closed up in tight formation. We'll use shields to batter our way in and lower the spears against anyone who creates trouble.'

'It's what I've been training 'em for. Time to see what they can do.' Macro trotted off to pass on the orders.

As soon as he returned, the two officers took their place behind the leading section of the Third Century, where they would be able to control the column's advance. The order was given and the men raised their shields and tramped along the road. Ahead of them the civilians parted, and they were able to progress at a steady pace. But as soon as they reached the edge of the shanty town, those fleeing the blaze presented a more compact mass and had to press themselves into the narrowest of alleys on either side as the soldiers approached. Just short of the city gate, people were packed into a dense tide of humanity and were only able to shuffle away from the danger.

'This is no good,' Macro observed. 'We'll never get through that lot. We need to shift them out of the way. Time for the spears.'

Cato nodded reluctantly.

Macro cupped his hands to his mouth and called out loudly enough to warn the mob as well as to be heard by the men at the front of the column. 'Front two ranks! Advance your spears!'

The first rank lowered the tips towards the crowd while those behind held theirs at shoulder height, the points extending over the shields of the men in front, presenting a bristling peril to the mob blocking their way. There were cries of alarm and surges towards the safety of the alleys and the flimsy shelters on either side, some of which collapsed under the pressure of the crowd. Alarm quickly transformed into panic, and people stumbled and fell. Many were trampled when they failed to regain their feet, but Cato knew there was no time to spare for them. He had to get his men into the city to join the other soldiers fighting the fire raging across the Boarium and threatening to engulf the crowded slums of the lower reaches of the Aventine Hill. Better a few died here than far more were burned alive should his men not be able to play their part in containing the conflagration.

The column kept moving at a steady pace, driving people before it and forcing the crowd to give way amid screams of terror and outrage. A moment later, a small rock was hurled from somewhere to Cato's left. Fortunately it missed its mark and passed over the column to fall amid the people on the other side.

'Shields up!' Macro barked. 'And keep 'em up, if you know what's good for you!'

The men needed no urging as more missiles rained from either side – stones, lumps of wood, shards from broken pots and handfuls of filth and shit. The air filled with the rattle and thud of impacts and the angry din of the crowd as the column passed through. Some projectiles struck home, clattering helmets and striking the men on exposed limbs. The few who were injured moved into the centre of the column while their places were filled by fresh comrades. A darker shadow fell over the head of the column, and Cato looked up to see the arches of the gatehouse directly ahead.

'Make for the left arch!'

The men at the front shifted their direction accordingly, and as Cato had hoped, the people crowded in their path hurried round to press their way through the other arch. As the front rank entered the wide street beyond, Macro called ahead, 'Clear the way!'

The crowd was less densely packed here, and was able to keep from the column's path as it quickened its pace and made for the curved mass of the far end of the Great Circus. Smoke, ashes and glowing sparks swirled overhead, and the roar of the flames and the occasional rumble of falling masonry and timber echoed off the buildings on either side. The crowd began to thin out as the column approached the blaze, and Macro gave the order to raise spears and lower shields now that the danger from the angry civilians had passed. The street gave out onto the broad space that surrounded the Great Circus, and there Cato saw Burrus and a handful of his staff officers coordinating the efforts to fight the inferno.

'Halt the men here,' he ordered before hurrying over to the

commander of the Praetorian Guard. Burrus looked up at his approach, but finished issuing instructions to one of his men before waving Cato forward.

'You took your time.' He did not pause to give Cato a chance to give an explanation and pointed towards the Boarium. Huge wavering sheets of fire spread across the market complex and warehouses, and even at a distance of a few hundred paces, Cato could feel the heat coming off the blaze in waves. 'We need to create firebreaks to try and stop it spreading beyond the market. I want your men to help the Praetorians demolish whatever buildings they can between here and the Tiber. Your other cohorts are already doing the same on the far side. The watch units and Praetorians are fighting the flames between the two. There's plenty of water in the aqueducts, but we've barely enough pumps and buckets.' He shrugged. 'That's the plan, and the part you play in it. Get to work.'

'We'll need tools – picks, hooks and rope.'

Burrus indicated a line of wagons beside the Great Circus. 'Over there. Take what you need, and hurry, man!'

The men of the cohort stacked their shields and spears beside the wagons and gathered round as their officers handed out the tools. Cato considered telling them to remove their armour to save them carrying the extra weight, but then decided they would be safer from falling debris if they retained it. Once they were equipped, he marched them in the direction of the fire. There were still civilians in the streets, hanging on until the end to protect their property in the hope that the fire would not reach them. Others turned and ran as they saw the soldiers approaching.

'Bloody looters,' Macro growled. 'Want me to do anything if we catch any in the act?'

'No time for that now. We keep going.'

The heat increased as they drew closer to the Boarium, and Cato felt the perspiration trickling down his face. They emerged from the last street and entered the marketplace. The fire was still a few buildings short of the market and rose in a terrifying wall of glittering red and gold flames beneath the billowing smoke. The roar and crackle was accompanied by tiles crashing and timbers bursting, and the shouts of the Praetorian officers as they coordinated the gangs that had started tearing down the warehouses backing onto the market. A tribune came running across as he saw Cato and his men arrive on the scene.

'Sir, we can manage the warehouses. Your men need to clear the market stalls and start work on the tenement blocks at the end there where they go down to the river. How many of you are there?'

'Four centuries.'

'Four centuries . . .' The tribune glanced at the column marching into the market. 'Where are the rest of the urban cohorts?'

'Already deployed on the other side of the fire.'

'Four centuries is not enough.'

'It's all there is, so you'd better let us get on with it and return to your men.'

'Yes, sir.'

Cato looked over the stalls covering the open ground between the colonnaded buildings either side of the Boarium. Many had been upended and their wares spilled over the flagstones. Others were still intact, laden with baskets of produce, piles of cheap pottery and bales of cloth. The more valuable commodities had been stripped by their owners or by looters.

'Macro, have the men break the stalls down and pile the debris on this side of the market. I want the space cleared of anything that will burn.'

'Yes, sir.'

'And make sure none of them try to put anything aside for later.'

Leaving Macro to organise the work parties, Cato went over to inspect the tenement blocks. As he approached, he saw that they were typical of the neighbourhood: old, decrepit and poorly maintained. The nearest of them was propped up by timbers wedged at an angle from the street. Cracks ran up the walls and the buildings had the sour tang of vomit, rotting vegetables and sewage left for many days. It would not present too much of a challenge to pull them down, but it would be hard and dangerous work given how swiftly it had to be done.

Macro had removed his helmet to mop his brow as he surveyed his men knocking over the stalls and breaking them up. What was left of the awnings, posts and display tables was heaped up against the side of the market furthest from the flames as the men laboured in the scorching heat. As soon as the space was clear, he ordered them over to the nearest of the tenement blocks, where Cato was testing the stability of one of the props. Macro looked up at the structure, four storeys in height. As was customary for such blocks in the slum areas of Rome, the best quarters were closest to street level, and the rooms became steadily smaller and the rents cheaper the higher up you lived.

'How are we going to go about this?'

Cato focused his tired mind. 'We'll take out these props first. That should bring this one down readily enough. There are a few more like this down the street to the river. They should go the same way. For the rest, we'll have to knock out supporting walls and try and control the collapse as best we can.'

'Easier said than done. The lads are going to have to move sharpish if the buildings fall the wrong way.'

'Well, yes. Quite. To work, then.'

Ropes were fastened to the four props of the first block and the lines drawn back towards the marketplace, where the men fell in and took up the slack.

'On three!' Macro raised his hand. 'One! Two! Three! HEAVE!'

The men strained with all their might, urged on by their officers, and the first prop lurched and fell. The soldiers on the line staggered back, some of them losing their footing. Cato saw the plaster give, and a crack opened on the first storey. The other props gave way almost immediately afterwards, and with a rumble the tenement collapsed in a choking swirl of dust that quickly cleared to reveal a mound of rubble.

Macro coughed, cleared his throat and spat. 'That was easy enough. How many more to go?'

'Another eight down to the river. Five of them are propped up like this one. The others are more stable and are going to be difficult to deal with. It'll take time.'

'Time's something we haven't got much of, lad.' Macro nodded towards the flames edging towards the street that would form the firebreak.

Cato examined the densely packed tenements, where his men were hurriedly preparing the next building for demolition. 'If the fire gets loose in that lot, there'll be no stopping it. We have to work faster.'

The next four buildings went the same way, three collapsing the moment the props were wrenched free. The fourth remained upright after the props were removed, and sturdy iron hooks attached to more ropes had to be used to finish the job. As soon as the dust had cleared, Macro had men scouring the rubble to remove as much timber and other combustible material as possible to add to the piled remains of the market stalls. All the while the inferno edged closer and the heat from the flames stung the exposed flesh of the men toiling to stop the fire in its tracks.

Cato had already inspected the exterior of the nearest of the remaining buildings and used charcoal from an ironmonger's shop in the next street to mark the sections to be attacked with picks and makeshift battering rams to weaken the structure. As

Macro and the century assigned to demolition duty gathered round, he hurriedly explained his intentions.

'The picks go in first and loosen the plaster and bricks on the corners. Then we'll use the ram. One corner at a time. I won't lie to you, it's going to be tricky work. The building could go at any moment, so keep your ears open. If I give the order to run, you drop the ram and get the fuck out of the way like you're the green team at the races.'

The greens were favoured by the Praetorians, taking their lead from the emperor, and this comment prompted some jeers and raspberries from Cato's men, as he had intended. He grinned. 'All right, faster than that, then! Now swing those picks! Show them how it's done, Centurion Macro.'

'With pleasure, sir.' Macro spat theatrically on his palms, then took up his tool and stepped towards the nearest corner. Bracing his boots, he took a big swing, and plaster and chunks of brick burst from the wall. The other men followed suit, while Cato stood back just enough to scrutinise the building and watch for signs of imminent collapse. The hot air and occasional billows of smoke made breathing uncomfortable as he willed his men on. A movement high up caught his eye, and he saw a narrow wooden balcony on the top storey drop at one end before it detached and started to fall.

'Look out!' he cried.

The nearest squad scurried out of the way as the balcony crashed into the street. One of the men laughed nervously before Macro rounded on him.

'What's so bloody funny? You haven't had a balcony fall on your head before? All in a day's work in the army. Now get your arse back to work. Caesar ain't paying you by the hour.'

The air rang with the sound of picks steadily biting into the building. It wasn't long before Cato saw a slight tremor, and several tiles crashed into the street.

'It's going! Run, lads!'

Macro and the others bolted away from the bottom of the block as cracks opened in the walls and the top storeys swayed towards the neighbouring building. Once again there was a loud roar and a burst of dust, and Cato shielded his eyes and covered his mouth and nose as it billowed over him. He waited an instant before cracking open his eyelids. Macro let out a whoop of satisfaction.

'Two for the price of one!'

The building had taken its neighbour down with it. All that remained was the ragged outline of the ground floor amid the ruins.

'Don't just stand there!' Macro yelled. He coughed, spat to clear his throat and continued. 'Clear the timbers!'

The men rushed forward as the two officers examined the situation. There was one more building to go, but already a gap of over a hundred feet had been created between the tenement blocks lining the Tiber and the warehouse district where the fire was raging.

'I hope it'll be wide enough,' said Macro.

'It better be.' Cato tipped his head towards the curtain of fire beyond the roofline of the last warehouse before the gap. 'There'll be no time to make it wider after the last block comes down. Let's do it.'

Macro led the men into position, then took his place round the corner from Cato. He found himself on the bank of the river. There was a narrow path between the wall and the piles that had been driven into the bed of the Tiber generations ago to support the foundations of the buildings crowding alongside – barely two paces' width before the sheer drop into the swift current ten feet below. A side door hung off one hinge to reveal a dingy hallway and the bottom of a flight of stairs.

'Watch your step here, lads. When the prefect calls time, I

don't want any of you falling into the river and ruining my day by having me jump in to save you.'

One of the soldiers shook his head in mock wonder. 'You'd do that for us, Centurion dear?'

'I might. Then again, I might throw you cunts in there just for fun . . . To work!'

They went at it with renewed effort as each man felt the increasing heat of the approaching fire. Lumps of grimy plaster came away easily, and then the bricks beneath, damp from years of proximity to the Tiber. Macro felt his muscles burning from the exertion and his limbs aching from two days of marching and precious little sleep. Sweat dripped from his brow and he paused to mop his face with the back of a hand. That was when he heard it – a plaintive cry, barely audible above the crackle of flames and the sharp notes of the picks striking home. For a moment he wondered if he had imagined it, and cocked an ear towards the source of the noise for a few heartbeats. It came again, loud and clear enough to dispel any doubt.

'There's a kid in there . . .'

The nearest soldier lowered his pick. 'What's that, sir?'

'Shh! Listen!'

There was no sound, and the soldier shrugged.

'I'm telling you, I heard it.' Macro glanced up to the fifth storey, where the shutters hung open. There it was again, fainter this time. He dropped his pick and hurried to the entrance, thrusting the broken door aside.

'Sir?' the soldier called out. 'What are you doing?'

'I'm going to find the kid. You lot carry on. I'll be back, quick as boiled asparagus.'

Then he was gone, and the soldier could hear boots pounding up the stairs. He shook his head and continued to batter the brickwork to pieces.

On the far side of the building, Cato looked towards the fire

210

and calculated that they would complete their work with a slender margin to spare. Nevertheless, he felt a tightness in his guts as he willed the tenement to come down.

'Now, you bastard . . . come on!' he muttered fiercely.

Then he heard a dull crunch, and the nearest wall gave a lurch as debris started to fall from above. He cupped his hands and shouted as loudly as he could above the din, 'She's going!'

The men, alert to the peril, scrambled over the rubble as fast as possible. Fortune at last seemed to show them some favour, and the tenement remained standing a little longer, giving them time to get clear. Cato waited, but there was no further movement. He feared he might have to order them back to complete the job and risk a sudden collapse that might bury them. Then he saw the wall that had faced the street fall in on itself, taking the roof down with it, before the remaining walls followed. As he shut his eyes and covered his mouth again, he felt a surge of relief that the firebreak was complete, for what it was worth. He and his men had done their duty well, and he was proud of their effort and courage.

As the dust began to settle, he called out, 'We're done here, lads! Get back to the far side of the marketplace and form centuries!'

Figures emerged from the rapidly thinning clouds of dust, men so covered in grime and dust it was almost impossible to distinguish between them in the lurid, wavering glare of the flames. He looked for the transverse crest of Macro's helmet. The fire was now starting to consume the warehouses on the far side of the firebreak, and the heat was almost unbearable. Some of his men were staggering with exhaustion.

'Get moving before we start cooking!'

The men passed by him and still there was no sign of his friend.

'Centurion Macro! . . . Macro! On me!'

As he blinked away the fine grit in his eyes and squinted at the debris, one of the soldiers approached him and spat to clear his throat.

'Sir . . .' he croaked, and gave a painful cough. 'He's gone.'

211

'What? What are you talking about? Who's gone?'

Even as he asked the question, a sensation of dread gripped his heart.

'Centurion Macro, sir. He was inside the building when it went.'

'Inside? What are you saying? What bloody foolishness is this?'

'He went in, sir. I was there. I saw him go in and up the stairs.'

'Why?' Cato snarled.

The wild expression on his commanding officer's face caused the soldier to recoil a step. 'Sir, he said he heard someone inside. He said it was a child. He said he would be back as quick as he could. But . . .' He made a helpless gesture towards the ruins.

For a moment, time seemed to stop as Cato stared at the piles of debris from the fallen buildings, now so intermixed that it was hard to tell where each had once stood. Every fibre revolted at the notion of believing that Macro was buried under it all, crushed to death.

He was about to shout at his men to go back and search for his friend when there was a loud crash, and the roof of the nearby warehouse gave way. Flames burst through the gap and licked up at the blood-red blanket of smoke covering the city. The searing heat struck at him like a physical blow, and he and the soldier ducked their heads and raised their arms to shield their faces. It was too late. There was nothing that could be done for Macro. Even if, by some miracle, he had survived the collapse of the final building, his body would be broken beyond repair and he was trapped under the rubble. And there he would be roasted, even if the firebreak stopped the flames spreading to the buildings beyond. The prospect sickened Cato, and he prayed that his friend had been killed outright and spared the horror of burning to death.

'Sir!' The soldier grasped the sleeve of his tunic and pulled him away from the ruins. 'We have to go! Now!'

Cato nodded mutely as the man turned and ran from the heat. He himself hesitated a moment longer, as much as he could bear, then set off, hunched over, forced to abandon the scene.

CHAPTER EIGHTEEN

Macro rushed up the first flight of steps and paused on the landing. The floorboards beneath his feet trembled slightly under the impact of the picks and the dull thud of the beam being used as a battering ram. He listened, straining his ears for the cry he had heard earlier, trying to locate it above the din of the demolition work and the roar of the flames.

There it was again. A thin, keening wail. He ran to the next landing, checking each of the four tiny apartments – dingy spaces reeking of human odours – and found nothing. There was only one storey left, and as he reached the top floor, he heard Cato shout his warning and the sound of the picks and the ram instantly ceased. 'Oh shit . . .' Macro cursed.

Bursting through the first door, he glanced over the threadbare bedrolls, abandoned rags and a handful of other belongings. The sound came again from the door opposite, and he spun round and crossed the narrow landing. Looking round frantically for the child, he spotted movement in a small box in the corner by the open window, and dashed to it. There, nestling amid some scraps of cloth, stood a brown puppy, tail wagging as it looked up at him, making the high-pitched mewling he had heard earlier.

'You are fucking kidding,' Macro muttered to himself. He felt the floor shift under his feet and snatched up the puppy, holding it in the crook of his arm as he turned and fled.

Tiles were already falling through the rafters and shattering on the floor as he reached the landing and sprinted down, taking the steps two at a time. Around him the structure shook and the air filled with the sounds of the collapsing building. At the next landing the stairs ahead fell away, leaving a yawning void and cutting off any hope of escape in that direction. Plunging into one of the abandoned apartments, Macro ran for the opening that gave out onto the rickety balcony. Tiles and bricks were tumbling down on all sides, and he acted on instinct. Bracing his feet for a second, he sprinted towards the opening and leaped across the narrow gap between the tenement block and the roof of the neighbouring warehouse. He felt debris strike him as he tumbled through the void before he struck the roof, the impact driving the air from his lungs. The tiles fell in around him as Macro and the puppy plunged down and thudded onto a heaped pile of kindling and old sacking.

For a moment all was black, and then he felt movement on his chest as consciousness returned. Something touched his chin, and a tongue played across his lips.

'Mmmmnurgh,' Macro mumbled as feeling returned to his limbs. 'Not now, Petronella. It's too early for that, love. I've got to . . .'

Full consciousness returned, and he blinked his eyes open to find himself looking up at the puppy.

'What the fuck? Off you get, mutt.' He grasped the animal by the scruff of the neck and sat up to survey his surroundings. The interior of the warehouse was lit by rosy shafts of light through gaps in the roof. Debris from the falling tenement block lay on the sacking around him, as well as a few cinders, some of which were glowing. The air was as hot as that surrounding a furnace in a blacksmith's, and Macro recalled that the fire had nearly reached the warehouse. He gave the puppy a gentle stroke on the soft fur on top of its head and was rewarded with a renewed bout of tail-wagging.

'We have to get out of here, my friend. And fast.' He rose swiftly and winced at a sharp pain in his side. Looking down, he could see no damage to his mail armour, but he had been lying on a wooden bar that must have winded him and damaged a rib or two. He grimaced at the puppy. 'Aren't you lucky Uncle Macro was there to break your fall, eh?'

He tried to inhale, but anything more than a light breath was too painful. In any case, the air was acrid with smoke and would have made him cough. Holding the puppy to his chest, he thought a moment as he took his bearings, then headed past piles of cloth, baskets of pottery and other stored items towards the end of the warehouse nearest to the river. There were two large doors that opened out onto the wharf, and a lurid glow lined the edges of them. He went to test them and found that they were locked from the outside. He heard the clink of a chain. 'Damn and shit.'

He saw a stack of wine jars and some tools on a bench to one side and made his way over, coughing as he breathed in a tendril of smoke. There wasn't much time left before the flames consumed the warehouse and everything in it. Putting the puppy down, he rummaged through the tools until he came across a rusty hatchet. He raised it and tested the weight. 'It'll have to do.'

He returned to the doors, the puppy scampering alongside him and letting out excited high-pitched barks as if it thought Macro was playing some kind of game. The left-hand door seemed the more worn of the two, and damp had caused the bottom of it to rot and start to split. Bracing himself, he swung the small axe and struck the door, splintering the timber. The puppy stopped barking at the sound and scurried over to scramble under the bench, shuffling round until only its muzzle was visible. Macro continued striking at the door, breaking up the worn planks and creating a small, ragged opening through which a lurid orange glow glinted like the eye of some nightmare monster. The air was getting steadily hotter and the smoke thicker so that it was harder to breathe. Working feverishly, he enlarged the hole and then leaned back to give one of the planks a kick. It gave way easily, and he began work on the next, calculating that three would provide a wide enough gap to let him escape the building. Escape to where? he chided himself. It was possible he would be surrounded by fire. He thrust the thought away, refusing to contemplate failure, and redoubled his efforts, chopping in a frenzy.

As soon as the opening was large enough, he tossed the hatchet aside and stripped off his armour, helmet and sword belt. Unravelling his neck cloth, he went over to the wine jars and kicked one over so that it shattered on the flagstones. Red liquid burst across the floor, and he soaked the cloth in it before tying it around his face so that it covered his nose and mouth. The odour of the wine filled his nostrils. 'What a waste of good Falernian,' he mumbled.

He saw that the puppy was still cowering under the bench. There was no time to coax it out, so he grabbed a handful of trembling fur and flesh and pulled the whining animal into the open. Smoke was curling through the ragged hole in the door, and Macro caught glimpses of flames running up the rigging and mast of a ship moored alongside the wharf.

He hesitated, then lifted up the bottom of the wine jar to douse the puppy. It howled in protest and shook its head, blinking as drops of the liquid stung its eyes. He tucked the furry bundle into the top of his tunic and held it steady with one hand before taking as deep a breath as he could and stepping through the gap.

Outside, one of the most terrifying scenes he had ever witnessed met his squinting eyes. Wild, glittering flames tore at the fabric of the warehouse and other buildings running along the wharf as far upriver as he could see. The air was filled with a deafening crackle, and a strong breeze seemed to be sucked in towards the inferno. There was no chance of escape in the direction of the firebreak, as piles of cargo were on fire. Ahead of him, ships and barges moored along the wharf were burning. But that way offered the only hope of survival. He felt his skin roasting, and the acrid smell of the hair shrivelling and smoking on his arm made him gag. The puppy squirmed, and Macro tightened his grip as he ran across the wharf and stopped to gaze down into the fast-flowing current of the Tiber. His tunic was already smouldering. He took one last look back, shielding his narrowed eyes with his hand. The fire towered over the buildings alongside the river, and through the flames he could make out the great columns of the Temple of Jupiter rising up on the Capitoline Hill, bathed in a wavering red light.

Steeling himself, he shifted along the wharf until he found a gap between two burning vessels and jumped down. The water closed over his head, and at once its coolness embraced him. But there was no time to enjoy the sensation. He kicked with his feet and worked at the water with his free hand as he strove to regain the dull orange glow of the surface. Then his head burst into the air and he took a gasping breath. The current had swept him down towards the hull of a barge. He thudded against the timbers, then pushed himself away so that he was carried on past the vessel. Freeing the squirming puppy, he held it clear of the water. It spluttered and shook its head vigorously while Macro looked round for something to grab on to. There was plenty of debris in the river besides the usual refuse and spoil washed into the Tiber from the Great Sewer. Feeling something nudge his shoulder, he turned to see a half-submerged wooden structure on the surface, and realised that it was the mangled remains of a balcony.

'Here you go.' He lifted the puppy up so that its forepaws were over the rail, and then gripped on either side to hold the animal in place as the current took them away from the fire.

There were others in the water as well. Macro saw a man

flailing helplessly some fifty feet away before he was carried under and did not resurface. Several were striking out towards the far shore, while some, like Macro, were clinging to whatever was buoyant enough to keep them afloat as they issued desperate cries for help. As he spun slowly round, he was afforded a good view of the fire raging along the riverfront for several hundred paces, the flames and their glittering reflection in the river terrifying to behold. The far bank was lined with spectators looking on in silence. For a moment he wondered why no one was trying to rescue those in the water, and then he realised that the craft that had caught light presented a hazard to any other vessel that attempted to venture out.

The puppy was whimpering again, and Macro did his best to comfort it. 'There now, lad . . . or girl.' He realised that he had no idea what sex the animal was and decided to settle on male for the moment. 'All right, boy. We're out of the frying pan and escaped the fire, so let's count our blessings, eh? We'll get through this, you'll see. And when we do, I'll take you home and you can meet Petronella and Bardea. You'll like them. They're a soft touch for puppies like you. Just do that thing with the eyes and the tail and you're home and dry. We could use a new dog since we lost Cassius back in Britannia. He was a loyal mutt. Ugly as fuck, so you have the edge there. Hold on, my little friend, and stop trembling . . .'

The current carried them away from the fire and beyond the walls of the city. The sound of the blaze diminished and so did the cries of those in the water. Many floundered one by one and were dragged under. The luckier ones who had found something to cling on to fell silent too, realising they were beyond help from anyone on either side of the fast-flowing river. Macro tried to kick out with his legs and use an arm to propel the balcony towards the nearest bank, but the pain in his chest forced him to stop almost at once and just cling on. The flames steadily receded

218

into the night, and as he passed round a bend in the river, they disappeared from sight, only the red loom against the pall of smoke still visible.

Overhead, the last clouds from the storm had dispersed and the sky was strewn with stars, sharp and bright against the velvet backdrop. As he felt the cold seep into his limbs, Macro realised how exhausted his body was. Two days of marching and being drenched by the storm and baked by the fire had taken its toll, and he feared that the last of his strength might fade away if he could not escape from the river. Then, a short distance ahead, he saw a dark shape in the water. It was a small skiff, no more than ten feet in length and lying low in the water.

The wreckage of the balcony bumped softly against the side of the vessel and Macro lifted the puppy aboard before transferring his grip to the small boat's beam and attempting to pull himself up. The skiff tipped towards him and he feared it might capsize. He stopped struggling for a moment and gathered his strength for another less clumsy attempt. The puppy was barking again, and he felt it nuzzle and lick his fingers.

'Give me a moment, mutt . . .'

He tried again and this time managed not to rock the craft as he attempted to pull himself aboard. But his strength gave out once more and he slumped back into the water. He closed his aching eyes briefly and the desire for rest and surrender stole upon him. He blinked and stirred himself.

'I'm not going to be bloody food for fish . . . And I'll not abandon you, my furry friend. Hold on, here I come.'

Summoning the last of his strength, he gritted his teeth and tried again, this time succeeding in hooking a foot over the side and using it to help lever his body until he rolled into the skiff, flopping into the water that sloshed about inside it. The puppy splashed over to him and pulled itself up onto his chest, lying with its head between its paws as it trembled with cold and fear. Macro found that the water came up as far as his ears and presented no danger of drowning him. He lay there stroking the puppy's wet fur as he stared up at the stars. His eyelids closed, and shortly afterwards he was asleep.

He woke with a start as he felt the skiff lurch. The stars had gone and the thin light of the coming dawn surrounded him. He thought about trying to rise, but his body refused and he merely rolled his head to the side as he heard splashing close by.

'There's a body in this one,' a voice called out.

'I ain't a body, thanks,' Macro croaked feebly.

'By the gods. He's alive!'

A figure loomed over him. A young man, soon joined by another. They grasped the side of the boat and hauled it into the reeds along the bank, grounding it on a patch of mud in front of a grassy rise. Macro was helped out of the waterlogged skiff and up onto the grass, where he was laid out for closer inspection by the pair. The light was bright and he had to close his eyes.

'Who is he?' said a different voice. 'Has he got anything valuable on him?'

Macro felt hands searching the folds of his tunic.

'Wait!' the first voice cut in. 'See that seal? He's a soldier.'

'So?'

'So we don't rob from soldiers. My father's a retired legionary. He wouldn't stand for it.'

'No one's asking him to. What he doesn't know won't cause him any concern.'

'Give me a hand with him. We'll take him to the old man's inn.'

Macro was hauled up, and the youths each took an arm across their shoulder.

'Wait,' said Macro. 'Get the puppy . . . In the boat.'

One of them returned to the skiff and came back with the

bedraggled animal hanging limply in his hand. For an instant Macro feared it was dead, but then he saw it give a wriggle and he felt a wave of relief.

They made their way up the riverbank and onto a path that overlooked farmland. In the distance Macro could see the road that connected Rome and Ostia. To the north-west the smoke over Rome was clearly visible.

One of the men, the son of the former soldier, asked, 'Care to tell us how you came to be in the boat?'

'Later,' Macro croaked, his tongue and throat feeling dry and swollen. 'After I've had something to drink.'

'Fair enough. But I'll warn you now, if you turn out to be a wrong 'un, my father will drag you in chains back to Rome, or wherever you came from.'

'Fair enough . . .'

The inn was set a short distance from the road, and the proprietor came hurrying over as soon as he was aware of their approach. 'What's this, son?'

'We found him in the river. Him and the pup.'

'Catch of the day, eh?' The innkeeper chuckled for a moment before scrutinising Macro.

'He's a soldier,' said his son. 'He's wearing a seal.'

'My eyes work, lad. So what's a soldier doing in the river?' The question was directed at Macro. 'You don't look like a marine to me.'

Macro ran his tongue over his lips to moisten them. 'Wasn't in the river. Was in a boat. Need a drink. Water.'

The innkeeper regarded his drenched tunic. 'Looks like you've had enough water for the time being. Casca, bring me some watered wine. And a bowl and sponge for this man to clean himself up.'

The lad who had rifled Macro's body looking for loot slunk off to carry out the innkeeper's instructions.

'Some food wouldn't go amiss,' said Macro.

'I'm sure it wouldn't, but I'm running an inn here, not a soup kitchen for vagrants. You might be a soldier, or you might have stolen that seal to pretend you're one and play on my kindness.'

'For fuck's sake . . .' Macro cleared his throat and straightened his back. 'Centurion Macro, late of the army of Britannia and presently assigned to the urban cohorts. Now if you don't mind, I'd like some refreshment for me and the mutt.' He took the puppy back and sat down at one of the benches set up beside the road.

'So what's a centurion doing washed up in a boat on our stretch of the Tiber?' the innkeeper asked again.

'Long story. Got separated from my unit while fighting the fire and had to jump in the river.'

'And the puppy? Was he fighting the fire too?'

Macro shook his head. 'He's the reason I got separated. I rescued him from a burning building.'

The puppy sat up on Macro's lap, rested his paws on his chest and licked his chin, tail wagging once again.

'Looks like love at first sight to me.'

'He's staying with me,' Macro replied. 'After what we went through together, he's earned his billet.'

The innkeeper was about to say something else when he paused and looked at Macro more closely. 'Don't I know you?'

Macro shrugged.

'Yes . . . yes, I recall now. You stopped here a few years back. You and another officer, a woman and a kid. There was also a dog. Big ugly thing. Looks like you found him a friend.'

'The other dog's dead. Died in Britannia during the rebellion.'

'Ah, that's too bad. Well, now that I recall you, Centurion, I'll get you and your pup watered and fed before you go on your way. Back to Rome, I imagine.' He turned to his son and sent him for some stew and bread and two bowls. Then he sat opposite

Macro and gestured in the direction of the city. 'We had news of the fire yesterday. Was it as serious as they say?'

'Worse. By the time I was washed downriver, most of the warehouses had gone, along with Boarium. The plan was to contain the blaze, but I don't know if that succeeded. On top of what happened at Ostia, I'm starting to think the gods might just be a little pissed off with Rome right now.'

'We heard about the storm. And if the gods aren't already angry enough, there's worse to come. If what I hear is true, Caesar's about to ditch his wife and marry that ambitious tart Poppaea. She's poison, that one. At least that's what they say. I'm in no position to judge,' the man went on hastily to cover up for his indiscretion in front of one of Nero's soldiers. 'Now, Octavia's a good one. Does Rome proud and makes a wife worthy of any Caesar. The people love her. Caesar would be unwise to divorce her. After that business with his mother, he's upset a lot of people, and he might be living on borrowed time, some might say.'

'Some might. Wise people might want to think twice about airing their views on such matters. Friendly advice.'

'I know. I get it. I watch what I say around the customers most of the time, but I'm talking soldier to soldier now. Ah, here comes the food and drink, and water to clean yourself up.'

Macro nodded his thanks and ate hungrily for a moment before he remembered the puppy. He poured some of the stew into the second bowl and set it down beside the bench. 'There you go, sunshine.'

It occurred to him that he still didn't know what sex the dog was. He picked it up. 'A boy, then. Well, my little friend, we've been through the mill together and I risked my bloody neck to save you. That's a debt you'll be paying off for the rest of your life. So, you better have a name . . .' He thought a moment. 'Flaminius, I think.'

The puppy was ignoring him, head down in the bowl, eating

ravenously, his little body jerking with each mouthful taken. Macro returned to his own meal, and when he had finished, he mopped up the last of the stew with a piece of bread and sat back with a cheery burp.

'Always nice to have my food appreciated,' said the innkeeper as he came over. 'I expect you'll be needing to get back to your unit now. Want my boy to saddle up a couple of mules for the journey?'

The idea of sitting astride some bony mount did not appeal, and Macro shook his head. 'We'll walk, thanks.'

He reached for his purse, then growled with frustration when he recalled that it had been attached to his belt. 'I'll have to settle up when I next come this way.'

There was a cynical look on the innkeeper's face. Soldiers across the Empire were notorious for refusing to pay their way. He smiled. 'No need, Centurion. But thanks for the thought.'

They clasped forearms in farewell, then Macro scooped up the puppy, who was set on licking every last crevice of his bowl, and set off towards Rome.

CHAPTER NINETEEN

The following dawn was marred by the dark grey haze that hung over the city. The acrid tang of the fire still clung to the air in the imperial palace, even though most of the blaze had been extinguished or burned itself out during the night. The two firebreaks had done their work and contained the flames in time to prevent them spreading to consume more of the capital. Even so, much of the warehouse district lay in ruins, along with most of the Boarium and some of the poor neighbourhoods nearby. Thousands had been made homeless and the city's merchants had lost a fortune, their valuable goods imported from across the Empire reduced to ashes. But it was not these commodities that presented the greatest loss to Rome. Of greater concern to the emperor and his advisers was the grain that had been lost or scorched in the fire, in addition to the vast quantity that had gone to the bottom of the sea during the storm the night before.

Nero's audience chamber was thick with incense, lit by the household slaves in a futile attempt to overcome the stench left by the fire. The emperor himself had not yet joined the meeting, and the small group of men waiting for him were tense and weary. Besides Seneca, Burrus and Tigellinus, there was the quaestor in charge of the city's grain distribution, the chief of the grain merchants' guild, the tribunes of the Praetorian Guard and the prefects of the city watch and the urban cohorts.

Cato and his men had continued to deal with the blaze throughout the night, and he had been summoned from the front line to join the emergency council in the palace. His exposed flesh was streaked with grime and he had not had more than a few hours' sleep in the last two days. Every muscle in his body ached with exhaustion. Even though he craved rest, he knew that would not be possible until he could break the news about Macro's fate to Petronella and Bardea. It was a task he dreaded.

He had thought he had lost his closest friend after the fall of Camulodunum to Boudica's rebels, but Macro had escaped and returned to the fight. However, surely even Macro's resourcefulness could not save him from having a tenement block collapse on top of him. This time it was certain that he had perished. And yet . . . Cato could not help nursing hope, however far-fetched, that his friend had somehow escaped death again. As soon as the last of the remaining fires had been put out, he would have the ruins searched for Macro's body. He owed Petronella that much.

The thick curtain at the rear of the hall was swept aside by one of the German bodyguards, who stood to attention as the emperor swept by. Nero jumped lightly onto the dais and settled himself on the throne as those before him bowed their heads in deference.

'Gentlemen,' he began, 'we have all but defeated the fire. Now it is time to count the cost. The most pressing matter is what we do about the grain that was destroyed, both here in Rome and in Ostia. At present the people are still reeling from the impact of the blaze and the news of the storm. They haven't yet grasped that one disaster coinciding with the other is about to cripple the supply of grain. When they start to go hungry, the mob is going to look for someone to blame. There will be some hotheads who will point the finger at me in order to rouse the anger of the people. I will not let that happen. *You* will not let that happen . . .'

His words sounded like more of a threat than an instruction, thought Cato.

'You will be tasked with keeping order. I want a show of strength on the streets in the days to come. There will be no opportunity for the Praetorians to lounge around their barracks. The same goes for the men of the urban cohorts and the vigiles. If there are riots, trouble of any kind, you will use whatever force is required to suppress it. Do I make myself clear?'

'Yes, Caesar,' Tigellinus responded. 'If the scum try anything, you can be assured they will be treated as they deserve to be by the Praetorians.'

Burrus coughed. 'They are not your men yet, Tigellinus.'

'Nor are they yours,' Nero cut in tersely. 'They are mine. And their officers are chosen, and dismissed, by me. I will not tolerate dissent among my officers. If you two want to squabble like old hens, I will find new men to replace you.'

It seemed to Cato that Tigellinus was about to object but thought better of it and kept his mouth shut. Burrus lowered his head. 'As Caesar commands.'

'For now the priority is keeping control of the streets,' Nero continued.

'Caesar,' Seneca spoke up, 'I would imagine the priority is to arrange for emergency supplies of grain to be found for your people. If they are fed, they are less likely to take to the streets. As the saying goes, no kingdom or empire is ever more than five meals away from a revolution. Food and entertainment offer the best means of keeping order.'

Nero nodded slowly. 'That is true.' He turned to the quaestor. 'How much grain is left in the city?'

'Caesar, we haven't had time to calculate—'

'I want an answer, not excuses.' Nero glared at him.

The young official consulted his waxed tablet quickly. 'As Caesar has been informed, the fire destroyed the warehouses where the grain is stored. I . . . I would imagine therefore that the entire stock has been destroyed or rendered unusable. There might be some that we could salvage,' he added brightly. 'It may be scorched, but it is edible, I think.'

'You think,' Nero repeated scathingly. 'I'd like to see *you* eat it.'

He turned his attention to the chief of the grain merchants' guild. 'Let's hope you have better news for me. How much grain do your members hold in Rome?'

The man moistened his lips before he replied. 'Not nearly enough to feed the populace, Caesar. The guild supplies the needs of those who are not eligible for the grain dole, or who have no need of it. If we were to open our storerooms to you—'

Nero raised an eyebrow. 'If?'

The chief of the guild shook his head. 'Forgive me, Caesar. Of course my members will do all in their power to help Rome in its hour of need.'

'That's very public-spirited of you. So how many days' supply can you and your cronies provide?'

'Two, perhaps three days, Caesar.'

'I see. So unless we find a solution, within three days the city will go hungry.'

There was a moment's silence as the others in the room grasped the fearful significance of the estimate. The grain dole was handed out to some quarter of a million citizens to feed their families. However, as Cato knew, it was barely sufficient to keep them more than a few steps from starvation. If it became known that there was only three days before that happened, there would be panic. Accompanied by desperation and the rage that only a man who had seen his children starve was capable of.

'Then we must act, gentlemen,' said Nero. 'I want word sent to every town within a hundred miles of Rome to bring us whatever reserves of grain they may have. In the meantime, we will announce that I have taken over the guild's stocks and will ensure that my people are fed. That will go a long way to reassuring them.'

Cato felt alarm at the emperor's words as his mind swiftly went over the practicalities of the situation. It would take days for the message to reach the furthest towns, and days more for them to send grain convoys to Rome. An ox cart barely covered twenty miles on a good day. By the time any supplies started to arrive, it was possible that order would have broken down completely and the streets would be running with blood. Nor would the city's poor be the only victims when they turned their rage against the rich. The emperor's orders, well-meaning as they were, were not sufficient. There had to be a better way.

Cato looked round at the others, fixing his eyes on Seneca. Surely Nero's wisest adviser must see the peril of his master's thinking. But Seneca said nothing, and his face was an implacable mask so that it was impossible to tell what he might be thinking.

Nero made to rise from his throne and Cato knew that he had only moments to point out the grave danger facing the city and its ruler.

'Caesar, if I may speak?'

Nero hesitated, then resumed his seat. The others glanced at Cato with a mixture of surprise, curiosity and, in the case of Tigellinus, barely hidden glee.

The emperor frowned. 'What is it, Prefect Cato? Whatever you say, it had better be good. We have little time to waste. I am prepared to indulge you in gratitude for your service of the last two days, and out of respect for the death of your comrade, Centurion Macro. As fine a soldier as ever lived, I understand.'

'Yes, Caesar.' Once again the grief began to well up in Cato's heart, but he suppressed it. There would be time for that later. 'It occurs to me that if the people are told you have taken charge of the guild's grain, it won't take them long to work out that the stocks will not last long. What they need is reassurance.'

'And how do you propose I go about that?'

'They need to believe that there is enough grain to get the city through the temporary shortage.'

'Are you suggesting that I lie to them?'

'When the truth leads to disaster, a deceit is generally preferable.'

'Ha!' Tigellinus snorted. 'You would have Caesar lie to his people! How dare you suggest such a calumny?'

'Caesar, hear me out!' Cato called out over the other man.

Tigellinus took a step towards the dais to continue his protest, but Nero stopped him with a raised hand. 'Be quiet. I want to hear what he has to say.'

As Tigellinus backed off, the emperor turned to Cato. 'Choose your words carefully, Prefect. It would be disappointing to have your recent appointment cut short.' He spoke the last two words with heavy emphasis.

'Thank you, Caesar. I am not suggesting that you lie. Just that you don't tell the whole truth. The people need to be confident that you have the matter in hand and that they will be fed. It would be wise to keep it secret that stocks of grain have been sent for. If word of that got out, they would know that the situation in Rome is desperate and there would be panic. They need to believe that there is sufficient grain in the city to feed them as things stand.'

'But there isn't, is there?'

'No, Caesar. But you must convince them otherwise.'

'How?'

'I suggest a gesture. The quaestor says there may be some grain that is salvageable from the stocks that were scorched or contaminated by smoke. I would suggest that you have it all thrown into the Tiber.'

'What?' Tigellinus could not restrain himself. 'Are you mad? What we salvage might be enough to feed thousands of people. Caesar, this is madness.'

'Thousands, perhaps,' Cato continued. 'But that will make little difference in a day or two's time. Indeed, if the people are offered spoiled grain, it would expose how desperate the situation is. As Caesar has pointed out, no one would choose to consume such grain.'

'Not in normal circumstances.'

'We are not in normal circumstances, and we need the people to believe that the emperor has the remedy to hand. If Caesar makes a public announcement that the damaged grain is to be disposed of and that there is sufficient supply to feed the people, they will be reassured.'

'And when it turns out there isn't?' Tigellinus demanded. 'They'll want our heads.'

'*Your* heads maybe,' Nero interrupted. 'That is what I will offer them if that's what it takes to appease the mob. Go on, Cato.'

'If we move fast, we can get the first grain convoys from the closest towns before the last of the remaining supply runs out. After that, it's a question of keeping just enough reaching Rome to perpetuate the illusion until a fresh grain convoy can reach Ostia. I admit, it will be touch and go. But what better course of action is there? If the people are told the truth . . .' Cato shook his head. 'In the meantime, it might be wise to offer them a diversion. Put on some entertainments in the Great Circus. Some racing would do. That, or gladiator games.'

Nero stroked his chin as he considered Cato's scheme. At length he sighed with frustration. 'This is all damnable bad timing. I had hoped to announce that I will be divorcing Octavia to marry my Poppaea. That's going to cause bad feeling. Now I daren't go ahead until we have taken care of the grain situation. That's also going to cause trouble. Poppaea is not the most patient of women.'

He bunched a fist and repeatedly tapped it against his jaw. 'Even the gods seem to disapprove of my plans. One thing after another . . . All that anger over the execution of the slaves, then the storm and the fire, and all of it will delay what must be done to rid myself of Octavia and provide myself with a fertile wife and an heir to the Empire. Can't those ingrates out there understand I am doing this for them? Unless there is a clear line of succession, there will be chaos when I ascend to the heavens to join the gods. I am determined to have a peaceful transition of power to my heir.'

The emperor's anguish was a bit ripe, thought Cato. After all, every previous accession of an emperor had followed a well-worn path strewn with conspiracies, murders and scarcely credible accidents before the succession was resolved.

Nero straightened up abruptly. 'Wait . . . There's more to all this than there seems.'

He paused, and Seneca cleared his throat. 'Caesar?'

'The storm is one thing. But a fire the night after? A fire that just happens to break out among the imperial grain warehouses? That cannot be a mere coincidence.'

'That is the nature of coincidence, Caesar,' Seneca said gently. 'There is often no connection between events, however much we might wish there to be for the sake of an orderly explanation. In any case, the grain was only one of a wide range of goods destroyed in the fire. I would suggest that you put this down to bad luck. Bad timing, as you yourself said. I can see no connection between the storm and the fire, other than the predicament both have plunged us into.'

Nero smiled. 'Good Seneca, you have a rare intellect, but the heart and mind of a philosopher. As such you are inclined to see too much good in people and overlook the darkness in men's hearts. As emperor, I cannot afford to share such naïve optimism. I see all. I see the brutish inconstancy of the mob. Drunk with affection for me one day and baying for my blood the next, only to be bought off by gifts and entertainments. They can be played like a cheap cithara. And as we both know, there is none better at playing the instrument than I.'

He smiled, and Seneca bowed his head and opened his palms to concede the point. Then Nero's expression became more rigid. 'I also see the raw appetite for conspiracy that so many of our senators and their followers are forever dabbling in. Such plotters are like vermin, rats scuttling from one dark sewer to the next to commune with their kind. Their loyalty to each other is as shallow as their personal ambition runs deep. And there are no limits to what they are prepared to do to achieve their aims. What does it matter to them if the people are starved into insurrection so long as they tear everything down and leave a clear field for those who would replace me?' His eyes widened in wonder. 'The arrogance of their presumption is scornful. Do such mortals seriously think they could run an empire as I do? The fools. The evil fools. I am Rome, and Rome is me. Without me there can be no Rome!'

He tilted his head back and stared at his advisers as if challenging them for a response. Tigellinus duly obliged, as Cato had expected.

'Caesar, you are the darling of the gods, and beloved of the Senate and people of Rome. If ever there is discontent, then as you say, it can only be down to the evil that men do in the shadows. There is no other explanation.'

'Quite so, my friend. Which is why I want you and Burrus to investigate the cause of this fire. You are to send your spies out into the city. They are to visit every inn, every gaming den, every brothel and every market. I want every senator watched. Someone knows the truth about who is behind it. Whether the fire was caused by accident or design, someone knows. When the culprit is found, we will make an example of them to ensure that everyone understands the price of failing Caesar and the people of Rome.'

'Every senator, Caesar?' Seneca queried. 'Is that really necessary?'

'No exceptions. We must root these traitors out, one way or another. Burrus, Tigellinus, you have your orders. Put them into effect at once. I want results and I want them quickly. Once we have caught those responsible for the fire, I will have them turned over to the mob, and we all know how those lambs treat criminals who fall into their clutches. As for you others, I want your men armed to the teeth and on the streets. There will be no tolerating disorder of any kind. Knock heads together, break up any crowds and arrest anyone you suspect of hoarding food. Return to barracks to issue your orders. You are dismissed.'

The small group of advisers bowed their heads and began to back away towards the entrance of the audience chamber.

'Prefect Cato, a moment.' Nero gestured to him to approach the dais.

Cato felt his heartbeat quicken. He had taken a risk in speaking up earlier, and it was clear that his fate hinged on the success of the deception he had talked the emperor into. Not just his fate. If the grain supply failed, or was too limited to stave off hunger, then the fate of many more hung in the balance. Possibly that of Nero as well. There was also the danger that the truth would slip out, and then the capital's rumour mill would start to work its poison and the panic and violence that Cato feared would grip the city.

He approached the dais and Nero waited as his other advisers left the chamber. Tigellinus was the last to go, pausing on the threshold to cast a final hostile look at Cato. Then the German bodyguards on either side closed the doors. The emperor regarded Cato sympathetically for a moment.

'Is there no hope that Centurion Macro is alive?'

'There is always hope, Caesar. Especially with regard to Macro.'

'Do you really believe that? Be honest with me.'

Cato hesitated a beat and then shook his head.

'That's too bad. I wish I had known him better. You were close?'

234

'As close as it gets. He was my best friend and like a brother to me. He is also a husband and father.' Cato caught himself. Weariness was fogging his mind, otherwise he would never have given any hint of Bardea's existence. If the truth of her origins was ever revealed, she would be at risk from those whose thirst to avenge the atrocities of the Boudican revolt was insatiable. He swallowed and quickly continued to try and cover up his error. 'I will need to break the news to his wife as soon as possible, Caesar.'

'Indeed.' Nero nodded reflectively. 'It's a sad tale. The stuff of tragedy. I might use it as inspiration for a lament. Or perhaps a poem. It has all the ingredients an artist requires.'

'Yes, Caesar,' Cato replied flatly. 'I am sure that will be a great comfort to his grieving widow.'

'I can imagine,' said Nero. 'To be honoured so . . . Maybe in the years to come I will be able to do the same for you.'

'You are too kind, Caesar.'

Nero nodded graciously and lifted a finger towards the doors. 'You may leave. Continue to serve me well, Prefect Cato, and you will go far.'

CHAPTER TWENTY

Seneca was waiting in the outer court and approached Cato as he emerged from the main entrance of the palace complex.

'You constantly surprise me, Prefect Cato.'

'Pleasantly, I hope.'

'Do you mind if I walk with you some of the way? I believe we are both going in the same direction.'

It was a loaded remark for all the senator's casual tone, and Cato realised that this was the man's stock in trade. The calm indifference he exuded was intended to be disarming. The impression was not that he was concealing any scheming; rather that he simply could not be bothered to be involved in such things. Therefore he could be trusted to a greater degree than those who wore their ambition as if it was a badge of honour. It was a shrewd artifice and one that had served him well.

'I understood you have a rather palatial residence on the Aventine. I am returning to the urban cohort camp. There wouldn't appear to be much overlap as far as us travelling in the same direction goes, wouldn't you say?'

Seneca smiled. 'Indulge me. Let's go your way for a distance. I could use the exercise and a little stimulating conversation. I find one is rather starved of the latter in the court of Caesar.'

'As you wish.' Cato set off for the ramp leading down into the Forum and Seneca had to scurry a few paces to fall in at his side.

'That was an impressive piece of work,' the senator said, clasping his hands behind his back as he walked. 'Not to mention courageous. I am not sure I could have got away with persuading Nero to lie so brazenly to the mob.'

'Oh, I am sure you could have managed it just as easily and with far more aplomb. Besides, if the grain can be supplied in time, there is no brazen lie, merely a certain economy with the truth. I imagine that's how a politician would justify such a stratagem to exculpate himself from any charge of dishonesty. As for whether he could so easily square it with his conscience, who knows?' Cato shrugged.

'You don't like those of us who have the honour of holding senatorial rank, do you? Do you really think you have more integrity?'

'My dislike is not a matter of integrity,' Cato replied. 'More a result of hard-won experience.'

'Then from experience you will know that there are always honourable exceptions within any aristocratic class, however venal the generality may appear.'

Cato gave him a wry glance. 'Such as yourself, I take it?'

Seneca laughed briefly. 'Oh, dear gods, not me. Not any longer. I used to be a more idealistic fellow in my youth. Quite the stoic philosopher that it suits Nero to think I am. However, that Seneca withered away a long time ago. Too much contact with the exigencies of guiding a wilful and flawed emperor to do the right thing in the execution of his duties.'

'Execution of duties, now there's an interesting choice of words.'

'Come now, Cato!' There was a trace of irritation in the other man's voice. 'Don't be so priggish. You've seen more than enough bloodshed during your army service. I'll wager that you accept much of that was necessary, or at least unavoidable, to achieve some noble aim or other. Well?'

It was a fair point, Cato conceded, but he did not respond.

'We both serve the Empire in different ways,' Seneca continued. 'The enemies of Rome die either way. So spare me any claim to the moral high ground. If there is a difference between soldiers and statesmen, it resides only in the fact that it is easier for you to identify the enemies you face. The challenge is rather harder for those in my position. Especially if the enemy, the man who is betraying the interests of the people of Rome, turns out to be its ruler.'

They had reached the bottom of the ramp and Cato paused mid step and looked round quickly. There were individuals and small groups passing them on either side, making for the palace or leaving it, but none seemed to be paying them any attention.

'You should watch your tongue, Senator,' he said quietly. 'Words have a way of finding their way back to dangerous men. Men like Tigellinus.'

'I was making an abstract point.'

'Of course you were . . .'

'Emperors come and go. The good ones tend not to make enemies of the Senate and work with us to run the Empire for the good of Rome. The bad tend to be removed, one way or another, before they do too much damage. Rome is a success story, Prefect Cato. And for it to continue to be so we must all remember one thing – in order for things to stay the same, things must change. Including emperors. That is how it has been since the time of Augustus. For the present, Caesar has played his hand well, under my guidance. He has honoured his promise to work alongside the Senate and resist any temptation to launch political prosecutions.'

'But . . .'

Seneca looked round before he continued in an undertone. 'I fear that he is on the cusp of changing direction and leading us into conflict between the palace, the Senate and the mob. When . . . if that happens, we will all have to pick a side.'

'And you, Senator? Will you do the right and brave thing and put Rome before your oath of loyalty?'

'I will do whatever is necessary.'

'Even if you have to burn Rome to the ground to do it?'

Seneca's eyes narrowed. 'I hope you aren't suggesting I had anything to do with the fire.'

'Did you?'

'No.'

Cato scrutinised the other man's expression for a moment, but the impassive mask had slipped back into place.

'Would you have the courage to put Rome before your life? I wonder . . .'

'I would, in a heartbeat.' Seneca drew himself up. 'And so would many others in the Senate. Not only them, but many in the equestrian class as well. People of your kind.'

'Then you won't need me.'

'At such times, men like you are precisely the kind who are needed.'

'You mean men backed up by thousands of soldiers.'

'There is that . . .'

Cato nodded. 'Good. Some honesty at last. You may find that sometimes speaking the truth carries more weight than flattery or lies.'

'I'll bear that in mind, though all three approaches have their merits, as you demonstrated admirably back there with Nero.'

Cato's mind was heavy with exhaustion, and it was hard to focus on the games the older man was playing with him. He needed to get away. Get away from the palace and return to camp. There he could rest briefly, clear his head and prepare himself to speak to Petronella and Bardea. He stifled a yawn and blinked his dry eyes to try and refresh them.

'This is where we part ways, Senator. I doubt we will be

travelling in the same direction in the days to come. If ever. Good day.'

He made to turn away, but Seneca extended a finger and pressed it against his chest. 'You need to think about what I said. There will come a time when you have to make a choice. Sooner than you think.' He fixed Cato with his dark eyes before lowering his hand. Then, scanning those leaving the palace, he called out a friendly greeting – 'Gaius Sertorius! Haven't seen you in months, old lad. Where have you been?' – and strode off with leopard-like litheness towards a pasty-looking man in a toga that struggled to encompass the considerable girth beneath.

Cato took a deep breath and set out across the Forum in the direction of the camp. To his left, thin columns of smoke were still rising from the scene of the fire. Seneca might be telling the truth about not having a hand in the burning of the warehouses, and it might be coincidence that it had happened on the back of the storm. If so, it played into the hands of anyone conspiring against the emperor. Too conveniently for Cato's liking. He recalled the group he had encountered at Vespasian's house a few nights before and wondered if they were capable of such a deed. The prospect of someone using the hunger of countless thousands as a weapon to attack one man sickened him. He could believe that the likes of Piso or Lucanus might entertain such a thing. Perhaps even Seneca, who would no doubt be able to use his superior intellect to rationalise the suffering as a price worth paying in the greater scheme of things. For such men, the poor and downtrodden rarely amounted to more than a background detail in their vision of Rome, and the significance of the part they played in perpetuating that vision.

It was Vespasian's possible complicity that troubled Cato the most. He had encountered the legate for the first time shortly after joining the Second Legion at its fortress on the northern frontier. From the outset, he had admired his commander and considered him to be one of the finest senior officers in the army. Intelligent, flexible, courageous, inspiring and driven by a sense of duty, he was also driven to prove that though he lacked the illustrious aristocratic pedigree of his rivals, he was no less a hero of Rome. That appealed strongly to Cato's sense of his own ambitions. Though he would never become a senator, he had risen higher within the army than he had dared to hope when he first enlisted and served as a lowly optio in Macro's century. If Vespasian had played a part in causing the fire, it would be a crushing blow to the faith Cato had placed in his superior's integrity.

Vespasian was a better man that that, he tried to reassure himself as he trudged wearily back to the camp. His thoughts inevitably turned to Macro, and he had to steady himself. The time to grieve was not now. He must ready his men to keep order on the streets of the capital in the days to come. The plan he had laid before Nero was a desperate measure and would succeed only if fresh grain reached Rome in time while the truth remained concealed from the people. If the enemies of the emperor chose to spread rumours about the true peril facing the city, the storm would break with such violence it would dwarf the destruction endured over the last two days.

Cato entered the camp, acknowledging the salute of the sentries on the gate. Around the parade ground men lay sleeping in front of their stuffy barrack blocks. Others were tending to the wounded, dressing burns and injuries from falling debris. Several men had been lost fighting the fire. There would be funerals to arrange for those whose bodies had been recovered and memorial addresses for those whose remains lay under the ruins, Macro among them. There would be little chance to deal with such formalities in the days to come. Every soldier in Rome would be needed to keep order on the streets. Cato decided to let his men rest for a few more hours at least before he began to send out patrols.

241

When he reached the headquarters tower, he found it deserted. Every man had been called upon to fight the blaze, and the clerks were no doubt resting too. Cato climbed the stairs, intending to have Trebonius bring him something to eat and drink before he took to his bed for a few hours. As he reached the commanding officer's quarters, he heard a deep rumbling snore and smiled. It seemed that even his servant had succumbed to exhaustion. That was too bad. He took a deep breath as he entered his office and prepared to issue his orders.

'Treb—' He stopped mid stride, his jaw slack with astonishment. On the couch below the open window lay Macro, mouth open, chest rising evenly as he snored and exhaled with a rhythmic snort. Cato's gaze was drawn to a movement beneath the couch, and a puppy emerged. It took a couple of tentative steps towards him before it opened its muzzle to yawn. Then, with a shake of its head, it trotted jauntily forward. He kneeled down to stroke the soft rolls of fur along its back.

'I wonder what your story is, my little friend? Time for that later. More to the point, what's Macro's story, eh?'

He straightened up and regarded his friend in wonder. Macro had more lives than a cat. Several cats, in fact. There was a sudden upwelling of emotion in Cato's heart – relief, joy and affection swirled within him, and he lurched towards his friend and shook his shoulder. 'Macro! By all the gods, man!'

Macro's eyes blinked open and he shook his head briefly before focusing on the grinning face looming over him. He gave a cough to clear his dry throat. 'Ah, it's you. What's the matter, lad? You look like you've seen a ghost.'

'Certainly feels like it!'

He rose and swung his boots off the couch as he saw the puppy trying to jump up the side of Cato's leg. 'Ah, I see you've met little Flaminius.'

'Flaminius?' Cato glanced down. 'You disappear, presumed

dead, and all the while you've been out and about looking for a pet? Tell me it isn't true.'

Macro grasped the puppy by the scruff of its neck and set it down in his lap. 'It's thanks to this one that I went into that tenement block. Did a passable impersonation of a baby crying out. By the time I found him, the building was a goner. We just got out in time but were cut off and had to go into the river to get away from the flames. The Tiber's pretty chilly and the current is bloody strong, I can tell you. Anyway, we were washed away down the river before we eventually got back onto dry land and made our way here. Caught up with Lemulus and his lads on their way back from Ostia just as they reached the city.'

Cato chuckled. 'Only you could make escaping death by a hair's breadth sound so straightforward.'

Macro affected a hurt look. 'What? Did you really think you'd seen the last of old Centurion Macro? Bloody hell, lad. You know me better than that. Charon's going to be working long hours of overtime before he gets his hands on me. I ain't going nowhere. Not least because Petronella would never forgive me if I was knocked on the head.' His expression became more serious. 'Speaking of which, the less said to her about what happened the better, eh?'

Cato nodded his assent. 'I think we could both use some wine.'

He left the room briefly and made for Trebonius's small pantry. When he returned with a jar of Falernian and two silver goblets, he found Macro gently rubbing the puppy's belly as it lay on its back between his thighs, legs flopped apart and eyes closed in bliss.

'What are you going to do with him?' Cato asked as he set down the goblets, pulled out the stopper and poured the wine.

'Given what he put me through, it would be just deserts if I kicked him onto the street. But the little feller's grown on me.'

'Puppies will do that.'

'Aye . . .'

For a moment both men recalled Cassius, the faithful mongrel that had attached itself to Cato before it was killed during the assault on Camulodunum by Boudica and her rebels.

'I've decided to keep him. I don't need a mascot trailing me around the camp, so I'll give him to Bardea to raise. Something for her to care for and to distract her from her woes.'

'Good idea.' Cato handed him a goblet and Macro raised it in a toast.

'To Fortuna. May she always spare her favoured sons.'

'And may she always spare me from having to break the news to Petronella that your luck has finally run out,' said Cato with feeling.

'That too.'

They drained the goblets in one, content to let the fine wine slake their thirst and warm their souls. Then Cato refilled them and pulled up a stool, and they sat for a moment sipping in silence. Words to express their pleasure were not needed. At length he sighed wearily.

'You'd do well to go home and get some rest. We're in for a hard time of it.'

'Oh? Do tell.'

Cato related the details of the meeting at the palace and the plan that Nero had agreed to.

'Desperate stuff,' said Macro. 'Do you really think the truth can be kept from the people long enough to make it work? You know what a rumour mill this city is.'

'What other choice is there? If they knew the truth, Rome would become a tinderbox and the next fire would be far more difficult to put out. I've got fewer than three thousand men under my command, and there are ten thousand Praetorians. The vigiles aren't real soldiers and won't be much help. If there's trouble then they'll be hard pressed to even defend their watchhouses.

Thirteen thousand men all told, tasked with keeping control of a population of over a million. Not great odds at the best of times. If the people start to go hungry, they'll be desperate. If they get to know the truth, it's a racing certainty that they'll tear the city apart.'

'I would think so, and who could blame them?'

Cato shrugged. 'Maybe, but we have a duty to keep order regardless of our sympathies. Whether we're facing barbarians on the frontier or our own people on the streets of Rome, we're bound by our oath and by the orders given to us.'

'Really?' Macro stared at him. 'I seem to recall you taking a fairly flexible approach to orders in the past. On many occasions. Why the change of heart?'

Cato was silent as he formed his answer. 'There are some in Rome who are prepared to use the situation as a weapon to remove Nero.'

'Aren't there always? Same goes for every emperor. What's new?'

'I've encountered them in person.'

'Ah.' Macro cleared his throat. 'When you say encountered . . .'

Cato related the details of the dinner at Vespasian's house and his exchange with Seneca. He hesitated before asking, 'What's your opinion of Vespasian? Is he a man you would trust?'

Macro reflected briefly. 'Hard to say. When we served under him, I was confident in his abilities as a commander and trusted that he wouldn't risk our lives unnecessarily. I respected him as a soldier. If that amounts to trust, then yes, I trusted him back then. But now? He's moved on from being a soldier to bigger and better things. These days he's a politician.' He shook his head. 'Tends to be the way for most of his kind. Only a rare few stick with the army and see it through to the end. Corbulo, for instance. That one will die in the garb of a soldier if I'm any judge of the man. Why do you ask?'

'I'm starting to wonder if our former commander is becoming rather *too* political. It's not just that he's involved with the group opposed to Nero. They're plotting something, that's clear enough, though I don't know how far their plans have advanced. Then there's the fire, hot on the heels of the storm. Two hits to the city's grain supply in as many days. The first was a freak of nature. The second? It feels like too much of a coincidence.'

'Are you saying they were responsible for the fire? You think Vespasian could be involved with something like that? I'm struggling to believe it, even if he ain't the same man we once knew.'

Before Cato could respond, they heard footsteps climbing the stairs and turned to see a man in the livery of the palace on the threshold.

'Prefect Cato?'

'That's me.'

'Message for you, sir. From Prefect Burrus. Most urgent.'

He approached and held out a small leather tube. Cato took it and the man stepped back.

'What now?' Cato asked wearily as he looked at the messenger. 'Do you know anything about this?'

'I'm not in a position to say, sir.'

'Will you require a reply from me?'

He shook his head, and Cato dismissed him. The messenger trotted back towards the stairs. Breaking the seal, Cato took out the flimsy-looking roll of papyrus, unravelled it and began to read.

CHAPTER TWENTY-ONE

Macro listened carefully as Cato read the message aloud. *'From Sextus Afranius Burrus, prefect commanding the Praetorian Guard, to Quintus Licinius Cato, prefect commanding the urban cohorts, greetings. Upon reflection, subsequent to the audience held earlier this morning, Caesar has resolved that the public announcement concerning the disposal of the burned grain should be delivered without delay and that the said grain should be dumped into the Tiber immediately after the announcement, in full view of the people of Rome. After consulting with his advisers Caesar has determined that the disposal of the grain should be carried out by the urban cohorts. Therefore, in Caesar's view, the announcement itself should be delivered by the officer in charge of the operation, from the rostrum in the Forum. You are therefore required to present yourself at the head of one of your cohorts at the appointed place upon receipt of this order.'*

As Cato lowered the papyrus, Macro shook his head. 'That has to be the wordiest form of saying "I'm dropping you right in the shit" that I have ever heard. The fuckers . . .'

Cato could guess at the reason for Burrus's uncharacteristic loquacity. He was trying to tip Cato off that those closest to Nero had put him up to this. Tigellinus, most likely. It was possible that Poppaea might have had a hand in it too.

'They're setting you up,' Macro observed. 'If things don't work out and the mob goes hungry, it will be your head they come for.

You'll be the one held responsible for tipping the spoiled grain in the river. Nero will throw you to the wolves. And if things do work out, you can be bloody sure that you won't get to mount the rostrum to receive the grateful thanks of the people. That'll be the golden boy.'

'Of course it will,' Cato agreed drily. 'Thus it ever was.'·

'It stinks.'

He nodded and gave a deep sigh, then straightened up, trying to shake off his fatigue. If there was going to be trouble, he wanted his best men at his back. Crossing to the window overlooking the interior of the camp he called out, 'First Cohort will fall in at once!'

He saw the men stir and turn towards the tower, many of their faces still streaked with grime. There was a palpable lethargy about them.

Macro lowered Flaminius to the floor and strode over to join Cato.

'You heard the prefect! On your feet and form up! If I catch any idle layabouts when I get down there, I'll kick 'em up the arse so hard I'll knock their teeth out! Move!'

He drew back from the window as the men below rushed to obey the order, and scooped up the puppy. 'Got a room I can shut him in?'

'Anywhere but the pantry. Put him on the terrace. He'll be safe there. You can take him to Bardea when we've finished our little excursion to the Forum.'

Macro and Cato led the First Cohort out of the barracks shortly afterwards. It was nearly noon, and even though the sun was struggling to break through the haze hanging over the city, the streets were stifling. The stench of burning made matters worse, catching in the throat and leaving a bitter taste on the tongue. There was a palpable tension in the expressions of the people they marched past, and Cato felt the hairs on the back of his neck prickle.

Before they'd left the camp, he had addressed his men, noting the exhausted and strained expressions on their faces. Despite being gratified that they stood to attention, shoulders back, heads raised, ready for duty, he was aware that tired men often made bad decisions. After relaying the order he had received from Burrus, he made it clear that the soldiers of the cohort must not provoke the mob. Whatever insults or missiles came their way, they must not react unless ordered to by Cato. He hoped his words would be heeded.

Later, there would be time to rest the cohort until the next day. The Second Cohort would patrol the streets when night came and then be relieved by the Third the following morning, when the First would become the reserve formation, ready to march swiftly to any part of the city to support their comrades. That would be the pattern for the coming days, perhaps months, until the grain supply was fully restored. It would place considerable strain on the men, but thanks to their recent training regime, Cato was confident they could deal with the challenge.

They reached the foot of the Capitoline Hill, where the column separated, with Lemulus taking two centuries down to the ruined warehouses and burned hulks of the grain barges. Cato had instructed him to make preparations to dump the scorched grain while putting aside any undamaged supplies they might find and keeping them under guard until they could be transferred to the cellars of the palace.

As Lemulus marched his men off, Macro regarded them longingly. 'We could do with them if things turn sour in the Forum.'

'If that happens, I doubt another two centuries would make much difference,' Cato replied. 'It's more important that I present people with the news that the disposal of grain has already started. It'll be too late for anyone to intervene then.'

'And it will be too late to change your mind if that turns out to be a mistake, lad. We might end up having our heads follow the grain into the Tiber.'

Cato had weighed it up before issuing his orders to Lemulus. Macro had a point, but he calculated that people tended to be more accepting of a course of action that had already been set in motion. 'Let's hope not, eh?'

As the Third Century came up, the two men resumed their place at the head of the diminished column and at the next junction turned in the direction of the Forum, passing between the Temple of Jupiter on the Capitoline and the imperial palace perched atop the Palatine. Cato wondered if Nero and his closest cronies were up there, waiting and watching to see how things turned out as he broke the news to the mob and did his best to placate them. The noise of the crowd gathered in the Forum was like the surf of a great ocean gently breaking on the shore. It was a sibilant sound, more subdued than the usual cacophony of merchants, street performers and others shouting to be heard above the general hubbub. There was an anxious expectation in the air. Cato could sense it as he led his men into the open area that stretched across the heart of the great capital.

At the sight of the column of soldiers, those closest drew aside and grew quiet. Cato and his men tramped across the cobblestones and made for the steps that led up to the rostrum. The public speaking platform had been constructed to resemble the bows of a large warship projecting into the Forum. It had stood for hundreds of years, and many of Rome's most prominent statesmen, and villains, had addressed the people of the city from there. Great victories had been celebrated, terrible defeats announced, heroes honoured and traitors vilified. Cato was aware of the weight of such history, and he hesitated before climbing the final flight of steps. Macro ordered the men to form up at the top of the stairs that surrounded the large reviewing area behind the rostrum. They stood closed up, four deep, shields raised and spears grounded.

As Cato came to the edge of the rostrum, he saw the expanse of faces turned towards him, wearing expressions of curiosity, anxiety and hostility. A hush steadily spread across the mob, followed by a stillness as they waited to see what his arrival portended. He felt his heart quicken as he became the focus of tens of thousands of pairs of eyes. He glanced at the terraces of the palace in the hope of catching sight of the emperor and his retinue, anything to divert the attention of the mob and spare him the need to begin his address. But if Nero and the others were watching, they were careful not to reveal themselves. Cato silently cursed them before drawing a long, deep breath and raising his arms.

'People of Rome! I am Licinius Quintus Cato, prefect of the urban cohorts.'

His voice echoed off the walls of the palace, temples and other public buildings that lined the Forum, amplifying his words.

'I have been sent by Caesar to reassure you that the last of the flames have been put out and the extent of the damage is being assessed. Caesar asks—'

'The grain!' a voice called out. 'What of the grain? The grain barges were destroyed along with the warehouses. Are we to go hungry?'

Cato shook his head in a deliberate gesture and raised his hands again as other voices joined in, demanding an answer.

'Quiet!' he shouted. 'Still your tongues!'

The harshness of his tone commanded their silence, and he waited until he judged he could be clearly heard once more. 'Caesar gives his word that no one will go hungry! It is true that much grain was lost in the fire—'

'What about the storm?' another man cried. 'The grain fleet was wrecked. There is no grain!'

251

Cato cut in quickly before the man's words could provoke the crowd. 'That is a lie! There is more than enough grain to feed Rome! Caesar has been wise enough to ensure that there is always a reserve stored in the great vaults beneath the palace! Even now, the quaestor in charge of the grain dole and his staff are arranging for you all to be fed.'

'Bollocks!' someone retorted. '*You* are the liar! There is no reserve! We will starve!'

Before Cato had a chance to reply, angry shouts and further accusations spread the length and breadth of the Forum. Fists were shaken and fingers stabbed at him as the mob vented its fear and disbelief. He raised his hands once more to try and quieten them, but the protests swelled. Abruptly he drew his sword and swept the edge along the granite parapet of the rostrum. A sharp metallic rasp cut through the noise as sparks flew, and the shouting quickly died away as all eyes once again focused on the solitary figure on the speaker's platform.

Cato lowered his blade to his side. 'No one is going to starve! Caesar has given his word! If any person here doubts the word of Caesar, than come forward and speak up!'

As he had anticipated, no one was foolish enough to respond, and he allowed a brief silence before he continued.

'You have Caesar's promise that he will ensure his people are fed. I believe him. I have seen the grain in the cellars. Mountains of it. More than enough for months to come! There is no need for concern! No need for fear that anyone will go hungry. Those who say otherwise, those who spread false rumours, are traitors! The agents of plotters conspiring against our beloved Caesar. Cowards who spew their lies from the shadows and seek to poison our minds against the very man who labours night and day to fill our bellies and lavish us with entertainments and gifts!' Cato pointed towards the palace. 'Even now he is drafting regulations to ensure that no unscrupulous merchant can hoard grain or try to raise his prices to take advantage of the temporary shortage caused by the storm and the fire! He does this for you! He puts your welfare ahead of all others! He does this because he loves you and seeks only to protect you. You, the people of Rome.'

'Bullshit!' A burly man some twenty paces into the crowd cupped his hands to his mouth. 'Nero loves only himself and that whore Poppaea! His abuse of Octavia is a scandal! He shames Rome!'

While some cheered, Cato could see that most looked anxious. Rightly so. Such words could get a man killed. The crowd stirred warily, as if waiting for a response from the soldiers behind the rostrum. He felt his stomach tighten with dread. The man had spoken the truth as far as Cato was concerned, but he dared not let the situation slip out of control. Already a rising chorus called out her name, a swelling rhythm whose four beats reverberated across the Forum.

'Oc-ta-vi-a!'

Nero could surely hear the chant, and Cato feared his reaction. Not just for his own sake but for the countless thousands in the crowd before him. If the Praetorians were sent in, there would be screaming, panic, a crush and a bloody massacre before the day was out. He cleared his throat and spat to one side before he cried out to be heard again.

'It is a lie to say Caesar does not love you! He has given over many of his gardens in Rome to you, his people. When you have suffered, he has wept alongside you. His greatest concern is to do right by Rome. To do that, he needs to ensure that there is order, and for that order to endure, he needs an heir. The lady Octavia is as noble, honourable and revered as any great Roman woman who ever lived. But she is barren. That is her burden. But it is also Caesar's burden and therefore our burden. That is why he must find another to be mother of his heir. He does it for you!' He punched his arm out and swept his finger over the crowd. 'For you! For Rome! The greatest empire ever to have risen anywhere in the known world!'

There was uncertainty in the expressions of those in the crowd, and Cato sensed that their mood was finely balanced. He needed to act swiftly to turn them against those who spoke up against Nero.

'Who among you would be so base as to utter dark lies about Caesar's integrity? Who would be so craven as to do the work of Caesar's enemies? Caesar's enemies are our enemies! Who among you is no more a true Roman than the foulest rat scurrying through the filth of the Great Sewer?'

He let his challenge echo off the walls of the surrounding temples and public buildings as his gaze swept over the mob, daring any to defy him. Then he raised his sword again and brandished it overhead. 'As Caesar has given his word, so I give my word! I swore an oath to serve and protect Rome. I have devoted my life to fighting the enemies of Rome and I bear the scars to prove it. I would willingly lay down my life for Rome, its people and Caesar. And if I, who have given so much, along with all the other soldiers who guard our frontiers, have willingly made such a sacrifice, then who among you would betray the blood we have shed on your behalf? Who would so dishonour themselves by echoing the cries of traitors? Who would stoop so low as to deny the love Caesar has for us?'

He searched out the burly man, who was backing away through the crowd, and pointed his finger as he shouted, 'You! You would!'

The man turned and began to push his way through towards the far end of the Forum. He managed no more than ten paces before he was punched. There were more blows as he staggered on and then dropped out of sight beneath a flurry of fists. The sight sickened Cato and he felt shame at his provocation. He told himself it was necessary. Like the orders he had been obliged to give many times to send men into peril, often at the cost of their lives. Necessity licensed his lies. He could imagine Seneca offering such a justification, but to Cato his words had felt like poison in his mouth, and the aftertaste of bitter shame and humiliation was almost unbearable. It took great effort to force himself to resume his address to the crowd.

'There will be no hunger. There will be no tolerance of those who spread rumours and lies against Caesar. There will be no tolerance of those who try to provoke violence. The grain dole will continue as before and there will be no tolerance of price gouging by merchants.' He paused and swallowed as he came to the matter he had been laying the groundwork for. 'Such is Caesar's confidence that there is more than enough to feed his people that he has ordered the disposal of all the grain damaged by the fire. Even now, it is being thrown into the Tiber, along with all the other ruined and damaged cargoes aboard the burned ships and in the warehouses . . .'

A silence settled on the crowd as they took in his announcement. Some appeared shocked, others afraid. Still others angry. But none dared to voice a challenge and Cato had no desire to give them enough time to do so. He raised his arm in salute.

'Hail, Caesar! Now disperse and go about your business!'

He gave them a final stern look before sheathing his sword, turning away and descending from the rostrum to join Macro and his men. He could not meet Macro's gaze for the shame that burned in his veins. It was not just the lies about the grain, but the pain of surrendering his sense of honour to try to keep the peace. If that sacrifice prevented riots and saved lives, he would live with the stain on his reputation that would endure to his dying day. If violence broke out, he was doubly damned in his own eyes and those of all who knew him.

Macro said nothing, but regarded his friend with aching pity. He knew what Cato's performance had cost him and he also knew that it was not something that could be spoken about for a while yet. Instead he saluted and addressed his superior formally.

'What are your orders, sir?'

'Orders . . .' Cato took a moment to clear his mind. 'We'll link up with Lemulus and finish the disposal of the spoiled grain. Then it's back to the camp.'

By the time the column reached the Tiber, a large number of people who had been in the Forum had already reached the scene. They looked on in numbed disbelief as the soldiers on board the surviving barges tipped the scorched jars and poured the blackened contents into the swift current. Other items of ruined cargo went the same way before those vessels that were beyond repair were cut loose.

Lemulus had been given strict orders not to allow his men to loot anything, nor to permit any civilians to do likewise. As Cato arrived on the scene, he saw a squad of soldiers pushing back a small crowd trying to enter the ruins of one of the warehouses along the river. The men used their shields to batter the looters, and when they were faced with defiance, they lowered the points of their spears and drove the civilians away.

Lemulus came over as soon as he spotted Cato, and the two men exchanged a salute.

'Any trouble?' asked Cato.

'Some. We had to clear the wharf and warehouses before we could start dumping the grain. We're not going to be the most popular people in Rome, sir.'

'I can imagine. Any casualties?'

'Not on our side. As for the others . . .' Lemulus pointed to several bodies further down the wharf, and Cato mentally winced at the sight. That was going to cause anger and resentment when the news was carried back to the neighbourhood of the victims. One more potential spark in the precarious tinderbox that threatened to burn Rome to the ground.

'Have our medics do what they can for the wounded. Get 'em patched up and sent on their way.'

'Yes, sir.'

'How far have you got with the grain?'

The centurion glanced round. 'We've finished with the warehouses. There's only a few more barges to deal with and then we're done.'

Cato nodded with satisfaction. 'Very good. As soon as you're done, we'll return to camp.'

'How did it go in the Forum, sir?'

He managed to keep his expression neutral as he replied. 'What needed to be said was said.'

He strode past the centurion and made for the edge of the wharf as if to inspect the progress on the remaining barges. Lemulus's gaze followed him for a moment before he turned to Macro with a questioning look. 'What's up with the prefect? I take it things didn't go as well as one might hope.'

'I wouldn't press the issue if I were you.' Macro glanced over the sullen crowd that had gathered to witness the disposal of the grain. 'Sooner we're on our way back to camp the better. Carry on.'

Lemulus made his way back to his men while Macro scratched his bristly chin and yawned so widely that his jaw made a cracking sound. They were all exhausted to the point of collapse, and that didn't bode well at a time when the teeming multitude of the city's population was teetering on the edge of violence. But there would be little hope of any rest and recuperation for a while yet. It reminded him of some of the hard-pressed campaigns he had served in throughout his army career. It seemed ironic that what should have been a comfortable billet in the great city might turn out to be the cause of more strain and constant vigilance than any march through the heart of enemy territory.

CHAPTER TWENTY-TWO

Nero held a spectacle three days after the fire. The arrangements were hurriedly put together by the palace officials tasked with entertainments. The programme contained the usual acts – a procession of the gladiators, animals and criminals to feature in the combats and executions that would take place on the sands of the Great Circus, an offering to the gods and a reading of omens by the Flaminian priests, followed by a morning of fights and hunts by the bestiarii as well as combat between a range of animals. At noon there would be a series of executions, where the condemned would be dispatched in re-enactments of myths and historical events. Once that was over, the main event of the day would take place: the gladiator bouts.

Given the short time available, the palace had done a decent job of it, thought Cato as he and his men policed the vast crowds attending the games or milling about outside. The organisers had located several lions and bears, and an elephant that looked old enough to have crossed the Alps with Hannibal. Terms had been agreed with the lanistas who ran the city's gladiator schools for the appearance of some household names among the gladiatorial elite. That should help distract attention from concerns about the grain. The first supplies from other towns and ports were starting to reach the city, but it was not nearly enough, and the meagre reserve left after the storm and the fire was at a perilously low level.

The men of the Third Cohort were patrolling the Great Circus, ensuring that any fights that broke out or any attempts at rabble-rousing were dealt with at once. The miscreants were arrested and hauled off to the cells of the Tullianum prison, given a beating and held long enough to discourage them from any repeat of their behaviour. A handful of other patrols were out on the streets further afield, but since a third of the city's inhabitants were either inside the Great Circus or close by, there was little danger of disorder elsewhere. The Praetorians were providing security within, an entire cohort surrounding the imperial box while thousands of their comrades were stationed around the stadium. So far, there had been little trouble for either unit to deal with.

In addition to his regular duties, Cato had been drawn into the inner circle of Nero's advisers and obliged to attend the morning meetings dealing with the growing threat of starvation in Rome. The emperor had taken a liking to him, but while this might have been regarded by most others as an honour and an opportunity for self-advancement, Cato treated it as a dangerous burden. Each time Nero turned to him for an opinion, he was aware of the hostile expressions on the faces of Tigellinus and some of the others. Men who would remain at Nero's side when the crisis had passed while Cato served out his time as prefect of the urban cohorts and returned to his farming estate. He was under no illusions about the appetite for revenge that men like Tigellinus harboured. As for Nero's present respect for Cato, well, that, like so much in the young emperor's life, was a passing fancy. Cato could be discarded as easily as a gaudy cloak, worn once and tossed aside. When that happened, it would only be a matter of time before Tigellinus began to undermine his standing and convince Nero that his former favourite was a traitor.

He thrust his private concerns aside as Macro approached, carrying a couple of pies.

'Here you go, lad. Have one of these. I imagine you could use it.'

Cato nodded his thanks and took a bite. Under the thick crust was a blend of diced pork and some sweet fruit that he decided was apricot. He found the flavour quite delicious and then realised how hungry he was, having not eaten since the previous day. He ate ravenously and Macro could not resist a chuckle.

'By the gods, I'd go and get you another if only the bastards weren't charging an arm and a leg for them.'

Cato swallowed the last of the pie and wiped his lips on the back of his hand. 'The rationing of grain puts pressure on other kinds of food across the board. It will get worse before it gets better. You can be sure of that.'

'My, ain't you the bright and cheerful person today.' Macro rolled his eyes and took a bite of his own pie, chewing steadily as they surveyed the crowd from their vantage point on the steps of a nearby shrine. 'Try and enjoy the moment. We've got sunshine, happy people and the chance of seeing some of the entertainment if there continues to be no trouble. And then there's these pies . . .' He licked his lips theatrically. 'Might just go and buy a few more, despite the price. A couple for you and me and some for the ladies at home. Petronella would love one.'

'I imagine so . . . How are things with her and Bardea?'

'The girl adores the puppy, though she's landed him with some unpronounceable Celtic name. Seems Flaminius wasn't good enough.'

'Good call on her part. Who wants to be reminded of that fire? Speaking of which, what did you say to Petronella?'

'I said I fell in the river when I rescued the pup. That's all she needs to know. No sense in adding to her worries. She's already worked up enough over the food shortages.'

'She believed you?'

Macro shrugged. 'Who knows? She's not making a song and dance about it at least. Which is good of her, considering I've been promising a quiet retirement for years now and it never seems to pan out that way.'

Cato looked at him sympathetically. 'Somehow I don't see you ever retiring from the army, brother. You're a soldier through and through and trouble has a way of beating a path right to your door, however much you might not want it to.'

Macro nodded slowly. 'That's the thing. Much as I love Petronella and have Bardea to care for now, I can't help knowing that I'd rather have a sword at my side and a vine cane in my hand than sit and grow old doing nothing. Truth is, I'd rather put my life on the line and feel like I'm living than face long years of being bored.'

'Maybe, but the years are against you. There will come a day when you're too old to be a soldier.'

Macro reached a finger to his mouth and picked out a shred of meat that was caught between his teeth. 'That day ain't yet. When it comes round . . . I'll see.'

'Good to know you'll be around for a while yet.'

The two remained silent for a moment as they watched the crowd stretching out before them. Then Cato saw a group of liveried men pushing people aside to make way for a group of senators in their red-striped togas, accompanied by wives and family. Behind them came some lesser aristocrats and equestrians. As they drew closer to the nearest entrance of the Great Circus, he could make out Vespasian and his sons. They were in the company of Piso and chatting amiably.

Vespasian looked round and caught sight of Cato and Macro. He hesitated a moment, then raised a hand in greeting before exchanging a few words with his companions and heading for the shrine. At the approach of their superior officer, Cato and Macro straightened up and brushed the crumbs off their scale vests out of a long-established habit with regard to presenting themselves to superior officers.

A smile played on Vespasian's lips as he came up the steps. 'Old habits die hard, eh, boys?'

The three men shared a knowing look before Vespasian continued. 'It's a far cry from our days in Britannia. I can still feel the clammy cold that closed over the island when winter came. Brrr. Not to mention those wild Celts and their Druid friends. Not the most hospitable of provinces.'

Macro was irked by the dismissive words. 'It has come a long way since you were last there, sir. Proper towns, roads, and the locals were starting to adapt to our ways. Now that the rebellion is over, the good work will continue. Britannia will become a province to be proud of, just like the rest of them.'

'I admire your optimism, Centurion Macro. We could do with more of that in Rome these days.' Vespasian glanced at the crowd. 'They're happy enough to enjoy a day or two of these entertainments, but once it's over, they'll go back to worrying about where the next meal is going to come from. Can't say I blame them, if the rumours are true.'

Cato regarded him closely. 'Rumours, sir?'

'Oh, it's probably nothing. You know how people are. Despite Caesar's promise that Rome will continue to be fed, there are some who say there's barely enough grain to go round from day to day.' He leaned forward and lowered his voice. 'Some are saying there is no reserve being held in the palace.'

'I would be careful about repeating such rumours, sir,' said Cato. 'They fly in the face of the guarantees given by Caesar. It would be wiser not to believe them and say nothing.'

'It's not just Caesar who offers a guarantee, is it? I heard about your address to the people in the Forum. Quite the orator. However, words are one thing and deeds another. If it turns out the rumours are true, your performance might well come back to haunt you.' Vespasian abruptly leaned back and opened his arms. 'Ah, but let's not spoil a fine day with such talk. I take it you are both on duty?'

'We are, sadly,' said Macro. 'First decent games held by Nero since we returned from Britannia and we're stuck out here making sure people behave themselves.'

'Such entertainments are less common than you think, Macro. While Caesar likes his chariot racing, he is not so keen on bloodletting displays. He prefers putting on poetry recitals, plays and musical performances. Not quite the ticket for those of us who like what the arena has to offer.'

Macro nodded with feeling. He had grown up with public executions and blood sports, as had most Romans, and he struggled to see the attraction of sitting and listening to actors and writers for hours on end instead.

'How about you, Cato? Do you share our taste in such things, or are you more of Caesar's mind?'

'Each to his own,' Cato replied tersely, sure that Vespasian was testing him in the same manner that Seneca had a few days earlier.

'I see.' Vespasian stared at him a moment before he clapped his hands together. 'I must rejoin my party before we miss much more of the show. It's good to see old comrades again. We have more in common than most here in Rome.'

He descended a couple of steps before he turned. 'If you can spare the time, I would be pleased if both of you would join my party for some of the events. We have good food, wine, and seating on the front row not far from the imperial box. A fine position from which to enjoy the spectacle.'

'That's kind of you, sir, but it wouldn't look good if we abandoned our post.'

'Spoken like a true soldier. Ah well, should you change your mind, we'll be there for the rest of the day.' He smiled broadly. 'Can't say the same for the food and wine, though.' With a quick farewell nod he left them and threaded his way through the throng to the nearest entrance.

'It was good of the old boy to search us out,' said Macro. 'And nice of him to invite us to join him and his mates. Not that he was really expecting us to take him up on the offer. That's the way of people of his rank. They assume lesser mortals will be too uncomfortable to accept. If we didn't happen to be on duty, I'd bolt in there just to see the look on their faces.' He grinned, then noticed the serious expression on his friend's face. 'What now? You look like a man who has lost a denarius and found a sestertius. Cato?'

Cato blinked and shook his head. 'Sorry, I was miles away.'

'I could see . . . Not for the first time since the fire. You're not still thinking that Vespasian had anything to do with it, are you?'

Cato did not reply at once, but stared after the senator until he passed under the arch of the entrance and disappeared from view. Then he turned to Macro. 'I think I'm going to take him up on the offer. You assume command in my absence. If there's any trouble, send a man for me at once.'

'Fair enough, but look here, lad, if that sort of entertainment ain't for you, feel free to let me go in your place.'

Cato felt guilty for denying him the pleasure, but he needed a further discussion with Vespasian. He forced a smile. 'Rank hath its privileges, brother. I'll see if I can bring you back a few snacks. Remember, any trouble, send for me.'

'I might just do that out of spite,' Macro grumbled.

The last of the beast fights had concluded as Cato emerged from the staircase and looked out on the Great Circus stretching away on both sides. It was filled to capacity and a loud murmuring filled the air, along with the odours of humanity made more abhorrent by the day's heat. Out on the immense sand-covered racetrack the carcasses of animals were being removed. Directly in front of Cato a team of slaves was struggling to shift the elephant. Hooks had been inserted into its grey body and men were pulling on ropes to haul the huge animal away from the blood-soaked sand around it. The beast's trunk, severed at the end, trailed behind it. Elsewhere slaves were dragging off the bodies of bulls, bears and a couple of lions, retrieving arrow shafts and broken and abandoned weapons, along with the bodies of several of the bestiarii who had been mauled to death. A pitiful sight, Cato reflected.

He paused to scan the senatorial seating area either side of the imperial box. For a moment his gaze alighted on Nero sitting beneath a huge purple awning with Poppaea at his side and his retinue of advisers, flatterers and entertainers standing behind a screen of Praetorians. He was struck by this proof of how fearful and untrusting the emperor felt. There were more Praetorians either side of the imperial box and in the seating above and behind, as well as a score of Nero's German bodyguards standing at the back of the box. A security cordon that must surely discourage any would-be assassin. He paused to look over hundreds of senators, their families and guests, picking out Vespasian and his group in the front row to the left of the imperial box. A selection of snacks and jars of wine had been set up on the perimeter wall before them and the senators appeared to be talking in a good-humoured way as they waited for the next item on the programme to begin. Cato picked his way down the steps, threading through those who had overflowed the seating, until he came to the low wall that separated the aristocrats from the common people.

A slave held a hand up at his approach. 'Senators and guests only, master.'

Cato showed his equestrian ring. 'Senator Vespasian invited me. Stand aside.'

The man hesitated long enough to make it seem that he was

doing Cato a favour before moving out of his way. Descending the last flight of steps between the ranks of the senators, Cato saw the cushions, hampers and other finery of Rome's elite and knew that these people would never know hunger or the fear of being burned alive in towering ramshackle tenements. If violence broke out, they would retreat behind the high walls of their palatial homes and bolt the doors, or decamp to their villas in Baiae or one of the other seaside resorts and wait for it to blow over. Such people were almost always immune to the hardships endured by the majority of their fellow citizens. Unless they were foolish enough to incur the displeasure of the emperor.

He reached the edge of the racetrack, where Titus, Vespasian's elder son, became aware of his presence and muttered a brief comment to his father. Vespasian eased himself round and his broad, homely face creased into a welcoming smile.

'Cato! Ah, I so hoped you would join us! Come, sit down, here at my side. Give the man some wine, Titus.'

Cato took the goblet he was offered and sat beside the senator. He exchanged a nod with Piso as Vespasian introduced the other members of his party, but the names were mostly forgotten the instant they were spoken. He was more concerned with how he was going to tackle Vespasian over who was responsible for the fire. There was some small talk about the upcoming gladiator bouts and a number of bets placed. His host briefly explained how he had come to know Cato, and recalled their first encounter, when a bedraggled Cato had turned up at the Second Legion's fortress on the Rhine frontier clutching a letter of introduction from one of Emperor Claudius's secretaries. It was not one of Cato's finest moments, but while he usually cringed over his youthful naïvety, he found that he was unconcerned at present. Too much was at stake to indulge in injured pride.

The men on the racetrack had worked swiftly to clear away the bloody detritus of the morning's entertainment, although

266

they were still struggling to get the dead elephant through a service gate beneath the spectator stands. At length they gave up and the grey mass was left where it lay in the hope that it would not present an obstacle for the rest of the programme. A figure appeared on the platform that ran along the top of the central spine of the racecourse, to the accompaniment of a fanfare blasting from a score of Praetorian bucina players. The drone of conversation quickly died as all eyes turned towards the man, who raised a speaking trumpet to his mouth and spoke in the clear, carrying tones of a trained public announcer.

'Great Caesar, and citizens of Rome! Greetings! We are but an hour away from the first of the day's gladiator bouts!'

There were cheers and applause, and the man waited until the sound died away. 'Before then, Caesar is pleased to offer for your entertainment the execution of several nefarious criminals, the first of whom will have the honour of representing the fate of the glorious Gaius Mucius Scaevola!'

The crowd cheered again and then subsided into eager anticipation as a large brazier was raised onto the central spine and set alight. Four attendants dragged the prisoner up the steps and chained his ankles to iron rings nearby before putting a manacle on his right wrist. Then two of them quickly made their way round the fire with the end of a length of chain connected to the manacle and stood ready.

Vespasian spoke just loudly enough for Cato to hear. 'Do you know why that man has been condemned?'

'Why would I?'

'Then let me tell you. He was found daubing a graffito on the back of a temple after having more to drink than was good for him. A rather accurate likeness of Nero being spanked by Poppaea, I'm told. For that he was arrested by the vigiles, taken to the palace, tortured and then condemned to death. I only know this because his father is one of my freedmen and he begged me to intervene and try to save the life of his son. I did my best, but . . .' He gave a shrug as he indicated the man waiting for his torment to begin. 'It's good that you are here to witness this. To see what is in store for those who dare make fun of Caesar.'

Cato glanced to the side and saw Nero give a wave for the execution to proceed. At once the two attendants hauled on the length of chain, drawing the man's arm over the flames of the brazier. The crowd watched in silence as it began to roast. For a while he strained every sinew in his body to fight the agony and not cry out. Cato guessed that he had been promised a reprieve if he endured the torment like Scaevola, who had held his fist over a flame to demonstrate the bravery of Roman men to King Lars Porsena centuries before. But then his courage failed him and he screamed and writhed as his limb turned black and red and the flesh curled. The crowd's jeers echoed round the stadium as the man twisted and howled before he eventually collapsed. At once he was hauled to his feet and the attendants on the opposite side of the brazier pulled him further forward so that his head and shoulders were drawn into the blaze.

Cato looked away and realised that the hand holding his goblet was trembling. He steadied it with the other and set the goblet down before he half turned towards Vespasian. 'The reason I came here was to talk to you about fire, as it happens.'

'Oh?'

'Is there somewhere we can speak more privately?'

'You would have me abandon my guests?' Vespasian affected a hurt look.

'Sir, let's not pretend pleasantries, or play any more games. You know what I'm talking about.'

'I'm not sure that I do, but I'll humour you.' The senator stood and turned to his companions. 'Excuse me a moment. We have business to discuss somewhere we can clearly hear each other. I'll be back soon.'

He led Cato to a covered flight of stairs descending into the heart of the grandstand. At the bottom, a passage extended on either side, lit by the arches that overlooked the broad thoroughfare outside. A handful of figures, slaves mostly, moved along the passage carrying jars of wine and baskets of snacks. Some fifty paces away a pair of Praetorians stood either side of another set of stairs that led up to the imperial box.

'Over here.' Vespasian indicated the nearest of the arches and they stood opposite each other, Cato in the full glow of the afternoon sunlight while the other man leaned back against the bricks, in the shade. 'So, what is it about the fire that preoccupies you so much you have me abandon my friends?'

'I need to know who started it.'

Vespasian stared back at him, his face fixed in a sober expression. 'Why? So that you can inform the palace and have them arrested?'

'I need to know.'

'Why are you asking me? Are you suggesting I had something to do with it?'

'You tell me.'

Vespasian's brow creased and he sucked in a deep breath. 'I'd be careful what you accuse people of, Cato. Your current position of favour with respect to Nero will not last long. Once he casts you aside, who do you think you can count on to protect your interests? After we parted company in Britannia, I followed your career with interest and always put in a good word for you among the senior military officers of my acquaintance. To date, you have justified any influence I have wielded to help advance your career. So you'll forgive me if I find your accusation rather ungrateful, not to mention offensive.'

His former commander's words stung, but Cato needed to know the truth and pressed on. 'Sir, I have not accused you. I have asked if you know who started the fire.'

'You have as good as accused me,' Vespasian shot back.

'However, for the sake of my past high regard for you, I will answer you directly. I have no idea how the fire was started or who started it. Will you take my word on that, or do you require me to swear a sacred oath that I speak the truth?'

There was a long pause as Cato scrutinised the other man's expression in an effort to determine if he was being lied to, but Vespasian gave nothing away. At length Cato nodded slowly. 'Very well. I have your word, then. For the sake of my admiration and loyalty to you, I will accept that what you say is true.'

'Well. That's very generous of you,' Vespasian replied, his words dripping with sarcasm. 'Now, if you don't mind, I'll rejoin my friends. My genuine friends. I don't expect we'll ever meet again as such. Not after this. Whatever bond there was between us as commander and subordinate, as old comrades, has been severed. I hope you discover who was responsible for the fire. I really do. If that happens, then may you recall this moment with every shred of the shame you deserve.' He gave Cato a look of contempt before easing himself out of the shadow and striding off without looking back.

Cato waited until the senator had reached the stairs and climbed out of sight. He could not help feeling a great sense of loss before he dealt with the frustration of being no wiser about the identity of those responsible for the fire. If it was not Vespasian and his circle, then who? He remained where he was for a while as he pondered the question. It seemed there might be another group of plotters in Rome, stealthier than those who saw themselves as latter-day Liberators. If so, the city was in more danger than he had thought. At the same time, he could not shake himself free of the possibility that Vespasian had lied to him.

CHAPTER TWENTY-THREE

The following morning, Nero announced that he was divorcing Octavia. Criers from the palace made their way through the streets to declare the news and a lengthy statement was fixed to the main gates of the imperial palace as well as the large public proclamation hoarding in the Forum. Nero, it stated, was greatly saddened to have to end the marriage. His wife was described as loyal and loving, embodying all the virtues and graces that exemplified the best traditions of Roman women. Her only fault lay in her failure to furnish the emperor with a child to continue the dynasty that stretched back through Augustus to the great Julius Caesar himself.

Octavia's infertility was no fault of her own, the announcement continued. She was an innocent victim of the will of the gods. Nevertheless, the emperor was obliged to find a new wife who could give him an heir, and he offered thanks to Jupiter that his intended, Poppaea, was with child. Their marriage would take place as soon as possible. In the meantime, in recognition of Octavia's loyalty, Nero had bestowed on her a number of great estates to enjoy as she retreated into private life with the grateful thanks of Caesar, the Senate and the people of Rome.

'Never heard such bullshit,' Macro scoffed as he stood beside Cato reading the details off the hoarding. 'Who's going to believe any of that pious crap?'

Cato glanced round anxiously, but dawn had barely broken over the city and there were not many people about, and none close enough to overhear Macro.

'Very few, I think,' he replied. 'Rather more are going to be angry, given how Octavia has been treated by Nero over the last few years.'

'Treated? Abused more like. I've heard he tried to choke her to death several times. And when he wasn't trying to kill the poor girl, he was treating her like shit. It's common knowledge, lad. I don't think bunging her a few houses he confiscated from his other victims is going to seal the deal quite the way he seems to think it will. Besides, he picks his moment. Doing this while the mob's temper is simmering over having the soldiers on the streets isn't helping matters.'

'True.'

So far the Praetorians and urban cohorts had managed to keep order day and night. The patrols had broken up any gatherings that might have got out of control and delivered beatings to pickpockets and any other petty criminals they encountered. After a drunken brawl broke out between rival supporters of the chariot-racing teams a few nights earlier, Nero had declared a curfew during the hours of darkness. The night patrols meted out more beatings to those who ventured abroad in defiance of the curfew. There were no more arrests, as every prison cell in the city was filled to capacity after the grain ration was cut less than five days after the fire and Cato's address to the crowd in the Forum.

'Ah, here comes Macrinus,' Macro announced, nodding towards the alley that the centurion and a section of his men had charged down in pursuit of a gang of boys who had pelted them with filth and insults. 'Looks like he's taken prisoners,' he added drily.

Macrinus carried two boys, one under each arm. They were

no more than twelve years old, Cato estimated. A third was being manhandled by a couple of his men. The centurion dropped his burdens to the ground and ordered the nearest men to take charge of them, pinning their arms behind their backs. He himself brought up the rear, looking over his broad shoulder for any sign that they were being followed by the rest of the gang.

Once they entered the Forum, he trotted forward to where Cato and Macro were waiting with the rest of the century. The men stirred and rose to their feet from the steps of the Senate House and the shrines nearby, and quickly formed up. They were keen to get back to camp for some food and rest and were not pleased to have been delayed while waiting for Macrinus and his section to reappear.

There was a satisfied expression on the centurion's face as the boys were thrust down onto their knees before Cato and Macro. 'We caught 'em, sir. Little buggers thought they'd got away from us, but they ran into a blind alley. Most managed to get over a wall, but we nabbed these three.'

Macro looked the boys over. Two were pale, thin creatures, barefoot and dressed in little more than rags. Too afraid to look up and meet his gaze. The third, larger and better dressed, glared back at him with a haughty expression.

'I hope they didn't put up too much of a fight, Macrinus. Otherwise you might have been in a spot of trouble. Nine of you against three. Not the best odds.'

Macrinus's eyes narrowed. 'There were at least twenty of the bastards when we went after them.'

'Oh, that's completely different then.' Macro turned to Cato. 'What do you reckon? Put him up for a medal?'

Cato raised a hand to stop Macro's baiting. He considered a suitable punishment. In truth he was more angry with Macrinus for breaking ranks and going after the gang. But the boys had been foolish enough to hurl insults and shit at the soldiers, and now that they had been caught, he could hardly release them without some penalty.

'What do you want me to do with them, sir? They need to be taught a lesson. Can't have them doing this and getting away with it.' Macrinus indicated a couple of brown stains on his shoulder. 'We need to set an example.'

'I'm well aware of that, Centurion,' Cato snapped irritably. He drew a deep breath. 'Since they have an affinity with filth, we'll take them back to camp and have them scrub out the latrines before we send them on their way.'

'We ain't cleaning your shit,' muttered the largest of the boys.

Macro raised his fist. 'Quiet, you!'

'Is that all?' Macrinus responded sourly. 'A day's latrine duty?'

'He's got a point,' said Macro. 'We could always crucify them to set an example to their mates.'

The youngest of the boys looked up with a terrified expression and Cato had to force himself not to smile. He stroked his chin as if deciding their fate, taking in the bruises, cuts and grazes, no doubt acquired when Macrinus and his men had got hold of them.

'Latrine duty it is. Though if the three of you are brought before me again, I'll hand you over to Centurion Macro to deal with.' He underlined the threat by drawing his thumb across his throat, and the boys winced with fright. 'Now that's sorted, let's get back to camp.'

As the soldiers formed a column, with the three boys grasped by the men of the rearmost section, Cato called Macrinus over.

'Sir?'

'A quiet word, Centurion,' Cato said in a firm undertone. 'Next time some street urchins give you a bit of lip and you break ranks to chase after them, it'll be you who gets latrine duty.'

Macrinus opened his mouth to protest.

'Don't!' Cato growled at him. 'You're a bloody centurion. You should know better. We're here to keep order on the streets, not beat up a bunch of kids. You might have served long enough in Rome to relish lording it over half-starved urchins, but you wouldn't last a heartbeat in the field against real opposition. If I catch you taking it out on them, or anyone else, and abandoning your unit, you'll have me to answer to. Latrine duty will be the least of your concerns. Clear?'

Macrinus swallowed his bitterness and answered through clenched teeth. 'Yes, sir.'

'Carry on.'

He gave a reluctant salute and walked away stiffly. Cato watched him with contempt. A cheap bully then, as well as corrupt. No wonder he was close to one of Tigellinus's cronies.

Cato had decided to take the men back to camp via the Suburra, in order to impress on the inhabitants of that district that no part of Rome was being overlooked by the urban cohorts' patrols. The Suburra was the most crime-ridden area of the city, occupying the slopes between the Quirinal and Viminal hills. Packed with crumbling tenements and cursed with an oppressive atmosphere, it was stifling in the summer months. Most of the city's brothels and seedy drinking holes were located there, along with the most powerful criminal gangs, living off the backs of small traders, pimps, prostitutes and rent boys. The poor and downtrodden of the slum lived in dread of the gangs, casual violence, starvation and the collapse or conflagration of their dwellings. Life there was short and miserable, and the other inhabitants of Rome avoided the area, unless they were seeking trouble or sexual depravity. For all that, the Suburra had also been home to a number of poets, and even Julius Caesar in his youth. As broad a cross-section of Roman society as could ever be encountered, thought Cato as he and his men advanced up the Argiletum, the main street that passed through the Suburra's dark heart.

'Never liked this place, even when I was a kid,' Macro remarked. 'You need eyes in the back of your head given all the pickpockets, muggers and cut-throats hanging around like vultures. It's a shame that fire didn't start here.'

Although the street was wide, the height of the buildings on either side and the overhang of the upper floors blocked out most of the light and created a patchwork of bright sunshine and various shades of gloom. Cato was obliged to slow the pace of the column to give people time to step aside. Hostile faces watched in silence as the soldiers tramped by, the same expressions worn by those looking down from some of the windows above. Even though it was not long after dawn, the air was uncomfortably stuffy already and would become more oppressive as the sun rose to its zenith, baking the city during the long afternoon and early-evening hours before giving some slight relief as darkness fell. At which point the dingy streets and alleys assumed a wholly human form of oppression as thieves and cut-throats filled the shadows, waiting for prey.

They were barely half a mile along the Argiletum when Cato heard a disturbance at the rear of the column, a chorus of angry shouts and screeches. He gave the order to halt, and he and Macro made their way back. He could see several women shouting and cursing the soldiers holding the three boys. The tallest of them had dark hair styled in braided loops and wore a green stola trimmed with white embroidered patterns. An unusually prosperous appearance given the area, he thought.

'What in Hades is all the fuss about?' Macro demanded as the two officers strode up. The optio in charge of the rear of the column was about to respond when the woman turned on Macro and stabbed a finger at him, thrusting her head forward.

'Fuss? You tell me! That's my boy you've got there.' Her voice was coarse and shrill and belied her finely appointed appearance. 'What d'you think yer fuckin' playin' at, hauling kids off to jail?'

'No one's going to jail,' said Macro, raising his hands to try and calm her down. 'These boys and their mates gave our lads a bit of grief and they need to be taught a lesson, that's all. They'll be sent packing at the end of the day. Now clear off.'

'Clear orf, 'e says!' The woman raised herself to her full height, which unfortunately was a few inches higher than Macro, and glared at him. 'Yer on our turf, mate.' She gestured at their surroundings. 'The Bronze Blades own this neighbour'ood. And my 'usband runs the Blades. So if yer know what's good fer you, hand over my boy and piss right orf aht of 'ere.'

She made a move towards the oldest of the three boys and clipped him round the ear. 'An' wot d'you think your father's going to say when he 'ears you gone and let yerself be caught like some fackin' tyro?' She grabbed his arm and tried to wrench him from the soldiers' grasp.

'Oi! That's enough!' Macro intervened and thrust her back. She tottered a couple of steps before falling on her backside with a shocked cry. The women around her looked stunned and fell silent.

'Your lad is coming with us. If he behaves, he'll be home tonight. If you give us any more lip, you'll be joining him in the latrines. Understand?'

She stared up at him, mouth open but wordless.

'Now piss off. You and your little coven.'

Cato faced the rearmost section. 'There'll be no more hold-ups. You keep a hand on these boys and you don't stop for anyone. If someone is fool enough to cause trouble, you give 'em a knock on the head. Macro, on me.'

As they retraced their steps to the head of the century, the woman got up, hurled some salty curses at the soldiers and scurried away with her companions up a side street.

'By all that's holy.' Macro shook his head. 'There's a voice that could shatter a thousand ships and no mistake.'

The column continued on its way, and Cato noticed that more and more people appeared to watch them pass by. The previous expressions of sullen resentment were replaced by looks of tense anticipation. Now and then he saw movement in the shadows of the alleys on either side as figures flitted along parallel streets.

'Macro . . .'

'I saw 'em. Looks like we might be in for a bit of bother.' Macro spat to the side. 'Thank you, Macrinus . . .'

A little further on, the street opened onto a square with a public fountain in the middle, around which a large group of men were waiting. They were carrying staves, studded clubs, hatchets and cleavers. At the approach of the soldiers, one of them climbed onto the edge of the fountain and stood feet braced apart, thumbs tucked into a wide leather belt. He wore a sword at his side, thick hide braces and greaves, a leather cuirass and a band of black cloth around his brow. He looked to be in his thirties, but it was hard to be sure due to the number of scars competing with wrinkles and creases on his broad face.

'That'll do!' he called out, raising his hand as the head of the column entered the square. 'Stop right there!'

When Cato made no effort to respond, the man's followers spread out, blocking the way, and he was obliged to give the order to halt and close up.

'That's better.' The man nodded. 'My wife tells me you've got my boy, Urso, and two of his mates. Let 'em loose and you and your men can go on your way without any trouble.'

Macro snorted. 'How about you and your men fuck off and we won't give *you* any trouble?' He patted the hilt of his sword to add weight to his threat. 'Who in Hades do you think you are, telling us what to do?'

The man raised a hand to slap his broad chest. 'Allow me to introduce myself. Tell him my name, lads!'

'Bullo!' his followers chorused, loudly enough for his name to echo off the surrounding buildings.

'And who are we?' he called out, spreading his arms.

'Bronze Blades!'

When the cry died away, he smiled. 'There you are. I won't ask for your name, Centurion, since you'll be off our patch soon and you won't be welcome back. But I know your mate well enough. Prefect Cato. I was there in the Forum when he spewed his bullshit about the grain supply.'

'Why, you . . .' Macro took a half-step forward, fingers closing round the handle of his sword. Cato held out his arm in front of his friend to stop him. 'Easy,' he muttered. 'Let's try to get through this without anyone getting hurt.'

Cato addressed the gang leader. 'Your son was arrested for causing a disturbance in the Forum. He'll be released at sunset, provided he gives us no more trouble.'

'You release him now, Prefect, or there will be trouble, I give you my word on that.'

Cato looked round the square. There were perhaps fifty of the gang members. Tough-looking men, it was true, but no match for well-equipped soldiers.

'If there's any fighting, your men will come off worse, Bullo.'

'You think so?' The man put his fingers to his lips and gave a piercing whistle. At once, shutters on the windows of the tenements on either side of the street and around the square crashed open and many more faces appeared. Men holding up bricks, tiles and small rocks for Cato and his soldiers to see. Over a hundred more gang members, he estimated. The odds were now in Bullo's favour.

'Shields up! Close ranks!' he called to the soldiers behind him. The column swiftly re-formed, four abreast, shields raised. The three boys were bunched together in the middle of the formation. 'Draw swords!'

Cato grasped the handle of his own blade and it came out of the scabbard with a rasp, followed at once by Macro's sword. They angled the tips in Bullo's direction.

'I suggest you tell your men to back off if they want to live,' said Cato.

Bullo stared back at him, trying to decide if he was bluffing. Then he gave a bitter, audible sigh and drew his own sword.

'Last chance, Prefect. Let the boys go.'

Cato called over his shoulder, 'At the slow step, advance!'

Neither he nor Macro was carrying a shield, but they took their places in the middle of the front rank as the column paced forward. There were no more than ten paces between the soldiers and the gang members, and the latter held their ground as they readied their assorted weapons. Cato clenched his jaw and tightened his grip on his sword as Macro drew his dagger and hefted it in his left hand, ready to strike. There was just time for Cato to hope that it was Bullo who was bluffing, and then the gang leader jumped down from the fountain, cupped a hand to his mouth and bellowed, 'Give it to 'em, boys!'

With a roar his men surged forward, while those in the windows began to pelt the soldiers with their missiles. The gangsters threw themselves at the head of the column, slashing wildly with their weapons. The men carrying shields on either side of Cato and Macro easily deflected the blows and struck back with their short swords. The two officers raised their own weapons, ready to fight for their lives. A skinny man with a pockmarked face came at Cato with a raised hatchet, and Cato leaned forward to grab his wrist while striking at his throat with his sword. It was a reflex blow that missed any vital blood vessels but nevertheless tore open the soft flesh of his neck. As the blood began to flow, Cato drew back his sword arm and smashed the hilt into his opponent's face. The man staggered to the side, where Macro stabbed him in the guts with his dagger and thrust him back against one of his companions who was shaping to strike Macro with a cleaver. Both went down and were finished off by the soldiers behind as the column edged forward across the square, pressing steadily through Bullo and his outnumbered followers on the ground.

The men in the windows quickly evened the odds, with the deluge of bricks, tiles and rocks striking several of the soldiers, dazing two who were hit squarely on their helmets. They were dragged into the centre of the column by their comrades and their positions filled. It might have been worse but for the presence of the three boys. The coarse voice of Bullo's wife screamed from one of the windows, 'Stop! You fackin' fools! Any one of you goes an' hits my boy an' ah'll cut your balls off and feed 'em to me dogs!'

The warning was sufficient. The barrage stopped and the gang members disappeared from the windows to descend the stairs and join the fight in the square. Taking a swift look round, Cato could see that the odds were swinging against him and his men. Their best chance to avoid getting overwhelmed was to push on and get out of the square and onto a street where the gangsters could only come at them on a narrow front. The head of the column had already edged past the fountain, and there was another twenty paces to the nearest thoroughfare leading off the square. He raised his sword and pointed. 'That way, Macro!'

He blocked a club with his sword guard and feinted at his attacker, forcing the latter to jump back to avoid the tip of his blade.

'Keep moving, lads!' Macro bellowed above the din of clattering weapons and the thud of blows landing on the soldiers' shields.

Step by step the century crossed to the far side of the square, cutting down at least a dozen of Bullo's men and wounding many more. In return, the gang inflicted only a handful of injuries, and those who were wounded fell back into the centre of the column to tend the cuts as best they could as they kept up with their comrades.

'The boys!' Bullo shouted. 'Rescue our boys!'

The attackers at the front of the column fell back and turned their attention to the rear, where Urso and his two companions were still being securely held by the men tasked with guarding them. The mob pressed in around them, hacking at the shields on each side of the column, or attempting to wrench them from the soldiers' grip. They paid dearly as they came on, easy victims for the swords thrusting out from between the shields.

The head of the column was free of the gang and had reached the street. It was tempting to pick up the pace, but that would have opened gaps in the formation that their opponents would exploit to divide the soldiers and destroy them in detail.

'Slow down, damn you!' Cato snapped at the men on either side of him and Macro as they edged ahead. 'Keep it tight!'

As soon as they entered the street, he sought out Macrinus and ordered him to take over at the head of the century and control the pace while he and Macro steadied the hard-pressed rear. Working their way down the centre of the column, they came to the section holding the boys. The two younger ones were wailing in terror. One had a cut on his shoulder where a brick or tile had caught him. The blood was flowing brightly down his skinny arms and leaving a crimson trail in his wake. The older boy, Urso, was hanging limply between two of Cato's men. His head was matted with blood. Cato's stomach knotted with anxiety as he lifted the boy's chin and saw that his eyes had rolled up and his jaw was slack.

'Shit . . .' He tried to feel for a pulse on the boy's neck, but it was impossible with the tight press of bodies about him. Urso was seriously injured, if not dead. It would be better to let his parents look after him than drag him back to the camp. Reluctant as he was to let Bullo take his victory and thereby undermine the authority of the urban cohorts, he decided it would be best to try to stop any more of the combatants being killed or injured.

'Let 'em go!' he called out, loudly enough to be heard by all around him. 'Bullo! We're releasing the boys! Tell your men to pull back! Now!'

There was a pause before he heard the gang leader shout, 'Let 'em be, boys! That's enough.'

After a last exchange of blows, Bullo's men broke away from the fight and warily retreated a few steps. A hush settled over the square before Bullo pushed his way through and pointed his sword at Cato.

'I want my kid and his mates.'

Cato crouched over the two younger boys. 'Your friend needs your help. Carry him to his father.'

He helped arrange Urso's arms over their shoulders, and they grasped the folds of his tunic and struggled through the gap the soldiers opened up to let them pass.

'The lad isn't in good shape,' Macro said quietly. 'Let's hope he's still alive, or this could get far worse.'

Cato nodded. 'We need to keep moving.'

'Close up!' Macro ordered, and the century hurriedly dressed its ranks. 'Advance!'

They marched steadily out of the square as Bullo hurried to his son. There was a flurry of motion behind him as his wife ran forward, then stopped and clapped a hand over her mouth at the sight of Urso's bloodied head. As he was lowered to the ground, his father bent over him before looking in Cato's direction.

'What have you bastards done to him?'

'It wasn't us,' Cato called back. 'He was hit by one of your men at the windows. He'd still be fine if you hadn't caused trouble . . .'

Bullo picked his son up carefully, the boy's head lolling back as his limbs dangled limply from his father's arms. 'Clear a path! My boy needs help. Camilla! Find a physician. Quickly!'

He had only gone a few steps before his wife let out an animal shriek and snatched up a bloodstained hatchet that had been dropped during the fight. She raised it above her head and ran at the rear of the column. 'You bastards! You killed me son! I'll fuckin' 'ave every last one of yer!'

She scurried down the street after them, her free hand holding up the hem of her stola, her face twisted into fathomless rage. The rear rank turned to face her and raised their shields in an unbroken line as they backed off, their optio calling the step. An instant later the woman caught up with them and hacked viciously at the shields, the blows echoing off the buildings crowding the street. She pursued them for several paces before she stopped and turned on the mob watching from the square.

'Why are yer just standin' there?' she screeched. 'They murdered my Urso! Bullo's son! Aintcha gonna do anythin', you bloody cowards!'

She turned away from them, chest heaving, and came on again. Behind her, Cato saw some of the gang members start forward. He knew he had to put a stop to the confrontation before anyone else got hurt.

He approached the rear rank, timing it so that he sprang between them just after a blow landed on one of the shields. She was raising the hatchet to strike again when he grabbed her wrist with one hand while disarming her with the other.

'That's enough! You've got the boys, Camilla. Go back and look after your son.'

She glared at him as she struggled to tear free, forcing Cato to seize her other wrist. She writhed violently and lashed out with one of her feet, kicking him on the shin. Fortunately it was a glancing blow. She hissed and spat in his face, then jerked her head to the side and attempted to bite his forearm.

'Damn you!' he growled, opening his right hand and slapping her hard across the face. For an instant she looked stunned, then her eyes narrowed and she made to strike him. Cato raised his hand again.

'Don't make me! Next time you'll go down and stay down!'

284

The woman hesitated, then snarled, 'Yer'll pay for what you did to Urso!'

'What happened to him was your own fault,' Cato snapped back. 'None of this would have happened but for you. Your son wouldn't have been injured, nor would any of my men or yours. Go! Get away from me. If you or your friends try anything else, I will hold you responsible for the consequences. I'll come back here with more men and hunt you down, and I swear to the gods I will show no mercy.'

She saw the anger and hostility in his expression and tried to back off. Cato tightened his grip on her wrist to underscore his determination, then released her abruptly so that she stumbled back and nearly fell over. The first of Bullo's men came up and caught her, but she shook him off.

'Leave me, yer fool!'

Cato turned away and strode quickly to rejoin the formation. Behind him the woman breathed hard for a moment before she called out, 'Yer'd better pray my boy is orlright! If he dies, then so help me Jupiter, Best and Greatest, I'll find you an' kill you with my own 'ands. Don't care 'ow long it takes, but I will kill you an' any family you 'ave. Stone dead . . .'

CHAPTER TWENTY-FOUR

In the days that followed, Cato was even more vigilant as he led patrols through the streets. The threat from Bullo's wife concerned him deeply. It was one thing for some barbarian on the frontier to swear to take revenge on him personally, but quite another when the threat extended to Lucius and Claudia. He had no doubts about the reach of the crime gangs of Rome. If they chose to, they could find a way to track down anyone in the city or its environs. He was relieved that he had already sent a message to Claudia after the dinner at Vespasian's house warning her to watch for any strangers who came to the villa or the nearby village. He also asked her to have men assigned to guard the villa itself and make sure that Lucius was not allowed out of their sight. Macro had also alerted Petronella in case Bullo discovered that the house in Rome was owned by Cato and had his men pay a visit.

There had been no sign that Bullo was hunting them, however, and after ten days Cato's anxiety began to fade and his mind focused on his primary duty of keeping order. Grain was no longer rationed now that a steady flow was entering the city, and the tense atmosphere had eased a little. There were still rumours circulating that there were no reserves stored in the vaults of the palace, but as long as there was a regular distribution of grain such rumours had little impact. Still, Cato reflected, if there was any serious disruption to supplies, it would not take long for restlessness to take hold. It was a truism that no civilisation, no matter how sophisticated and ordered, was ever more than a few meals away from revolution, and Rome, for all its might, was no exception. The feeling of living day to day as the temper of the mob simmered close to the point where it could easily boil over placed great strain on the commander, officers and men of the urban cohorts. A strain that was marginally lifted for Cato by Tigellinus reassigning Centurion Macrinus for service in the imperial palace.

The tension in the streets was made worse by Nero's cavalier treatment of Octavia and his flaunting of Poppaea in public. Even though the spectacle that had been provided in the Great Circus had distracted the mob from their concerns over grain, the sight of the emperor fawning over his lover had drawn jeers and calls for Poppaea to be banished. At first Nero had affected not to notice, but on the third and last day of the spectacle, he had been goaded into taking action. A cohort of Praetorians had waded into the most vociferous section of the stands, wielding canes, and driven them out of the stadium, killing scores and injuring hundreds more. The rest of the spectators had risen to their feet at the sight and begun to howl their protest, until more Praetorians entered the stands and took up positions facing the crowd. Their cries had died away and they'd watched the beatings in silence before Nero had risen from his couch to address them. This, he had said, was a warning to all who dared to abuse the woman he had chosen to be the new empress. Henceforth all must show her loyalty and affection or pay the price.

The result of that afternoon was to raise the temperature among the people of Rome, who were already enduring the stifling heat of an unusually early summer. No rain had fallen for over a month, and the accumulated stench of sewage rising from the drains seemed to settle on every building and fill every street so that each breath was a constant reminder of the filth in which the people lived. It felt like Rome was cursed and that the gods themselves had turned against the city. The tide of sickness that came with every summer and claimed its harvest of the old and weak was more lethal than usual, and every day saw hundreds of bodies carted away for burial in the vast necropolises that extended along the roads stretching out of Rome. The smoke of funeral pyres trailed up into the harsh azure of cloudless skies.

Within the walls of the city, those who could avoided the streets and open spaces during the hottest hours of the day. Those without a home took shelter in the shade of dusty trees amid the parched brown grass of public gardens and rested or slept until the unbearable heat had passed. Only the rich had respite from such conditions, with many abandoning Rome for their estates in the cool highlands or the resorts dotted along the coast. At another time Nero would have done the same, but the danger in Rome was so acute that he had been persuaded by his advisers, including Cato, that it was vital he remain in the capital to be seen to share the privations of his people.

It was no more than a gesture, since he spent his days beneath the awnings erected over the terraces and gardens of the palace, lounging on soft couches and cooled by fan-wielding slaves as he slaked his thirst on watered wine chilled with ice from the store rooms deep beneath the building.

As May drew to a close and the heat showed no signs of abating, Cato and Macro made their way to the palace for the daily briefing held by Caesar to monitor the grain situation and the mood of the people. It had already been a long day. The urban cohorts had arrested more than fifty people when a large crowd had gathered outside the house of a merchant rumoured to be hoarding grain. They had overwhelmed the merchant's bodyguards and stormed his home, killing the merchant, his wife and children and most of his household. They were still looting the place when Cato turned up with Macro and two centuries to surround the house. Those arrested were taken to the overcrowded cells of the Tullianum to await their fate.

Holding their helmets under their arms and perspiring freely, the two officers climbed the ramp from the Forum to the palace.

'Is it really necessary that I accompany you?' asked Macro. He was hot and tired and yearning to get home to be with his wife and daughter. Since the encounter with Bullo, he was anxious about their safety. 'I doubt there's anything I can add to proceedings that you can't say for me. Besides, after that business during the storm, I'd rather keep a low profile.'

'I need you by my side. Nero knows your face and will recall the time you saved his life some years back.'

'You played a large part in that too, lad.'

'Then he'll be twice as likely to look on us with favour, won't he? Besides, if anything should happen to me, I'll need you to let Claudia know as soon as possible. I don't want her or Lucius still at the villa if Nero's henchmen turn up to confiscate the place.'

Macro gave him a doubtful look. 'Do you think that's likely?'

'Who can say? I'm safe as long as Nero thinks I'm of use to him. And he will think that only for as long as someone doesn't poison him against me.'

'Someone like Tigellinus or Poppaea?'

'Quite. Or until he needs a scapegoat to throw to the mob. Either way, it feels like I'm living on borrowed time. So if anything happens to me . . .'

'I'll make sure I get word to Claudia, right after I've helped myself to the best jars in your wine cellar and looted your money chest.'

Cato sighed patiently. 'Always good to know how much I'll be missed.'

The Praetorians on duty passed the two officers into the palace, and Macro, who had not been there for many years, was struck by the contrast between the edgy tension on the streets and the ordered calm and luxury of Nero's surroundings. The stench of the slums surrounding the palace was overwhelmed here by the sweet odour of incense emanating from small platters hanging amid the oil lamp stands. While it was a relief for a moment, the sickly, cloying scent soon became almost as repellent as the pervasive stink of the city outside. The decor that Macro recalled from Claudius's reign had been replaced with gaudy wall hangings and gilded murals replete with expensive gold and azure details. The emperor seemed to have an insatiable appetite for gold without any awareness of how it betokened crass taste rather than wealthy sophistication.

They were halted outside one of the entrances to Nero's private suite, what had once been a cluster of large aristocratic houses dating back to the time of Augustus. Since then, his successors had adapted them to form a lavish single household that appeared labyrinthine to any visitor.

'Caesar has ordered his advisers to attend him in the stadium garden,' the Praetorian optio explained. 'I'll have a man escort you there. But first . . .' He indicated a small table on which lay a handful of sword belts and daggers.

Cato and Macro surrendered their weapons and were searched by one of the Praetorians before they were ushered through the entrance. They followed a man along some corridors and emerged into an elongated open area that was a scaled-down version of the Great Circus, some fifty paces in length and twenty across, with shaded alcoves running around the perimeter. Some contained statues while others had benches within, or potted plants. The open area was covered with flagstones. At the far end was a curved retaining wall around twenty feet in height. Beneath a large canopy was a raised area upon which Cato could make out Nero and Poppaea reclining together on a couch. A small group of men were seated on stools below them. The notes of a flute carried along the length of the garden, and he saw a slender young man playing the instrument in one of the alcoves behind Nero.

As they approached, Macro let out a soft whistle. 'Do you see?' he muttered. 'There to the left.'

Cato spotted a woman sitting in the shadows of one of the other alcoves. It was Octavia. She was quite still, head slightly lowered and clasping her hands in front of her.

'What's she doing here?' Macro whispered. 'I thought Nero had done with her.'

'So did I.'

Nero looked up as he became aware of the three men approaching. He frowned slightly as he recognised Cato and glanced fleetingly at Macro. Then he rose to a sitting position and called out, 'You're late, Prefect Cato.'

Cato bowed deeply and Macro followed suit. 'I beg your forgiveness, Caesar. We came as swiftly as we could.'

'Hmm,' Nero responded. 'Well, you are here now. Be seated. You and . . .' His gaze shifted to Macro, and he paused. 'Ah yes. Centurion Macro, as I recall.'

'Yes, Caesar.' Macro bowed again, fervently hoping that Nero had forgotten his unfortunate language on the night of the storm. 'I am honoured that you remember me.'

'I never forget a face. Nor a favour. Nor a wrong done to me,' Nero said flatly. 'That is something you should never forget in turn. There are some who have forgotten and paid for it with their lives.' He suddenly grinned and clapped his hands. 'Do take a seat! Now that we are all here, I have some excellent news to relate. Not an hour ago, I received a message from the commander of the fleet at Misenum, Ancietus, who tells me that a fresh grain convoy has set sail from Sicilia. If the wind and weather hold, it should reach Ostia within the next five days or so. Given that Burrus has calculated that we have sufficient grain in Rome and en route to feed the city for at least that long, it appears that we are finally out of the woods!'

He beamed at those seated before him and was rewarded with expressions of relief and smiles as his advisers vied to be the first to congratulate him. Tigellinus was quickly on his feet, and he indicated the others with a sweep of his arm as he addressed Nero.

'Caesar, I am sure I speak for us all when I say we are lucky indeed to be ruled by a prince as wise and far-sighted as you. It is through your judgement and concern for your people and the will of the gods that we have come through these dark days and can now look forward to a golden age in confidence. You have fed Rome and maintained order on our streets, and your resolute bearing has been an example to us all.'

Macro leaned towards Cato and whispered sourly, 'You'd think we had nothing to do with keeping the mob in line since the storm and the fire.'

As Tigellinus sat down to applause and nods of approval from those around him, Nero gave a modest inclination of his head. 'Kind words, my dear friend, and never more truly spoken. But we should not underestimate the influence of the gods in such matters, nor the contributions of those who acted on my orders to such good effect. Men like our loyal servants Centurion Macro and Prefect Cato.'

Faces turned towards them and Nero paused expectantly. Cato hurriedly formed a response. 'Caesar, we merely did our duty and obeyed your orders. I am sure any other officers would have done the same. As Tigellinus has already said, we can only count ourselves lucky to serve at a time when you are Caesar.'

'Such modesty,' Nero said, touching his hand to his brow. 'I am, in turn, fortunate to enjoy such loyalty and affection from those who serve me. Fortunate and touched . . .'

For a moment it seemed to Cato that the emperor was moved almost to the point of shedding a tear, before he realised it was merely a performance. A gesture that Nero had picked up off an actor in his artistic entourage.

He brushed away an imaginary tear and straightened up. 'Enough of that, and on to today's agenda. Although the grain crisis has preoccupied us for a while, there are other, pressing matters that need to be addressed. Foremost of which is the situation on the eastern frontier. The long-standing rivalry between Rome and Parthia over control of the kingdom of Armenia has plagued me since the start of my reign, as it did my predecessor. It is time this struggle came to an end.'

Cato gave a nod of approval. In his view, and that of many other soldiers, too much treasure and blood had been shed in a conflict that seemed to be more about the pig-headed pride of Roman and Parthian rulers than any strategic advantage. A permanent peace treaty between the two powers was long overdue, and the recent arrival of the Parthian embassy to negotiate such a peace was welcome.

Nero's brow creased into a frown as he continued. 'For too long the Parthians have defied us, secretly planning new wars against Rome and her allies while mouthing platitudes about peaceful co-existence. They need to be taught a lesson. More than a lesson. Parthia needs to be . . .' He paused as he searched for a suitable phrase. 'Parthia needs to be utterly obliterated so that it can never again pose a threat to our eastern dominions. We have sufficient legions in the region to do the job, as well as one of our finest generals, Corbulo. Just the man to serve up a great victory for me to celebrate here in Rome.'

Cato could see that Nero's words were causing consternation among some in the room, and Seneca rose hesitantly to respond.

'Caesar, General Corbulo has been obliged to spend more than a year reversing the disastrous defeat suffered by Lucius Caesennius Paetus. He is barely able to contain the Parthians as it is. We should be grateful that he has managed to persuade them to accept the neutrality of Armenia and the withdrawal of both sides from its territory. The embassy has been sent to finalise the terms of the treaty. Caesar, we are on the verge of a historic peace that would remove the threat of Parthia. Isn't peace what you seek?'

Nero's lips curled with distaste. 'Peace? Yes. Roman peace. Peace on our terms. Peace under our rule. Anything else is a sign of weakness that our other enemies will exploit. For too long Rome has extended carrots rather than sticks to our foes. The time has come to make them recognise Rome's greatness again.'

Seneca shook his head. 'But what about the embassy, Caesar? What will you say to them? They expect to hear words of peace, not war, more war, no end to war . . .'

'Send that rabble back to their king. I will not dignify them by speaking to them directly. Tell them that Caesar is tired of their scheming ways. Caesar demands they recognise that Armenia falls within Rome's sphere of influence and that Roman troops will defend its lands if need be. If they refuse, we will crush Parthia and turn it into a vassal of the Roman Empire.'

Seneca's eyes briefly widened with shock before he recovered his wits and turned to Burrus. 'You are the most senior soldier at Caesar's side, and therefore best placed to speak on the military situation. Tell us, is Corbulo's army sufficient to carry out the will of the emperor?'

The Praetorian prefect's face, already thin and drawn due to his illness, seemed to sink into further despair as he considered how to respond. When he spoke, Cato was aware of a hoarseness to his voice that he had not heard before. The man's strength was bleeding out of him and it could not be long before the end came.

'It is true that Corbulo is a fine general,' Burrus began, 'and a good soldier. He has forged his men into a fine weapon. However, as Seneca has pointed out, his forces are stretched along a vulnerable frontier. He can hold what we have, but he lacks the strength to take Armenia, let alone consider invading Parthia. It cannot be done.'

'It will be done!' Nero shouted angrily. 'Because I say so. Am I surrounded by cowards and traitors? We all know the fate awaiting such people!'

He leaned forward, hands clutching the arms of his chair so tightly that the knuckles blanched bone-white. His jaw trembled with rage and his eyes blazed, and Cato feared for the life of every man in the room.

CHAPTER TWENTY-FIVE

The flute player had lowered his instrument in response to the outburst, and Nero rounded on him at once. 'Did I say you could stop, Eucaenus? Play for us, or I will have that flute rammed so far down your throat you will choke to death on it.'

The man instantly put the instrument back to his lips and played a few wavering notes before he could control his fear and settle into a more even melody.

Burrus paused for a moment. When he spoke, it was in a calm, measured voice. 'Caesar, I have served you loyally for many years. In that time I have always done my duty to further your ambitions for the good of Rome. As a soldier I have proved my courage in battle and have never betrayed my oath of loyalty. I speak to you now on the basis of that record. When I tell you that Corbulo cannot carry out your wishes, it is so. If he were to try, it would only end in disaster, given the force he has at his disposal.

'I am no traitor. I have always been honest with you and I believe that is a quality you cherish. Some soldiers crave glory, but that is because they lack the wisdom to recognise the value of peace. If war comes, it is only because those who command soldiers have failed at peace. The price of that failure is measured in dead men. Always. Surely it is better to take the peace that the Parthians offer us? Particularly when we are not in a position to wage a successful war against them. Caesar, I speak from the heart, unlike those who merely echo your wishes and compete to drown you with false praise. For the sake of the long years of my faithful service, I beg you to heed my advice. Take the peace.'

There was silence in the chamber, and Cato looked from the stunned expressions of the advisers to that of the emperor. Nero's face was blank, as if he could not understand what had been said and had no notion of how to respond. Cato realised that he had lived so long in the shadow of deference and dishonesty that he was incapable of dealing with honest, unadorned opinion.

It was Poppaea who broke the silence, as she examined a sprig of grapes she had plucked from a nearby platter of fruit. 'If Corbulo lacks the power to carry out Caesar's will, then send him more legions. There are enough of them sitting idle in peaceful provinces after all.'

'My lady, those provinces are peaceful precisely because of the legions stationed there,' Burrus explained patiently, as to a child.

She looked at him directly. 'Not all of them, surely? Do you really believe Aegyptus, Hispania or Africa would go up in flames if their legions were temporarily reassigned to defeat Parthia? There has been peace in those provinces for over a hundred years. They have become so used to being part of the Empire that they cannot imagine living without Rome. Wouldn't you agree?' She smiled sweetly. 'Of course, with such enhanced power concentrated in Corbulo's hands, there would need to be some consideration given to discouraging him from misusing it. His family is still in Rome . . .'

It was at that moment that Cato recognised the shrewdness of Nero's mistress. She was no mere beauty. Her mind was as sharp as that of anyone in the chamber, and as ruthless. Nero might rule Rome, but if Poppaea ruled Nero, she was the force that must be reckoned with.

'Poppaea is right,' Nero announced. 'We must strengthen our forces in the east. After all, Parthia is not the only challenge we are facing. Our towns along the northern shores of the Euxine Sea are under threat from Scythians. We must protect our interests there. Corbulo will be too busy dealing with the challenges at hand to contemplate treason. Besides, as my beloved has pointed out, he would hardly dare to move against me while I have his family in my clutches.'

'All the same,' said Poppaea, 'it would be wise to limit any temptation that might come his way. The reinforcements for his army could be concentrated somewhere other than Syria until the moment they are required to be used against Parthia. Aegyptus, for example. A quiet backwater, under the control of an equestrian prefect directly appointed by Caesar. It's close enough to Syria to quickly locate the reinforcements when they are needed, but far enough away to prevent feeding Corbulo's ambition.'

'Very good!' Nero smiled and bent down to kiss her on the forehead before turning to his advisers again. 'You see? There is no reason to fear confronting Parthia. This time we shall deploy enough men to finish the task and turn the place into a mere footnote of history. The way is open to us, gentlemen. We have only to summon the heart to take that path to victory.'

Cato saw Seneca's shoulders slump in defeat, but Burrus was not ready to give in. He coughed with a pained expression before he challenged Nero again.

'Caesar, it is not just a question of numbers. Crassus once led a mighty army to its destruction and his death in Parthia. The great Marcus Antonius could not subdue the enemy with an even more powerful army. Why should it be any different for Corbulo? The land itself is hostile to the invader, as those who have served there will attest. Is that not so, Prefect Cato? You and Centurion Macro know the region better than any man . . .' he gave a nod in the direction of Poppaea, 'or woman here.'

All eyes turned on the two officers. Cato sensed Macro go

rigid at his side while he himself swiftly composed a response. If there was the slightest chance of swaying Nero towards peace, it must be taken.

'Yes, the centurion and I served in Syria, Judaea and Armenia. I was also sent to Parthia by General Corbulo to speak with their king. Prefect Burrus is correct when he says it is not just about numbers. Let no one doubt that our soldiers are the best in the known world. Man for man they could beat any army that Parthia deployed in a set-piece battle. But first they would have to march across trackless deserts beneath a merciless sun by day and bitter cold by night, all the while plagued by thirst. By the time they encountered the enemy they would be in no fit state to fight.

'Moreover, I have faced the Parthians. They do not fight as we do. They know how to sacrifice space to win time to wear the enemy down before they strike. Their horse archers will steadily pick us off as we advance. If we send our cavalry after them, they will lead them on to the heavily armed cataphracts, who will dash them to pieces as waves break on a rock. Only when our men are exhausted, whittled down and weakened by thirst and hunger will they offer battle. By then it will be too late and retreat will not be an option. As the army of Crassus discovered . . . Caesar, given what the centurion and I have experienced, I would counsel peace as the better course of action. Let Armenia be neutral. I can assure you that the king of Parthia will never tolerate allowing it to become a vassal state of Rome.'

'That is why it must be ours!' Nero shouted, his eyes wide with anger. 'I am the emperor! It is my will that Armenia will belong to Rome. We cannot permit some mongrel, barbarian dog from out of the desert to defy the will of Caesar. You talk of peace, when any fool can see that to the mob it would look like shameful surrender. Is that what you would have?'

Cato feared that any further response would put him in danger of his life, and perhaps Macro too. He said nothing but kept his eyes unwaveringly on Nero until the emperor switched his attention back to Burrus.

'Am I the only one here with the courage to do what is necessary to protect the reputation of Rome? Will no one speak up for the honour of our people?'

On cue, Tigellinus rose to his feet. 'Send the Parthian embassy back, Caesar! Let them tell their king that Rome does not surrender to their will. Tell them that Rome does not negotiate with barbarians. If there is to be a peace, it will be on terms that Caesar dictates, or they will face war of a kind the world has never experienced before.'

His cronies nodded in support, and Nero raised his chin with a look of cold satisfaction before he waved Tigellinus back to his seat.

'Very well . . . Our message to Parthia is this. Armenia will be annexed by Rome. If Parthia accepts that, there can be peace. If not, there will be war.' He nodded to the scribe sitting on a stool at the side of the room. 'Have that written up and handed to the leader of the Parthian embassy, and tell him that he and his companions are to leave Rome before the end of the day if they wish to avoid my wrath. Go!'

The man hurriedly finished his note and packed his writing materials into his satchel before rising, bowing and backing out of the chamber. Cato looked round at the other advisers and saw despair on the faces of Burrus, Seneca and those who sympathised with them. Tigellinus, by contrast, could not hide his pleasure at being at one with the emperor. It was clear that there had been a shift of Nero's favour in his direction, and that Burrus's moment of honesty had cost him dearly.

'There is one final matter to deal with today, my friends.' Nero turned to Octavia, who had been sitting still throughout the previous confrontation. No doubt, thought Cato, hoping that she had been overlooked and forgotten. She flinched as the emperor's gaze fell upon her like a hawk diving out of the sun, shrinking in on herself as he continued to stare at her. Cato felt a wave of disgust as he saw the visceral expression of cruel delight on Nero's face, while Poppaea casually dropped the last of the grapes into her mouth and tossed the bare sprig onto the floor in front of the couch.

'It has come to our attention that the friends and followers of my former wife have been attempting to turn the affections of my people against me. That of course is treason, a capital offence. However, out of respect for the memory of her father, the *divine* Claudius . . .' Nero paused to enjoy the smirks and sycophantic laughter of those responding to his sarcasm, 'and the affection, however undeserved, that some of the common people still have for her, I have shown her mercy thus far.'

'Here it comes,' Macro muttered.

'Yet far from being the demure model of virtue that she pretends to be, I have recently discovered that my former wife, while married to me, was engaged in an illicit affair.'

'No!' Octavia cried out. 'It's not true.'

'Silence!' Nero commanded, stabbing a finger at her. 'You will speak when I say. If you dare interrupt me again, I will have one of my Praetorians gag you. You will have your chance to speak when you are put on trial.' Octavia wilted back into the alcove. 'That's better. As I was saying, an illicit affair with a low-born individual of my household. Indeed, the affair has continued to this very day, when the name of my former wife's lover was made known to me. The name of a man who is in this room with us now.' He paused theatrically before slowly sweeping his gaze across the faces of those seated before him, every one of whom felt the cold dread of being singled out. At length he looked up at the ceiling and sighed.

'You may stop performing now, Eucaenus. In both senses of the word.'

The notes of the flute ceased and the musician responded in a strangled voice. 'Caesar?'

'You heard me. You are the treacherous villain who has committed adultery with Octavia.'

Cato saw the blood drain from the man's face, and Eucaenus began to tremble. 'No! It is not true! Caesar, I swear it, on my life!'

'Are you calling me a liar?' Nero asked calmly.

Too late Eucaenus saw the trap and in a panic tried to blunder out of it. 'No, Caesar. Of course not.'

'Then if it is not a lie, it must be the truth.'

A movement caught Cato's eye, and he turned to see Octavia rising to her feet. As she opened her mouth to protest, Poppaea hurled a silver goblet, narrowly missing her target, and screamed, 'Silence, slut! You were told what would happen if you tried to speak. Sit down before you are tied down.'

Cato, Macro and the others sat rigidly as they watched the accused flute player shaking like a newborn lamb on one side of Nero and his mistress, while on the other Octavia regarded them with disgust. She summoned up her courage and defiance to address them.

'Do with me what you will, but know this. I will proclaim the truth to my dying day. I was never an adulterer, unlike you, Nero. You philandered your way through the torturous years of our marriage, fornicating with any woman foolish enough to part her legs for you, and forcing yourself on those who would not. You are a foul monster, and a tyrant so foolish and vain that you believe every word of the praise lavished on you by your cronies. I shudder when I recall your hands on my body on those thankfully few occasions when you tried to impregnate me. Once, I blamed myself that I could not give you an heir. Now I rejoice that I could not. I would not want to bring a child into this world who carried your vile blood in his veins.'

'See!' Nero shouted. 'See how she speaks treason! You are all witnesses to it. She condemns herself by her own words.'

He turned to the nearest of the Praetorians. 'Take the bitch away from here! Throw her in a cell while I decide on her fate.'

The Praetorians obeyed the order instantly, almost as if they had been primed for the moment, thought Cato. They held her between them, one of them muffling her attempt to speak out as she was dragged from the room.

Nero turned to Eucaenus. 'Since you both deny the allegation, the only way to get at the truth will be through torture. If you are wise, you will confess quickly. If not, then should you survive, I dare say you will not be in any condition to resume your flute-playing. Instead, you will be reduced to a blind cripple begging on the streets, if I am any judge of the imperial interrogators. Guards, remove him from our presence. Place him in a cell close to Octavia, where she can hear his screams and his inevitable confession.'

Before the Praetorians could react to the order, Burrus rose from his seat and drew back his shoulders. 'Wait!'

The soldiers hesitated, and in that instant Cato saw that their first, instinctive loyalty was to their commander rather than the emperor. While Nero might dismiss or appoint their prefect, it was Burrus they looked to for orders. Cato saw the look of fear that passed over the emperor's face, but Burrus continued before he could respond.

'Caesar, this is wrong. To treat Octavia in this fashion is unconscionable and unwise. Every person in this room knows it, whether they speak up or not. You have what you desire. The divorce is complete and you can marry Poppaea, and when your child is born, all Rome will share your joy and celebrate the event. There is no need to persecute your former wife. What good will come of making a martyr out of her? She is regarded with affection by the people of Rome, from the humblest street beggar to the most august of our senators. And with good reason. She poses no threat to you and wishes only to live out her days in peace. Why can't you let her do that?'

The question hung in the air, with Nero too startled by the Praetorian prefect's audacity to respond, and his advisers too terrified to do more than remain quite still and barely breathe.

'I am, and always have been, your loyal servant, Caesar. I have tried to tell you the unadorned truth, and on the rare occasions when I have disagreed with your decisions I have done so out of concern for your reputation. That is why I tell you now, to your face before your advisers, that you are doing wrong. Worse, you are making a mistake. Whatever your personal reasons for this, I beg you to put them aside and think of how it will look to your people. They will not only question your wisdom, they will condemn your treatment of Octavia. Their disapproval will turn to scorn, scorn to anger, anger to violence, and none of us knows where that may lead. Let Octavia be. Let Eucaenus go. Exile him if you wish. If not . . .' Burrus left the sentence unfinished. The threat was clear enough to be unspoken.

Nero's face was white and his lips trembled. Whether it was from rage, or fear, or both, it was impossible to say. Poppaea leaned towards him and whispered into his ear as she took one of his hands and stroked the back of it soothingly with her thumb. The emperor kept his eyes on Burrus as he listened to her, and when she had finished, he nodded and eased himself back down beside her. He took a deep breath before he addressed the prefect calmly.

'Out of gratitude for your years of service, and because your sickness grows steadily worse, I am prepared to overlook what you have just said. Illness has a way of affecting men's minds, and you are not yourself, Burrus. We can all see that. However, there may be some wisdom in your words. I need time to reflect before I decide what happens to Octavia. It is true that sometimes

I am inclined to act too swiftly without sufficient thought for the consequences. I am glad that there are some among my advisers who have the courage to speak plainly to me, as you do. For the time being, she will be held in the palace. I will announce her fate once I have considered the facts. You are tired, my old friend. You need rest. Leave your duties here to your officials and return to your headquarters at the Praetorian camp. Put aside your burdens for the rest of the month and you can return to duty when your strength returns. Go now.'

Burrus's shoulders slumped in resignation before he bowed and turned to leave the chamber. Nero waited until he had gone before he focused his attention on the men who remained. 'Let none of you think that I will tolerate such insolence again. Whatever the merits of what Burrus said, I am Caesar. I decide what is best for me, my people and Rome. No one else. I advise you to bear that in mind so that there is no repeat of what just occurred. You too are dismissed. Leave us.'

Cato, Macro and the rest stood and bowed before backing away a few paces and turning towards the entrance of the chamber. Cato hung behind and was the last to leave. He saw Poppaea reach for a fresh sprig of grapes. Eucaenus put his flute into its case and made to follow the others, but was halted by a curt command from Nero.

'Not you.'

The emperor pointed to the nearest of the Praetorians, and then at Eucaenus, and Cato had no doubt as to the man's fate.

CHAPTER TWENTY-SIX

'Sweet fucking Jupiter,' said Macro as they left the palace and descended into the Forum. 'What was Burrus thinking back there? Does the man have a death wish?'

'You saw how ill he looked. I would say he has weeks, maybe days, left in him. Perhaps he is beyond caring about the consequences of speaking up for what is right.'

'All the same, I have to say he genuinely impressed me for the first time. I never would have thought old Burrus had balls of iron. Did you see the look on Nero's face?' Macro let out a low whistle. 'I don't think anyone in that room is going to forget it. For a moment there I thought he was going to give the order for Burrus's head to be served on a platter to that woman of his. And Poppaea? She was ice cold throughout. That's one woman whose heart is never going to melt. I'm not sure who I should fear more, Nero or her.'

'Both of them are dangerous. When you add Tigellinus to the mix, that trio will be each contributing their own dose of poison to ruling Rome. They'll ignore what Burrus had to say about Octavia. Poppaea wants her rival for the affections of the mob removed. Tigellinus wants Burrus pushed aside so he can become prefect of the Praetorian Guard, and he's not even prepared to wait until illness claims Burrus's life. And Nero wants whatever the other two tell him he wants.' Cato shook his head. 'Shit, being caught up in palace politics is the last thing I expected to have to survive when we came back from Britannia.'

'Yet here we are, in the thick of it again. I tell you, Cato, trouble just seems to follow us around like a bad smell.'

'Well, yes. Quite.' Cato reflected on the drama they had just witnessed. 'Did you catch that moment when Burrus countermanded Nero's order?'

Macro took a moment to recall the incident. 'Yes, when he told the guards to wait and they obeyed.'

'Revealing, don't you think?'

Macro glanced at him. 'How so?'

'If it comes to a choice of who to obey in a crisis, Nero or Burrus, I'm not sure how the Praetorians will react. I wonder if sending Burrus back to the Praetorian camp might not be a mistake for Nero.'

'Maybe, but what crisis is there? You heard it yourself, the danger posed by the grain supply is over.'

'Not quite. The situation in the city is still tense. We saw that earlier. Rumour feeds on rumour and people are restless, and that's dangerous. The games did good work in distracting them, but now they're going to have something else to provoke them into action. This business with Octavia is going to be like adding fresh kindling to dying flames. As soon as word hits the streets that she's been arrested and put in a cell, there will be protests.'

'There's always a few loudmouths trying to stir the mob up.'

'More than a few this time. And there will be plenty who have sympathetic ears open to their message.' Cato paused and took off his neck cloth, then mopped the perspiration from his brow. 'This heat doesn't help. I don't know about you, Macro, but it feels to me like the city is a tinderbox. One spark will be enough to set it all off. I think it would be wise if you got Petronella and Bardea out of Rome as soon as possible. Have them go to my farm until it's safe to return.'

'You really think they're in danger?'

'I think we're all in danger. You, me, them, the people of Rome. Even Nero, if he doesn't handle the situation carefully.'

'After today, I'd say that was a racing certainty.' Macro nodded. 'All right, I'll see to it as soon as I go off duty. That is, if you're happy for me to be away from the camp for a few hours.'

'Of course. Just make sure they understand the need for haste. I don't know how long we've got before word gets out about Octavia.'

'There's always the hope that Burrus's advice hit home with Nero.'

'There's always hope,' Cato agreed. 'But if experience proves anything, it's that hope rarely delivers.'

Macro gave a dry laugh. 'If there's one thing certain in this life, lad, it's that you'll always find a way straight to the amphora that's half empty.'

It took two days for the first rumours to reach the streets of Rome. Cato and Macro had ventured into the Forum in old tunics, frayed at the sleeves and hard worn. With strips of cloth tied about their heads and cheap sandals on their feet, they easily passed off as two of the many thousands of casual labourers scraping a living in the capital. While the constant patrols conducted by the urban cohorts were keeping a lid on the tensions stewing away in the unseasonal heat, Cato knew that he needed first-hand intelligence on the mood of the people. Particularly now that Nero was fanning fresh flames that would ignite the resentment and fury of many.

In the hour before noon, they picked their way through the markets, listening for exchanges between customers and merchants or groups of idlers sitting by the fountains, and looking for signs of the kinds of furtive conversation that suggested people's views were changing. The trick was not to be too obvious about the eavesdropping or to linger too long among those who were wary of being overheard.

From a baker talking to a regular customer Cato discovered that news of Octavia's arrest had leaked out of the palace. He and Macro tailed the woman, who had brought two loaves and a pie, and observed her telling an acquaintance about the arrest in a low voice. It was clear to Cato that before the sun set that evening, most of the city would be aware of what had happened. The woman suddenly glanced round and fixed her gaze on the two men, her eyes narrowing suspiciously as she recognised them from the bakery. She abruptly ended her discussion with her companion and scurried away, looking over her shoulder to see if she was being followed. There was little point in pursuing her, and Cato crossed to the fountain in front of the Temple of Vesta. The water in the basin was low due to the lack of rain and the dregs appeared too murky and unwholesome to drink. He took off his headband and soaked it to provide some comfort.

'I think we've heard enough to know which way the wind is blowing,' he decided. 'And I could use a drink.'

'That's the best thing I've heard today.' Macro looked round for the nearest chop house. The crowd in the Forum was steadily thinning as people sought shelter from the glare of the midday sun. He pointed out a place on the corner of a street fifty paces away. Sausages were hanging from hooks and wisps of steam curled off the pots of stew set into the counter facing the Forum to lure in customers. A brightly painted sign hung from an iron bracket. It depicted in lurid colours two smiling men raising their cups in a toast beneath the florid legend *The Happy Brothers*.

The clientele was the usual mix of labourers, layabouts and louche young aristocrats out to experience the authentic street life of the capital. Cato and Macro took the only empty table, in the corner of the room near to the grates that heated the stew. The atmosphere was sweltering, and as they sat down, Cato realised why the table had been unoccupied. But before they could leave in search of another eatery, a serving boy was at their side asking for their order.

Cato looked across at Macro. 'Want to try somewhere else?'

'No point. We'd be lucky to find anywhere with a spare table at this time of day.'

Cato looked at the boy. 'What's on offer?'

'Stew of the day, or stew of yesterday.'

'What's the difference?'

'Stew of yesterday is half the price.'

Macro snorted with derision. 'What if we go for stew of the day before yesterday? That should be given away free, right?'

The boy regarded him blankly.

'We'll have the stew of the day,' said Cato. 'And a jug of watered wine.'

'Better make that wine of the day,' Macro added.

Before he could be subjected to any more such comments, the boy turned on his heel and headed towards the counter to place the order. Looking round the interior, Cato took in the mood of the customers. Some sat eating or drinking alone, but most were in small groups clustered on benches around the tables. A group of men two tables away must have been drinking since earlier in the day and were well into their cups. Enough to be speaking loudly and indiscreetly. They were complaining about the brevity of the recent games put on by Nero and recalling the far more spectacular exhibitions that had taken place under previous emperors. At least they weren't discussing the grain supply or Octavia, thought Cato.

'Not the happiest of clienteles, despite the name of the place,' he said to Macro.

Macro nodded. 'Must have been thinking of Romulus and Remus when they came up with the sign.'

The boy returned with a tray and set down two bowls of stew, a small jug and two samianware goblets. Macro indicated the jug.

'Here, boy, what do you call this?'

'A wine jug, sir.'

'Do we look like pygmies? I want something to drink, not merely moisten my lips. Get us a proper jug.'

'That'll be extra, sir.'

Macro eyed him harshly. 'I take it you don't earn many tips.'

'I'll see what I can do, sir.'

'You do that.' Macro handed him the jug. 'And tell the owner that if he just tops the order up with water, I'll be having a word with him myself.'

When the boy had gone, Cato shook his head. 'We're not supposed to be drawing attention to ourselves. Anything else you want to complain about?'

In response, Macro dipped his spoon into the stew, raised it and let the thin, greasy liquid slop back into the bowl. 'Where should I start?'

'Enough. Keep your head down, ears open and try and ignore the meal.'

The boy returned with a jug twice the size, and Cato and Macro hunched over their workman's lunch, pausing now and again to sip enough wine to wash away the taste of the stew. Not long after they started eating, a man entered and paused on the threshold for his eyes to adjust to the gloom of the interior. He was spotted by someone at the table close to Cato and Macro and beckoned over.

'Apullius! Come and join us, lad.'

As the newcomer drew closer, Cato saw that he was young, no more than twenty, and wearing the purple-fringed tunic of an imperial freedman. At once his senses heightened and he strained to catch the details of the conversation. A drink was poured for Apullius, and his cronies leaned in. 'What news from the House of Poppaea?' asked one of them.

That caused a ripple of laughter from around the table and more than a few glances from other customers.

Apullius took a swig and gave a theatrical sigh. 'He's only gone and done it. Caesar's going to put Octavia on trial for adultery.'

'Old news,' one of his companions scoffed. 'Heard that this morning. Some bollocks about her and a flute player.'

'Eucaenus?' Apullius shook his head. 'Not him. I've a mate who takes scraps down to the cells. He heard that Eucaenus gave up nothing, even under torture. So that put the top boy on the spot. The word now is that he's cut a deal with Ancietus, the admiral of the fleet at Misenum. He gets a comfortable exile if he admits that he was having it off with Octavia when she was married to Nero. Her goose is well and truly cooked now.'

'Pah! Rubbish, you're making it up!'

'The fuck I am,' Apullius shot back. 'I got it from the taster who was in the room when Ancietus agreed to take the pilum for Nero. That was no more than a couple of hours ago. Dare say Ancietus is already packing his bags.'

'And Octavia?'

'Writing her will, if I'm any judge of things. She'll be lucky if Nero gives her the same treatment. That witch Poppaea will settle for nothing less than her head.'

There were growls of protest from those around the table, and Cato saw that others in the room had turned to listen to the exchange. Now one of them, an older man, frail-looking but eyes gleaming with anger, stood up and brandished his fist. 'It's a bloody outrage what Nero's doing. Him and that conniving bitch of his! He owes everything to Octavia's father and this is how he repays the favour.'

One of the men at the table laughed. 'Sit down, you old fool. What are you going to do about it? Wave your walking stick outside the palace gates? Fat lot of good that'll do.'

'Down with Poppaea! Down with Nero!' The old man looked round and urged others to join in with his chant, and one by one most of the customers did so. The landlord of the chop house

312

looked on in alarm for a moment before he raised a metal skillet and struck it with a ladle from one of the stew pots.

'Oi! That's enough of that! You trying to get the urban cohorts down on me? I don't want my business closed. You want to cause trouble, do it out there in the streets, or better still, outside the palace! Shut your traps or get out!'

'All right,' one of the men at the table responded. 'We'll go, right, lads? Let's all go. Everyone here. Come on!'

He and his companions abruptly rose and made their way outside. Too late, the landlord cottoned on to the ploy and hurried out from behind the counter.

'Oi, just you wait! You pay for your food and wine first, you bastards!'

But now the rest of the customers pushed past him and piled out into the street, joining the chorus of voices chanting in protest against Poppaea.

Cato lowered his spoon and pushed the bowl aside as he leaned across the table to address Macro. 'That's it. The city's going to erupt once the news spreads. I'm going back to the camp to get the men ready to march. You join me there once you've seen to Petronella and Bardea. Get them out of Rome as quick as you can, and have my steward bolt the doors until it's over.'

Macro hesitated, torn between his duty as a soldier and his duty as a husband and father. Cato reached over and pressed his shoulder.

'Get going, brother. Before it's too late.'

Macro nodded, standing up and hurrying out of the chop house. Cato was about to follow him when he saw the landlord step across the doorway. He reached into his purse and took out a gleaming denarius, holding it up for the man to see before slapping it down on the table.

'Why, thank you, sir!' The landlord dipped his head in gratitude and moved aside.

Cato paused on the threshold. 'If I were you, I'd close for the day and board the place up.'

Then he stepped into the street and broke into a run as he turned in the direction of the camp of the urban cohorts.

CHAPTER TWENTY-SEVEN

'Come on!' Macro pounded on the door with the heel of his fist. 'Bloody well open up!'

He paused as he heard a rush of footsteps a short distance up the street. Gripping the handle of the dagger concealed under his tunic, he backed into the porch. A moment later, a group of fifty or so men surged past, heading in the direction of the Forum. Some carried clubs and other weapons and wore neckerchiefs to hide their faces. When they were gone, Macro released his grip and turned to strike the door again.

He saw the slot behind the grille at eye level slide open, and the steward peered out. As soon as he saw Macro, he pulled back the bolts. Macro stepped into the atrium, closing and locking the door behind him.

'Where's my wife?'

'In the garden, master. Under the awning to the rear.'

'I want you to prepare two haversacks with food and drink to last two days. And put a good sharp knife in each bag.'

'Master?'

'Just do as I say, damn you. Do it quickly.'

'Yes, master.'

Macro brushed past the man and strode down the corridor that gave out onto the garden. Although it was mid afternoon, it felt somewhat cooler here than on the street, and the herbs and flowers that Petronella tended lent the air a pleasant scent. The awning that she had arranged to be set up stretched across the far end of the garden, up against the rear wall of the house, close to the modest fountain. Petronella was lying on her side, eyes closed as she wafted air over her face with a small fan. She blinked as she heard the crunch of Macro's sandals on the gravel path.

'Get up!' he ordered.

At once she swung her legs over the couch, fully alert. 'What's happened? I wasn't expecting you back until you came off duty.'

'You and Bardea need to get out of the city at once.'

Her jaw fell slightly in surprise before she quickly recovered her senses. 'Macro, tell me what's going on.'

'Looks like the place may go up in smoke.' He briefly related the details of Nero's move against Octavia and the reaction of the mob. Not long after he had parted from Cato, he had come across an angry crowd making their way down to the Forum to protest outside the palace. The uncertainty of recent days, the unrelenting heat and the news about Octavia had tipped the public mood over the edge, and now they had an excuse for the outpouring of their pent-up frustration.

Petronella listened anxiously, and when Macro had finished, she shook her head in wonder. 'I was out shopping this morning. There was no sign of trouble. I can't believe things have got out of hand so quickly.'

'Believe it. I've ordered some rations for you and Bardea. You'll need them when you are on the road.'

'On the road?' she repeated. 'What are you talking about?'

'Like I said, I want you out of Rome. Go to Cato's villa and wait for word from me there. I'll let you know if and when it's safe to come back.'

She made to protest, but he leaned down and kissed her hurriedly. 'Don't argue with me, love. Just do as I say. Besides the food, I've told Taurus to provide you with some knives, just in case. I hope you don't have to use them.'

He looked round. 'Where's Bardea?'

'She's not here.'

He felt his heartbeat quicken. 'Where in Hades is she?'

'Visiting a friend, to show them the puppy.'

'What friend?' Macro frowned. Like any new arrival from a strange land, Bardea had been bewildered by the scale and chaos of the capital and had been reluctant to go out on her own. Then he noticed the guilty expression on his wife's face.

'I was going to tell you when the time was right,' she began.

'Tell me what?'

'She's met a boy. Son of the merchant I went to for the cloth to make the awning. He's a good lad. Quiet and polite and they get on well enough. It's all quite harmless.'

Macro slapped his forehead in frustration and anger. 'Ye gods! What were you thinking? She's not used to city ways. A boy like that will eat her for breakfast.'

'I doubt it. Not after all she went through in Britannia.'

He took a deep breath. 'There's no time for this. We'll speak about it later. Where does he live?'

'Over on the Caelian.'

'Shit . . . shit,' Macro fumed. It would take too long to cross the city to track her down. Even if they found the house, there was no guarantee Bardea would still be there. He had visions of her going along with the boy to the Forum to be part of the crowd gathering outside the palace.

'She said she would be back well before dusk,' said Petronella.

'And you believed her?'

'Of course. Why wouldn't I? I trust her. So should you.'

Macro saw the warning signs, the way his wife's eyebrows drew closer together and her lips tightened into a defiant pout. But there was no time to pander to her. 'All right . . . You at least can get ready. Change into some plain clothes, something that won't stand out, then wait by the front door. I'll join you once I'm done. Go.'

As Petronella scurried off towards the house, Macro paced up and down impatiently, working out the best course of action. If Bardea didn't return soon, he resolved to get Petronella out of Rome at least, and his daughter would have to take her chances in the house, along with the servants and slaves, hopefully safe behind the locked street door and high walls. As deeply as he regretted it, he could not afford to waste time looking for her. Cato was expecting him back at the camp as soon as possible. At least he could send his friend a message explaining the situation and promising to join him as soon as the women were as safe as each could be.

He took a last look around the walls bordering the garden and was satisfied that they would deter any casual looters at least. Then he returned to the atrium, where the steward was waiting with the two haversacks. He held them open so that Macro could check the knives within and satisfy himself that the blades were substantial enough to deter anyone rash enough to threaten Petronella and Bardea. Along with the weapons were water canteens, small loaves, cheese and apples.

'Good job. Now one last thing . . .' Macro made his way to the kitchen, where the cook was cutting up meat for the evening meal. His assistant, a boy of ten by the name of Helos, was sitting on a stool peeling vegetables. Both bowed as Macro entered.

'Boy, I need you to run an urgent errand for me. You know the camp of the urban cohorts?'

Helos nodded.

'I want you to go there and deliver a message to the prefect. Tell him that I might be delayed briefly. I'll explain when I get there. Tell him that if they have already marched on the Forum, I'll come and find him there. You got all that?'

'Yes, master.'

'Go, and be double quick. Don't stop for anything.'

The boy scampered out of the room and Macro turned to the cook. 'Leave the meat. I want you to hand out whatever knives and cleavers you have to the rest of the household.'

'Master?'

'Just do it, and take your orders from Taurus when my wife and I have gone.'

'Yes, master.'

Macro returned to the atrium just as the door to the street closed behind the kitchen boy. The steward resumed his place by the grille and watched as more people flowed by, this time accompanied by angry chants against Poppaea and Nero. Petronella emerged from the corridor and crossed the atrium. She had changed into a plain brown stola and black cloak and wore a sturdy pair of sandals. A spare cloak for Bardea was bundled under her arm, and she set it down beside the bags. Macro regarded her and gave a nod. 'You'll do.'

She cocked her head to one side. 'Thank you for the high praise, husband.'

He was glad that she had regained her spirits after his instructions for her to leave Rome.

'Are you ready to go?' he asked.

'Not until Bardea is back.'

'There's no need to wait for her. She'll be safe enough here when she returns.'

'If that's so, why are you so keen to get me out of Rome?' Petronella folded her arms. 'If Bardea will be safe here, so will I.'

Macro let out an explosive hiss of frustration. 'All right. She won't be as safe here as she would be at the farm. I admit it. But if I can only get one of you to safety, then that's what I must do. No arguments. You're going.'

'Make me.'

'For fuck's sake, Petronella. How do you think I can do my duty while I'm worrying about you and Bardea? I'm trying to do the best for both of you. It's not my fucking fault she's gone off to see her boyfriend. It's not my fucking fault I had no idea that she even *had* a boyfriend. That's down to you. Right now, I need you to help me do what I can under the circumstances. And that's to get you to safety.'

'I'm not going.'

'Yes, you bloody are!'

They were interrupted by the steward. 'Here she is, master. Bardea.' He slid back the bolts and opened the door.

Bardea was carrying the puppy in a sling, and she looked surprised to see them both by the door, obviously angry with each other.

'Has something happened?'

Macro turned his gaze on her. 'You've just been out in the streets. Did you somehow miss the angry crowds heading for the palace?'

'Oh, I wondered about that.'

He rolled his eyes. 'Never mind. Change into that old cloak. Do it now.'

'Why?'

He felt his blood begin to boil. 'What is it with you two? Just bloody do as you're told.'

Bardea was still for a beat, then she set the puppy down and put on the cloak that Petronella had brought for her. When she went to retrieve Flaminius from where he was sniffing around by the pond, Macro shook his head. 'Leave him here.'

'Leave him?' Bardea looked surprised, then angry. 'No chance. Anyway, are we going somewhere?'

'You're both leaving Rome for a few days. I'll not have any argument about it. You can see your boyfriend again when you get back.'

Bardea exchanged a guilty look with Petronella before picking up the dog and returning it to the sling she had put back across her shoulder. As she turned to Macro with a serious expression that reminded him painfully of her mother, Boudica, another group passed the door, shouting their slogans, and he decided there was no time to waste in a stand-off with either of the feisty women in his life.

'All right. Bring the bloody dog. Now pick up your bags. There's food, drink and a weapon in there. Don't ask why, Bardea. Just pick it up and let's be off.'

As the two women completed their preparations, Macro turned to the steward. 'Keep the doors locked and don't let anyone in. If there's trouble, do your best to keep 'em out. If you can't, don't try to be brave. Give them what they want. There should be enough food and water in the house for several days. By then, things should have settled, or the city will have been burned down. You are in charge here. Do whatever you need to do to protect the others. I'll be in the city and will check on you when I can. Good luck.' He stuck out his hand and the steward took it.

'May the gods protect you, master.'

The street was empty when they emerged from the house. Macro had already planned which route they would take to get to the Colline gate and the road that would take them in the direction of the farm. He wished to avoid the neighbourhoods he considered unsafe, but some risks had to be taken as he was also aware of the need to get back to the camp as soon as he had seen the women safely out of the city. As things stood, he would be fortunate if he rejoined Cato before nightfall.

They set off up the street towards the crest of the Viminal Hill and the low ridge that linked it to the Quirinal. A crime-ridden slum lay in the vale between the two hills, and he skirted it. In the distance he could see the dark band of storm clouds edging

321

towards the city. They were passed by more and more people heading in the opposite direction, but there were others, no doubt sharing Macro's concern, who hurried along the same way. He kept Petronella and Bardea moving as quickly as possible. By his estimate there was no more than three hours of light left, and he could hear the cries of protest from the centre of Rome as clearly as the din from the racegoers at the Great Circus on other days. That meant there must already be tens of thousands thronging the Forum. The three cohorts under Cato's command would not be able to contain the swelling crowd for long, and soon Nero would be forced to call on the ten cohorts of Praetorians if there was to be any hope of restoring order. Every soldier would be needed, and the thought drove Macro on as the two women struggled to keep up with his pace.

The three turned onto the street that led directly to the Colline gate, some five hundred paces ahead. Macro was relieved to see that it was almost deserted. The doors of most of the shops and small businesses were already shuttered and the proprietors of those that weren't were busy clearing the last of their wares from the pavements and closing up. Bardea looked from side to side anxiously as she cradled the puppy, now fully aware of the danger. Macro heard more voices raised in protest from ahead, and as they turned the final corner, he saw a crowd of perhaps two hundred people gathered in front of the closed gate. They drew closer and saw that a double line of Praetorians was keeping the angry crowd back.

'Why are the gates closed?' asked Petronella.

Macro shook his head. Normally, they would be left open day and night, with only a token presence of armed men from the city watch to keep an eye open for slaves attempting to escape.

'Wait here,' he said pushing his way through the crowd towards the Praetorians and the young, nervous-looking optio who commanded them.

'What's the meaning of this?' he demanded. 'Why are the gates closed?'

'Orders,' the optio said tersely. 'Now push off.'

Macro stood his ground. 'You better show a centurion of the urban cohorts the respect he is due, lad, unless you want me to take your insubordination up with your superiors.'

The optio regarded him suspiciously before he recognised Macro's military bearing and relented.

'I have orders to seal the gateway, sir. Until further notice no one is to enter or leave the city.'

'Orders? Who from?'

'Tribune Rufrius Gallo, sir. Signed off by Burrus himself. It's the same for all the other gates.'

A large man brushed past Macro and stabbed a finger at the optio. 'You ain't got no right to stop us leaving.'

'I have my orders,' the optio replied.

Macro could see that the large man was in the mood for a fight, and he intervened between the two and spoke in a reasonable tone. 'I expect your orders are intended to stop anyone joining the crowd down in the Forum. These people want to leave the city before there's any trouble. What harm is there in letting them through, eh?'

'My orders were clear, sir. No one goes through the gate, either way.'

'There are women and children here. At least let them through.'

'Sorry, sir. I can't permit that.'

'Then let me speak to your superior at the camp. I'm sure he'll see reason.'

'No.'

'Dammit, man! I'm a senior officer. I'm ordering you to let me through.'

Macro made to push his way past, but the optio thrust him back and gripped the handle of his sword. 'It's against orders.

Particularly for soldiers, or men sent from the palace. No one gets through . . . I'm sorry, sir. There's nothing I can do about it. Now get back. Get back, all of you!' he shouted over Macro's head as the crowd began to press forward.

Someone lobbed a clod of mud that struck the helmet of the Praetorian next to the optio. The officer flinched and shouted the command. 'Draw swords! I'm warning you! Get back or I'll have my men strike you down. Back, I say!'

As the gleaming tips of the Praetorians' swords emerged from between their shields, those at the front of the crowd retreated, pressing against those behind. The sudden crush caused panicked and angry shouts. Macro forced his way back to rejoin Petronella and Bardea.

'We can't get you out this way, and the optio says all the other city gates have also been closed.'

'Why?' Petronella frowned. 'What's the point of that?'

'I don't know . . .' Macro was trying to think of an alternative plan even as he pondered the reason for the optio's orders. And why had he been explicitly told to prevent soldiers and palace officials from leaving the city? He could make no sense of it at present; it was something he would have to consider later. Right now, he needed to get the women to a place of safety.

'We'll have to go back to the house,' he decided. 'If we can't get out of Rome, there's no other choice. Come.'

As they turned away from the angry confrontation at the gate and retraced their steps, the optio shouted a final warning to the crowd. Shortly afterwards, the air was split with the sounds of screams and howls of rage.

'Don't stop. Don't look back,' said Macro. He felt sick with anxiety. They were trapped inside a city on the edge of exploding into violence, and there was nothing he could do to keep his wife and daughter from danger.

CHAPTER TWENTY-EIGHT

A distant peal of thunder from the approaching storm vied with the roar of the crowd from the far side of the Capitoline Hill as Cato led his three cohorts along the avenue that ran parallel to the Tiber. They had made good progress since the streets were almost empty. Those who had not gone to the Forum to demand Octavia's release were staying indoors, a self-imposed curfew while they waited to see what the following morning would bring. Cato had brought with him every man fit enough to fight and had left the camp in the hands of one of the optios injured during the fire, together with a handful of walking wounded to defend the entrance if part of the mob came their way. The optio had been told to send Macro to join the main body should he return to the camp. Cato was worried about his friend and hoped that he had managed to get Petronella and Bardea out of the city without any trouble. There had been no time to waste in getting the cohorts assembled and setting off for the palace, and Macro would have to catch up as best he could.

There had been no word from the palace since they had left the meeting of Nero's advisers a few hours before. Cato was acting on his own initiative in leading his men to the Forum, and hoped that his pre-emptive action would be seen for what it was: an attempt to forestall violence rather than part of a plot against Nero. If he managed to get his cohorts in between the mob and the palace and the confrontation turned violent, there was every chance the blame would fall on his shoulders. It was not a question of choosing the right course of action, he reflected, merely hoping that he was pursuing the least dangerous.

The column had reached the junction of the road leading to the bridge that crossed the river to Tiber Island when a figure in palace livery came running towards them. Lemulus, leading the small vanguard party, halted him and there was a hurried exchange as Cato trotted forward to join them.

'This man says he has a message from Tigellinus, sir.'

'What is it?' Cato demanded.

The palace servant was breathing hard and took an instant to gather himself. 'Thank the gods you are . . . already on the way.'

'Speak up, man!' Cato snapped. 'The message! What's the message?'

His tone forced the servant to attention. 'The mob are at the gates of the outer courtyard, sir. Tigellinus fears they may try to force their way in at any moment. He has sent for the urban cohorts to protect the palace.'

Cato felt some small relief at this vindication of his decision to call out his men. Then something else occurred to him. 'What about the Praetorians?'

'There's only the men on guard duty, sir. A message was sent to the Praetorian camp to order them to march on the Forum, but there was no response and there's been no sign of Burrus and his men. That's why I was sent to find you, sir.'

'What in Hades is going on?' asked Lemulus. 'What is Burrus playing at?'

Cato had a shrewd idea about what was unfolding, but there was no time to discuss it with the centurion. He focused his attention on the servant.

'How many Praetorians are at the palace?'

'Just the duty century, sir, and a few others who happened to be there for other reasons. A hundred and fifty or so. We can't expect any help from the vigiles. Those that aren't bottled up in their watchhouses are busy dealing with outbreaks of looting in other parts of the city.'

'What about the German bodyguards?'

It was a desperate query. The German mercenaries had served a number of emperors before Nero, as they had been considered less likely to be drawn into conspiracies if they could not speak Latin. Nero had decided they were uncouth and barbaric and had reduced their number. Only a small company of them remained in their barracks attached to the palace.

'They have already been alerted, sir. They're guarding Caesar's private suite.'

A last line of defence then, Cato mused. Not that they would be able to protect Nero and Poppaea for long if the mob broke into the palace. It was vital to get his men into position as swiftly as possible to prevent a massacre of the imperial family and the hundreds of servants and slaves who lived in the palace. If the mob was already pressing forward at the entrance to the outer courtyard, there was no question of the cohorts fighting their way through to reach the gate. He would have to lead them in another way.

'Which way did you come?'

'Through a service entrance at the rear of the palace. This end of the Great Circus, sir.'

'How many people have gathered there?'

'Not that many when I set off, sir. Most of them are in the Forum. Thousands and thousands of them,' the man added, his voice trembling.

'Then that's our way in. I want you to go back to Tigellinus as fast as you can. Tell him that the urban cohorts are on their way and will enter the palace complex by the same way you came. Go.'

As soon as the servant had sprinted off along the street, Cato turned to Lemulus. 'Change of plan. We'll go via the Boarium. At the quick step. Give the order, but pass it down the line quietly. Let's not attract any more attention than we have to.'

Despite the lack of bellowed commands, the noise made by the boots of nigh on two thousand heavily armed soldiers in the confined space between the tenement blocks was loud enough. Thankfully the rising din from the direction of the Forum drowned out the advance of Cato and his men. At the junction of the street leading to the Forum and the palace, they continued on into the mostly ruined Boarium. A sharp odour still clung to the stifling atmosphere even this many days after the fire. On the fringes of the market were the buildings that had been saved from the blaze, but even some of these carried the dark streaks of grime from the smoke and drifting embers. Being closer to the heat had caused the plaster on the walls to shrink and crack.

They came to the remains of the buildings that marked the firebreak. Paths had been cleared along the lines of the streets and the rubble piled up on either side. Cato saw a handful of people digging through the ruins to try and find anything of value that might have survived the inferno. They paused in their labours to watch the soldiers pass by with wary stares, but he ignored them. There was no time to arrest the looters or chase them away, and they returned to their work as soon as they realised they would not be bothered on this occasion. Cato made a mental note to increase patrols across the ruins once Rome was no longer in peril. Assuming he survived what was to come, he reflected grimly.

The column crossed the blackened stretch of wasteland and entered the tightly packed tenements of the slum beyond before turning up the slope towards the curved end of the Great Circus. There were some in the buildings on either side who had caught the rebellious mood of the moment and dared to hurl insults down from the windows and rickety balconies overhanging the street. Emboldened, they began to throw the contents of their sewage buckets too, and Lemulus, marching beside Cato, was caught by a deluge of piss.

'What the fuck?' he snarled, and paused to look up at the woman holding an empty pail who was laughing at him from the safety of the third storey. 'I'll have you!'

'Not now,' said Cato. 'Keep moving.'

Lemulus pointed at the woman. 'Best not be here when I come back this way . . .'

The soldiers continued, heads hunched down as they were subjected to further indignities. Cato, amused by the misfortune of Lemulus, had thought he had escaped a similar humiliation, but just as they reached the edge of the neighbourhood and the end of the Great Circus loomed above them, he was struck by a bucket of slops, a foul-smelling concoction of rotten food, piss and shit. He paused mid stride, disgusted and enraged. Lemulus glanced sidelong at him.

'Not now, eh, sir? Best we keep moving.'

Cato continued without a word, brushing as much of the muck from his shoulders as possible as they emerged into the open ground that surrounded the vast stadium. As elsewhere in the city, the chop houses, inns and other small businesses were closed up. A crowd had started to form on this side of the palace as well, but their angry chants died away as they caught sight of the approaching soldiers. Those directly ahead of the column melted away from the small service entrance where they had been shouting abuse at the handful of Praetorian Guards in front of the sturdy-looking gate. Beyond was the jumble of structures that had once been grand houses in the days of the Republic but now served as storerooms and accommodation for the large number of slaves and freedmen who made up the staff of the imperial palace.

'Open up!' Cato ordered as he approached the gate.

The Praetorians hurriedly obeyed the order, grateful for the presence of more men to bolster the perimeter of the palace. There was a large yard beyond the gate where several heavy wagons were parked ready to have their supplies unloaded. That morning, however, the slaves who normally carried out such duties were absent. Many had locked themselves into their quarters. The rest had been armed with an assortment of weapons to help defend the palace. There was just enough space for the three cohorts in the yard, and Cato turned to the tribune commanding the Second.

'Marcellus, have one of the Praetorians guide your men through the palace to reinforce the outer courtyard. I'll send you further orders once I find out how the land lies.'

'Yes, sir.'

As the men tramped off along a narrow alley leading up through the service area, Cato assigned Lemulus and his men to guard the yard while the Third Cohort stood by in reserve.

He knew the layout of the palace well enough to negotiate the labyrinth of narrow alleys and corridors to the imperial suite occupying the heights above the Forum. He was admitted past the screen of German bodyguards by their centurion. It was late afternoon and the sun was low in the sky, burnishing the tiled roofs of the surrounding temples and public buildings in a fiery red that reminded Cato of blood. An ill omen, he thought. Most of the Forum was in the shadows, but even in the absence of direct sunlight, the heat was sweltering and further aggravated the restless anger of the mob. Through a large arched window he saw that the entire expanse of the Forum was now one heaving mass of people, gesticulating with their fists and thrusting their fingers up at the imperial quarters as they shouted their abuse at Poppaea and Nero and called for the release of Octavia.

Tigellinus and a small number of the emperor's inner circle were with Nero and Poppaea as Cato was admitted to a high-ceilinged room with openings out onto a narrow garden terrace that overlooked the Forum. Four of the German bodyguards stood to one side, looking on impassively. They seemed to be the only unperturbed people in the room. The roar of the mob filled the strained atmosphere of the chamber as Cato approached and bowed his head to Nero.

'Prefect Cato!' The emperor hurried to him. 'Thank the gods you are here! Where are your men?'

'I sent one cohort to the outer courtyard, Caesar. The others are at the rear of the palace awaiting orders.'

'Good, good . . .' Nero clasped his hands together. Then his lips curled in contempt. 'Now we have enough men to keep the rabble out of the palace.'

Cato quickly thought over the size of the palace complex and the location of the various entrances. He did not have nearly enough men to defend them all, even with the assistance of the servants and slaves who had been armed, in addition to the small number of Praetorians and German bodyguards on the scene.

'Are Burrus and his men on the way here, Caesar?'

A dark look crossed the emperor's face and he exchanged a glance with Tigellinus and Poppaea before he responded.

'It seems there is treachery afoot. Orders were sent to the Praetorian camp telling Burrus to bring his men to the palace at once. However, the man carrying the orders was turned back at the city gates and was unable to get through to the camp. He tried to pass through three more gates before returning with the news. The city has been sealed off and we can't expect any help from the Praetorian camp or anyone else outside Rome.'

'I see . . .' It was as Cato had suspected ever since he had encountered the messenger on the way to the palace.

'Either Burrus has been overthrown by conspirators among his officers, or he is part of the conspiracy,' Nero continued. 'If it's the latter, I shall have him torn to pieces by wild beasts on the sands of the Great Circus in full view of the mob. Him and every other treacherous dog who is plotting against me. Let all Rome see what happens to those who dare to break their oath of loyalty to their emperor.' There was a savage gleam in his eyes as he savoured the prospect of the revenge he would exact on his enemies. 'Them and their families. They will be hunted down, even to the ends of empire. Hunted down and exterminated . . .'

Nero was now staring over Cato's shoulder into the mid distance, apparently deaf to the rising chorus of protest from the Forum and blind to the imminent peril facing himself and his household. Cato cleared his throat gently and the emperor jerked his head as his thoughts returned to the present.

'Caesar, we must prepare the defences.'

'What? Oh, yes, yes. I'll leave that to you and Tigellinus. That's your field, not mine. Deal with it, Prefect Cato. See us through this and you will not find me ungrateful. Loyal men are always rewarded.'

Until the moment you decide on a whim that they are not loyal, thought Cato. He nodded. 'As you command, Caesar.'

Nero retreated to stand beside Poppaea, who had moved to one of the openings and was staring down at the seething mob, many of whom were now calling for her death.

'Listen to them,' she sneered. 'Filthy rabble . . . No better than animals. I can smell their stench from here. Disgusting.'

Nero put his arm around her and kissed the back of her neck. 'Ignore the plebs. I know your worth and I am Caesar. I chose you and soon they will love you as I do. The world bends to my will.'

'Apparently not,' Cato muttered to himself as he paced over to Tigellinus.

'How many men have you got with you?' Tigellinus asked without preamble.

'Almost two thousand.'

'Not nearly enough to hold the entire perimeter against that lot.'

'Well, I can't pull any more out of my arse, so we'll have to make the best of it.'

Tigellinus smiled briefly. 'All right, rivalry aside, you're the one with the military experience here. What's the plan, Prefect Cato?'

'Firstly, I am not a rival, I'm a soldier doing his duty,' Cato replied directly. 'I have no interest in competing to be Nero's lackey, whatever you think.'

Tigellinus regarded him coolly. 'I've heard that before. I've even said something similar myself. No one means it. So let's understand each other, Cato. You made a good first impression on Caesar and it bought you some political capital, but I'm the one who gets to speak to him every day and that makes me top dog.'

'Really?' Cato nodded discreetly towards the emperor and his lover. 'I think not.'

Tigellinus smirked. 'She and I understand each other. There's room for both of us at Nero's side. No one else, though. No role for you, I'm afraid. As the saying goes, two's company, three's a crowd.'

'Seems your maths is as poor as your judgement,' Cato responded. 'You are the third person in your little coterie.'

Tigellinus frowned and made a dismissive gesture with his hand. 'Enough. How do we deal with the mob?'

'If you want to cut a deal with them, then just give them what they want. Set Octavia free and abandon her prosecution. You might throw in banishing Poppaea if you want to seal the deal. But as we both know, that isn't going to happen. So we can't pacify them. The best we can do is try and keep them out of the palace. My men can cover the entrances to the complex. You can take command of the Germans and any of the Praetorians who are here. Might as well get some practice in, since you'll be elevated to prefect of the Praetorians when this is over, if we survive.'

'Not you, then? No ambition to replace Burrus instead of me?'

'No. I just want to go back to my farm and be left alone. The job's yours and you're welcome to it. In all seriousness, though, the best thing would be to release Octavia as soon as possible. That'll go a long way to mollifying the people out there in the Forum.'

Tigellinus's gaze shifted and he looked down. 'That's not going to be possible.'

Cato felt a sudden chill in his heart. 'What have you done to her?'

'Nothing. Not yet. Nero ordered that she be taken out of Rome and escorted to the island of Pandateria. I gave the job to Centurion Macrinus and a hand-picked party of Praetorians.'

'Macrinus? He's one of your men, isn't he?'

'I promoted him, yes. He's been loyal to me and is someone I can trust to get a job done. As for Pandateria, that was Poppaea's idea. She insisted on it. Told Nero that as long as Octavia was in Rome, her supporters would use her arrest to stir up the mob against him.'

Cato shook his head. 'Well, that worked out well. Listen to them. They sound pretty stirred up already to me. Imagine how much more stirred up they're going to be when they discover their favourite has been banished. You'd better pray that nothing happens to her on the way to the island, or while she's there. It won't just be Macrinus who is held responsible.'

'She was sent into exile, Cato. Not to her execution. I swear it.'

'If she dies, the mob will tear Nero and Poppaea and the rest of his coterie to pieces. Including you.'

'Not me. I'm a survivor. Worry about yourself, Cato.'

'If Octavia dies, I may well be on the side of the mob. Me and my men.'

Cato let his threat settle in the other man's mind before he continued. 'We've wasted enough time. You take charge here. You're the emperor's last line of defence. Not that you have much chance if the mob gets past me and my men. I'll deal with the outer perimeter. Good luck.'

He turned away and left the chamber, unnoticed by Nero and Poppaea, who were still embracing and speaking softly to each other as they looked down on the mob. He descended to the outer courtyard, where Tribune Marcellus had his cohort formed up behind the gate, several ranks deep, with two centuries held back in reserve. On the other side of the gate and the walls stretching out on either side, the mob threw insults and jeers at the soldiers, accompanied by whatever they could use as missiles. Most were harmlessly deflected by the men's shields, but Cato noticed two men on the steps leading up to the inner courtyard being treated for wounds to their faces.

'All under control here, sir.' Marcellus saluted. 'Those bastards won't get past us.'

'It's not just this gate that concerns me. There are a number of smaller gates and entrances on this side of the palace. At the moment they are being held by a few Praetorians and palace staff. Find someone who knows their way about, then take one of your centuries out of the line, along with one of the centuries in the reserve, and have them distributed among the other entrances.'

'That's going to leave us a bit thin on the ground here, sir. When can we expect the Praetorian cohorts to join us?'

'They're not coming. We're on our own.'

The tribune made no effort to hide his surprise. 'What's that? Surely Caesar has sent for them?'

'He did, but the order never got through. It's down to us now. If the mob gets violent and breaks in, it'll be all over for us and the emperor.'

'I understand. Me and my lads will hold the line here. You can depend on us.'

'I know. Now get those two centuries in position. If you need me, I'll be with the Third Cohort outside the audience chamber.

If fighting starts, I'll feed them in wherever they're needed. Let's hope that lot out there grow tired of shouting and drift off once they've vented their spleen.'

The other man nodded, but it was clear he did not anticipate a peaceful resolution to the mood that was building outside the palace walls any more than Cato did.

'If there are any developments to your front that I need to know about, send a man to me at once.'

'Yes, sir.'

Cato took a last look at the faces on the far side of the iron gates and noticed that the barrage of missiles had intensified while he had been talking to the tribune. It was only a matter of time now before the mob took matters further. He strode away up the steps and ran across to the rear of the palace, where Lemulus had ordered his men to drag the wagons into position behind the gate. He repeated the orders he had given to Marcellus and then led the reserve cohort up to the huge anteroom of Nero's audience chamber, on the crest of the Palatine. From there they could be rushed to any point on the perimeter as quickly as possible.

Once they were in position, Cato mentally went over the preparations and tried to anticipate what might happen if the mob attacked. To be sure, they would be outmatched by the soldiers on a one-to-one basis, but the main peril was that they would force a way into the palace before he could react to plug the gap. Once enough of them got through, they would be able to rampage through the complex. At that point the game would be up for Cato's men and the other defenders. It would be every man for himself, and the best that could be hoped for was to barricade themselves into a room until the mob had sated their appetite for violence and looting. The danger then was that some might be tempted to set fires, and those trapped in the palace would perish in the flames . . . If only Nero had been able to produce Octavia for the mob to see that she was unharmed, and then set her free, there would be a way through this without violence. But he might as well have wished for the moon, Cato told himself.

The other pressing concern related to the Praetorian Guard's behaviour. What precisely was Burrus, or whoever was in charge at the camp, up to? The Praetorians were being held back, as if someone was waiting for the mob to do their dirty work and then step in to take control when the palace fell and Nero and Poppaea along with it. Cato wondered if this was part of the plot that he had been made aware of the previous month. But then it was Nero's actions that had triggered the mob. The conspirators could not have planned for that. Maybe they were taking advantage of the opportunity gifted to them by the emperor, just as they might have done by causing the fire on the back of the storm.

The fact that the plotters had never mentioned that Burrus was one of their number troubled Cato. He did not consider Burrus the kind of man who would be open to conspiracy. His sense of duty and moral integrity was too rigid for him to have thrown his lot in with Piso and his group. In which case he must have been neutralised and some of the other officers had taken control of the Praetorians. The question was, did their men know that they were being played? That did not seem credible. It was one thing to bring a handful of officers into the conspiracy, quite another to suborn the loyalty of some ten thousand soldiers to turn against their emperor. If the Praetorians had gone over to the conspirators, there was no chance of Cato and the defenders of the palace holding out against them as well as the mob. The men of the urban cohorts would be given a stark choice – stay loyal to Nero and die at his side, or throw their lot in with the plotters and survive.

He pushed his thoughts aside as he became aware of an upswelling in the roar of the crowd in the Forum. He feared that it meant the start of their attack, but there was no corresponding sound of clashing weapons or shouts from his officers. Something else was happening. He hurried through the audience chamber towards the source of the sound, which seemed to be loudest beneath the imperial quarters. Hurrying onto the narrow balcony that ran along the side of the chamber overlooking the Forum, he glanced up and saw the familiar figure of Nero standing at the balustrade of the garden terrace. The emperor had raised his arms and stretched them out at an angle.

'Dear Jupiter, Best and Greatest,' Cato prayed urgently. 'Please don't let him speak. Not that. Not now.'

The volume of the crowd's protests continued to increase. Nero's hope that his presence alone might quieten them had failed to pay off. He raised his hands several times to call for silence, but they ignored his entreaties. He turned away briefly to retrieve something from one of his slaves standing behind him. The next moment he hurled a fistful of silver coins out into the Forum, burnished by the honeyed glow of the setting sun. More followed, raining down on the people below him, and the crowd's chants died away as they surged towards the falling coins.

Taking advantage of the distraction, he called out, 'Romans! Caesar welcomes you to the Forum and lavishes silver on you just as he feeds and entertains you. For Caesar loves you as if you were his own children!'

He hurled another handful of coins as far out as he could, and now Cato could hear some in the crowd cheering him. His initial dread over Nero's attempt to address the mob began to ease. Perhaps he might be able to turn the mood of the mob around. Nero acknowledged the cheers with a modest bow of his head, and touched a hand to his breast before he spoke again.

'I have never taken you for granted and I understand the strong feelings that have brought you here today. I am the father of the nation. Like any father, I need an heir. A child that I can present to my beloved people. A son to rule Rome and love you in turn after I am gone. And if not a son, then a daughter who will be the mother of the emperor who will come after me! You all know that Octavia was unable to bear me a child, and for that reason alone I needed another wife. It was not for lack of love or respect that I have been forced to divorce her!'

He paused to let his words echo back off the buildings surrounding the Forum. To Cato's surprise, almost every face in the mob was looking up towards the emperor as they listened to his impromptu address. He had their attention and had stilled their anger, and Cato reluctantly conceded that he might just be a talented enough performer to win them over.

'I need an heir! Rome needs an heir! For the sake of order and peace. And, may the gods be praised, Rome was blessed with one who could satisfy that need!'

Cato's hopes sank almost as swiftly as they had just risen.

'The gods have gifted me, and Rome, the most beautiful and loving of women to fulfil the duty that our dear Octavia could not. I present you with my new wife, your new empress, Poppaea!'

As he ushered her forward to join him, her fine blonde hair took on an incandescent glow in the dying sunlight of the day. Nero indicated the slight bulge of her stomach as he called out once again. 'See! My child grows in her womb. My child. My heir. I share this joy with you!'

'Throw the hussy in the Tiber!' a voice cried out, and the mob roared with approval as more insults were shouted up at Nero and Poppaea.

Nero tried to quieten them again, but he had lost control, and even another shower of coins failed to distract them. Anger flowed through them more strongly than ever and the cacophony of their cries drowned the emperor out so that his further attempts to speak to them only looked more and more humiliating. Matters were not helped by Poppaea, who brandished her fist at the crowd, then turned her back on them and walked away out of sight, followed by the laughter, jeers, whistles and catcalls of the people crammed into the Forum.

The mocking mood turned into anger that built up into rage, and with a sick feeling in the pit of his stomach, Cato saw the crowd close in on the gates to the outer courtyard. Some among them had fetched rope, and the ends were quickly tied to the iron gates before the strain was taken up. Before the defenders could react to untie or sever the ropes, one gate lurched as the hinges gave way, then twisted and toppled, crushing those who could not get out of the way. The crowd surged forward through the gap, some pausing to push the other gate aside, and charged Cato's men as their tribune ordered them to form a shield wall and strike at will.

Cato clenched the edge of the balcony tightly, his heart sinking as he watched the enraged mob crash into the front line of his soldiers. He saw more surges pressing in on the other entrances to the palace complex as Nero's people thirsted for his blood.

'Oh shit . . . Here we go.'

CHAPTER TWENTY-NINE

Cato leaned out as far as he dared to observe the attack on the main entrance to the palace. The crowd was pushing up the ramp, through the now opened gates, and shoving against the shields of the soldiers lined up across the courtyard. They had drawn their swords but were trying to use their shields to drive the crowd back rather than cut them down. But it was only a matter of time before blood flowed and the confrontation turned into carnage.

His instinct told him to get down to the outer courtyard and try and keep control over his men in person. However, he knew that he had to stay in command of the overall situation, and that meant remaining where he was. His subordinates needed to be able to send reports to him and request backup if needed. It was frustrating for him to observe from a distance, but he had been a soldier long enough to know the vital distinction between being a line officer and the overall commander.

The men of the Second Cohort were holding their own for now, and Cato looked along the perimeter of the palace, where a number of smaller confrontations were taking place at the other entrances. Try as they might, however, the mob could not push aside the better-equipped defenders.

There was a piercing shriek from the outer courtyard, and he turned to see a space open up around a woman who had collapsed. A man bent over to try and raise her to her feet, but she was as limp as a child's doll and he released her and raised his blood-smeared hands for the crowd to see as he shouted, 'Murderers! Murderers!'

A roar of animal rage rippled through the mob, and they drew back from the shields and subjected the soldiers to a frenzied barrage of missiles, ripping up loose stones from the streets to hurl them at Cato's men. In the gathering gloom of dusk a flicker of light caught his attention, and he saw that a brazier from one of the temples was being carried forward by a small group of men. Some of their companions cleared a way through and they set the brazier down outside the broken gates, where combustible materials were added to it – broken up pieces of wood, baskets and whatever else could be looted from nearby shops and market stalls. More small fires were started along the Forum, and soon flaming materials were inscribing shallow arcs as they were lobbed at the defenders at the gates or hurled over the outer wall of the palace complex. A fire had already started on one of the lower garden terraces, and a fir tree, dried out by the hot weather, burned fiercely, bathing its surroundings in a lurid glow. Brilliant embers swirled up, and though most faded and died after a short distance, others landed elsewhere in the garden and a few flickering spots showed where other fires were starting.

Short-handed as he was, Cato was forced to return to the reserve cohort and detail half a century to go to the perimeter and fight the fires as best they could. The men had just trotted off down the corridor when another soldier came running up and drew a deep breath to make his report.

'Centurion Lemulus says . . . that thousands more of the rioters have . . . joined the crowd at the back, sir.'

'Have they attacked?'

'Not when I left, sir. But they were getting worked up. The centurion is concerned that he may need to be reinforced.'

'Follow me,' Cato ordered. He led the man to the balustrade so that he could see the fighting and the fires running along the foot of the Palatine Hill. 'You tell Lemulus what you see, and that I can't spare any men from the reserve cohort for now. If he is attacked, he is to let me know at once. If he fears he can't hold the line without reinforcements, he can ask for them then, but not before. Tell him the main attack is here.'

'Yes, sir.'

Cato shook his head bitterly. He had hoped that Lemulus would show more resolve than this. He must know that the men of the urban cohorts were thinly spread and that Cato could not afford to send him reinforcements at such an early stage. 'Damn the man,' he muttered.

There were now enough fires burning for the Forum to be lit up by the pools of light, and he could make out a wagon being wheeled through the crowd towards the ramp leading up to the outer courtyard. As it reached the gates, it slowed down as those around it struggled to get it over the iron bars. Then a torch was brought up and lobbed onto the materials heaped in the wagon. As the flames spread, a large group of men heaved the burning vehicle towards the soldiers and the crowd let out a savage cheer. The blazing wagon gathered pace, and those pushing it had to dip their heads to shield their faces from the searing heat.

Cato could not tear his gaze away from the spectacle as the wagon rumbled across the flagstones and the soldiers attempted to brace themselves for the impact. There was only one way the collision could end. The wagon burst through the lines, scattering Cato's men and knocking two of them down, crushing them under its heavy wheels. The mob poured through the gap and hurled themselves on the disordered soldiers on either side, gripping the edges of their shields and wrenching them aside before hacking at the men with makeshift weapons and their bare fists.

The burning wagon came to a stop in the middle of the courtyard, and Tribune Marcellus ordered his men to fall back to the steps. It was the only course of action open to him. They were using their swords freely now, and scores of rioters were being struck down as the soldiers retreated in small groups and singly. Cato saw the mob overwhelm several of his men and beat them to the ground, where they were stabbed, battered and torn to pieces. Their swords, daggers and shields were instantly snatched up to be used against their remaining comrades.

Within moments the situation had become extremely perilous. If the Second Cohort gave way, the mob would have free rein across most of the palace complex. Returning to the reserve cohort, Cato ordered two centuries to support the men battling to hold the outer courtyard.

The struggle had barely begun, and nearly half of his reserve had been used up. He needed more men. The only force he could think of was the small body of German bodyguards protecting the emperor. If the perimeter collapsed, they would be overrun in moments. They would be more use bolstering the outer defences, he decided.

He sought out Tribune Pantella. 'You take command here. I'll be back as quickly as I can. If Lemulus asks for reinforcements, make sure he really needs them before you send anyone.'

'Yes, sir.'

Cato hurried through the audience chamber and up the stairs beyond to reach the imperial suite. Twenty or so of the German bodyguards, under the command of one of their Roman officers, stood guard at the entrance.

'Let me through, I need to speak to Caesar.'

'Nothing doing, sir. He's ordered us to admit no one.'

'It's urgent, dammit! You must know who I am.' Cato made to push past the optio, but two of the burly Germans closed up in front of him, blocking his way. Their long hair, trailing

344

moustaches and beards, tribal armour and weapons reminded Cato of his first confrontation with their kindred barbarian warriors on the Rhine frontier, and he felt a spasm of the terror he had experienced at the time. These men were killers, selected for their warrior prowess and loyalty to their paymaster. They would cut him down rather than let him get close to Nero. He pulled back a step.

'Listen, I have to speak to Caesar. I need him to place most of these men under my command. They're needed to keep the rioters out of the palace and they'll be more use on the battle line than up here. Let me through.'

'No, sir. My orders are clear and they come straight from Caesar himself.'

The man was not going to budge. Cato could see it in his unrelenting expression. He needed to try another approach. 'Who else is in there with him?'

'Just Poppaea, sir. He sent the rest away.'

'What about Tigellinus?' Cato asked. For all his faults, Tigellinus would be sure to recognise the grave danger facing them and back up Cato's request.

'Tigellinus is gone, sir. Caesar sent him to find you and report back on how the defences were holding up. He never returned.'

'And he never came to me . . . No doubt he's already well away from the palace.'

'That figures,' the optio said sourly. 'Always out for himself, that one. I could see it plain as day.'

Cato nodded vaguely. Tigellinus had been his best hope of getting through to Nero. Now that he had fled to save his skin, the only other person who could get the emperor to place his German bodyguards under Cato's orders was Poppaea, the very person who had been the cause of the dire situation. She would be too busy consoling her lover to listen to Cato's request, no matter how urgent it was. He sighed with frustration.

345

'I just hope you and your men will stay here until the end.'

'We will. Some of us know the meaning of loyalty, Prefect Cato. Good luck, sir.'

Cato nodded and turned to run back to his command post, cursing Tigellinus for fleeing before he could finally do something honourable.

By the time Macro had escorted Petronella and Bardea back to the house and then reached the Forum, the sun had set. The ramp leading down into the heart of Rome afforded him a far-reaching view over the vast crowd that surrounded the palace. Many were carrying torches, and their flames flickered as they cast wavering looms over the angry faces of those around them. Others brandished fists and weapons and shouted insults and demands up at the palace and its defenders. The gates at the main entrance were down and beyond them a wagon blazed fiercely as a line of soldiers defended the steps leading up to the inner courtyard. A number of fires had started on the lowest terraces.

'Jupiter's balls . . .'

He took the entire scene in within moments before his sense of duty to Cato and his comrades compelled him to action. He broke into a trot and descended the ramp. The crowd was ebbing and flowing in waves against the palace entrances, and he was able to thrust his way through without much difficulty until he reached the approaches of the main gate. There he came across the first of the casualties being carried away by their companions. Men and a few women with sword wounds and head injuries caused by missiles thrown by other rioters. Some were already dead, but many were writhing in agony and crying out or moaning as they were helped to the pediments of nearby buildings to have their wounds dressed with whatever strips of cloth came to hand.

Being shorter than most men, Macro had to use the heights of the Palatine Hill to keep his bearings as he fought his way

346

through the press of bodies that was shifting one way and then another. At one point he found himself caught amid a group brandishing their fists as they chanted, 'Death to Poppaea!'

When he said nothing and tried to edge his way through them, a man who was clearly drunk grabbed him by the shoulder. 'Come on, mate! Death to Poppaea! Give it all you got!'

Macro bunched his hand into a fist and shook it above his head. 'Death to Poppaea!'

The man grinned but held on to Macro's shoulder. 'There you go. Feels good, dunnit?'

'Almost as good as this.' Macro rammed his knee into the man's groin and pushed him gently to one side as he doubled over. One of the others looked round, and the centurion shook his head. 'Poor bastard can't hold his drink.'

He continued to work his way forward, over the gates and into the courtyard. The din of the rioters was deafening and the air filled with enraged curses as stones and bricks flew overhead. Then, through a break in the crowd ahead, he saw the line of soldiers, their helmets above the trim of the shields that were held up just below eye level. The points of swords, some smeared with blood, protruded between the shields, and many dead, dying and wounded rioters lay at their feet. A space had opened up between the two sides, and every so often one of the mob boldly pounced forward to strike a blow or get a grip on the edge of a shield and rip it from the man holding it. The soldiers simply stepped back, drawing their attacker on, where he could be stabbed by those on either side, or forcing him to release his grip and rush back into the crowd.

It was a dangerous moment, Macro knew. If he called out to the soldiers and identified himself, he risked being seized by the mob and hacked and beaten to death. If he rushed forward and tried to get between the shields, he was likely to be stabbed before he could make himself recognised. It would take careful timing to pick his moment. Before he could do anything, however, he was caught by a surge from behind and forced towards the shields. There was no hope of edging back through the press, which bore him on remorselessly.

'Oh fuck!' he snarled.

Time seemed to slow enough for him to feel bitter about the prospect of being killed by one of his own. At the last moment, he dropped down at the feet of the nearest soldiers, risking being trampled by the rioters behind him, and scrambled beneath two shields, crawling a short distance further on before turning onto his side and raising his hands. An optio loomed over him in the gloom, sword lifted to strike.

'Friendly!' Macro bellowed. 'Centurion Macro!'

It was too dark for the optio to recognise him, and the sword came down. Macro jerked his torso to the side, and the point of the sword narrowly missed his stomach. Sparks burst from the metal as it grated on the flagstones. Macro seized the optio's wrist and wrenched the man off balance so that he fell to one knee beside him.

'For fuck's sake, you moron. I'm Macro! Centurion Macro!'

The man froze for an instant before he relaxed his sword arm. 'Macro?'

'The bloody same. Now help me up, you blade-happy arsehole.'

He was on his feet and almost at once back in a crouch as a small rock sailed over his head. He ducked down as he spoke to the optio.

'Where's the prefect?'

'Up the hill, sir. Command post is outside Caesar's audience chamber. Do you need a guide?'

'I know where I'm going. What I do need is a shield.'

The optio scurried off towards the equipment left by the injured soldiers who had been carried up to the safety of the inner courtyard, while Macro examined his scraped and bleeding knees. 'The things I do for Caesar and Rome . . .'

The optio returned with a shield and handed it to him.

'You and your lads seem to be holding on well enough.'

'For now,' the optio replied.

Macro could sense his fearfulness. 'First time in a fight?'

'On this scale, yes.'

'I've seen far worse, many times over. You'll be fine. Just keep your sword up and your face to the enemy, eh?'

'Yes, sir.'

Macro patted him on the shoulder, reflecting that it felt odd to be describing his fellow Romans as the enemy. When they were battering you with stones and rocks and trying to rip you apart, however, there was no other word for them.

Raising the shield to cover his head and torso, he backed away up the steps towards the inner courtyard, wincing every time a missile cracked off the surface. He passed through the inner gate, where the men of the reserve century eyed him warily before he lowered the shield and was recognised.

'Let none of those bastards get by, lads!' he called to them before heading for the stairs that led to the audience chamber.

Cato had just issued an order to one of his men, who hurried off to the rear of the palace as Macro approached.

'You're a sight for sore eyes.' Cato grinned. 'I was worried you might have better things to do than join us for this scrimmage.'

'Hardly worth turning up for, sir. But I had nothing else in the calendar.'

The soldiers standing nearby smiled and laughed at the exchange as Macro and Cato shared a grin and clasped arms.

'How are we doing?' Macro asked in an undertone, and Cato ushered him into the comparative quiet of the audience chamber.

'Did you get Petronella and Bardea safely away?'

Macro shook his head. 'Some bastard's ordered the Praetorians to seal off the city. I had to take them back to the house. That's why it took a while to catch up with you and see the mess you're in. Feels like old times.'

349

'I wish it didn't. So much for retreating into a quiet retirement, eh? Starting to feel like it isn't ever going to happen for either of us.' Cato's rueful smile faded as his manner became serious. 'Whoever is keeping the Praetorians from intervening is taking advantage of the riots for their own purposes.'

'They're trying to topple Nero?' Macro arched an eyebrow.

'What else could it be? And they don't give a shit if you, me and every man in the urban cohorts goes down with him.'

'Fucking scheming politicians . . .' Macro clenched his fists at his sides. 'If we ever get out of this, I'll have more than a few words to say to those concerned.'

'Doubtless, but first we have to survive.'

Cato detailed the position of his men and the dangers facing them before he concluded, 'It's too large a perimeter to hold for long. We have to assume the rioters will get in somewhere. When that happens, they'll be able to use the alleys and corridors of the palace complex to attack our contingents from all sides. At that point, I'll give the order for every man to fall back on the imperial quarters. Just hope they all hear the signal if it comes to that.'

'Then it's a last stand for us and Caesar, I suppose.' Macro shook his head. 'I really hoped that if I had to give my life for a cause, it would be a better one than trying to save Nero's skin.'

'Soldiers rarely get to choose what they die for, brother. If not for Nero, we fight for each other.'

'That'll do for me.' Macro nodded.

'Find yourself some kit, and then I want you to take charge of the men on the other side of the palace. I'm not sure Lemulus is made of the stuff I thought he was. I need someone in command who can be trusted to hold the line and only call for help when it's needed.'

'I'll make sure Lemulus plays his part.'

'I know. Keep your ears open for the signal and move quickly when it comes.'

'*If* it comes.'

Cato forced a smile. 'Yes, if it comes.'

Macro turned away, and Cato returned to the balcony overlooking the Forum to reassess the situation.

His men fighting in the pockets around the service entrances showed no signs of giving way, and those dealing with the small fires that had broken out on the garden terraces and lower yards were keeping them under control. Over in the outer courtyard, the Second Cohort was holding firm. The rioters had pulled back, leaving a gap of five paces or so, from where they subjected the defenders to a constant barrage of missiles and deafening tirades. Cato felt he had some grounds for hope, despite what he had said to Macro a moment ago. The line was holding, even without the Praetorians, and he was proud of the men he and Macro had whipped back into shape. To be sure, this was no battle such as those they had fought before. One side consisted of well-armed and well-trained soldiers, while the other was a rabble armed only with whatever weapons they had to hand and a fickle sense of grievance that would fade as quickly as it had flared up. Be that as it may, few would forget the bloodshed, rage and fear experienced that night.

The shouting down in the outer courtyard faded away and the rain of missiles eased up and stopped as the mob drew back and parted to make way for a loose column of men advancing up the ramp. Some four or five hundred, Cato estimated. Several of them carried torches, and by their light he could make out the formidable array of armour and weapons with which they were equipped. There were tied bundles of kindling on the shoulders of many, and at their head strode a man who wore a silvered cuirass, leather bracers and greaves. He carried a curved sword in one hand and a torch in the other, which he held aloft. Cato felt his stomach tighten as he recognised the man's face. Bullo. The leader of the Bronze Blades.

351

He stopped ten paces short of the line of soldiers and turned to address the mob. Even though the shouting continued further off, Cato strained his ears and could just make out his words.

'You all know me! You all know my reputation. I am Bullo, the chief of the most powerful gang in Rome! Some call me a thief. A criminal. You know who they are. The fat pigs who sit in the Senate and live in luxury while the common people of Rome go hungry and live in squalor! But the fattest of all the pigs lives up there!' He thrust his arm up at the Palatine, and to Cato it seemed as if Bullo was pointing directly at him. He added another entry in the record of injustices that Nero had dealt him since recalling him to duty.

'Up there he lives in luxury that few can even imagine. Surrounded by the choicest foods, gold, silver and other treasures. Treasures that could be ours. Should be ours! It is there for the taking, my friends. All that stands between us and enough riches for all are the bullies and cowards of the urban cohorts. They call themselves soldiers . . .' The contempt of his words was palpable. 'They are thugs in uniform. Caesar's henchmen and killers, paid to keep us from all that is rightly ours. Too long have we endured them.'

Bullo paused, and when he resumed, there was a slight tremor in his voice. 'They murdered my son. The bastards murdered my only son! Just as they have murdered many of your children, your fathers, brothers and even your women! They must die, along with everyone in the palace who stands in our way. Who is with me?'

He thrust his sword into the air and his followers did the same, brandishing their weapons and their fists at Cato's men.

'Death to Poppaea!' Bullo shouted. 'Death to Nero! Death to the enemies of the people of Rome!'

His cry was echoed by his thugs and quickly spread through the mob, becoming a rhythmic chant that reverberated through the night air so that Cato could feel its impact upon his body even from where he stood. As it reached a pitch of imminent violence, Bullo lowered his sword and waved his men forward. They did not charge, but approached to within a few paces of the soldiers, weapons braced. Behind them, torches were applied to the bundles of kindling, which swiftly blazed with fierce intensity. Bullo swung his sword forward, and the bundles were pitched towards Cato's men, bursting over their shields in showers of sparks and embers. Some landed harmlessly on the far side of the line, while others fell through the gaps in the shields and sprayed the soldiers with burning fragments. Only fire had such a propensity for causing panic, and the men beat at the flaming matter on their tunics and exposed skin. The line wavered and became disrupted as they recoiled from the fresh peril.

Bullo cupped his hand to his mouth. 'Come on, boys. Let's have 'em!'

Yelling a war cry, he charged the line, his followers close behind. They punched through the wavering centre of the Second Cohort and instantly turned to both sides to open the gap for the mob to pour through in their wake. Cato looked on with a sickening sensation of dread as his men were thrust aside and forced to clump together in small protective rings to fight for their lives. Those who were isolated, or tried to flee up the steps, were run down by their pursuers and slaughtered.

The moment he had feared had come. The perimeter could not be held. All they could do now was fall back on the imperial quarters and make that their redoubt. There they would have to hold on and hope that heavy losses, wavering resolve and a sated desire to loot the palace would see the mob dissolve and the defenders survive until the following dawn. If not, they would at least save their honour by fighting to the last man. He turned and called for the bucina man. As he came out onto the terrace, Cato nodded to him.

'Sound the signal to fall back.'

CHAPTER THIRTY

As the notes of the signal echoed across the palace, Cato hurriedly made plans for the defence of the audience chamber and the imperial quarters beyond. There were over four hundred men from the Third Cohort under his command in the antechamber. The space had a number of doorways besides the main entrance and was unfurnished apart from a few benches along the walls. It would be hard to defend, Cato decided. Better to fall back on the audience chamber itself, where there were only two entrances. One connected it to the antechamber, while the other, behind the dais upon which the thrones sat, led up a short flight of stairs to the imperial quarters. There were several openings high on the walls to admit light, but he decided that they were unlikely to be used by the rioters to enter the chamber.

Indicating the benches, he ordered the nearest men to carry them through to the audience chamber. The room was similarly sparsely furnished, containing only Nero's gilded and cushioned throne, and two lesser thrones set back behind it on either side. Years before, his mother had broken protocol by insisting on sitting in on matters of state, and now Poppaea had taken her place. Nero was as dominated by his women as he was by his flatterers, Cato reflected.

He set two centuries to cover the entrances to the antechamber to keep them open for any of his men who managed to arrive

354

ahead of the mob. He knew that his scattered forces were at risk of being overrun, and he trusted that his officers would do as he himself was doing and find a place to barricade themselves in if they could not reach the antechamber. Most should be able to reach the command post in time, he calculated. There would be casualties, though. Those men who were wounded and had to be left behind, those too slow to escape their pursuers, and those who chose to stand their ground and go down fighting.

He returned to the audience chamber and gave an order to one of the optios. 'I want the thrones over here by the door, ready to barricade it. They look solid enough to do the job.'

'That's just it, sir,' the optio replied. 'I tried shifting them just now. The gods only know how much the bloody things weigh.'

'Then use as many men as it takes. Just get them in position.'

'Yes, sir.'

Cato continued through the chamber and mounted the stairs to the imperial quarters. The officer outside took a step towards him.

'What's the meaning of the trumpet signal, sir?'

'The rioters have broken through the perimeter. Tell Caesar that I am pulling as many men as I can back to the audience chamber and will hold the mob off from there. However, if that's not possible, my intention is to fall back on the imperial quarters as a last line of defence.' He emphasised the last few words. 'If Fortuna favours us, we'll live to see another day. If not . . . Caesar needs to make whatever arrangements he chooses while there is still time. I dare say he might not want to be taken alive. Same goes for Poppaea.'

'I'll let him know, sir.' The officer lowered his voice and spoke urgently. 'Is it really as bad as that?'

'It is now. Be sure that Ceasar understands the situation.'

Cato hurried back to the antechamber as the first of the men summoned by the signal stumbled through the entrances, gasping for breath and bent double from the effort of climbing the stairs and ramps from the lower levels. There was no sign of Macro, Lemulus and the men of the First Cohort.

'Go through to the audience chamber,' Cato ordered the arrivals. 'Form your units in there. Move!'

He went to the entrance of the antechamber and looked down the length of the corridor that led to the inner courtyard. Men were rushing towards him. Most still retained their shields and weapons, he was pleased to see. The triumphant cries of the mob carried clearly to his ears, and he felt a tremor of fear at the bloodthirsty tone. Stepping aside for the first men to pass, he trotted towards the end of the corridor and stopped one of the soldiers, a young optio. When the man tried to brush past him, Cato grabbed his arm.

'Where's the tribune?'

It took a moment before the man controlled his panic sufficiently to respond to his superior. 'He's with the rearguard, sir.'

'Very good. Before you join the others, you'd better get a grip on yourself. Officers set the example, you understand? The men look to you. So you walk tall the rest of the way.'

The optio drew a deep breath and nodded. 'Sorry, sir.'

'It's all right, son. Just don't let it happen again.'

Cato released him and continued to the end of the corridor. Several more men passed by, barely acknowledging him in their desire to reach a place of safety. At the top of the stairs, he stopped. Beneath him he saw some fifty or so men from the First Cohort steadily falling back as one of the centurions called the time. Tribune Marcellus stood to one side clutching a hand to his arm to stem the flow of blood from a wound. Cato hurried down the steps to join him. He glanced at the soldiers and the seething crowd beyond, extending back along another broad stretch of corridor towards the inner courtyard. In the confined space, the din of their shouting and the clash of weapons and thuds of blows landing on shields was deafening. Many of the rioters had looted the swords, shields and helmets of the soldiers they had already killed.

He leaned close to Marcellus and spoke loudly into his ear. 'Where's the rest of the cohort?'

The tribune shook his head and shouted his reply above the noise. 'This is all I can account for, sir. Some of the men may have escaped into other parts of the palace. We lost a fair few when they broke the line. I managed to rally this lot and we've been fighting them every inch of the way as we retreat.'

In the confines of the corridor and staircase, the closed-up ranks of the soldiers were more than capable of keeping the mob at bay. At the same time, Cato knew the layout of the palace well enough to be aware that there were plenty of ways for the rioters to work their way round, and they might be able to cut off the rearguard before it reached the audience chamber.

'You need to increase the pace, Tribune. Keep your line intact but fall back on the command post as soon as you can. I'll form up a party to cover the last stretch of the corridor. Carry on.'

'Yes, sir.'

As Cato climbed the stairs, something struck him between the shoulders. He staggered a step and turned to see a dagger lying on the steps. Luckily, it was the handle of the spinning weapon that had struck him. The impact had numbed his shoulder, however, and he hunched his head down as he took the steps three at a time to ensure he got out of range of any further missiles as swiftly as possible.

He found Lemulus and most of the First Cohort in the antechamber when he returned.

'Where's Centurion Macro?'

'Just coming, sir. He sent me and the lads on ahead, together with the slaves and servants, and kept a century back to hold the gate while he waited for the outliers to have a chance to get back to the position.'

'I see.' Cato felt a moment's frustration. It was typical of Macro. He was a centurion down to his bones and fully subscribed to the centurionate's code of being the first into the fight and the last to leave it. Valour over judgement every time.

'Tell him that he and his men are to fall back on the command post at once.'

'Yes, sir.' Lemulus turned to one of his men, and was about to speak when a spurt of anger got the better of Cato.

'You go, Centurion.'

'Sir?'

'You take the message. Better be quick. I don't want to lose any more men.'

Lemulus was about to protest, then thought better of it and turned to run out of the antechamber.

Cato saw that more men were coming through the side entrances, and he stationed the last of his fresh reserves there in case the rioters were already getting close enough to mount an attack on the position. He also had the wounded taken directly through to the audience chamber to have their injuries dressed. He was about to make for the terrace to get one last overview of the attack when he was approached by one of his centurions.

'Sir, you better come through to the audience chamber.'

'What is it?'

'It's Caesar, sir. He's demanding to speak to you.'

'Now? Fuck.'

'At once, he said, sir.'

From the man's tone, Cato could guess that Nero was in a rather more imperious mood than normal. 'All right. Let's go.'

On the other side of the imposing doors that separated the two chambers, the emperor was standing feet braced apart, hands on hips, as he directed several of Cato's men to drag his throne back to the dais. As soon as he saw Cato, he addressed him furiously.

'How dare you treat my throne in such a cavalier fashion,

Prefect Cato! I'll not have it! The bloody thing is priceless. That's gold, you fool. And there are the most priceless of duck feathers under the leopard-skin covering. But of course, coming from your background, what would you know about the value of such things?'

Cato weathered the vitriol, clamping his jaws together until Nero had finished.

'Caesar, the rioters are in the palace and making their way here as we speak. If I can't seal the doors to this chamber and barricade it with whatever comes to hand, we're all dead. I need the throne to block their way.'

Nero regarded him closely, his face in an agony of indecision. Then he nodded. 'Put like that, I see your point. All right. Have your way, Prefect, but next time, ask first.'

'Next time?' Cato said before he could stop himself. 'Yes, Caesar. I'll do my best to make sure your throne comes to no harm. Is there anything else?'

Nero glanced at the soldiers, who quickly looked away and tried to appear preoccupied with checking their kit. Then he leaned towards Cato and spoke in an undertone. 'My officer said that you thought we should be prepared for the worst.'

'That's right, Caesar.'

'I see . . .' Nero looked uncomfortable. 'The thing is, I'm not terribly sure about the best way to . . . I, er, I'm not sure that I would do it properly, you understand. Wouldn't want to make a mess of it. It's important for posterity that I meet my end well. If it comes to that.'

Cato shrugged. 'There's always a first time for suicide, Caesar. Tends to be the last for those who do it well. I'm sure you'll know what to do.'

'I've never killed anyone in my life,' said Nero. 'I've had people killed, but any fool can do that. You, on the other hand . . . you've made a career out of killing people.'

Cato felt a cold anger stir within. 'I've made a career out of serving Rome, her people and her emperors, Caesar. I didn't do it out of any desire to kill.'

'Of course not.' Nero smiled weakly. 'I meant no offence. I just wanted to be confident that if the end comes, you'll see to Poppaea and myself.'

Cato felt his stomach turn in disgust as he gave his reply through clenched teeth. 'Willingly, Caesar.'

'That's good.' The emperor sighed with relief. 'I'd better let you get on with it here, then. Just, er, try not to do too much damage.'

'Yes, Caesar.'

Nero turned to the men surrounding the throne. 'I've changed my mind. Put it back where it was. Quickly now!' With a click of his fingers, he paced to the rear of the audience chamber and disappeared up the steps to the imperial quarters.

Cato glanced at the men and frowned. 'You heard the emperor. Get the bloody thing back by the doors!'

He allowed himself a moment to relish the thought of putting an end to Nero, then he returned to the corridor. By the light of the oil lamps along the walls, he could see that the rearguard of the Second Cohort had reached the top of the stairs and was backing towards him. Beyond them the mob pressed forward, hacking at the soldiers' shields. Someone had impaled the head of one of his men on a spear, and the grisly trophy was being waved to and fro to taunt the defenders. Time was running out for Macro and his men, Cato realised. They had to reach the antechamber before they were cut off by the rioters.

Hastening to the terrace at the rear of the chamber, he looked down to the yard that was being defended by Macro and his rearguard. There was no sign of them. The crowd between the palace and the Great Circus had swollen in size and was almost as numerous as that in the Forum. The gates of the yard were open and the rioters were streaming through.

Returning to the corridor, he hurried to the side of the wounded tribune and indicated the opening where Macro should appear.

'You need to halt your men just short of that and hold your ground until I give the order to fall back to the audience chamber. We're waiting on the last men to get through to the command post,' he explained.

The tribune puffed his cheeks. 'We'll do our best, sir.'

'I know you will. The lives of our comrades depend on it.'

Cato could see that the rearguard was vastly outnumbered by the mob and it was only a matter of time before they were pushed back and cut off from their comrades. He was tempted to go and look for his friend, but he knew his duty was to remain where the rest of the men were. A commanding officer must put personal feelings aside. One of the many burdens that went with high rank, he reluctantly accepted. Where was Lemulus? He should have returned by now. Had the message not got through to Macro? Had Lemulus let his nerves get the better of him and instead gone to ground in some corner of the palace? That was an unworthy thought, Cato chided himself. The man was better than that. The only thing certain was that the gate and yard that Macro had been defending was now in the hands of the mob. It was possible that Macro and his small force was already well on their way. Cato offered a quick prayer that it was so. If the gods were listening, they were cutting it fine.

A shout of alarm came from the antechamber, and he dashed inside to see that the first group of rioters had reached one of the openings and were engaging the men he had posted there. The gap was narrow enough for three men to deploy their shields and there was little hope of the rioters breaking through until they arrived in greater numbers. Cato considered defending the antechamber and the corridor beyond. It could be done, at the cost of more of his men. No, it was better to fall back on the audience chamber, barricade themselves in and wait for the storm to pass. Besides, the antechamber was already filling up with his men and those from the palace who fought alongside them. The larger audience chamber would be needed to fit them all in.

There was a sudden rush of movement and a group of armed slaves entered, followed by Lemulus and most of the men from the rearguard. Cato crossed to him. 'Where's Macro?'

'He's right behind me, sir,' Lemulus said defensively.

Cato pushed past him into the corridor. Macro and a score of others were fighting off the rioters as they retreated up the last few stairs. At the same time, the rearguard that was holding the space open for them had been forced back close to the entrance of the antechamber. Beyond them Cato could hear Bullo urging his supporters on.

'Come on, boys! One final push and the riches of the imperial quarters are ours for the taking!'

Cato called out to the tribune. 'Fall back! You too, Macro! On me!'

The soldiers of the two cohorts merged, folding around Cato and edging towards the open doors. Believing that victory was in their grasp, the mob pressed home their attack with renewed savagery. One of his men fell back against Cato, his sword arm ripped open and gushing blood. Cato caught him and dragged him inside. One by one the soldiers passed through, Macro among the last, and their comrades began to close the doors. For a moment the pressure from outside resisted their efforts before the soldiers regained their momentum and the doors thudded into place. Macro jammed his sword through the iron rings to lock them in place and stepped away, breathing hard. 'That won't hold for long.'

'Long enough,' said Cato as he handed the casualty over to one of his comrades to escort to the audience chamber. He looked round and saw that the rioters were now at all the openings on one side. It was time to make for the final redoubt.

'Lemulus!'

'Sir?'

'Except for the men holding the openings, get the rest of them out of here. You too, Macro. You've done your bit.'

'Fuck that,' Macro replied, bending to pick up a bloodied blade abandoned by one of the wounded.

There was no time to offer an argument, and Cato nodded as he ordered two sections to form up on either side and withdraw slowly across the marbled flagstones. As they passed each opening, the men there joined them and the rioters began to enter the chamber and press home their attack on the retreating soldiers. Some set their eyes on the wall hangings and ignored the fighting as they tore the valuable fabrics down and bundled them up. It took a moment before one of them had the presence of mind to go to the door and try to wrestle Macro's sword free. The pressure from outside made the task difficult, and it took all his strength to wrench the end of the sword from the iron ring. At once the doors swung inwards and Cato saw Bullo at the head of his men as they burst into the chamber.

But they were too late. The soldiers had reached the doors to the audience chamber, and the last of them passed through and sealed the heavy timbers in the faces of the rioters. While some of his men held them in place, Cato ordered the thrones to be pushed hard up against the doors and the benches wedged in position. As the rioters pounded the solid wood, Cato and his men stepped back and gasped for breath, bracing themselves for the imminent onslaught.

CHAPTER THIRTY-ONE

After the appalling din of battle in the corridor, the audience chamber seemed quiet, even with the sound of blows landing on the doors. Across the room, the men looked at each other in numbed relief. Cato could see that the slaves and servants of the palace were badly shaken, and so were many of the soldiers. He had to give them something else to occupy their thoughts at once.

'Officers! Form your units and take a roll call. Report to me as soon as you have the numbers! You people from the palace, if you haven't yet got a weapon, take one from our wounded and be ready to use it. There's only one way those bastards outside can come at us, and that's through those doors. If they can get through them. Even if they do, we can hold them off indefinitely at the entrance, so you're safe enough for now.'

The slaves and servants did not seem comforted by his words, but Cato had nothing better to offer them. While it was true that the audience chamber could be held, it was possible that Bullo would find a way to break in. He had already proved that he was a man of imagination and initiative. He might even try to starve them into surrender if the rioters remained in the palace over the coming days. There was no food or water for the hundreds of men in the audience chamber, and the hot weather would lead to unbearable thirst very quickly. Cato had bought them breathing space. Nothing more.

The hammering on the other side of the door ceased and the angry shouts in the corridor died away.

'What are they up to now?' asked Macro.

Cato shook his head.

Then Bullo called out, his voice carrying easily to those inside. 'Prefect Cato! I know you are in there. Hear me! You and your men are trapped, along with Caesar and that viper he is consorting with. There is no escape for any of you. So me and my friends here are making you an offer. If you open the doors, lay down your arms and surrender, your men will be spared and allowed to leave the palace. Our argument is with Caesar. Nero will be spared if he agrees to free the lady Octavia. Poppaea will be given to the mob to decide her fate. There is only one other life we will claim, and that is yours, Prefect Cato. Because of you my son is dead, and I will avenge him. Those are our terms. Accept them or none will live!'

Cato felt the eyes of the soldiers and slaves fix on him as they waited for his response.

Macro spat at the doors. 'Let me tell him to go fuck himself . . . All of them can go fuck themselves.'

Cato took a moment to respond to his friend. 'I don't believe him. This isn't about Octavia and Nero. Bullo's a gang leader. He doesn't give a shit about any injustice Octavia has suffered. He's saying that to keep the mob onside. He wants to loot the palace.'

'What about you?'

'Oh, he wants my head all right. That's true enough. As for the rest . . .' Cato turned away from the door to face the men in the room. 'He's lying about letting you leave. He'll hand all of you over to the mob to massacre. We stay in here and wait it out.'

'Wait it out?' One of the servants shook his head. 'Wait for what?'

'They'll abandon the palace once they've stripped it of anything of value. We can leave then. Alive and with our weapons in our hands, just in case.'

'And what if they're lying in wait?' the servant responded. 'We'll be wiped out. I say we surrender!'

Several voices echoed his demand.

Macro strode over to the man and knocked him down with a powerful right hook. 'And I say you should shut your bloody mouth.' He turned and glared around at those in the chamber. 'Anyone else got anything to say? No? Then the matter's settled. No surrender.'

There was a sharp rap on the far side of one of the doors.

'Prefect Cato? What is your response to our offer?'

Macro returned to Cato's side and arched an eyebrow.

'Be my guest,' said Cato.

Macro cleared his throat. 'I speak on behalf of Prefect Cato, commander of the urban cohorts, who has better things to do than bargain with a common criminal from the gutters of Rome. Prefect Cato's response is that you and your rabble should bugger off and go fuck yourselves.'

There was a pause before those outside roared with anger. Bullo shouted above the din. 'Then you will all die!'

Cato looked at Macro and nodded. 'Well said, Centurion Macro. I think they got the message.'

There was renewed pounding on the outside of the thick timbers, and Cato muttered, 'I wonder what they will do now?'

'Not much they *can* do. We've got ourselves a stand-off.'

'I hope so . . .' He sighed. 'Right, let's get some order in here.'

The mob had largely fallen silent and only the distant sounds of revelry from around the palace could be heard. Outside, a band of clouds now blotted out the heavens and plunged most of the city into darkness, pierced only by torches and braziers and the fires still burning across the Forum and in the palace. The very

366

air felt smothering, thought Cato, as thunder rumbled ominously in the distance.

Macro had been conferring with the other officers, and now he came to the bottom of the stairs leading up to the imperial quarters to speak to Cato, who was standing in an archway overlooking the Forum. 'I have the strength returns, sir.'

'Go on.'

'Two hundred and sixty-three from the First Cohort made it to the command post. Together with three hundred and two from the Third Cohort. The Second suffered most. Only eighty-one of them.'

Cato closed his eyes briefly. Of the men he had led into the palace only a few hours earlier, less than half remained under his command.

'Of course,' Macro continued, 'there's bound to be plenty of our lads who are in the same situation as us, barricaded in somewhere around the palace.'

'Let's hope so.'

Both were silent as they looked down on the Forum. Thousands of people were still there. Drunken groups gathered around wine jars looted from nearby inns. Individuals and small bands were making off with whatever valuables they had looted from the palace. Rowdy crowds were lynching anyone they suspected of being a supporter of Nero.

'So much for the greatest civilisation in the known world,' Cato mused. 'I would never have believed it could sink to this so swiftly.'

'Rome is not the Empire,' Macro replied. 'Sure, it's our capital city, but it's always been a hotbed of intrigue, tension and violence. This is no worse than it was in the last decades of the Republic. Bloodshed and collapse of authority was pretty much the order of the day.'

Cato glanced at him wryly. 'You've become quite the student of history.'

'What else do you do when you're retired? Can't spend all your time drinking and playing dice.'

'You're right, though. I'd just hoped that the stability Augustus bequeathed Rome would endure. Seems like we're slipping back into the bad old ways. We've replaced back-stabbing senatorial factionalism with a succession of corrupt dictators. Nero may turn out to be the very worst of them. I can see it in him already. He's vain and selfish and cares nothing for others. We are all a means to his self-gratification. He'd throw us under a wagon to save his hide in a heartbeat. Worse, he knows nothing about what is required to run a powerful empire. He makes far-reaching decisions on a whim and reverses his decision a few days later . . . It would be no great loss to Rome if Bullo killed him along with the rest of us.'

'Perhaps.' Macro shrugged. 'I'm not in this to protect Nero and his tart. I just want to live to see my Petronella and Bardea again. In the meantime, I'll fight for my comrades and we'll live or die on the whim of the gods. Same as always, eh, Cato?'

Cato smiled grimly. 'Same as always, brother.'

'Sir!'

They turned to see Lemulus at the foot of the stairs.

'What is it?' Cato demanded.

'You'd better come quickly. Looks like Bullo is making his move.'

Smoke was already curling under the doors, which were illuminated by a faint glow from the flames on the far side. Cato pursed his lips.

'I feared he would do this. Seems he'd rather have his revenge on me for his son than get his hands on Nero's treasures. So much for any hope of them leaving once they had their fill of looting.'

'It puts an end to any notion of surrender, though,' Macro

pointed out. 'There's no way out through a fire. That'll put some spine into those in here who are wavering. Not that having a spine makes you any more fireproof . . .'

Cato turned to Lemulus. 'Get cloth stuffed under the door and around the edges. It'll keep the smoke out for a while at least.'

While Lemulus saw to the task, Cato examined the high openings in the walls. He pointed one out to Macro. 'See there? The glow? Bullo's lighting more fires around the chamber. And I'll bet he's intending to do the same to the imperial quarters. Like I said, he's after blood, not booty.'

'I wonder how he's squaring this with the mob?' asked Macro.

'Would you want to go up against him and his band of thugs? Besides, if there's one thing the mob likes for sure, it's the spectacle of people dying. As far as they're concerned, we're part of the entertainment now.'

As quickly as Lemulus and his men managed to block the smoke from the door, more entered through the openings, carried on a light breeze that had picked up in advance of the coming storm. It billowed across the blue-painted ceiling with its depiction of the heavens, studded with glass to give the impression of stars. The glow from the fires below the openings swelled and the crackle of the flames was clearly audible to those in the audience chamber. Once again panic seized the palace staff and some of Cato's men. One of the servants, a bronze plate on a chain about his neck identifying him as a freedman, was pushed forward to speak for his companions.

'Prefect, we must surrender, while there is still time.'

Cato shook his head. 'Even if they can still extinguish the flames outside the door to let us out, we'd all be killed. As long as we remain in here, there's still hope.'

'If we stay here, we'll be burned alive!'

Macro gave a dry chuckle. 'Then we are dead either way, so what does it matter?'

The freedman thought desperately. 'What if we open the doors and put out the fire? You still have plenty of soldiers. We could try to fight our way out.'

'No,' Cato replied firmly. 'We've nothing to put the flames out with. No water. No mats to smother them. Even if we had, what chance is there of a few hundred of us cutting our way through tens of thousands of them? It would be little better than suicide.'

The freedman paused, then nodded towards Macro. 'Like your friend said, we're dead either way. So what have we to lose?'

Macro turned away from the freedman and muttered, 'You know, he's got a point . . . We might get some nasty burns, it's true. But we'll have a fighting chance.'

Cato cleared his throat and spoke loudly enough that everyone in the chamber could hear him. 'We stay where we are. The situation may change. Until then there will be no more talk of surrender.'

He stared round, daring anyone to defy him. No one did, and the freedman backed away among his comrades.

They waited in silence as the flames licked up around the openings and the smoke steadily thickened and began to catch in their throats. After a few minutes, the officer in charge of the German bodyguards came hurrying into the room and paused as he took in the scene before approaching Cato.

'The rioters are lighting fires around the imperial quarters.'

'Welcome to the club,' said Macro.

'Caesar demands that you and your men put them out. At once.'

Cato indicated the doors, the edges of which were now glowing as the wadding stuffed into the gaps began to smoulder. 'How does Caesar propose we go about it? Beyond the flames outside, there are thousands of rioters waiting to hack us to pieces. We'd never get through. So, my friend, if Caesar has a better plan, I'm all ears.'

The officer scratched his jaw. 'What should I say to him?'

'That's your problem,' said Macro. 'You could always tell him he's welcome to come down here and sort it out in person.'

The officer drew himself up and spoke formally. 'Caesar has given you an order. It's your duty to carry it out. I will tell him that I have communicated that order to you. If you fail to obey, you will answer to him and face the consequences.'

Cato felt an urge to laugh in the man's face. What hold did he think Caesar had over them any more? As things stood, the prospect of Nero's wrath was not the most concerning of prospects. At the moment of death, all men were equal. Rank counted for nothing. All that mattered was the manner in which they faced their end.

'I suggest you return to Caesar and explain the situation. I can no more put out the fires than I can fly to safety across the city. Tell Caesar he has a choice of death . . .'

Macro grinned at his friend's reference to the sentence that was handed down to aristocrats who were condemned by the emperor and offered the chance to kill themselves or be executed by the Praetorians. What goes round, comes round, he mused. Even for Caesar.

The officer's shoulders sagged. 'I'll tell him . . . May the gods help you.'

'May they help us all,' said Cato.

As the officer turned and left the chamber, there was a sudden swirl of smoke that left almost every man coughing and spluttering. Outside there was a brilliant flicker of lightning, and shortly afterwards a shattering crash of thunder followed by a rolling rumble that shook the fabric of the palace. Then, above the crackle of the flames, they heard the hiss of rain, quickly turning into a downpour as the wind strengthened and the storm that had been building for many days finally broke over Rome.

More lightning filled the openings high on the wall and

bleached the faces of the men within the chamber. In the bursts of illumination Cato could make out their expressions of fear and awe, but importantly, hope.

Macro laughed with relief. 'Seems like the gods are out to help us after all.'

But Cato's relief was short-lived. He heard shouting from the corridor outside. The doors had almost burned through, and light showed through the splits in the timber. Then he saw the glow fade and blink out before water seeped under into the audience chamber and spread across the flagstones.

'They're putting out the flames . . . Form up!' he ordered. 'Lemulus, get the First Cohort over here!'

There was a rush as the soldiers snatched up their shields and took up their positions. Cato ordered the palace staff to the rear and joined Macro and Lemulus in the front rank as the fire outside was steadily extinguished.

'Looks like Bullo's impatience has got the better of him,' said Macro.

'Then he's a fool,' Cato responded. 'If he wants a fight, it'll cost him dearly.'

'Maybe it's a price he's willing to pay . . .'

They stood, shields up, swords ready, muscles tensed, listening as the men on the far side of the doors extinguished the last of the flames and moved the debris aside. Then the doors thudded under the impact of a heavy object and the timbers splintered further.

'Hold steady, lads!' Macro called out. 'When they come through, make 'em pay for every one of the lives of our comrades they've taken tonight!'

The scorched thrones began to shift, grating as they moved across the flagstones. The gap between the doors widened and Cato could see the gleam of blades and armour in the gloom of the corridor. Then, with a sudden lurch, the doors burst open and Nero's throne toppled onto its side. Cato raised his sword, braced his feet and clenched his teeth, ready to defend himself.

The first two figures stepped through the opening. Praetorians. They drew up at once, swords raised as they beheld the smoke-streaked faces and shields of the men formed up across the chamber before them. Then a third figure entered the room. Tigellinus's eyes fixed on Cato and he grinned.

'Well met, Prefect Cato!'

CHAPTER THIRTY-TWO

The storm lasted most of the night, lashing the city with rain that gushed down the slopes of the hills and coursed through the Forum before emptying into the Tiber. The fires lit by the rioters in and around the palace were soon doused, and as dawn broke, the clouds passed towards the coast and the sky cleared.

First light revealed the devastation caused by the previous night's violence. Bodies littered the Forum and the approaches to the palace complex. Many more lay within. The vast majority had been part of the mob, hunted down by the Praetorians when they entered the palace. They had gone in hard, cutting down any who resisted and many who didn't. Some had tried to pass themselves off as members of the palace staff when the latter emerged from their hiding places, but were quickly picked out. Many prisoners had been taken, including Bullo and some of his men. As the sun rose over Rome, they were formed into work gangs and forced to begin clearing up the mess in and around the palace.

The bodies of the rioters were hauled out and heaped in the outer courtyard while the dead of the urban cohorts and the palace staff were laid in lines so that they could be identified and preparations made for their funerals. Nero had ordered that the corpses of the rioters were to be carted out of the city and buried in a mass grave beyond the necropolis. There would be no ceremonies for them and nothing but a mound of earth to mark the place of their interment.

Over half the men missing from the rolls of the urban cohorts had managed to find somewhere to hide during the hours of darkness after the Praetorians had retaken the palace. Cato had moved his men to the inner courtyard and they were joined by their comrades who had not been able to fall back to the audience chamber. As Cato and Macro oversaw the collection of the dead men's seals and recording of their details, they were approached by a young tribune of the Praetorian Guard. He bore the strain of the night's action as well as a bloodied dressing on his hand, in which he held a waxed slate.

'Prefect Tigellinus sends his compliments, sir. Here are your orders.'

'Prefect Tigellinus?' Cato arched an eyebrow. 'What's happened to Burrus?'

The tribune hesitated before he replied. 'The previous commander died shortly after the transfer of command to Tigellinus, sir.'

'Died? How?'

'I am told that he succumbed as a result of his illness, sir.'

'Natural causes, then,' Macro remarked cynically. 'Seems to happen a lot among those in high office in Rome. I'd be careful not to get promoted too quickly, young man.'

Cato glanced over the lines scored into the wax before he addressed Macro.

'The urban cohorts are to return to the camp, taking our dead with us. It seems the Praetorians are in charge here.'

'Typical. We do the hard fighting and they turn up in time to claim the glory.'

The tribune stiffened. 'I resent that remark. It was us that saved your necks.'

'It was your failure to obey orders to march to the palace in the first place that put our necks in danger,' Macro pointed out.

'We were unaware of such orders until Prefect Tigellinus entered the Praetorian camp bearing Caesar's letter of appointment. We marched on the palace as soon as we could.'

'Is there anything else?' Cato intervened. 'Any other instructions?'

'Yes, sir. The prefect instructs you and Centurion Macro to attend Caesar once your cohorts have left the palace. That's all I have been told to relate to you.'

'I see. Is there anything you could relate to us that you haven't been told to say?'

The tribune frowned as he tried to untangle the question. 'Sir?'

'Like the reason why the urban cohorts, my men, have been ordered to return to camp without us.'

'As I said, sir. The Praetorian Guard is protecting the palace and the emperor now. You and your men are no longer needed. I imagine that you will be returned to duty patrolling the streets as soon as possible. Is that all, sir?'

'Yes. You are dismissed.'

Macro frowned as the tribune strode off. 'Glad to see the Praetorian ruperti maintaining their high standards of arrogance and ignorance. Nothing that a hard kick up the arse wouldn't improve.'

'Indeed . . . I wonder why Nero wants to see us *after* our men have left the palace? I don't like the sound of it.'

'Me neither.'

The imperial quarters had been one of the few sections of the palace complex to escape the ravages of the mob. It maintained its ambience of serene luxury, despite the odour of smoke that clung to the soft fittings and furnishings. Macro and Cato were disarmed by the German bodyguards and escorted to a garden terrace overlooking the Forum. Nero was surveying the scene, hands clasped behind his back. Tigellinus, wearing a black cuirass picked out with silver wreath designs, stood at his side. Poppaea lay on a couch under a large white awning, fanned by a slave wielding an arrangement of large feathers. Nero and Tigellinus ceased their conversation as Macro and Cato approached. The German escort halted them three paces away and indicated that they were not to get any closer.

Nero looked tired, but managed a thin smile of greeting as he waved the German bodyguard aside. The latter bowed deeply and retreated a few paces but kept a hand on the pommel of his sword.

'Prefect Cato, Centurion Macro, I'm glad you two were spared as well, thanks to the quick thinking of my friend Tigellinus.'

His companion bowed his head modestly. 'You are too kind, Caesar.'

'Nonsense, man. We owe you our lives. If you had not got through to the Praetorian camp and exposed that traitor Burrus and his cronies, we'd all be dead and the palace a smoking ruin by this morning.'

'Indeed, Caesar,' said Cato. 'I have to say, I was surprised to see Tigellinus leading the Praetorians to our rescue, given the haste with which he left the scene earlier on.'

Tigellinus frowned for an instant before responding calmly, 'I had to do something to safeguard Caesar once I learned that the Praetorians were refusing to respond to his orders. I took it upon myself to forge Caesar's order to dismiss Burrus and appoint me to command the Praetorians in his place. It was all I needed to get through the Praetorians at the city gates and into the camp. Fortunately, Burrus and his followers were rather fewer in number than those men loyal to Caesar.'

'So that's how it was done,' Cato mused.

Nero smiled. 'Yes! And I am mightily grateful to Tigellinus for his initiative and boldness in our hour of need. That is why I have appointed him this morning to command the Praetorians. With a genuine letter of appointment this time, eh?'

He nudged Tigellinus who managed to look suitably abashed.

'Burrus is dead, sadly,' Nero continued. 'I would have liked to see him join Rufrius Gallo and his fellow conspirators and the ringleaders of the mob in the arena when they are put to death. The wild beasts are going to gorge themselves on their flesh,' he added with cruel relish.

'Conspirators, Caesar?'

'Yes, Cato. Surely you must see it? Burrus was acting with other plotters to depose me. They were responsible for the violence stirred up in our streets over this business with Octavia. I wouldn't be surprised if she and her supporters were behind it all. You were there when Burrus spoke up for her.'

Cato was wary of responding too directly, and he thought carefully before he spoke. Even though he was aware of the group of plotters associated with Vespasian, it was hard to believe that they had sufficient influence to cause a popular uprising. 'Yes, Caesar. But the lady Octavia has always been a favourite of the people of Rome. I think their anger over her treatment, misguided as they undoubtedly are, was spontaneous. It would be difficult for any group of plotters to provoke the mob so swiftly and so violently as we witnessed yesterday.'

'That may be so . . .' Nero said thoughtfully.

Tigellinus intervened. 'It may be so, Caesar, but it's more than likely that Burrus and his friends took advantage of the uprising to stand down the Praetorians while the mob did their dirty work for them.'

'Yes, the treacherous cowards . . . They must pay for it, and they will.'

'Of course they must be punished,' said Cato. 'However, given what Rome has been through, I would suggest that Caesar treads carefully while the mob is in its present febrile state. It might be wise to offer them something to appease their mood.'

Nero considered this for a moment. 'What do you suggest, Prefect?'

'The spark that set them off was the news that Octavia had been arrested. If you want to win the mob over, set her free. That should go some considerable way towards repairing the situation.'

'It could equally look like weakness, Caesar,' said Tigellinus.

Nero stroked his jaw and then glanced towards the couch where Poppaea had been following the discussion. 'What do you think, my love? Should I recall Octavia from exile?'

Given the venom Poppaea had vented against Nero's former wife on previous occasions, Cato was expecting further vitriol. However, she barely stirred as she gave her response in a languid tone.

'Do as you wish, Caesar. Send for her. Leave her in exile on Pandateria. It does not concern me any more.' She slowly swung her legs off the couch and eased herself to her feet as she touched her brow. 'I have a headache. I should go inside to sleep for a bit. Given my condition.'

She stroked the curve of her belly, and at once Nero went to her and kissed her tenderly. 'You must take every caution, my love. So much is riding on the child in your womb. Go and rest. I will deal with this matter.'

She walked steadily away, back through the faintly wafting curtains of the entrance to the imperial quarters, attended by the slave, who continued fanning her. Once she was out of sight, Nero returned to the waiting men.

'It's important that Octavia returns safely to Rome. It needs to be handled by men I can trust.'

'I am sure Centurion Macrinus is more than capable, Caesar,' said Tigellinus.

'Perhaps . . . But just to be sure, I can think of no better men than Cato and Macro here.'

Cato started. 'Caesar, the urban cohorts need to be reconstituted and returned to their former duties. I should attend to that.'

'Tigellinus can take care of that in your absence.'

'But . . .' Cato stilled his tongue as he saw the irritation in Nero's expression. He swallowed and bowed his head. 'As Caesar wishes.'

'Tigellinus, have the authority drawn up for me to put my seal to, and arrange for fast horses to be readied for the prefect, the centurion and ten Praetorians. They will leave as soon as the document is ready.'

Three days later, at dawn, Cato and Macro were standing on the foredeck of the bireme in which they had set off from the naval base at Misenum. Some five miles ahead of them they could make out the tiny strip of Pandateria. To the left and slightly closer was the companion rock, which rose from the sea like a molehill. Pandateria appeared to be no more than a mile in length and a quarter of that in width. A grim, isolated retreat that had served as a prison for a number of members of the imperial family since the days of Augustus.

'I can think of nicer places to live out your exile,' said Macro as he strained his eyes to make out the details. 'I'd be surprised if she hasn't already gone stir crazy.'

'I'd be pleased if that is all that has happened to her,' said Cato.

Macro looked at him sharply. 'What do you mean, lad? You really think Nero would risk having her killed? After what the mob did, he'd be mad to.'

'If he did, he would have given the order *before* the riot broke out.'

'Aye, that's true. Then he'd better be praying she is still alive if he wants to avoid any further violence.'

'I'm not sure praying would be much help.'

There was only the faintest of breezes and the bireme was under oars, moving across the gentle swell with a rhythmic splash and a lurch of the deck beneath their boots. Both men were silent for a while before Macro spoke again.

'Don't know about you, but I ain't too happy about Tigellinus being given command of the Praetorians. Burrus may have been a crusty, old-fashioned bugger, but he was a proper soldier through and through. Seems to me that Tigellinus's sole quality – if you can call it that – is his loyalty to Nero.'

'Maybe that's all that matters these days,' said Cato. 'With Burrus gone, Seneca will be the next to go. Then you'll see a steady replacement of governors, generals and others with those who are loyal to Nero, Poppaea and Tigellinus. Frankly, by the time we get back to Rome, I'd be surprised if I was still the commander of the urban cohorts. Maybe that's why they were sent back to camp so quickly, and why you and I were dispatched to retrieve Octavia.'

'You really think so?'

'We'll know soon enough.'

'And what then for us, lad?'

'If we're lucky, I'll go back to my farm to live out my days with Claudia and Lucius, and you'll go back to Petronella and Bardea and finally get to enjoy your retirement.'

'If we're unlucky?'

Cato puffed his cheeks. 'There's always room for two more among those being sent to the arena for execution . . .'

Just over an hour later, the bireme nosed its way into the small bay that served as the island's only harbour. Apart from a signal tower at the end of a narrow breakwater, a cluster of fishermen's huts, a couple of trading posts and an inn, the only other structure was the modest villa perched on a hillock overlooking the harbour. Augustus had once intended it to serve as a holiday home, but having spent a few days on the island to inspect the work in progress, he had abandoned the project, and since then the half-completed buildings had served as a prison. Pandateria was the kind of place that suited simple fishermen and sheep herders, thought Cato. Anyone else would soon be driven mad by the isolation.

As the bireme turned towards the strip of beach where a handful of fishing boats were drawn up, he saw an imposing figure in military garb standing on the shingle watching them.

'That's Macrinus, isn't it?'

'Yes,' Macro answered. 'I wonder if we're who he was expecting?'

The trierarch of the bireme gave the order to ship oars, and the long shafts rumbled inboard as the vessel glided the remaining distance to the shore and softly ground to a halt in the pebbles of the shallows. Two crewmen lowered the gangplank, and Cato and Macro descended and splashed into the ankle-deep water. They strode ashore and exchanged a salute with Macrinus.

'The urban cohorts have missed you, Centurion,' said Macro. 'Not exactly acceptable of you to piss off without giving us any notice.'

'I had no choice. Tigellinus summoned me to the palace, handed me my orders and sent me here with four men to guard Octavia.'

'A likely tale.'

'But the truth nonetheless.'

Cato fished out the leather tube containing the order to transfer Octavia into his custody and handed it to Macrinus, indicating the imperial seal as he did so.

'I've been hoping for fresh orders,' said Macrinus. 'Sooner I get off this island and away from the smell, the better.'

Macro raised his chin and sniffed, then shrugged. 'If you say so.'

Macrinus broke the seal, extracted the small scroll of papyrus and read the message. As he did so, Cato noticed him swallow anxiously, and his hand gave a slight tremble. He reread the short document and then looked up and shook his head. 'I don't understand this.'

'What don't you understand?' Cato demanded, a sick sense of foreboding creeping over him. 'It's simple enough. You're to hand your prisoner over to us to take back to Rome.'

Macrinus chewed his lip. 'You'd better come with me, sir.'

He walked quickly up the beach to the path that climbed the short distance to the villa. Cato turned to the Praetorians, who had started to descend the gangplank, and ordered them to accompany him. The party followed Macrinus towards the entrance to the shell of the villa, where Cato could now see four other men. They rose to their feet and stood to attention as they spied the two officers behind Macrinus.

There were no gates at the entrance. They had never been fitted. There had never been any need for them, as the island's prisoners had nowhere to escape to on the barren rock of Pandateria.

'Wait here,' Cato ordered the Praetorians.

He and Macro followed Macrinus into the courtyard of the villa, an open space no more than thirty feet across. A well stood in one corner, supplied by the cisterns that had been completed in the first stage of construction. There were finished structures on one side only. The rest had only been partially built, or they lacked roofs, doors and shutters. Macrinus pointed to one of the rooms without a roof.

'She's in there.'

They crossed to the entrance, but before they reached it, Cato heard the buzz of flies and caught the sweet smell of decay. Macrinus stood to one side of the doorway and ushered them through. It was a small room, little more than a sleeping cell. On the far side was a low wooden-framed bed with a thin, frayed mattress. A woman's body lay on it, mostly covered by a blanket. Her exposed shoulders and arms were already mottled blue and black. Her wrists and forearms had been cut open in several places and were dark with dried blood, on which the flies were feeding. Her head had been cut off and placed in a basket beside the bed. The tresses of her hair covered her blotched face.

Cato felt his throat tighten as his stomach heaved. It took all his self-control not to vomit. He heard Macro suck in a deep breath at his side and let it out in a soft growl of rage and disgust. Swallowing the rising bile in his throat, Cato managed to speak.

'How long ago did this happen?'

'As soon as we arrived, two days back,' Macrinus said from the doorway. 'My orders were to offer her a choice of death the moment we landed on the island. She refused to take her own life. So me and the others had to hold her down and cut her wrists. She resisted as much as she could and . . . you can see the result. I was told to make it look like suicide, before we took her head off. And that a ship would be sent to bring her body back to Rome and present her head to Poppaea. That's why I don't understand the orders you just gave me. They don't make sense.'

Macro coughed to clear his throat. 'Who told you to do this to her?'

There was the briefest of hesitations before Macrinus replied. 'Poppaea. Just before we left for Ostia. We brought the prisoner here on one of Nero's yachts.'

'Poppaea . . .' Cato repeated slowly. 'You claim this is her doing?'

Macrinus nodded.

'Did she give you that instruction in writing?'

'No. She said it was Nero's decision.'

'And you didn't think to check that with Caesar?'

Macrinus looked at him accusingly. 'Would you dare to second-guess the word of Poppaea?'

'I might, if I thought my life depended on it.'

'Easy for you to say, Prefect Cato. You weren't there. What do you think would have happened to me if I had questioned her orders? She'd have had me killed at once.'

'Maybe, but at least she would have spared you the trip . . . Macro, hold him.'

'With pleasure.'

Before Macrinus could react, Macro rounded on him and

384

slammed him backwards against the door frame. His head crashed against the weathered wood, and while he was still dazed, Macro swung him round, pinning his arms behind his back. Cato had drawn his sword and set the point at an angle against Macrinus's stomach, leaning close to his face as he spoke.

'If you want to save yourself from what Octavia went through, I suggest you keep still.'

Macrinus's eyes widened in terror and he managed to gasp, 'No! Please! I was just obeying orders! I swear!'

'Tell it to Charon.'

Cato bunched his muscles and rammed the sword up under Macrinus's ribcage and into his heart. His head snapped back and his mouth stretched open in an explosive cry as his body strained every sinew to try and break Macro's grip, but despite his size, he was no match for the stocky centurion, and he steadily weakened as he bled out. The two of them lowered his limp body to the ground outside the cell, and Cato wrenched his blade free and wiped the blood off on the dead man's tunic before he sheathed his sword.

'What now?' Macro asked quietly.

'We were sent to bring Octavia back to Caesar. So that's what we must do.'

Cato crossed the yard to the entrance and addressed the officer in charge of the party who had accompanied them from the palace.

'Optio, you'll find the body of a woman inside. She is to be wrapped up in blankets and bound. Place her head in with the body and then use these men's belts to secure the package. Once you have killed them.'

'Sir?'

Cato nodded towards the four men who had helped Macrinus butcher their prisoner. 'You heard me. Carry out your orders and kill these men . . .'

CHAPTER THIRTY-THREE

There was silence in the small private chamber of the imperial quarters. Nero was sitting on a couch behind his writing desk. Poppaea stood behind him, playing with the curls that hung down the back of his neck. Tigellinus, in a finely spun toga, was wearing the chain and pendant of the prefect of the Praetorian Guard that he had inherited from Burrus. Before them stood Cato and Macro. The latter had just unbuckled the belts that had bound the blankets around Octavia's body and head. Her mutilated corpse was further tinged by the hues of decay arising from the journey back to Rome, and the stench of it reached all those in the room.

Poppaea's nose wrinkled as she muttered, 'Disgusting . . .'

Nero looked as if he might throw up. The blood had drained from his face and he was covering his lips with one of his hands as he swallowed hard before he managed to speak. 'How can this be? I gave orders that she be sent into exile. Not . . . this. Explain yourself, Prefect Cato.'

'She was long dead before we reached Pandateria, Caesar. Centurion Macrinus said he offered her a choice of death. She refused suicide, so he and his men murdered her.'

'Murdered? Massacred, more like. Poor Octavia. She didn't deserve this.'

After Nero's previous expressions of hatred for his former

wife, Cato found it hard to put much store by the sincerity of his current display of sorrow. 'No, Caesar. She did not.'

Poppaea leaned forward and spoke softly to Nero. 'Whether she deserved it or not is irrelevant. She was the cause of the riot. It was because of her supporters that we were nearly torn apart by the mob. You, me and the baby. It's sad that she is gone, but at least she won't be around to inspire any more trouble. By all means grieve for her if you must, my dear, my love, but never forget the damage she is responsible for.'

Nero nodded slowly, then shifted his gaze from the corpse and addressed Cato. 'Macrinus would never dare to kill her on his own account. He must have been told to do it by someone. Who would give him such an order?'

Cato paused before he replied, making sure that he did not look at Poppea directly. All the same, he was aware that her fingers had frozen and she was no longer playing with Nero's hair. 'He did not say, Caesar.'

'Well, where is he? Have him brought to the palace at once. Get your interrogators to work on him, Tigellinus. I want to know who was responsible for this.'

'Caesar, Macrinus is dead,' Cato said. 'I executed him and his men on the spot as soon as I discovered what they'd done.'

'That's a pity. Your actions were understandable, Prefect Cato, but now we have no way of finding out who gave the order to carry out the murder.'

'Perhaps it's better that way,' Poppaea suggested.

Nero twisted round to look at her. 'How do you mean?'

She gave a slight shrug. 'If you discover who ordered Macrinus to kill Octavia, you give the mob another target for their ire, and that may give them an excuse for more violence.'

'But if I don't find out who was behind it, the mob will blame me, likely as not. Or they will say I am covering up for the person who is responsible. Neither option does me any favours.'

She cupped his cheek in her hand and kissed his forehead. 'Nero, darling, you don't have to do either of those things. Turn around and look. The answer you need is lying right in front of you.'

He did as he was told, with some reluctance as his eyes once again fell on Octavia's body.

Poppaea gently kneaded his shoulders as she continued. 'What if she had committed suicide? Racked by guilt over her adultery with Ancietus, she chose an honourable death. All Rome knows what a stickler for honour and integrity she was. Suicide was the only way out for her, and she accepted her fate bravely.'

'But she didn't kill herself . . .'

Cato saw Poppaea roll her eyes before she increased the pressure of her fingers on the emperor's neck. 'No one needs to know that. If you tell the people that she died, bravely, by her own hand, they won't have anyone to blame for the deed, will they? Instead we can all put on a show of grieving for her and use this as an opportunity to unite the people of Rome and their Caesar. Do you understand now?'

Nero smiled slowly. 'I see. That's good. Yes, very good.'

Poppaea gestured towards the body. 'Of course, we need to make sure that she is covered up in a shroud, laced with fragrance, for the public funeral. Get Seneca to write a moving valediction and you'll have the people eating out of your hand. There's only one further matter to be attended to.' She looked at the other men in the room. 'The three of you must not breathe a word of what has been said today. It is more than your lives are worth. Do we understand one another?'

'Absolutely.' Tigellinus nodded.

Cato stared back at her without blinking. 'The centurion and I understand.'

Poppaea shook her head. 'I'm not so sure that you do. Or maybe you understand only too well. In which case it would be a good idea for the pair of you to absent yourselves from Rome for a few years until all this is forgotten.'

'Absent, as in exile, my lady?' Macro asked pointedly. 'Rather than absent, permanently.'

Poppaea laughed at the centurion's hubris. 'Oh, I like these two! They may be fine soldiers, but they're hopeless at politics. They need to be sent far from Rome if only for their own protection.' She lowered her head to speak to Nero. 'I believe I overheard some talk the other day of another campaign on the eastern frontier.'

'Yes, the danger posed by Parthia never seems to fade. Then there's the threat to our lands along the coast of the Euxine Sea.'

'There we are then!' Poppaea smiled. 'Send them east. They can kick their heels there until we – you – permit them to return. They have family in Rome, so we can trust them not to speak of this under the misapprehension that such gossip never reaches the ears of Caesar or his wife. Tigellinus . . .'

'My lady?'

'You can take responsibility for drafting their appointments to the eastern armies.'

'Yes, my lady. I've already appointed a replacement to command the urban cohorts, so there's no reason to delay their departure.'

Nero pulled himself free of her grip. 'Now just a moment! I am Caesar. Not you. I give the orders!'

'Of course you do, my darling. Pardon me, I only meant to relieve you of some of the burdens of ruling that vex you so. You give the order to Tigellinus.'

Nero puffed himself up as he turned to the Praetorian prefect. 'You are to send these two officers east.'

'Yes, Caesar.'

'I am tired now. I need to rest. Come, Poppaea!'

Cato, Macro and Tigellinus bowed as the emperor, arm in arm with his mistress, left the room, steering clear of the body. Once they had gone, Macro let out a sigh.

'Well, we know who wears the toga out of those two.'

'Not the wisest of comments,' said Tigellinus. 'She's right. You'd last less than a day in politics. It's as well you are being sent east.'

'Oh, come on!' Macro protested. 'Caesar is going to forget he gave that order an hour or so from now. He'll have other things on his mind if I'm any judge of how Poppaea plays him.'

'He might forget. She won't. I know her well, and believe me, the two of you won't be safe in Rome.'

Macro shook his head. 'Oh fuck. We've only been back in the city for a matter of months and we're already being kicked out. Petronella's going to throw a fit.'

Cato shared his friend's anger and frustration but dared not make any mention of his own domestic arrangements.

'Come on, Macro. Tigellinus is right. We're pushing our luck every moment we remain in the palace. We need to go.'

His friend nodded sullenly and turned to the door. Cato paused and fixed his eyes on the Praetorian prefect. 'One thing I need to ask. Did you know about this?' He nodded towards Octavia's body.

'No. I gave Macrinus his instructions personally. He was to take her to Pandateria and keep her there until further orders. I swear that's the truth.'

'But you must have a pretty clear idea who told Macrinus to murder her, whatever orders you may have given him.'

Tigellinus was still for a moment, then he nodded.

'I'd watch your back if I were you,' said Cato. 'For all the riches and finery that comes with being a close adviser to Nero, you may find that you'd be better off wherever you send Macro and me. How long do you think it will take for Poppaea to turn on you? Something to think about. Farewell, Tigellinus. I don't expect we'll meet again, not that either of us would want to.'

He fell into step alongside Macro as they left the chamber and strode out of the palace. They didn't speak again until they had crossed the Forum.

'I'll see you back at the house,' Cato said. 'There's something I need to deal with first.'

'Oh? There's no need to return to the camp to retrieve our kit. We can send for it.'

'It's another matter. Something I need to know before we leave Rome. I won't be long.'

'All right. Suit yourself. At the house then.' Macro made his way up the ramp that led out of the Forum. Cato watched him for a moment before turning in a different direction.

Vespasian was having a massage in the bathhouse of his villa when Cato arrived. After stating that he needed to speak to the senator on an urgent matter, he was shown to a veranda overlooking the modest but neatly manicured garden. He sat on a bench and leaned back against the wall. There was a fountain in the centre from which the pleasing sound of water added to the serenity of the setting. After the events of the previous month, he could not help feeling a sense of unreality about the carefully trimmed bushes, graceful statues, colourful flower beds and whitewashed walls and pillars of his surroundings. Far from feeling relieved by having the command of the urban cohorts taken away from him, he felt weary to his bones, his spirits equally subdued and numbed by what he had experienced. However, he was still firmly resolved to pursue answers to some of the questions that plagued his thoughts. While he waited, a slave brought him some lemon-infused water that had been cooled in the villa's cellar. He sipped at it without appreciating the flavour any more than the bucolic scene around him.

At length Vespasian approached along a path shaded by the trees on either side. He was wearing a simple white tunic and sandals. The hair that fringed his pate was wet and his face was flushed from the heat of the bathhouse. He did not offer a smile or hold his hand out in greeting as Cato rose from the bench.

'So what urgent matter brings you here, Prefect Cato?' he asked curtly.

'I have been relieved of my command and Centurion Macro and I are about to be posted to the eastern frontier.'

Vespasian eased himself down at the other end of the bench and Cato resumed his own seat. 'That is a pity. I know how much you and the centurion were looking forward to a peaceful interlude from your army service.'

'Interlude? We'd hoped to retire.'

Vespasian gave him an amused look. 'I don't think the Fates have done with either of you yet. Some of us are born to be soldiers to our dying day. You and Macro are two such examples, from my experience of you. Peace is not the ultimate goal for your kind. It is merely an interval between doing what you live for. It is no different for me. I lead a similar life of service to Rome. As it happens, I am also leaving soon.'

'Oh?'

'I am bound for the African province to take up the governorship. At least I can do some good there, instead of sitting on my arse in Rome and watching things go from bad to worse under Nero. Now that Burrus has gone and Seneca has decided to retire to his estates, there will be no restraining the emperor's baser instincts. The man will become a monster.'

'I believe so.' Cato nodded. 'History may judge that you and your friends did the right thing in plotting against him.'

Vespasian turned abruptly and stared hard at him. 'Are you here to accuse me of treason? Did Tigellinus send you?'

'No. I came here for answers for my peace of mind.'

'Really?' Vespasian raised an eyebrow. 'You should be wary of that, Cato. Some answers cause more pain than they are worth.'

'That may be so, but I must have them all the same.'

'I see . . . Before we go any further, do I understand that what passes between us will not be shared with anyone else? On your sacred word as an officer of Rome?'

'You have my word.'

Vespasian considered briefly. 'From most other men that would not be enough. But you are not most other men, Cato. Very well. Ask your questions. I will answer what I can.'

'How far were you and your friends responsible for the fire and the attack on the palace?'

'They are not my friends any more. I have cut ties with them. Not because I don't share their aims, but because they are rank amateurs who lack the foresight and means to mount a successful conspiracy to topple the emperor. They are sloppy about the need for security and present more of a danger to themselves than Tigellinus and his agents ever could. Piso and Lucanus are arrogant dilettantes unsuited to power play. That is why they failed to depose Nero this time, and why they will continue to fail, until the day their plotting is exposed and they are rounded up and put to death.'

'So there *was* an attempt to get rid of Nero?'

Vespasian gave a bitter laugh. 'If you can call it that. Lucanus and his friends were responsible for the fire. I did not know that when I spoke to you last. I found out later. Just as I found out that they intended to arrange for Octavia to be murdered by one of their agents.'

Some of the pieces of the puzzle suddenly shifted into place in Cato's head. 'Macrinus?'

Vespasian nodded. 'How did you find out?'

'I hadn't, until just now. I was sure he was Tigellinus's man.'

'He was, but like most men who attach themselves to the likes of Tigellinus, he had his price. We needed someone as close as possible to Nero's favourite. When Piso heard that Macrinus had been assigned to escort Octavia to Pandateria, he decided to have her killed in order to feed the rage of the mob directed at Nero and Poppaea. I told him I would have no part of that. The mob was already incensed. It would be unconscionable to murder Octavia. He eventually came round to my point of view. By that time I had already realised that there was no hope of a successful plot being carried out here in Rome. Burrus came over to us very late in the day and closed off the city and confined the Praetorians to their camp, but even he could not carry a sufficient number of officers with him to guarantee the Praetorians would support the overthrow of Nero. In the event, all it took was for Tigellinus to turn up waving his commission from Caesar and a promise of a bonus for the soldiers, and Burrus's support crumbled. Now he's dead and the officers loyal to him are condemned. The truth of it is that if Nero is to be toppled, it will only be achieved by someone at the head of the legions outside Italia.'

'Someone like you, perhaps.'

Vespasian smiled. 'Maybe me. Most likely someone else. I won't be able to exert much influence as a provincial governor. But if I ever achieve command of a large enough army, who knows? For now, my money is on Corbulo. He has enough men to see it through, but does he have the ambition? That's the question.'

Cato had been half listening as he prepared himself for what he had to say next. 'You say that Piso did not proceed with his plan to murder Octavia.'

'That's right.' Vespasian frowned. 'Why?'

'Octavia is dead. Murdered by Macrinus.'

Vespasian gasped, and then his eyes narrowed in fury. 'That bastard Piso! He lied to me.'

'Maybe not,' said Cato. 'Before I killed Macrinus, he said that he had been ordered to make Octavia kill herself, and if she refused, to make it look like she had.'

'Who told him to do it? Nero?'

'Poppaea, he said. I don't believe Nero was involved. From what I have seen of Poppaea, she's more than capable of being the one behind it. No doubt because she saw Octavia as a rival for the affections of the mob. Her position at Nero's side was not safe as long as Octavia lived and Nero could not count on the loyalty of the people.'

'Sweet Jupiter.' Vespasian clasped his hands together. 'Rome is well and truly fucked now it's in the hands of those two. Someone will have to get rid of them . . .'

'But not me. I have had enough of politics. As far as I'm concerned, all those who play political games are as bad as each other. Nero, Tigellinus, Poppaea, Piso, Seneca . . . even you.'

Vespasian rounded on him angrily and glared for a moment before he spoke. 'You may think that, Cato. The truth is, you have already taken your place in the equestrian order. You are a member of the aristocracy now. Who knows how much further you will rise? Like it or not, a man of your rank is already part of our world, and one day you will find yourself in a position like mine. What will you do then?'

'I will do what is right. As I have always tried to. I will remain a soldier and have no part to play in politics.'

'For the gods' sake, Cato, wake up. You are more intelligent than that. It's time you stopped behaving like some neophyte at Plato's academy. The world around you is a complicated mess. There are no philosophical or moral certainties. We live, act and die as a result of the contingencies that confront us. That is how it has always been for those who serve Rome. That is the truth that we have hidden beneath stories about honour, glory, tradition and some divinely ordained mission. We do what we do to survive and gain power to guarantee that survival. If that coincides with what is good for Rome, that is how we justify it to others, and ourselves when we lack sufficient self-awareness. If you don't see it all now, you will one day. Trust me.'

'Trust you? After a speech like that? I wouldn't know where to begin to trust a man who speaks as you do.'

'Very well then.' Vespasian stood up abruptly. 'It's time for you to go. We both have to make our preparations to depart from Rome.'

He escorted Cato to the door of his villa, and the two men faced each other on the threshold. There was an awkward pause before he offered Cato his hand.

'Good luck, Cato. Whatever you may think of me, I wish you well and will pray for your safety and success. You and that rogue Macro.'

Cato hesitated, then took the senator's hand. 'Good luck to you too, sir.'

Releasing his grip, he turned and stepped through the door, descended the small flight of steps and headed in the direction of his own house. His mind was more burdened than ever, as Vespasian had warned him it would be. Answers were often more of a curse than the questions that prompted them.

As he strode through the streets of Rome, he yearned to escape the city and all those who conspired and connived as they competed for power, not caring how many bodies they had to climb over to pursue their ambition. He understood, as never before, that the best that could be hoped for was to find friends and loved ones he could trust with his life, and return their affection and loyalty in kind. His heart lifted at the thought, and he looked forward to serving with Macro again. Before that, he would relish every moment he could in the company of Claudia and Lucius. Only the gods knew how little time they would have before fresh orders came and they were obliged to fight for Rome once again.

AUTHOR'S NOTE

Almost as soon as he had died, Emperor Nero became an object of vilification by many of his contemporaries, a tone picked up by the Roman historians who wrote about him subsequently. As Mary Beard has pointed out in her admirable analysis of the emperors, *Emperor of Rome,* those who died violently tended to be regarded afterwards as evil despots. Understandably, those who had suffered under the rule of such men would be inclined to portray them in unflattering terms. Equally understandably (though not commendably) there were those who were quick to heap their opprobrium on the dead even though they had profited mightily under their reign and presented themselves, while he lived, as friends of the emperor. No one likes to be associated with a tyrant, and such sycophants did their best to distance themselves from the deceased Nero at the first opportunity. Just as many of those on the wrong side at the end of World War Two were quick to announce that they were always secret opponents of the fascists. No doubt the same will apply to latter-day tyrants once they are gone.

In Nero's case there is little doubt that he was a mediocrity whose narcissism was never adequately reined in by those around him, who were therefore complicit in his excesses. He was instinctively vindictive, and cut down those who he saw as surpassing his modest talents as a singer, musician, writer or actor.

He murdered his mother and was instrumental in the death of his former wife. Far from serving the interests of his people, he left the day-to-day running of the empire to others while he wallowed in self-gratification, while at the same time asserting that no one knew better than him.

That said, either Nero, or his advisers, or both, understood the need to pander to the appetites of the mob. He laid on lavish entertainments and kept the people of Rome fed. After the great fire, he took care to be seen to offer support for the victims while at the same time singling out a handy minority to be presented as the villains behind the disaster. In much the same way, scapegoats have been violently targeted by populist political figures throughout history in order to distract the masses and use their grievances to turn them against each other rather than against those who oppress them. In that respect, (sing along, folks) Nero was the very model of a modern megalomaniac . . .

Like all tyrants, Nero relied on military muscle to protect himself from assassins, persecute his enemies and enforce his will. In that regard he was loyally served by the commanders of the Praetorian Guard, Burrus and Tigellinus. It is well known that the Praetorians were often involved in the succession 'system' of the empire and were responsible for the overthrow and anointing of many emperors. That is why emperors took great care to secure their loyalty through generous rewards. At the same time, even as early as the reign of Augustus, the first of the emperors, it was apparent that the Praetorians posed something of a danger. And so Augustus reassigned three of the Praetorian cohorts to form a separate body – the Urban Cohorts. This went some way towards balancing military power in the capital and allowed the emperors to play off one formation against the other.

Further afield, the legions and numerous auxiliary cohorts were spread out across the empire. Emperors made sure that their soldiers were paid well and were given hefty bonuses every so often. At the same time, the dispersal of forces made it difficult for commanders to pull together sufficient strength to challenge the emperor. The danger occurred when large armies were required for campaigns, and generals like Corbulo were watched closely to make sure that they were not tempted to use their military power for their own purposes. Towards the end of his reign Nero's advisers became increasingly concerned about the loyalty of a number of field commanders; they summoned them to report to Nero, then promptly had them done away with. That fate ultimately befell Corbulo as well.

The final crisis of Nero's reign occurred when the generals and their armies turned on him. He awoke to the danger too late to save himself and was forced to flee Rome before the Praetorians, seeing which way the wind was blowing, turned on him as well. Pursued by his opponents, he took his own life, or had someone do the job for him, before he could be arrested. A bitter year of power struggles followed his death before a new emperor stabilised the situation.

Cato and Macro's ongoing tales will increasingly interweave with these political crosscurrents as they chart a course through the perils to come. For now, they have survived the political infighting and are bound for the frontier of the empire once again to face the enemies of Rome.

CAST LIST

The Urban Cohorts

Prefect Quintus Licinius Cato, hoping for peace and quiet and not finding it under Nero's regime

Centurion Macro, not coping well with balancing peaceful retirement with being a born soldier

Tigellinus, transitioning from Commander of the Urban Cohorts to Commander of the Praetorian Guard

Tribune Gaius Albanius Ferox, Second in Command of the Urban Cohorts

Centurion Brocchus

Vibius Fulvius, a put-upon but savvy clerk

Centurion Aulus Lemulus, of the First Century, First Urban Cohort, an old sweat with little sympathy for slackers

Tribune Marcellus, Commanding Officer of the Second Cohort

Centurion Macrinus, an exemplar of corruption

Tribune Pantella, an exemplar of corpulence

The Praetorian Guard

Sextus Afranius Burrus, Commander of the Guard, frail from years of managing Nero's foibles

Tribune Rufrius Gallo, fed up with Nero's foibles

Nero's Court

Nero Claudius Augustus Germanicus, Emperor, aiming to make Rome great again, in his own image . . .

Poppaea Sabina, Nero's consort, a woman with a heart of cold . . .

Claudia Octavia, Nero's wife, victim of a tragic arranged marriage . . .

Seneca, a smooth-tongued senator with a great future behind him

Vespasian, a senator carefully considering his future

Titus and *Domitian*, sons of Vespasian, apples that will fall not far from the tree

Pallodorus, director of the palace banqueting division, harassed and anxious to please

Severus and *Celer*, architects by appointment to an overly ambitious client

Calpurnius Piso, an aristocrat with unlimited ambition

Lucanus, nephew of Seneca, a poet rather better at writing than plotting

Eucaenus, a talented flautist, possibly a player

Roman civilians

Claudia Acte, wife of Prefect Cato, in hiding from her previous husband

Petronella, wife of Macro, hoping for peace and quiet while knowing her husband well enough to be aware that is unlikely

Lucius, son of Cato, hoping to grow up and be like his dad, or better still, Uncle Macro

Bardea, daughter of Macro with Boudica, struggling to find her place in Roman society

Taurus, Macro's steward, solid and loyal

Helo, assistant to Macro's cook, motivated by financial reward

Trebonius, Cato's manservant, occasionally over-familiar, but steadfast

Horangenus Titus, a landlord, aiming to make himself grate again

Flaminus, a stray puppy, a survivor living his best life

Bullo, leader of the Bronze Blades gang in the Suburra, a ruthless robber and rabble-rouser

Urso, son of Bullo and Camilla, a wayward youth

Camilla, wife of Bullo and mother of Urso, well turned out but with the mouth of a sewer

Ancietus, Admiral of the fleet at Misenum, a loyal fall guy of Emperor Nero

RAISING READERS
Books Build Bright Futures

Dear Reader,

We'd love your attention for one more page to tell you about the crisis in children's reading, and what we can all do.

Studies have shown that reading for fun is the **single biggest predictor of a child's future life chances** – more than family circumstance, parents' educational background or income. It improves academic results, mental health, wealth, communication skills, ambition and happiness.[1]

The number of children reading for fun is in rapid decline. Young people have a lot of competition for their time. In 2024, 1 in 10 children and young people in the UK aged 5 to 18 did not own a single book at home.[2]

Hachette works extensively with schools, libraries and literacy charities, but here are some ways we can all raise more readers:

- Reading to children for just 10 minutes a day makes a difference
- Don't give up if children aren't regular readers – there will be books for them!
- Visit bookshops and libraries to get recommendations
- Encourage them to listen to audiobooks
- Support school libraries
- Give books as gifts

There's a lot more information about how to encourage children to read on our website: **www.RaisingReaders.co.uk**

Thank you for reading.

hachette
UK

---

[1] OECD, '21st-Century Readers: Developing Literacy Skills in a Digital World', 2021, https://www.oecd.org/en/publications/21st-century-readers_a83d84cb-en.html

[2] National Literacy Trust, 'Book Ownership in 2024', November 2024, https://literacytrust.org.uk/research-services/research-reports/book-ownership-in-2024